The fiery brilliance of the Zebra Hologram Heart which you see on the cover is created by "laser holography." This is the revolutionary process in which a powerful laser beam records light waves in diamond-like facets so tiny that 9,000,000 fit in a square inch. No print or photograph can match the vibrant colors and radiant glow of a hologram.

So look for the Zebra Hologram Heart whenever you buy a historical romance. It is a shimmering reflection of our guarantee that you'll find consistent quality between the covers!

FORBIDDEN KISS

"We will not be disturbed again tonight, all the others are already asleep," he reassured her softly.

"How can you be certain?" Bianca asked shyly.

"Because yours is the only room with a light." Reaching out to catch her hand, Evan pulled the stunning blonde down across his lap. "Let's not waste another moment," he whispered seductively as his lips sought the same sweet taste of surrender he'd enjoyed so much earlier that evening. He hesitated a moment, concentrating upon the delectable flavor of her kiss. She tried to pull away then, as he'd known she would, but he held her captive in his powerful embrace.

Bianca's flesh grew warm, eager for the first knowledge of his well-muscled body, and Evan felt a great sense of satisfaction. He knew he could have Bianca now, steal her innocence and be gone, shaming Paolo with a bride who'd already savored every delight a man could give. It was a temptation he swiftly discarded, however, for he wanted to make his brother's murderer suffer greatly for his crimes, not simply humiliate him!

Bianca had no hint of the turmoil which tore at Evan's soul; she felt only the tide of pleasure which swelled to an ever-heightening crest within her heart. This man had fascinated her at first glance, that he frightened her as well as thrilled her no longer seemed important. She'd have no other chance to share the rapture he was creating, and she wanted to savor it until dawn. . . .

Taylor—made Romance From Zebra Books

WHISPERED KISSES (2912, $4.95/5.95)
Beautiful Texas heiress Laura Leigh Webster never imagined that her biggest worry on her African safari would be the handsome Jace Elliot, her tour guide. Laura's guardian, Lord Chadwick Hamilton, warns her of Jace's dangerous past; she simply cannot resist the lure of his strong arms and the passion of his *Whispered Kisses*.

KISS OF THE NIGHT WIND (2699, $4.50/$5.50)
Carrie Sue Strover thought she was leaving trouble behind her when she deserted her brother's outlaw gang to live her life as schoolmarm Carolyn Starns. On her journey, her stagecoach was attacked and she was rescued by handsome T.J. Rogue. T.J. plots to have Carrie lead him to her brother's cohorts who murdered his family. T.J., however, soon succumbs to the beautiful runaway's charms and loving caresses.

FORTUNE'S FLAMES (2944, $4.50/$5.50)
Impatient to begin her journey back home to New Orleans, beautiful Maren James was furious when Captain Hawk delayed the voyage by searching for stowaways. Impatience gave way to uncontrollable desire once the handsome captain searched *her* cabin. He was looking for illegal passengers; what he found was wild passion with a woman he knew was unlike all those he had known before!

PASSIONS WILD AND FREE (3017, $4.50/$5.50)
After seeing her family and home destroyed by the cruel and hateful Epson gang, Randee Hollis swore revenge. She knew she found the perfect man to help her—gunslinger Marsh Logan. Not only strong and brave, Marsh had the ebony hair and light blue eyes to make Randee forget her hate and seek the love and passion that only he could give her.

Available wherever paperbacks are sold, or order direct from the Publisher. Send cover price plus 50¢ per copy for mailing and handling to Zebra Books, Dept. 3193, 475 Park Avenue South, New York, N.Y. 10016. Residents of New York, New Jersey and Pennsylvania must include sales tax. DO NOT SEND CASH.

ZEBRA BOOKS
KENSINGTON PUBLISHING CORP.

ZEBRA BOOKS

are published by

Kensington Publishing Corp.
475 Park Avenue South
New York, NY 10016

Third printing: April, 1990

Printed in the United States of America

This book is dedicated to my sons, Jeff and Drew, who provide a constant source of inspiration for my dashing, romantic heros.

Prologue

Early Spring, 1785

Evan sat with the soles of his highly polished black leather boots nearly touching the flames, the slim fingers of his left hand only lightly grasping the stem of the snifter of fine brandy which was balanced precariously upon his brass belt buckle. The library was dark except for the illumination provided by the bright blaze upon the hearth, and the fire's glow cast the young man's superbly proportioned features in high relief. His deep auburn hair reflected the coppery hues of the flames, while the brown of his eyes shone with a soft golden glow. His pose was relaxed, yet his expression revealed his deep despair. When his stepfather spoke, moments elapsed before he turned toward him.

"You know what must be done," Lewis Grey remarked sadly.

"Of course. I must bring Charles's murderer to justice myself, for it is plain the Venetian authorities never will. They have dismissed his death as the unfortunate killing of a traveller during a robbery, but you and I both know that's a blatant lie."

Lewis nodded in agreement, his expression as despondent as Evan's. "I would gladly go myself, but I dare not leave your mother alone with her grief. To have lost Charles in such a brutal and senseless fashion is almost more than she can endure."

"You need not even consider making the trip," Evan advised the older man. "I am the one who should go for I have no obligations of any kind. Charles resembled you and bore your name; no one will recognize me as his kin when I arrive in Venice. I will not arouse the suspicions your presence would surely raise, and we do not want Charles's killer to have the advantage of any such warning." Evan glanced back at the fire, disappointed that the flames provided so little in the way of warmth for he was chilled clear through. "We have few clues, but they will have to be enough."

"A woman's lace-trimmed handkerchief embroidered with the letter *A*, and effusive praise for that mysterious lady in Charles's journal. With such scant information, do you think you can find the golden-haired goddess who lured your brother to his death?"

Evan stretched languidly, inching dangerously close to the leaping flames. "I will find her if I must go to the gates of hell, but surely she is not the one responsible for Charles's murder. It has to be a man, one whose love is an obsession. Her fiancé or lover—her husband, perhaps even her father—a man who would not allow Charles's flirtation with the young woman to continue and who chose desperate means to assure that it didn't. Whoever he might be, I'll seek him out and make him curse the day he was born."

His stepson's bitter tone prompted Lewis to issue a warning. "You must be cautious, Evan. We can not lose you too. Neither your mother nor I would survive that blow." His voice softening, he continued. "You were only eight when I married Marion and fathered Charles, but I never saw a single spark of jealousy pass between you boys. You were all an elder brother should be, an example I encouraged Charles to emulate. It is fitting you should be the one to avenge his death, and yet I can not bear to have you put your life at risk to do so."

With a steady hand, Evan reached over to grip his stepfather's arm in an affectionate clasp. "Cease to worry. If the British did not succeed in killing me in all the years of the war, one Venetian never will."

Lewis covered the handsome young man's hand with his own momentarily then leaned back and closed his eyes to hide his tears. Content to remain silent for a long while, he at last regained his composure and then changed the subject abruptly. "I know tonight may seem like an inappropriate time for such a discussion, but when you return home I want you to marry. You should have a wife and a family of your own. Your mother needs the laughter of grandchildren to surround her with happiness, and I know you must long for a woman's love."

Evan shot his stepfather a disapproving glance for he lacked nothing when it came to the delights of feminine companionship. "A wife, Lewis? You can not be serious," he scoffed.

"Oh, but I most certainly am. Just consider the benefits of marriage for a moment. Newport News is filled with young beauties who would be proud to become your bride, Sheila Blanchard, for example. If no one here pleases you then you're in Richmond frequently, that city must also abound with lovely young women. Choose one, and begin your own family before another year goes by. You are thirty-two, wealthy in your own right. You would undoubtedly already have a family had the War for Independence not taken so many years of your youth."

Evan knew better than to shock a man so strict in his morals as Lewis by stating that the joys of marriage were already his without its stifling commitments. Since his stepfather had enough grief at present, he'd not add to it by revealing his nature had an active sensual side Lewis didn't even suspect existed. "I will give your advice careful consideration when I return," he promised instead; but his mind was already closed on the subject. Charles had been eager to wed, far too eager apparently, and his zeal had gotten him a villain's blade thrust clear through his heart. "For the present, I will be occupied with the preparations to sail."

"Yes, of course. You must leave as swiftly as the *Phoenix* can be loaded with provisions. The sooner you strike the more unexpected your vengeance will be, but I beg you again to take care so that you will be able to return safely to us."

Their conversation concluded, Lewis bid Evan good night but the young man remained by the fire allowing memories of his half brother to flood his heart as well as his mind with sorrow. Charles had been fair haired and blue eyed, always in high spirits, so full of laughter and fun, whereas he himself was dark in coloring and possessed a far more serious nature. How had someone as likeable as Charles inspired a jealousy so deep it had led to murder? What sort of man would do such an evil thing to keep the love of the young woman Charles had described as a green-eyed enchantress whose silken tresses had been kissed by the sun? The last pages of the young man's journal had been filled with poetic references to the lady's beauty, but other than the initialed handkerchief, there was no clue as to her identity. Was it possible Charles did not know it? Had he only seen this fascinating young woman, longed to meet her, and in openly expressing his desire met his death? Those are the very questions I intend to answer, Evan promised himself.

Finally alone after an exhausting day spent with

solicitous relatives and caring friends who'd remained to offer comfort after the memorial service for Charles, he gave in to his grief and wept for the handsome young man who'd found not only love, but death in his twenty-fourth year. Charles should not have died, certainly not in such a senseless fashion. He'd been a romantic fool, on his way to meet the woman he'd adored when he'd been struck down from behind. It had been no robbery, certainly not. Money had been found in his pockets, a gold ring had been left on his hand. No indeed, Charles had been carefully stalked and slain but the motive hadn't been robbery. But what manner of man had committed such a despicable crime? That was the question which tormented Evan, burned in his soul to be answered, and as the hour grew late a plan began to take shape in his agile mind. It was so perfect in its simplicity he knew he could find no better way to trap a murderer so, inspired by his own brilliance, he hastily wiped away the last of his tears. Raising the snifter in a silent toast to Charles's memory he swallowed the last drop of the old brandy and after stirring the ashes, which were all that remained of the fire, he wearily climbed the stairs and fell into bed. He slept soundly, satisfied that he would soon make Charles's murderer pay the ultimate price for the life he had so needlessly taken.

Chapter I

After carefully studying the array of vibrant hues dabbed upon his pallet, Stefano Tommasi attempted to mix precisely the shade he wished to use for the highlights in Bianca Antonelli's golden blond hair. He was satisfied that he had captured the delicacy of her exquisite features, the sparkling emerald of her long-lashed eyes, and the creamy softness of her flawless complexion; but the glorious shade of her gleaming tresses eluded him still.

"I can not hold this pose for another minute, Stefano. Can't we please stop for today?" The lovely young woman called to the preoccupied artist, her usually melodic voice plaintive and forlorn.

"You have the fair beauty of Botticelli's Venus, my dearest. Can you not find her patience as well?" Seeing that his subject was even more restless than usual, however, Stefano painted a few feathery strokes upon his canvas and then granted her request. "It is hopeless, I see. Carnival season leaves you yawning all day, but I doubt you'd consider missing Paolo's ball tonight in order to provide me with a well-rested model tomorrow."

Bianca stood, stretching her slender body with a languid, feline grace as she replied, "I love the Carnival parties, Stefano, and why shouldn't I? The music and dancing are better now than at any other time of the year." Curious, she moved to his side, taking care not to brush against the wet canvas. "How many more days must I endure this torture to provide my parents with this portrait?" she asked, with a bewitching toss of her sun-kissed curls.

"One or two only if you will sit still, two weeks if I must attempt to work while you fidget constantly," Stefano replied, then chuckled; but he was clearly serious in his estimate.

"Don't tease me, Stefano. I've never been able to sit still for more than a few minutes, no matter what the reason. You'll be doing Raffaella next, just look forward to painting her."

At the mention of her name, Bianca's cousin looked up from her reading. Seated near the window, she'd not moved the entire afternoon. "I'm sorry, did I miss something?"

Stefano turned to look at the petite, dark-haired girl. While her bone structure was similar to that of Bianca, she lacked the striking beauty Bianca's unusual coloring created, and he found little reason to look forward to doing her portrait. He smiled, however, as though he regarded her beauty highly. "Yes, indeed. I think I shall paint you with a book in your hand, my dear. That is your most typical pose, is it not?"

Raffaella smiled shyly as she rose to her feet and reached for her cloak. "Yes, it is. I'll not deny it."

Stefano picked up a rag to clean his hands as he turned back to his present subject. "Perhaps after I complete Raffaella's portrait, you'll give my proposition further thought, Bianca."

Bianca laughed as she turned away. "I am only sixteen. What do you think would happen if my parents learned I'd posed in the nude for you? Then there are Paolo

Sammarese's feelings to consider as well."

"But neither your parents nor Paolo need ever know," Stefano assured her confidently. "I would not display the work here in Venice, but in Florence instead."

"Even that precaution would not protect my reputation," Bianca argued sensibly, "All who see such a painting would believe you had seduced me. My identity would not remain a secret for long with such a scandal." Coming back to face the artist, who was a scant two inches taller than she, Bianca whispered in a sultry voice, "How would you answer such a charge?"

"Perhaps I would say you were the one who seduced me," the quick-witted artist replied. At thirty-six, his thick black curls and slender build still gave him a boyish appearance, but the gaze in his sparkling brown eyes was a worldly one. He had too many wealthy patrons to fear the threat in Bianca's words.

While she frequently spoke to men in a teasing fashion, Bianca did not enjoy having her jests countered so handily, and she turned away to hide her frown. Donning her cloak, she secured it beneath her chin with a hastily tied bow. "I think this portrait will be enough, Stefano. I've no desire to pose for another, especially not in the nude."

Stefano chuckled at the sudden seriousness of her expression, "Bianca, I would never sully your reputation, although saying you had seduced me would greatly enhance mine. Your family is one of the most powerful in Venice, and I am but a humble artist. Your face and figure have the perfection of a goddess, but I wish only to paint, not possess, you. Here in my studio your virtue is quite safe." Seeing a bright blush fill the attractive young woman's cheeks, he wondered if in fact Paolo Sammarese had not already succeeded in seducing this high-spirited beauty. That was too dangerous a matter upon which to speculate, however. He smiled in what he hoped was no more than a brotherly fashion as he showed the two young women to the front door, which opened onto a narrow canal where a sleek black gondola awaited. The silver paint adorning the elegantly carved prow shone, and the immaculate condition in which the graceful craft was kept instantly proclaimed the wealth of its owner. The handsomely dressed gondolier leapt to his feet to reach for his mistress' hand, seeing that she was comfortably seated before he helped Raffaella to the adjacent seat and reached for the single oar he used to propel the distinctively Venetian craft.

"I will do my best to complete your portrait tomorrow, Bianca, if only you will give me your full attention. It will be my masterpiece until you are willing to sit for another," Stefano assured her with a sly wink, but her smile was a slight one and he did not feel encouraged as he returned to his studio.

"Nude! How dare the man suggest such a thing?" Raffaella whispered anxiously. "You will come with me each time I pose for him, won't you?"

"Of course, I will, although how I'll pass the time I don't know. You needn't worry about Stefano, though. He was merely teasing me since I've been such a difficult subject." Bianca did think he was merely teasing, but sometimes the way he looked at her was most unsettling and she was happy she'd have to pose for him just one more time. More than once she'd noted that his glance was not directed at her face, and she now wondered if he hadn't been the one who'd delayed the completion of her portrait by inattention, not she. At any rate, the tedious sittings were nearly over, and she was grateful that her portrait had turned out so well. Stefano was the finest artist in Venice when it came to portraiture, her father considered his exorbitant price money well spent, but no respectable young woman posed nude for any artist, regardless of his talents. The mere thought of doing such a scandalous thing made Bianca's clear green eyes sparkle with mischief.

When the two young women arrived at the Ca' Antonelli on the Grand Canal, they hurried up the wide marble staircase to Bianca's room, where they found a wide selection of Carnival costumes from which they would make their selections. After their baths, Bianca was in a playful mood as she selected her gown for the evening's ball. As usual, she shocked her far more conservative cousin with her wit and daring.

"I think I shall be the goddess Flora tonight, this yellow silk is very pretty. If I were to wear nothing beneath it—"

Shocked, Raffaella declared in a hoarse gasp, "Bianca! You might as well pose nude for Stefano if you're going to embarrass us all with such an immodest display!"

Striking a provocative pose, Bianca drew the filmy veil of golden silk across the fullness of her bosom, "Do not be so hasty in judging me, Rafaella. As Flora, I'd need little more than my mask and a long-stemmed rose to play the part. Perhaps a gown isn't necessary at all."

"You wouldn't!" Rafaella cried, not at all certain Bianca would not arrive at the party in such a scanty costume. For herself, she chose a gown of midnight blue velvet with stars embroidered in golden thread, and she planned to say she was Andromeda. Fearing Bianca was making fun of her modesty, she asked in a hushed whisper, "What are you trying to do, make Paolo break your engagement? He would, you know. He'd not stand for even the hint of impropriety from you."

Bianca tossed the veil aside with a careless shrug. "I know how proper a gentleman Paolo is, Raffaella. You need not remind me."

"Not only is he a proper gentleman, but your father is one as well. He would not allow you to leave the house were you to plan to wear no more than a mask to Paolo's ball. The gown you had created for Flora is nearly transparent. Isn't that daring enough to suit you? You enjoy boldly teasing all the young men, but what will you do if one responds in kind?"

Bianca only laughed at the ridiculousness of that question. "You know Paolo has considered me his fiancée since the day I was born. I am merely another of his many possessions. My father encourages him so openly, which young man would dare to do more than flirt with me? The evening holds no mystery despite the requirement that we wear masks until the last stroke of midnight."

Raffaella frowned, confused by her pretty cousin's words. "Paolo is handsome, wealthy too. Don't you want him for your husband?"

When Bianca slipped on the elegant silk gown, its tiny Grecian pleats hugged the fullness of her high firm breasts seductively. She held her hair aside while Raffaella fastened the hook at her nape, then responded truthfully. "I don't believe anyone has ever asked me that question before, Rafaella, least of all my father. I think Paolo is handsome too, and his wealth is the envy of all, but I do not wish to be his bride. He disapproves of all I do, that I smile when he wishes to be serious, that I laugh before he has time to understand what makes a joke humorous. I am quick and he is methodical; we are a poor match. If only he would admit it and choose another for his bride, we would both be far happier for it."

Raffaella watched the lively girl wind her golden curls atop her head and secure them with a yellow satin ribbon and combs decorated with pearls. Bianca left a few tendrils trailing down her neck to complete the classical style which complimented her features and was in keeping with her flattering gown. "Your father is too ambitious a man to allow you to refuse Paolo's proposal. I am surprised a date for your wedding has not already been set."

Bianca spent only a few seconds turning in front of her mirror; then she stepped aside so Raffaella could complete her grooming. "He and Paolo are waiting for me to mature in my attitude. They believe in a year or two I will make not only a beautiful wife, but a sensible and serious one. They are badly mistaken, however, for I shall not change." Her posture erect, the golden-haired beauty put on a small pair of pearl earrings and a matching bracelet, then picked up her mask. Made of a thin sheet of papier mâché delicately hand-painted with wild flowers, it was light in weight and covered only her eyes. Her preparations complete, Bianca crossed the bedroom and stepped out upon the balcony to look down on the Grand Canal. The water flowed smoothly out to the lagoon, then on to the sea and the world that lay beyond, that fascinating world Bianca feared she might never see, for the life she led in Venice, while pleasant, was highly restricted. After a moment, she commented wistfully, "The night is clear, splendid for a party. I wish only that—"

"Wish what?" Raffaella asked curiously as she finished brushing out her glossy dark curls.

"Nothing which can come true," Bianca replied softly. Words could not express the longing which filled her heart, and that evening it was almost painful. Paolo was handsome and rich, yet the thought of seeing him that night, or any other night, brought not the slightest bit of joy, only dread, which threatened to flood her sparkling green eyes with tears of sorrow. Finally distracting herself with more pleasant thoughts, she turned back to Raffaella, "Marco Ciani will be there tonight, won't he?"

The petite brunette blushed deeply as she replied, "I hope so, but I doubt he'll take any notice of me."

Bianca knew better than to ask the reason for that sorry opinion. Raffaella was the daughter of her father's youngest sister, a woman who had married a man of extremely modest means. Were she not a guest in the Antonelli home, she would not have been invited to any of the wonderful Carnival parties. "Perhaps you should smile just a little more sweetly when he strolls by, Raffaella. You are so terribly shy, I doubt the man realizes you find him attractive."

"I am no flirt!" Raffaella responded primly, obviously appalled by Bianca's suggestion.

With a weary sigh, Bianca took her cousin's arm and propelled her toward the door, "I did not tell you to tap his chest with your fan as you speak to him; just smile as though you look forward to dancing with him and that will do for a start." Bianca knew Raffaella considered her to be a terrible flirt, but she thought of herself as merely friendly, polite, not brazen in her appreciation of male company. If only she were as interested in Paolo as Raffaella was in Marco, then the anticipation of the evening would bring a delicious excitement, rather than the mere promise of amusement.

The two attractive cousins had been at the ball for more than an hour when Marco Ciani arrived with a tall man clad in a flowing black cape, which he swiftly tossed aside to reveal a black velvet suit richly embroidered with gold thread. All eyes were upon him as he crossed the crowded room to be introduced to Paolo Sammarese, his host. Intrigued by the unexpected appearance of so dashing a figure, Bianca moved to Paolo's side in the hope of being included in the introductions. All the influential members of Venetian society were well known to her, and she recognized each of them easily, even in costume. This man, however, let Marco speak for him, and Bianca soon realized he understood none of the conversation he had inspired. Not only was he a stranger to Venice, but a foreigner as well. His elegantly tailored costume showed off his broad shoulders and muscular build to every advantage, but his gold mask and plumed hat concealed all but a well-shaped mouth and a firm chin, mere hints that the rest of his features would be as fine. Thinking a man who moved with such easy grace would surely prove to be handsome, Bianca spoke the moment they were introduced. "How do you do, Mr. Sinclair. My mother is from Great Britain so I speak English fluently, and I will be happy to translate for you this evening should Marco grow weary of that task."

Evan inclined his head in a mock bow, then quickly refused her offer, his mask muffling the sound of his deep voice only slightly. "I am no longer a British citizen, but an inhabitant of the United States, and I am certain I shall be adequately entertained tonight without your help, Miss Antonelli."

At first Bianca did not comprehend that her politely worded offer of assistance had been rudely rejected, yet his abrupt refusal brought a deep blush to her cheeks, which her mask only partially hid. "As you wish, Mr. Sinclair," she replied coldly, disappointed that this fascinating stranger had proved himself an arrogant ass. When he and Marco moved on, she looked up at Paolo. "Do you suppose all Americans are as rude as that one?"

"Was he rude to you?" Paolo asked absently. He was quite tall for a Venetian, nearly six feet in height, but the American had towered above him. He was sorry Carnival time dictated masks had to be worn for he would have liked to have had a better look at the man. Paolo was quite pleased with his own appearance that night for his tailor had fashioned for him a harlequin suit of silver and blue satin which he thought exceedingly flattering to his slender build. He knew women considered the wavy brown hair and brown eyes which accented his patrician features handsome, but he left nothing to chance. He was always fastidious in his grooming and dress in order to make the most of his physical assets. On his part, he was delighted that Evan Sinclair had shown no interest in

Bianca, for he allowed no one to compete for her love. It was a relief to find that he'd not have to prove that to the American. "I will forgive his lack of manners since he is here in Venice to do business. When Marco requested an invitation for his guest for tonight's ball, he told me that Sinclair has access to a ready market for our glass. I'll not insult a buyer eager for Venetian wares when I stand to make a large profit from him."

Bianca turned away, disgusted because Paolo considered his business interests more important than her feelings. She had known that he would, of course, but it still hurt to hear him say money was his primary concern. It was obvious to her that he would always place a higher value upon profit than upon her happiness, and she felt like telling him that his greed was the foremost reason she had absolutely no desire to marry him. She held her tongue, however, as she knew a lady must, but she promised herself she'd let Paolo know exactly what she thought of him the first time an appropriate opportunity presented itself.

Hardly daring to hope Bianca would have the answers to her questions about the elaborately costumed stranger, Raffaella approached her shyly and whispered, "Who is the man with Marco?"

"His name is Evan Sinclair. He's a client of Marco's who has come from America to purchase fine crystal, but why barbarians need expensive glassware, I do not know." Bianca responded with icy sarcasm.

"Barbarians?" Rafaella asked in surprise. "Did Marco actually call him that?"

"No, of course not, I did!"

Bianca spent the remainder of the evening flirting with young men she usually considered immature, but she had no desire to remain at Paolo's side. The gaiety of the party did not improve her mood, and at midnight, when all were asked to remove their masks, she found herself searching the crowd for Evan Sinclair. He'd not spoken another word to her all evening, not that she would have replied, but she was curious about him still. Standing at the edge of the festively decorated ballroom she had a clear view of all the guests, and she realized, with a sigh of frustrated disappointment, that Mr. Sinclair had apparently departed early. Since his manner had been so discourteous, perhaps he'd not been handsome after all. Still she wanted to know for certain. When a man walked up behind her and touched her shoulder gently she stepped aside so he might pass, but the sly grin which greeted her as she looked up was so disarming she gasped with delighted surprise. Evan did no more than nod and move on, but Bianca stared after him until he'd disappeared into the crowd. He had removed his hat as well as his mask. His dark auburn hair was striking, and she'd never met anyone else with eyes more gold than brown. His features were as perfect as she'd imagined, yet fully masculine and strong. His teeth were straight and very white, making the brief smile he'd given her glow radiantly against his deeply tanned skin. He was the most attractive man she'd ever seen and the warm rush of emotion his sudden appearance had evoked was not due to embarrassment but to a flood of desire so heady she feared for an instant she might actually faint. Certain she was being very foolish, she began to converse again with those standing nearby, hoping none would guess the cause of her bright blush. She was mortified to think Evan Sinclair could stir such powerful emotions within her heart when he'd not even had the courtesy to be civil! It was devastating to think this exciting newcomer to their midst did not like her simply because her mother was British. The American Colonies' War for Independence was over and won. Why would he be so bitter? Since he'd not even speak with her, she doubted she'd ever learn that secret, and when it came time to depart, she was nearly in tears, so depressed was she by the evening's unexpectedly sad turn of events. She'd always been surrounded by the smiles of eager men, and she had no idea how to win the admiration of an attractive but hostile stranger.

Mistaking her downcast expression for fatigue, Paolo bid Bianca good night, kissed her lightly upon the cheek, and then busied himself with other guests who were preparing to depart. The fetching blonde was standing with her cousin, waiting for their gondola to reach the front of the line, when Evan Sinclair suddenly moved to her side. With one easy gesture, he wrapped her in the folds of his flowing cloak and lifted her into the gondola which had just reached the steps. Bianca had time to do no more than glance back at Raffaella, who had just been joined by Marco Ciani. That Marco was in league with the American was clear, but she had no opportunity to scream for help for Evan pulled her down onto the seat beside him and covered her mouth with his hand. He held her so tightly that she could not draw a deep breath, and she began to tremble for she feared this handsome man meant to do her some dreadful harm.

The sleek boat moved out into the waters of the Grand Canal, but instead of proceeding in the direction most of the other guests had taken, it swiftly veered off into one of the numerous narrow canals that branched off from the larger waterway. Once he was certain his actions had not been observed by the departing guests and that they would not be followed, Evan whispered softly, "Be still, I will take you home in a moment."

The lanterns on board provided barely enough illumination for recognition, but Bianca found the forceful stranger's appearance far more pleasant than his tight embrace. When she continued to struggle against him, he simply pulled her across his lap and pressed her face into the soft folds of his velvet cape.

"Be still I said! I want no more than a word with you; you needn't fight me." Satisfied that no one was close enough to give pursuit should she scream, he lowered his hand.

"How dare you treat me so roughly!" Bianca demanded as she gasped for air. "We attended the same party. There was ample opportunity for us to converse, but you wanted nothing to do with me there. Now you say you want no more than a word." Clearly, she thought the man was a liar and a poor one.

"Forgive me for disappointing you so badly," Evan apologized with a deep chuckle. "I had to know certain things before I spoke with you, and it took me far too long to learn them."

Her curiosity piqued, Bianca's glance swept Evan's even features intently, for they were mere inches apart as they sat whispering in the darkness. As before, she was fascinated by the golden gleam of his eyes. They seemed to glow with liquid fire. Surely the devil himself possessed such eyes, and she could not suppress a shudder of fear as she forced her gaze away from them.

Believing her chilled, Evan drew her closer still, pressing her supple body against his own as he fought the rush of desire her nearness had so swiftly created. She was an enchanting creature, even when angry, and to save himself further torment, he sought her lips hungrily, bruising her pretty mouth with the savagery of his passion. When she placed her palms upon his chest in a futile attempt to push him away, he caught her wrists in a firm grip to hold her captive in his arms. Her lips parted then, to voice a protest, and stealing that advantage, he deepened his kiss. His tongue caressed hers with a lazy insolence, but she did not relax against him as he'd hoped she would and the moment he released her she cried out to the gondolier for help.

"I have paid him well to work for me tonight, Bianca.

Do not expect the man to come to your rescue," Evan warned her in a hoarse whisper, his voice deepened by unfulfilled desire.

Still breathless from his seemingly endless kiss, Bianca nevertheless continued to argue. "You are a fool to think you can rape me tonight and live to see the dawn! My father will kill you for this outrage, even if he has to pursue you all the way to America to do it!"

Evan swore under his breath and again clapped his hand over her mouth, but her threat provided him with an inspiration he'd not even considered. Unable at the moment to ponder the wisdom of luring Charles's murderer away from Venice, he spoke to reassure the volatile young beauty. "I am not trying to rape you. Don't be absurd!" He thought the idea preposterous since he considered the gondola no more seaworthy than a large canoe. Indeed, he doubted any man could rape a woman in such a craft without running the risk of drowning his victim and perhaps himself as well, but Bianca was trembling so badly he finally realized she was truly frightened. His manner growing tender, he kissed away her tears and promised softly, "I would never harm you. How can you believe that I would?" Lowering his hand slowly, he awaited her reply.

Although confused by the gentle words of this maddening stranger who still held her far too tightly, Bianca again responded defiantly. "First you insult me rudely. Then you ignore me. Now you have kidnapped me, tried to ravish me, but you say you want merely to exchange a few words? You are no more than an obnoxious bully and I want to go home!"

Disappointed by her response, Evan replied with equal hostility. "This is no time to question my character, damn it! I need to know whether or not you are Paolo Sammarese's fiancée. Yes or no?" Marco had told him she was, but he'd seen her so seldom by the dandy's side that he doubted she could really be betrothed to the man. He'd been almost certain of her identity the moment he'd entered the ballroom and seen her glorious golden hair, and it had taken more patience than he'd thought he possessed to wait for her to remove her mask so he'd be positive she was the beauty he thought her to be. Now he wanted to know everything about her, but whether or not she belonged to Paolo was too vital a piece of information to delay acquiring.

Cradled in his warm embrace, Bianca found it difficult to think at all, especially about Paolo. "Of what possible concern is that to you?" she finally managed to ask, with what she hoped would sound more like sarcasm than fear.

"Look, I have little more than a week to spend in Venice, and I do not wish to waste what time I have in courting another man's fiancée," Evan declared.

"I am not for sale like Paolo's fine crystal, Mr. Sinclair." Bianca again tried briefly to move off his lap, but she gave up the effort when, rather than releasing her as she'd hoped, he tightened his confining hold.

"I have no intention of offering your father money for you, Bianca. I mean simply to win your heart with love."

Dumbfounded by that declaration, Bianca stared up at Evan, too surprised to respond for several seconds. Nothing he said or did made the slightest bit of sense to her, yet she could not deny that she found him enormously attractive. He was far more physically appealing than any other man she'd ever known. She'd not admit that to him, however. "You are either insane or a fool, Mr. Sinclair. Now I wish to return home immediately." She was still frightened by his strength despite her continued show of bravado, and she hastened to rebuke him again. "You promised to take me home."

"Is that what you really want me to do?" Evan whispered seductively, his warm breath caressing her cheek as sweetly as a kiss.

"As you said, you will soon be gone, but I do not want my reputation ruined for a few nights of pleasure. Must I insist you escort me to my home?" Bianca turned away, thinking she would sound more convincing if she didn't have to fight the hypnotic appeal of his bright golden gaze.

Evan sighed sadly. "I thought you possessed more spirit than that, Bianca. You seemed like the sort of woman who would take any risk to find the true beauty of love. Obviously, you are far younger than I had first thought."

"No. It is precisely because I am no child that I know what is best for me! If you wished only to learn whether I am engaged to Paolo you could simply have asked me at the ball. You need not have taken advantage of me," the furious blonde scolded.

"Taken advantage of you? I've not done that, my dear." Not yet, he thought to himself with a sly smile, enormously pleased that she would describe nights spent with him as a pleasure. He found her naïveté more charming than he'd thought possible, and that surprised him for she was unlike the sophisticated beauties with whom he usually spent his time. "Just tell me the truth about your engagement to Paolo, if it exists, and then I'll take you right home."

Since she'd no hope of getting home any other way, Bianca replied truthfully. "Paolo likes to think that I am engaged to him. My father encourages that fantasy, but I do not. Is that answer enough for you?"

Rather than respond with words, Evan wound his fingers in her softly upswept curls to turn her face toward him and again he pressed his lips to hers. He found her sweetness delicious despite her lack of appreciation for his affection, but he released her before she could again begin to struggle. "I did not mean to frighten you. I'll take you home now and your parents need never know we were alone together unless you wish to tell them."

"I'd not ever do that!" Bianca assured him breathlessly.

"Simply to protect me from their wrath?" Evan asked hopefully.

"No. I wish only to protect myself, Mr. Sinclair."

When she again attempted to move from his lap, Evan slipped his arms around her tiny waist to hold her still. "My ship is the *Phoenix*. You will find me there tomorrow morning."

"I shall not even bother to look!"

"Then meet me at the Piazza San Marco at noon instead," Evan suggested.

"No, I will not. You are no gentleman, Mr. Sinclair, and I'll do nothing to encourage your attentions since I do not wish to receive them."

"It is too late for such caution, Miss Antonelli, for you are already mine." To seal that vow, Evan kissed her again, his tongue languidly plundering her mouth, enjoying the sweetness of her taste until she ceased to struggle. He wanted far more of her then, wanted to undress her completely and savor every inch of her delectable flesh, but he restrained himself from taking any further liberties that night, other than allowing his fingertips to trace the smooth swell of her breast. He laughed at her responsive shudder of revulsion and after releasing her, he signaled to the gondolier to return to the Grand Canal. "Marco will be waiting for us so you will arrive at your door in your own gondola with your cousin as is expected. You see, I have taken great care to safeguard your reputation." It was not her gratitude he wanted, however. He simply desired to provoke the same villainous reaction to budding love which had led to Charles's murder. He was saddened that he'd not been able to arouse her passions as she'd aroused his. That was an unexpected complication. He'd not imagined her fair beauty would affect him as strongly as it had his half brother, but he could not deny that it had. Just as Charles had written in his journal, she was an enchantress, a spirited young woman with a remarkable aura of sensuality, and he was sorry she'd not spent the evening flirting with him rather than countless other young men. "You have a sizable dowry, I suppose?"

"What?" Bianca's reply was a startled gasp.

"Surely your father is rich and will provide a dowry worthy of you." Evan grabbed for Bianca's wrist as she swung her hand toward his cheek. "Do not try to slap me again, my love, for I promise you will not like the spanking I will give you in return." With a devilish chuckle, he gave her an affectionate hug but all too quickly he sighted the gondola in which Marco awaited with Raffaella and their brief interlude came to an abrupt end. He sat staring into the darkness then, amazed by the haste with which Bianca had left him.

"Is she not all that I described?" Marco asked slyly, certain he'd pleased his wealthy client.

"Indeed she is," Evan agreed, but his satisfied smile gave no hint that his heart lusted for revenge, not the thrill of romance.

Chapter II

Bianca pretended not to hear Raffaella's endless stream of whispered questions as they mounted the wide staircase of her home, but when they reached the third-floor landing she turned toward her cousin and explained hurriedly, "The American wished only to speak with me privately. Lacking all manners, he thought a gondola the place to do so. I demanded he see me to my home, and since I am here, the matter is closed. It never happened, do you understand? Now I will bid my parents good night and then go right to sleep."

"But—" Raffaella began to protest, her heart still aflutter with the excitement of having spent a few minutes alone with Marco Ciani. She wanted to remain up all night talking about the two handsome young men, and was gravely disappointed that Bianca didn't intend to confide in her.

"Hush!" Bianca ordered fiercely, directing the shy girl toward her room with an emphatic gesture. "Good night!" She drew in a deep breath as she approached her mother's bedroom, but at that point her courage swiftly deserted her. Her parents had declined the invitation to Paolo's party. However, a light was showing beneath her mother's door so Bianca knew they would be expecting to speak with her. For as long as she could remember she'd found her father in her mother's room at night. She doubted that he'd ever slept in his own bed in the seventeen years he'd been married. Why she'd had no brothers and sisters she didn't understand, but that was not a question a young lady dared ask her parents. Forcing herself to play the part expected of her, she rapped lightly upon the door and, hearing her mother's response, entered her room.

Catherine Antonelli was already in bed, propped upon a half-dozen satin pillows. She was reading while her husband sat near the fireplace. "Come give me a kiss, beloved. How was Paolo's party?" she inquired sweetly.

"Lavish. Exactly what you'd expect from him." Bianca kissed her mother's cheek lightly, then crossed the spacious room to bid her father good night, but rather than let her go, he reached out to catch her hand.

"Just a moment, I want a word with you." Francesco's hair, once jet black, had begun to turn silver long ago. Nonetheless, at forty-five he was still a very handsome man. While his words were teasing, his manner was as usual a strictly formal one. "Is it Paolo who is responsible for the pretty blush that fills your cheeks? I have despaired of ever hearing you say you cared for him. Has he at last won your heart?"

Bianca tried to smile but found her features frozen by an unaccustomed numbness. "Perhaps it is only the chill of the night air, Papa, not a blush at all," she finally managed to mumble.

"You did not answer my question," Francesco pointed out sternly. "Paolo is pressing for a wedding before summer. What am I to tell him?"

"What?" Bianca gasped sharply, "But I thought he considered me as yet too young for the responsibilities of a marriage."

Francesco shrugged. "Your beauty grows more bewitching with each new day. It is no wonder the man has reconsidered his plan to wait a year or two."

"Well I have not!" Bianca replied quickly. "I am not eager to wed, not this year or the next!"

"You see, Francesco. I told you she would not be pleased by your news," Catherine called softly from the comfort of her bed. "Paolo spends too much of his time counting his money and too little courting Bianca. You must tell him how to win our daughter's love since he obviously does not have the sense to discover how to do so himself."

"He need not court her, Catherine. The matter was settled between us last year," Francesco explained impatiently.

Caught in the midst of her parents' conversation, Bianca looked first at the lovely blonde snuggled in the spacious bed and then at her father's determined expression. "Let's discuss this another time," she begged. "We are all too tired to debate Paolo's failings tonight."

Francesco rose to walk his headstrong daughter to the door, but he cautioned her before she left the room. "You must think only of the many fine qualities Paolo possesses for as his bride you should flatter his vanity, not criticize his faults."

"Is that how Mother treats you?" Bianca asked coquettishly, smiling in the hope of distracting him from a line of conversation she had no wish to pursue.

"Your father has no faults." Catherine's declaration was followed by a lilting giggle.

As Bianca closed the door she saw her father smile as he turned toward the bed and she heard her mother's sultry laughter. She envied her parents, for the magic of their love was an everlasting joy while she had no hope of discovering such bliss with Paolo Sammarese.

Once alone in her room, Bianca could not find the

energy to undress, and was grateful when her mother's maid appeared to help her. She sat fidgeting nervously while Lucia brushed out her hair, then dismissed the woman and climbed into bed, but she found the peace of dreams elusive. Only that night she'd hoped for more excitement in her life, had dreamed of romance and had longed for the thrill of love, but Evan Sinclair's attentions had simply frightened and confused her. He posed more problems rather than providing a solution to the dilemma of what she was to do with her life. Well, he would soon be gone, and while she might have to bear his presence at a few more parties, she'd be rid of him. Paolo, on the other hand, would be there forever. Tears filled her eyes as she thought of the wealthy Venetian. Like the elegant palaces of Venice, he, too, had a pleasing façade, but that was all. He had no heart. The Antonellis were a powerful family, just as Stefano had said, and her father had instructed her from childhood that such prominence brought responsibility. Paolo was the very soul of responsibility, but the light kisses he occasionally placed upon her cheek had never stirred her heart or warmed her blood as did Evan Sinclair's slightest glance. She'd not been able to suppress a shiver of delight when he'd caressed her breast lightly, yet she was relieved that he'd not pressed for any further advantage when she undoubtedly would have had little strength to resist. By dawn she was no more certain of what she should do than when she'd gone to bed, but when she finally fell into a fitful sleep her graceful body was warmed by memories of the handsome stranger's magical touch, while his golden glance burned brightly in her dreams.

In stark contrast to Bianca's restlessness, Evan's sleep was undisturbed. The next morning he visited the glass factories on the island of Murano, to complete the business dealings which were supposedly the reason he'd come to Venice; then he returned to San Marco to meet Bianca. From a peddler woman he bought a small bag of corn to throw to the pigeons while he paced up and down the spacious Piazza San Marco, and though he made every attempt to appear carefree, he was almost certain the delicate beauty would not appear. That possibility frustrated him greatly. Perhaps he had misread her glance as well as her words and she did not find him attractive. That possibility had not even occurred to him the previous evening until he'd found her a difficult young woman to handle. Not difficult, impossible, he finally had to admit. If only he had realized beforehand what a volatile creature she was, he would not have been so foolhardy as to have kidnapped her, no matter how briefly. That had been a grave error on his part, one he'd not risk repeating.

Not a man to waste his time brooding over mistakes, however, Evan continued to play the part of a tourist, and took a moment to admire the ornate marble façade of the cathedral, the basilica of Saint Mark, which faced the square. He marveled that it had once served as a private chapel for the dukes of Venice when it could comfortably hold a thousand worshipers. The city, built upon one hundred eighteen islands, fascinated him for there was nothing in America to compare with it. Located between East and West, Venice had once been the gateway to the Orient, so prosperous a trading center that her most ambitious citizens had amassed fabulous fortunes and had lined the Grand Canal with their palaces. In the fifteenth century Venice had been an important center for the exchange of goods, as well as the mightiest seapower of the Mediterranean. The Venetian shipyards, still known by the Arabic word for a house of construction, the Arsenale, had launched a new galley every few hours, a rate Evan found staggering to contemplate. But he had learned all their secrets of prefabricated construction, and he planned to implement certain improvements in his own firm when he returned home. The power of Venice had declined rapidly with the discovery of the New World and the sea route to India, but Evan found the study of history a most worthwhile pursuit since it provided a key to the future.

With a weary sigh, he turned back to the pigeons encircling his feet, tossing them the last of the corn one kernel at a time and feeling very foolish for having come to the piazza. He'd had scant experience in courting respectable young ladies, but he'd found Bianca Antonelli intriguing and so he could not have stayed away simply to save his pride. If she did not arrive soon, he was determined to try to impress her at the next party he attended, and the next, until someone found his attentions annoying and came after him. If only he had some clue as to what Bianca had thought of Charles, but there was no way for him to ascertain that without tipping his hand. "Blast!" he muttered under his breath, furious that his plan was proving to be so difficult to carry out when he'd thought it would all be so easy.

While Evan passed his time recalling the glories of Venice as he paced the granite stones of the piazza, Bianca stood in the shadows at the base of the brick campanile, observing him, for the American provided a most entertaining sight. In a well-tailored navy blue coat, maroon brocade vest and white breeches he was every bit as handsome as he'd been in the black velvet costume. Tall and well built, he radiated a stirring masculine vitality, even at a distance. The cuffless coat allowed bits of his ruffled shirt sleeves to show against the backs of his hands, and the contrast between the snowy linen and his dark skin made her wonder if perhaps that deep bronze tan graced every inch of his powerful body. She had seen statues of males, though never a live man nude, and her imagination painted Evan Sinclair with a vividness which provoked the bright blush he continually brought to her cheeks. More than once she tried to force herself to flee to the safety of her gondola, but before she could depart, he chanced to glance in her direction and it was too late to leave unobserved. Nodding slightly toward the cathedral, Bianca walked toward the entrance with a purposeful step as though she were late for her daily devotions. Once inside, she waited for Evan to appear before she continued down the left portico and turned into the small chapel of St. Isidore and knelt at the rail before the altar.

"You are late," Evan scolded hoarsely, attempting to appear more interested in the splendid golden mosaics which adorned the cathedral's high, vaulted ceiling than the beautiful young woman as he knelt by her side.

"And you are an arrogant fool!" Bianca responded in a hushed whisper. "I came only to beg you to forget we ever met. My life is too complicated as it is, and nothing can come of this infatuation of yours save grief."

"Infatuation?" A slow smile curved Evan's well-shaped mouth, for he found that term highly amusing. Infatuations were for lovesick youngsters and he was a grown man. Still, it served his purpose to let her think he'd simply been smitten by her beauty. He raised his hand and then lowered it gently to cover hers. "Aren't you being overly dramatic, my dear? How can either of us come to grief? Surely we do not deserve so tragic a fate." Rejoicing in his heart, Evan was certain Bianca had just revealed an important clue. She was warning him. If he could encourage her to tell him whom it was she feared, his task would be completed swiftly.

Bianca found the heat of the persistent young man's touch impossibly distracting, but when she tried to pull her hand from beneath his, Evan slipped his fingers around her wrist so she'd not escape him. Angered by his sudden show of strength, she whispered emphatically, "I must go and I'll not ever see you again."

Although astonished that this spirited blonde had so little interest in knowing him, Evan had no intention of allowing her to flee. "No. You must wait. I showed few manners last night and beg your forgiveness. I meant you no disrespect, but my time here is very brief and I'll not waste a minute of it. Now, tell me precisely why you've no desire to see me. Who might cause us this grief of which you spoke?"

Exasperated by his insistence that she remain when she had clearly expressed her desire to leave, Bianca explained through clenched teeth, "I told you, both my father and Paolo consider me to be engaged." Yet that excuse rang false even in her own ears. She had come there that day because she could not have stayed away. He fascinated her, but he frightened her; and she feared her heart was beating so rapidly he might actually be able to hear it's frantic flutter.

Evan needed one name, not two. Again he attempted to win her confidence. "But you do not consider yourself to be engaged?"

"No! I do not!" Bianca responded with a defiant burst of spirit.

Seeing the sparkle of angry tears begin to glisten upon her long lashes, Evan relaxed his hold upon her, certain that she'd tell him no more that day. Instead of simply releasing her hand, however, he brought it to his lips; kissing her slightly moist palm tenderly. "I will accept your word as the truth then," he told her with what he hoped would be a reassuring smile.

Before he could request another such secret meeting, Bianca withdrew her hand, which was still trembling from the heat of his lips, and hurried away. It had been lunacy to meet him, she knew that now, and she could not still the rapid pounding of her heart until she'd rejoined Raffaella in the safety of their gondola. She'd told herself she'd come more out of curiosity than for any other reason, yet she did not now attempt to lie to herself. She knew this was certainly not infatuation on her part, but something far more primitive. The desire he created within her heart with no more than a sly glance and light kiss appalled her for there was no possible future in pursuing such an attraction, none whatsoever. The man was very handsome, perhaps more of a gentleman than she'd dared hope, but how could an American help her avoid a marriage she'd fooled herself into believing wasn't inevitable? What could Evan Sinclair possibly do to help her? Nothing that she could see, nothing at all.

Not one to give up so easily, Evan followed Bianca through the piazza to the edge of the lagoon passing between the two columns bearing the statues of the patrons of Venice: Saint Theodore and the lion of Saint Mark. He waved to a gondolier waiting to be hired, intending to pursue the young lady. It took a moment for him to explain that he wished to follow the golden-haired beauty whose gondola was rapidly disappearing in the distance but at last the man understood. Evan sank down low in his seat, hoping that if Bianca glanced back she'd not see him, and that tactic seemed effective. However, she did not return to her home as he'd expected, but instead went in the opposite direction. Curious, Evan followed until she stopped at the door of a modest home painted a bright shade of yellow. She and her cousin were welcomed inside, and when she did not soon reappear, he gave up his vigil and returned to the *Phoenix*.

Bianca had more than a dozen costumes for she loved Carnival, but her father had again reminded her that

Paolo would not only be her escort for the night, he would soon be her husband, and she was thoroughly depressed by that dreary prospect. Choosing an elegant gown which matched her mood she dressed in black velvet and hid her golden tresses beneath a lacy black veil. "I think I shall say I am Death should anyone inquire," she told Raffaella calmly. "Why should Death be portrayed as a skeleton, why not as a young woman for a change?"

"Death? Where did you get so morbid an idea?" Raffaella had chosen a vibrant yellow dress, and her mask was painted with the bright plumage of an exotic tropical bird. "Why not something more festive? Carnival season should be full of gaiety, not gloom." She was in a merry mood. Having found Marco to be a most charming companion during the few minutes they'd spent alone together, she was eager to see him again, and hoped he would be looking forward to seeing her.

Not wishing to justify her comments, Bianca turned slowly in front of her mirror, surprised by the way the somber folds of the black gown showed off her slender figure while the color of the midnight sky made her own fair beauty all the more vivid. She picked up a silver mask and matching fan before moving toward the door. "I will wait for Paolo downstairs. Join us as soon as you are ready."

"Oh, Bianca," Raffaella called after her cousin, "Evan Sinclair plans to attend every party at which you are present. Marco told me so last night. Isn't that unusual devotion for a barbarian?"

The blonde young woman hesitated momentarily, uncertain what to do if that were truly the case. She could give Paolo an excuse and remain at home, but since she was never ill, doing so would only worry him and make him suspicious. She'd discussed the American in as limited a way as possible that morning, but she could see by Raffaella's amused expression the girl was enjoying making her uncomfortable for a change.

"Well, what is it?" Raffaella asked pointedly. "If you don't wish to see him again, you need not leave Paolo's side. That should discourage him quite thoroughly."

"The man means nothing to me; I told you that this morning!" Bianca responded in a sudden fit of temper.

"Which one?" Raffaella asked with a teasing giggle, "Paolo, or Evan Sinclair?"

"Both!" Bianca replied, then slammed the door behind her. She hurried down the stairs to escape her cousin's teasing, though she knew she was only avoiding the issue.

Paolo Sammarese was dressed in bright red that night, an unusual choice for so serious an individual, and he made no comment upon Bianca's selection of a costume. He escorted her and Raffaella to a ball being given by one of his associates in one of the palacial homes located upon the Grand Canal. No sooner had they entered the ballroom, which was brightly illuminated by the candles flaming in four magnificent crystal chandeliers, than he excused himself to discuss a business matter with their host. Distressed because she'd now have no way to avoid Evan Sinclair's attentions should he arrive as predicted, Bianca tapped her fan nervously against her palm in an agitated rhythm. When the American finally did appear he was dressed as an Indian, in buckskins, and the soft suede suit accented his unusual height and muscular frame, endowing him with a sensuous grace that male and female guests readily turned to admire. Instead of a mask, he wore a streak of warpaint on each cheek, and feathers were braided in his auburn hair. When he glanced about the crowded room, obviously searching for her, Bianca hoped her mask would hide her blush, but the pretty rose color which flooded her cheeks was plainly visible to his practiced eye.

Her obvious reluctance to speak with him was not lost

upon Evan, so he paused at her side only briefly. "Forgive me if my attentions last night, or this morning, simply annoyed you but—"

"There is nothing to forgive," Bianca replied with a graciousness she truly didn't feel.

"You are much too kind, Miss Antonelli." With a courtly bow, Evan moved on to rejoin Marco, who had stopped to greet several young men. His brief exchange with Bianca had taken only a few seconds, and Marco had not even noticed that his American client had strayed away.

Accepting a goblet of wine from a passing servant, Bianca found its refreshing coolness did not sooth her ravaged feelings. It was not the American's fault that he was so terribly handsome, rather hers for finding him so irresistibly attractive. Yet she could not encourage his attentions when her father insisted Paolo would soon be her husband. While she had always loved the elaborate costumes and festive parties of Carnival, that night she felt as though she were suffocating in the boisterous crowd, and moving to the end of the dance floor she stepped out upon the balcony to breathe deeply of the crisp night air. Removing her mask, she cooled herself with the silver fan, wondering meanwhile how long she might enjoy the pleasant solitude before someone else felt the need for fresh air. Lights sparkled along the canal, their reflection glistening on the water like stars fallen from the heavens, and she sighed wistfully as she admired their calm beauty.

"Have you grown weary of the evening's festivities so swiftly?" Evan inquired as he stepped to her side. "I waited to see if another man would follow you, but when none did, I thought perhaps you were waiting for me."

"For you?" Bianca asked incredulously. "Why would I be waiting for you?"

Evan smiled as though he found the insulting tone of

her question amusing. "Despite what you told me last night, and again this morning, I do believe you are engaged to Paolo Sammarese, but fortunately for me, the man means nothing to you."

"Mr. Sinclair, you should not allow your imagination such free rein," Bianca advised him, boldly tapping her fan upon his broad chest but she instantly regretted that flirtatious gesture when he moved closer still.

"Is this no more than my imagination?" Evan asked as he drew her into his arms. He had meant to kiss her only lightly, but he could feel her trembling again and he wanted it to be from pleasure this time, not fear. She fit so perfectly in his embrace, and she could not escape him as his hands moved slowly down her spine pressing her close as he savored the delights of her small moist mouth before at last stepping away. The surprise in her glance made her eyes seem enormous as she gazed up at him, her lashes so long and thick he wondered for a moment if they were not part of her costume. "Does Paolo's kiss make you tremble with desire as mine does?" As he leaned down to whisper softly in her ear he was entranced anew by the subtle yet intoxicatingly sweet fragrance of her perfume.

Unable to offer any coherent reply, Bianca brushed past him, reentering the festive atmosphere of the ball and hurrying to the group of men that included Paolo. She placed her hand upon his sleeve and smiled brightly. "Must you speak of nothing but business and politics at such a gay time?" While their host and the other men laughed, clearly charmed by her question, Paolo gave her a disapproving glance.

"It is not time yet for the dancing to begin. Can't you find someone else with whom to converse for a while as you did last night? I am quite busy."

Horribly embarrassed by that curt rebuff, Bianca quickly avoided the other men's startled glances and turned away. But Evan Sinclair, who had observed what had happened, smiled at her in the sly knowing fashion she found so unnerving. The man seemed to have recognized her despair although she'd not voiced it, and it was not a comforting feeling to be so transparent in her emotions. What did the man see with those golden eyes of his? All her secrets laid bare?

Evan found himself observing Bianca with growing admiration, for rather than being crushed by Paolo's rude rejection she seemed stubbornly bent upon charming every other man in the room. Paolo Sammarese was a great fool in his opinion. He'd clearly hurt this captivating blonde's feelings, and she was paying him back by flirting quite openly with the other young men present. Was this what had happened the night Charles had met her? Had she merely been trying to get back at Paolo, and had Charles been enchanted by her? Reminding himself that the other men in the room also bore watching, Evan was disappointed to find so many had chosen to wear the *bautta* that night. It was a Carnival costume, but he'd learned that the *bautta* was frequently used as a disguise. It consisted of a black silk cape with a hood which left a small opening for the face. Its wearer added a mask to cover his eyes and nose, and then topped the hood with a tricorne hat. The most popular of costumes, it was worn by men and women, by rich and poor. Evan did not know the other guests well enough to correctly guess their identities in that garb so he kept his eyes upon Bianca, seeking clues as to the men who found her company especially fascinating. Unfortunately, as at the previous evening's party, she was extremely popular, amazingly so for a young woman already engaged to be wed.

On her part, although she danced each dance with a new partner, Bianca found the evening passing far too slowly. From time to time Paolo would seek out her company, as if to remind her as well as the others that she was his, but while he had remarkable skill upon the dance floor, he was a difficult partner. To him, dancing provided an opportunity to put on an exhibition, and Bianca felt as though he were constantly testing her, expecting to find her lacking in grace just when that lack would be most evident. Other men kept her entertained. They laughed with her so frequently that she scarcely noted what music was being played, but when Paolo took her hand, she found it difficult to even smile. It was quite late when Evan Sinclair appeared at her side. By that time she did not feel up to parrying his verbal thrusts, but he surprised her with his request.

"I have been exploring the house a bit, a liberty I hope will not be considered rude. If you have not seen more than this ballroom, I shall be happy to show it to you. I promise to behave as a gentleman should for a change. Wouldn't you like to escape this crowd for a moment or two?"

Bianca first turned to see where Paolo was, and she found him deep in conversation with their host and several others. Why had she stopped to consider his reaction? she wondered. Clearly he cared little what she did. He would neither notice that she was gone, nor care. Still, she did not feel comfortable with the handsome American. However, when she looked up at her tall companion, her initial suspicion as to the purpose of his invitation and the fear of her own lack of restraint with him faded under the warmth of his engaging smile. "Yes, to enjoy a few minutes of quiet would be delightful," she finally agreed, and placing her fingertips upon Evan's sleeve, she followed his lead. They quickly left the happy confusion of the crowded ballroom, traversing the adjoining rooms until they arrived at a study whose walls were decorated in brilliant yellow silk woven with an oriental motif depicting chrysanthemums and exotic birds.

"This is a lovely room, don't you think?" Bianca wandered about for a moment, taking time to admire the delicately carved jade statuary displayed on three teakwood tables before she sat down upon the window seat to rest. Looking out at the star-filled heavens, she mused softly as she again removed her mask, "It must be close to midnight."

"It is a pity I did not arrive in Venice sooner. Carnival season is nearly over, isn't it?"

"Yes, everything ends at the stroke of midnight on Shrove Tuesday, the day before Lent begins. That is next week."

"Is the last ball the best?" Evan remained standing, hoping not to frighten her away as he had earlier in the evening.

"Oh, yes." Bianca's smile was impish. "All of Venice celebrates that night. It is impossible to walk through the Piazza San Marco; the crowd is so thick. There are jugglers and acrobats, musicians; it is a wonderful celebration, and all of Venice is there."

"Your parents allow you to mingle with the common folk?" Evan asked, with a teasing grin.

"No, not really. But I have been there on Shrove Thursday when the Doge takes part in the festivities. That will all take place tomorrow, and you should not miss it. There are fireworks to commemorate the victory at Aquileia in 1162 and—" Suddenly embarrassed by her enthusiasm which had made her overly talkative, Bianca blushed deeply and looked back out at the night.

"The Doge is your president, is he not?" Evan asked calmly, but he did not understand her sudden reticence, nor her refusal to continue her colorful description.

"Yes, and my father is one of his advisors," Bianca explained with undisguised pride.

That was something Evan already knew. But the fact that Bianca's father could call upon the most powerful man in Venice for aid if his daughter attracted a troublesome suitor did not excuse murder. "I have yet to meet your father. Why is it your parents did not attend Paolo's party or this one?"

"Because they attend very few." Bianca realized as she spoke that her words explained little about the devoted couple. "They have many friends, but usually prefer their own company to that of others. They entertain in our home frequently, however. They are not reclusive."

Evan shifted his weight uneasily. It was not that his moccasins were uncomfortable; Bianca's soft voice and sweet manner aroused feelings he had no wish to savor at the moment. He'd come to avenge his brother's death, he reminded himself sharply, not simply to seduce the young woman whose distracting beauty was responsible for it. Still, if there was no other way to discover the murderer's name, he'd damn well do that. "Since Paolo is your father's choice, not yours, what are you going to do about it?"

Shocked by the impertinence of that question, Bianca rose quickly, certain she'd made a serious mistake in tarrying so long with him. That carelessness had apparently inspired him to again become impudent after she had made every effort to converse with him pleasantly. "I must return to the others."

"Wait." Evan reached out to catch her arm, but attempted to make his grip upon her light, not confining. "Is there someone else, another man you'd prefer to wed but to whom your parents object?" A very jealous man who tolerated Paolo, but who had murdered Charles, he thought.

"Mr. Sinclair, really it is—"

As she looked up at him the harshness in his expression suddenly softened. She saw him incline his head yet was powerless to resist the heady excitement he created within her as his lips again conquered hers. She could not struggle for his warm expression of affection was so inviting she had no wish to continue to object to the love he seemed intent upon giving. Instead, she wound her arms around his neck and returned his deep kiss with a passion which shocked him. He drew away with a startled frown. Surprised to find that this time she had made him blush, Bianca began to laugh. "Well, isn't that what you wanted?"

Evan again told himself his mission was one of revenge, but the fire this lovely blonde's delectable kisses had ignited in his blood made such reasonable thought impossible. Pulling her back into his arms, he vowed hoarsely, "No, I want far more." Crushing her in a forceful embrace, he could feel the wild beating of her heart through the soft suede of his fringed shirt. Once again she did not fight him, instead her lithe figure melted gracefully against his lean frame. Her kiss was teasing, gentle, inspiring in him a desire for more than he had any right to take, and when his knees grew weak with desire he pulled her down upon the cushioned window seat to savor her surrender to the fullest. His lavish kisses strayed down her slender throat, finding the taste of her creamy smooth flesh delicious, but as his hand moved tenderly over the soft swell of her breast she suddenly shoved him away.

Unwilling to allow her to stop him now, Evan reached out to encircle her waist, hoping to lure Bianca back into his arms, but he understood the abrupt change in her mood when he followed the direction of her panic-filled glance and saw Paolo Sammarese standing at the doorway silently observing them. The Venetian scowled angrily as he swiftly strode forward and reached for Bianca's hand. Without speaking a word, he swept her to her feet and promptly escorted her from the room but the terrified gaze in her eyes had told Evan all he wanted to know. With a slow smile of satisfaction he returned to the party, but just as he'd expected, Paolo and Bianca were already gone.

Chapter III

Evan lay awake long into the night, carefully plotting the strategy of his next move. He'd finally learned that Paolo Sammarese would take action if forced to, but the fact that Sammarese had not demanded satisfaction the moment he'd discovered Bianca in Evan's arms revealed a great deal about him. The dandy was clearly a coward or he'd have issued a challenge the instant he'd found Bianca enfolded in such a passionate embrace. Instead, the Venetian had done nothing but spirit the lovely blonde away with great haste. What would such a man do next? Evan wondered. Send out a hired assassin, or merely make certain there were no further opportunities for Bianca to meet him alone before his ship left Venice? If Paolo had killed once to keep Bianca for his own, would he attempt the same evil deed again, or would he be more cautious this time and simply wait for the *Phoenix* to depart?

Puzzled by the man's reluctance to fight him, Evan found himself forced to consider other possibilities. Bianca's father seemed to pay as little attention to her as did Paolo, but was he in reality a more determined man, one who would not stop at murder to protect his lovely daughter's virtue? Only one person would know for certain. Having found sleep impossible, Evan rose and dressed in dark clothing, bent upon learning all he could before the first light of dawn lit the sky.

Although Venice was totally unique, a labyrinth of islands connected by four hundred bridges and intersected by nearly two hundred canals, he'd spent a good many hours studying an accurately drawn map of the city, and he swiftly made his way to the Ca' Antonelli in a small boat he rowed himself. There was only one light showing in the three-story palace, in a room on the top floor. He prayed it would be Bianca's for he doubted she could sleep any more easily than he could that night. He secured his boat to the mooring posts which bore the coat of arms of the Antonelli family, then began to climb up the delicate Gothic stonework which decorated the marble façade of the palace. The quadrafoil motif above the windows provided convenient footholds for a man used to the complexities of a ship's rigging. He scaled the building in a matter of minutes and climbed up upon the balcony outside the single illuminated room. Edging toward the French doors, he leaned over cautiously to peer inside, and found to his relief it was, indeed, Bianca's bedchamber. The slender blonde was now dressed in a sheer linen gown and lay stretched out upon the bed, her cheek resting upon her arm, but she was sobbing silently rather than sleeping. Evan found the graceful beauty's tears strangely moving, and he hesitated a moment before disturbing her. He'd never meant to hurt her, merely to court her in order to lure Charles's murderer out into the open. He had used her very badly, he realized with a sudden stab of remorse, but that had been unavoidable. Reminding himself his cause was a just one, he tried the door, and finding it unlocked, stepped into the dimly lit bedroom.

Bianca sat up abruptly, badly startled by Evan's sudden appearance. "How dare you come here?" She whispered in a voice hoarse with tears, obviously astonished to find he'd somehow gained entrance to her room.

Evan raised a fingertip to his lips in a plea for silence, then crossed the room to make certain the door was locked. To his dismay he found it had been secured from the opposite side. Returning to the disheveled Bianca's side he spoke softly. "I feared you might have been punished for what happened tonight, and that indiscretion was entirely my fault, not yours."

Pleased to find him in so contrite a mood, Bianca hastily wiped away her tears and attempted to smile. "Does marriage strike you as an appropriate punishment?"

"Marriage to whom?" Evan asked suspiciously, for he'd not expected to be forced to marry Bianca simply because Paolo had seen him kissing her.

The lovely young woman stared at Evan's intense expression for some moments before replying. "You needn't look so stricken, Mr. Sinclair. Your name was not even suggested as a possibility. Paolo and I are to be married two days hence, on Saturday."

"What?" Evan found that news deeply troubling. He'd wanted the arrogant Venetian to devote his energies to coming after him, not merely to tightening his hold upon Bianca. "When was this decided?"

"Tonight," Bianca explained sadly. "To marry so swiftly will surely cause a scandal, but Paolo insisted I marry him before Lent begins or he threatened to break our engagement. My father knew that would have brought me even greater disgrace. My good name has been ruined apparently, and all because of you." Yet, as she looked up at him, Bianca could think only of how compelling his fiery kisses had been. He had provided affection in such abundance, perhaps all she would ever know. Her eyes again flooded with hot tears.

"You must not weep over this. Please don't." Evan sat down by the fragile beauty's side and gathered her into his arms, cradling her head gently against his chest. A subtle trace of perfume still lingered in her golden hair, and he lifted his hand to brush a stray curl away from her damp cheek before he bent down to kiss her temple lightly. "Why did you not object to Paolo before this if you did not want him for your husband?"

"Oh, I have always objected to him!" Bianca replied angrily, "But my objections were ignored. He is very rich you see, and my parents consider him the finest match I could make."

Evan continued to stroke her golden tresses gently, sorry he'd not thought of a plan which would have resulted in a less unfortunate circumstance for her. "It sounds as though your father and Paolo are very close," he murmured softly, hoping still to draw some useful information from her lips before he left her for the last time.

"No, not really. They respect one another, that is true, but they are not good friends." Relaxing in his warm embrace, Bianca found it difficult, as always, to concentrate upon anything other than the warmth of his powerful body and the strength which he now kept in check as he held her. Her heart was beating too rapidly, and she realized with sudden embarrassment that the sheer fabric of her gown revealed far too much of her figure. Sitting up very primly to remedy that unfortunate circumstance, she spoke with forced calm. "You must go. If we are found together again—"

For a reason Evan could not even begin to comprehend, the fear which lit her green eyes with emerald fire drew him nearer rather than making him eager to depart. There were many ways to take the revenge he sought, and to give free rein to the desire he could no longer suppress suddenly seemed to be one of the best. "We will not be disturbed again tonight, all the others are asleep," he assured her softly.

"How can you be certain?" Bianca asked shyly.

"Because yours is the only room with a light." Reaching out to catch her hand, Evan pulled her across his lap. "Let's not waste another moment," he whispered seductively as his lips sought the same sweet taste of surrender he'd enjoyed so much earlier that evening. Unlike her black velvet costume, the fine linen of her gown presented no barrier to his touch and his fingertips teased the soft pink tips of her breasts until they became firm peaks. His tongue met hers in a lazy caress, drawing her ever deeper into the intoxicating spell of romance he was taking such care to weave. Then his fingertips strayed down her ribs and across the flatness of her stomach to rest at last upon the fullness of her thigh before drawing the soft folds of the linen gown ever higher until he'd revealed the smooth flesh of her leg. Her lightly perfumed skin was soft and creamy, a delight to touch, and he gently traced the distance to her knee before returning to her bare hip. He hesitated a moment, concentrating upon the delectable flavor of her kiss before he slid his hand down to the triangle of soft curls nestled between her thighs. She tried to pull away then, as he'd known she would, but he held her captive in a confining embrace. Knowing well how to give a woman the greatest of pleasures, he swiftly conquered all resistance to the intimacy he'd longed to share. His fingertips filled her with the first rush of ecstasy then his hand again strayed down the graceful line of her thigh before returning to torment her anew with his magical caress. Her flesh grew warm and moist, eager for first knowledge of his well-muscled body, and Evan felt a great sense of satisfaction. He knew he could have Bianca now, steal her innocence and be gone, shaming Paolo with a bride who'd already savored every delight a man could give, one who would never be satisfied with an unfeeling husband such as the haughty Venetian would surely make. It was a temptation he swiftly discarded, however, for he wanted to make his brother's murderer suffer greatly for his crimes. He did not want merely to humiliate him.

Bianca had no hint of the turmoil in Evan's soul; she felt only the tide of pleasure swelling to an ever-heightening crest within her heart. This man had fascinated her at first glance; that he frightened as well as thrilled her no longer seemed important. She'd have no other chance to share the rapture he was creating, and she wanted to savor it until dawn. She held him locked in her own embrace, his mouth now a captive of hers while she bent her knee gracefully to encourage him to take his tantalizing caress ever deeper. Her mind refused to consider the consequences she'd have to face; instead, she longed only to return the gift of pleasure he was so generously lavishing upon her.

Reason swiftly fled Evan's mind once Bianca began to enchant him with the delights of her incomparable affection. Her lips were warm and pliant, and her slender fingers moved slowly through his thick auburn hair as she held his mouth pressed tightly against her own. As the hunger of his kisses grew more desperate, she undid the buttons on his shirt so she might savor the warmth of his deeply tanned skin more easily. His broad chest was covered with a tangled mat of auburn curls which tapered to a thin line as they grew across the hardened muscles of his flat stomach. She found his brass belt buckle a simple matter to unfasten, and slipped her hand inside his breeches to explore the last secret his magnificent body had to reveal. Then she matched the rhythm of her caresses to his, teasing, taunting, igniting a fire within his loins only she had the means to quench.

Evan had been with more women than he could count

let alone begin to name, but never had he encountered a beauty with the skills this exquisite blonde possessed. How did she manage to project the demure countenance of a virgin when clearly she was no stranger to love? Her possessive touch held not the slightest trace of shyness, but encircled him with a thrilling caress which drove him to the brink of rapture before he found the strength to draw away. "Your gown," he urged gently, peeling it away with one deft tug. He then tore off what remained of his own clothing before he stretched out beside her upon the enormous bed. His golden glance traveled slowly down her superb figure, noting that her creamy skin was flushed with the same radiant desire that had turned his blood to fire. She was posed gracefully upon the pillows, her long slender legs tempting not only his eyes but the very marrow of his being to claim her for his own. He leaned down to kiss her breast, and found he could not draw away. His tongue slid over the delicate pink tip, savoring that intimacy with an overwhelming joy as she drew him into her arms. That was her secret, he realized with only a dim awareness. Not merely content to accept affection, she gave love in abundance. Her touch, her kiss, her sultry glance, each gesture she made was filled with the most generous expression of love he'd ever felt, but he'd not be satisfied until he'd taken far more.

The sweetest of smiles lit Bianca's face as she let her fingertips slide down Evan's spine. His body was as perfect as she'd imagined it would be, more splendid than any classical statue carved of marble, for he was vibrantly alive. She pressed him closer still, drinking in his intoxicating warmth as though she would never have her fill. This was the true beauty she'd known love to possess, and she would never give herself to Paolo with the same fiery abandon. This would be her most precious secret, one she'd take to her grave: that she'd loved Evan Sinclair with all her heart and soul, and although they had shared that wonder for no more than one night, the splendid memory would live within her heart forever.

Evan slowly turned the slender blonde in his arms as his eager lips traced the perfection of her graceful form. She was all any woman could ever be, and he paused for no more than a fraction of a second, the question only in his glance before he moved to possess her fully. She raised her hands to his shoulders to welcome his advance, her fingertips light yet demanding as he lowered his mouth to hers and his first forceful thrust seared their bodies into one. Instantly he realized his mistake, and although it shocked him to learn she'd been a virgin, he did not withdraw. He lay motionless within her, hoping the pain he'd caused her would swiftly subside so their union would bring her the same deep pleasure he knew it would bring to him. He kissed her cheeks, the long sweep of her eyelashes, and bit her lips playfully, but when he could no longer ignore the urgency which throbbed within him he began to move again. Although he had meant to be slow and sweet, the strength of his desire soon forced him to strike a far more rapid pace as he plunged ever deeper into the soft sweet center of her being, which now belonged solely to him. To his dismay, that knowledge sent his spirit soaring while his smooth sleek body dominated her lissome figure with masterful ease. He had been the first to savor her charms; that was not a gift he'd regard lightly. No indeed, she was his woman now, and he meant to keep her.

Bianca held Evan tightly, each of her senses filled to overflowing with the splendor of his loving. She had not expected him to be so tender a lover, to be so gentle and considerate of her, but that thought brought tears to her eyes. She wanted to stay with him forever, to taste the ecstasy of his kiss every day, to spend each night as she had this one: locked in his arms, enveloped in his loving embrace. She arched her back to meet his thrusts as the intensity of his motions made further dreams impossible. She was simply his, their bodies and hearts so in tune the rapture which flooded through him burst within her in shimmering waves, pleasure coming in endless ripples of delight which left her as breathless as he. When at last she lay contentedly resting in his arms, the realization that they would soon be parted was one she couldn't bear to face.

While he appeared relaxed with Bianca's head cradled upon his chest, his fingers slowly combing through her glossy curls, Evan was busy thinking of how best to alter his plans to take advantage of this sudden bit of good fortune. He had her to thank for the inspiration to take her home with him to America. Surely that ploy would force the villain who'd slain Charles to take up their trail, and that would place the advantage squarely in his own hands. He'd not have to take steps to avoid the authorities of Venice who'd back Paolo or her father, then. No, he'd be free to do as he wished on the high seas. The *Phoenix* was heavily armed, and was manned by a skilled crew who'd fought with honor during the Revolution, loyal and hardworking seafarers all. He could ask for no better men to fight by his side. Yes, her idea was the best. He'd take her with him, and then, when Charles's killer pursued him to claim her, he'd take his revenge. "It is nearly dawn. Pack only the belongings you can't bear to leave behind and we'll set sail for America immediately."

Bianca raised herself upon one elbow, then had to toss her heavy cascade of curls aside so she could look down at the man who fascinated her still. The bright blush of passion filled her cheeks with a rosy glow as she replied, "I can't go with you. I told you I must marry Paolo, it is all arranged."

Outraged by that ridiculous response, Evan sat up and

yanked Bianca up beside him. "You have only used me then? You meant this night to be a good-bye rather than a beginning?" That he was also using her seemed irrelevant at the moment. "Do you think Paolo is so stupid he will not realize you are no longer a virgin?"

The fury of his temper both shocked and angered Bianca, and she begged him to be quiet. "Please, my situation is desperate enough. Do not make so much noise someone will come and find us together!"

"So you'll not even deny it?" Evan asked again, his voice only a fraction lower in volume. "You have merely used me?"

The fire in his glance again turned the warm brown of his eyes to molten gold, and Bianca searched her mind frantically for the words to soothe him. "No, I have not used you, of course not, but destiny has allowed our paths to cross only briefly. Soon you'll be gone and I'll be married to Paolo," she explained sadly. "If my first child is yours, I will not be sorry."

The prospect of Paolo Sammarese raising his son was so appalling that Evan wound his fingers in her golden curls, capturing her mouth in a savage kiss he did not end until her surrender was complete. He made love to her with deliberate care this time, meaning to conquer all resistance to his plan. He carried her spirit aloft with his own, letting the pleasure which flowed so easily between them again fuse their bodies into one before he paused to demand, "I am the one you'll marry Bianca. You'll be my wife. Now say yes!"

Her mind blurred from pleasure so intense it was nearly pain, Bianca could find neither the strength nor the resolve to argue. She wanted only for him to end the torment which filled her loins with longing, to complete what he'd begun before she perished in the anguish of her desire. "Yes," she whispered in a desperate plea, her mouth then seeking his and the release only his loving could bring. She had the wild spirit of a gypsy. He could not deny the intensity of her unspoken demand, and he enfolded her in his embrace, the fire of his passion now contained and directed solely at pleasing her.

The next time Evan spoke, his mood was an exuberant one, "Well, my love, get up and pack. We must be on our way before the first light of dawn. We've not a second to waste." He moved to the side of the bed then, meaning to get dressed, but when Bianca did not move, he turned to look down at her, regretting the haste with which they had to depart for her loveliness made him long to remain in bed.

Bianca was uncertain, not exactly comprehending what he'd enticed her into doing, and she sat up slowly, hoping she could make her point now. "Today is Shrove Thursday, when the Doge joins in the celebrations in the Piazza San Marco. Everyone will attend and I can slip away then to meet you."

Evan saw the lovely girl's chin tremble slightly, and doubted she was speaking the truth. He was unwilling to risk leaving without her, but he didn't want to call her a liar to her face. "No, my pet. You must come with me now. The morning tide beckons and we can't tarry."

"But I cannot leave like this," Bianca implored him. "Last night everyone was so angry with me. My father was furious to learn I'd left Paolo's side to meet secretly with you, and my mother simply sobbed over the disgrace. I have hurt them both with my thoughtless behavior. Can't you understand I need some time to say good-bye?"

Evan shook his head. "Do you honestly believe your father will allow you to marry me if you give him the opportunity to say no?"

Bianca looked down at her hands, which were

wrinkling the sheets nervously as she tried to decide what to do. "I want to come with you, Evan, but I know I should not."

"You've never called me by my name, Bianca, and you say it so nicely I can not bear not to hear it each and every day of my life. Now if you won't get up and dress, I will simply get back in bed with you and we will let your parents decide whom you'll marry when someone finds you in my arms in the morning."

Astonished by that threat, Bianca cried out, "You wouldn't do that to me, you wouldn't dare!"

Evan slipped back under the covers and made himself comfortable before he gave her his most disarming grin. "It is your choice: elope with me or be forced to marry me tomorrow. Since you consider it a disgrace either way, I will do whichever you choose."

This man has been an impossible bully since the night we met, Bianca thought. He was doing what he always did, professing to admire her while he created the worst of situations for her to face. "Oh, all right!" she exclaimed angrily. "I will come with you now, but you must at least do me the courtesy of allowing me a moment to write my parents a note."

"I insist that you do, my dearest. I don't want them to worry. I want them to know exactly where you have gone and with whom. Please tell them I am a very wealthy man, though perhaps not the one they had chosen for you." Evan turned away to hide his smile as he got dressed. If he'd not been successful with his first attempts to flush out Charles's killer, surely he couldn't fail with this one. That Bianca Antonelli would also be his bride was only an added bonus.

Bianca heard Evan's sly chuckle and turned quickly, but he was keeping his back turned while she dressed. That he could be a gentleman at times was a fact for which she was grateful, but she'd never expected to marry him. She wished she had time to soak in a hot bath instead of hurriedly rinsing away the evidence of their passion, but she dared not provoke him again.

Only when Bianca was dressed and ready to go did Evan realize she could not climb down the front of her home with the ease he'd demonstrated in climbing up. "Do you have a hairpin?" he asked hopefully.

"Yes, of course, but why?"

"Just give me one. I'll use it to unlock the door," Evan explained, and true to his word, he knelt down by the door and, in a matter of seconds, unlocked the ornately carved portal. "There, my dear, now we can leave your home by the stairs."

Bianca looked around the room anxiously, hoping she'd forgotten nothing of importance in her haste to flee. He might make light of their being found together, but glancing at the rumpled bed she knew exactly what he'd risked: his life, and that was not a price she'd allow him to pay for her love. Smiling bravely, she took his arm. "Yes, let's hurry. We will have to race the dawn as it is."

Evan smiled but he did not reply until he had her comfortably seated in his boat and they were out of sight of her home. His grin was a charming one as he reassured her. "You will never regret your decision to marry me, Bianca, I promise you that. I may have come to Venice meaning to do no more than purchase fine crystal, but I found a priceless treasure in you."

Bianca smiled shyly, although she barely heard his flattering words. The Eastern sky already held a faint blush of pink, and she wanted to be well out to sea before the sun rose. This would surely be the most exciting day of her life, but she dared not contemplate the fury of her father's wrath when her elopement with Evan Sinclair was discovered. What Paolo Sammarese would do was too horrible to even imagine. "I hope your ship is a fast one," she prayed aloud.

Understanding her concern, Evan's grin grew wider still. "It is the *Phoenix*, beloved, and I can make her fly." That was a promise he meant to keep, for the race was on and it was one he intended to win.

Chapter IV

When they reached the *Phoenix* Evan wasted no time in escorting Bianca to his cabin. He swept her along beside him as he strode up the gangplank, crossed the deck swiftly, and hurried down the steep stairs of the companionway leading to his well-appointed cabin. He tossed her cumbersome bundle of belongings upon a chair, then turned to give her a rakish grin. "It would be best if you climb into my bunk and go to sleep. I'll have the captain marry us when we're out at sea, but first we must set sail and that task will require my full concentration for the next few hours."

As Bianca untied the bow which secured her cloak, her fingers trembled nervously despite her best efforts to appear calm. "You are not the captain of the *Phoenix?*" she asked hesitantly.

Evan rested his hands on his hips, certain the charming young woman deserved a more detailed explanation than he had just supplied. "I build ships for a living, Bianca. The *Phoenix* is indeed mine, but I hire another man to be her captain so I needn't spend my time managing the ship's routine. You needn't be concerned. I'll be too busy to keep you entertained until we're safely out of the harbor, but when we're at sea I'll be the most attentive husband you can imagine," he promised, then winked slyly.

Bianca's fair complexion was flooded by a bright blush, but she was still curious despite his teasing. "I thought you'd come to Venice to buy crystal. Why would a man who builds ships bother with such an errand?"

She was a very bright young woman, and since her point was well taken, Evan made no effort to avoid answering this question truthfully. "I enjoy travel, and having a profitable cargo makes any voyage far more worthwhile. Please excuse me, but I really must leave you now. Take a nap, and I'll wake you in plenty of time for our wedding. You'll kiss me good-bye, won't you?" he inquired playfully, his own anxiety well hidden.

As Evan drew her into his arms, Bianca was overwhelmed with sorrow. She clung to him as she returned his deep kiss, her response desperate, not simply because of the passion he'd always been able to arouse within her, but because of fear. She wanted him to stay with her, to tell her the decision she'd made was the right one, not a horrible mistake, but he interpreted her panic-filled affection as an attempt at seduction, gave her another lingering kiss, and then stepped back.

"You mustn't tempt me any further, Bianca, for while I'd like nothing better than to make love to you all day, I really must go and speak with the captain."

Embarrassed that he thought her demanding, Bianca forced herself to apologize calmly. "Of course. I did not mean to delay you." But she had to restrain herself so she didn't shriek hysterically until he realized that her happiness was more important than any message he might have for the captain of the *Phoenix*. She smiled sweetly as he left, however, certain she should not risk angering him before they were married, for if he were to decide he did not want a wife so temperamental as she, whatever would she do?

That she was now totally dependent upon Evan Sinclair was a terrifying prospect, but Bianca was far too clever not to realize she'd chosen a life of exile the instant she'd surrendered to his passion. That knowledge now brought her no comfort, and being unable to rest, she paced the spacious cabin with an anxious stride. Her choices had been very clear: to marry Paolo whom she knew she'd never love, or to elope with Evan whose roguish charm promised not only romance but endless adventure. Tears filled her eyes as she thought of the note she'd written so hurriedly. Her dear mother would weep for days, her father would simply be outraged that she'd run off with an American. It had been cowardly to disgrace her parents as she had, but how could she have lived a contented life with Paolo when his love was no deeper than the brief kisses he'd placed upon her upturned cheek? Surely a man who displayed so little passion before their marriage would have been the coldest of husbands. Yet, taunted by doubts over what she'd done, Bianca grew increasingly distraught. Evan was right; the best course was to leave Venice with all possible haste . . . but there were so many people she loved and should have bid farewell. A profusion of tears trickled down her cheeks in a continuous stream as she thought of the beloved friends and relatives she'd never see again. Finally exhausted by lack of sleep and the pain of her sorrow, she cast her dress and all but her lace-trimmed camisole aside and slipped under the covers of Evan's bunk. The sheets held a faint trace of his masculine scent, and she found that sensuous reminder of the handsome man wonderfully comforting. Sleep overtook her in an instant softening the strain from her features until only the beauty Stefano Tommasi had admired so greatly remained.

Once on deck, Evan found William Summer, quickly drew him aside, and shook his hand enthusiastically. "It is high time I made you the captain of the *Phoenix*. It is a promotion long overdue in fact, so from this morning forward you shall have all the privileges afforded that rank. Congratulations."

William Summer had become Evan's mate after fighting by his side during the Revolutionary War, but he'd never expected to become a captain on such short notice. While he knew he was fully qualified, he was nonetheless shocked by so unexpected an announcement. Just under six feet in height, he had light brown hair, deep blue eyes and the powerful build of a wrestler. While he lacked Evan's dashing good looks, his features were pleasant and his manner always so open and friendly he did quite well with the ladies too. "It is not that I am not grateful to be hired on at what I am certain will be a generous raise in pay," he began in a teasing whisper, "but I can not help but feel I owe the lady you brought on board for this honor rather than my own skill."

Evan chuckled at his friend's attempt at humor, but he could not deny the truth of the mate's words. "Bianca Antonelli has done me the honor of consenting to become my wife. Since I can not possibly preside at my own wedding, I have promoted you so you may do so but your new rank is permanent."

Well aware that Evan had come to Venice to discover the identity of the mysterious beauty whom Charles had described so lovingly, William was nonetheless taken aback that he'd chosen to marry her. "How can you even consider such a thing?" he asked with a strangled gasp. "I know you do not suspect her of being a murderess, but still she is to blame for your brother's death."

Evan lay his finger against his lips before issuing a stern warning. "Never, and I mean never, are you to let Bianca hear you say such a thing. She must not even suspect the reason for our marriage is any save the love I have sworn to feel for her. Charles's murderer will come after her, I'm certain of it. That she will, by then, be my wife will enrage him all the more. The angrier he is, the easier he'll be to kill and the sweeter his death will be."

William knew Evan to be a fierce adversary and he'd never seen the man more serious but he was still not convinced he wanted to perform a marriage ceremony under such unusual and, he was certain, unwise circumstances. "I don't know," he began uneasily. "If you're merely using Miss Antonelli to trap Charles's murderer, why must you marry her? Isn't that involving her too deeply in your plan?"

A gentleman despite the way he chose to conduct his private life, Evan would not even consider what William was suggesting. "She is a lady, Summer, and as such deserves to be treated well no matter what my motives for bringing her on board. I have offered marriage and she has accepted. The matter is settled." He'd no intention of revealing that he'd seduced the beautiful young woman with shocking ease. That had been a most enjoyable experience, but it had sealed Bianca's fate. He would not simply rob her of her innocence and send her home to face that disgrace alone. That idea was totally unacceptable to him. "What do you think I should do, Will? Dangle Bianca in front of the murderer to distract him while I slit his throat and then return her to her parents? Provided, of course, that her father is not the man I'm after."

William frowned, and then took a moment to gather his thoughts. He knew he was not nearly so clever as Evan, but he thought the man had gone too far this time. Finally he cleared his throat and attempted to explain his hesitation to agree. "I have to admit your offer of marriage is the most gallant solution for Miss Antonelli's future, but I still doubt it is a wise one."

"You let me be the judge of that since I'll be her

husband." Hoping he'd made his point, Evan remarked forcefully, "I don't expect you to neglect your duties, the ceremony needn't take place until we're well out at sea."

Summer was an honest man in all his dealings with others, and Evan's plan still pained his conscience badly. Despite their discussion, he truly didn't want any part in it. Suddenly thinking of a respectable alternative, he quickly proposed it. "This city abounds with churches, wouldn't a priest be better able to perform the wedding than I?"

"No! There is no time to locate a priest, we've not a moment to lose," Evan insisted sharply. "Now, I want to see how quickly you can have the *Phoenix* under way. We must be gone before Bianca's absence is discovered as she left a note which will swiftly set the murderer on our trail. I'll not have my chance for revenge ruined while we stand here and argue. Get moving. A good head start is vital!"

"Aye, aye, sir," William responded smartly, for despite his promotion, the *Phoenix* still belonged to Evan. He'd not dare again to offer his opinion of the dangerous course the man had set, but he was not at all pleased. Charles's murderer deserved to die, but he doubted the wisdom of involving a young woman in the plot. Women made wonderful companions on shore, to that he could readily attest, but aboard ship they were no more than a nuisance. He didn't understand how Evan could have devised so ridiculous a plan, the success of which relied upon a madman's lust for a beautiful woman.

Evan remained on deck. No longer issuing orders for William to relay, he was too restless to return to his cabin when there was so much at stake. As the sky began to brighten in the east, he paced with long, easy strides, but he did not draw a deep breath until William had given the order to cast off the lines which held the *Phoenix* to the dock. The morning tide swiftly carried the sleek

Baltimore Clipper out into the Adriatic Sea, where the fore-and-aft-rigged sails on her two raked masts billowed out with the brisk wind and the *Phoenix* began her gallant race with fate.

The sun was high overhead before Evan assembled the crew and announced to all aboard William Summer's promotion and his own plan to wed. He knew Bianca must be wondering what was keeping him, but when he cautiously opened the door of his cabin, he found her fast asleep and saw no reason to awaken her. There was no sign of pursuit as yet, and he was far more tired than he'd dared admit to himself that morning. He removed his clothing quietly, taking care not to wake her, and then slipped into his bunk. Snuggling against her to achieve a comfortable position, he promptly fell asleep.

It was the warmth of Evan's muscular frame which awakened Bianca, but his arm encircled her waist and she could not rise. Being in his arms was very pleasant, so comforting that she lay still, languidly enjoying his presence. He was breathing easily, lost in the world of dreams, and she wondered if his thoughts were of her. She thought him such a handsome man, deeply tanned, tall and strong. Dark brows and thick fringes of eyelashes accented his finely chiseled features while a slight growth of beard detracted not in the least from his good looks. The soft curls which covered his chest were the same deep auburn shade as his hair, and Bianca thought his appearance impressive in every respect. That he would soon be her husband, however, was a strangely unsettling thought. When they had made love, she'd thought she'd have no more than that one glorious memory. Now he would be by her side forever, and when she stopped to contemplate the fact that she scarcely knew this man, she found her situation extremely disconcerting.

Evan could feel Bianca fidgeting restlessly, but he pretended to be asleep for a while. Taking her had been almost too easy, but she was not his bride yet and he wanted to make certain she did not change her mind before she spoke her vows. Raising his hand slowly, he caressed her cheek lightly as he called her name. "Bianca? This bunk was not designed for two, would you rather I slept elsewhere for the voyage?"

Startled as much by his question as by the deep resonance of his voice, Bianca didn't know what to say for a moment until she realized he was teasing her. Turning on her side, she leaned over to brush his lips sweetly with her own before she replied. "No, I think we belong together now, don't you?"

The green of her eyes was so appealing a shade, Evan could not recall what his question had been. He knew that he wanted this lovely creature too badly to discuss any topic save their wedding, but even that conversation could wait for the moment. He pulled her close, pressing her soft curves against the hardness of his chest as he lowered his mouth to hers. Again she returned his kisses with an affection so lavish he was content this time to let her take the lead. Her touch was light, yet tantalizing as one hand moved down his side then over his hips drawing him closer still. She was clad in her chemise, yet did not seem to think his nudity odd. As her fingertips strayed over the flatness of his stomach then dared to move lower, her touch was knowing, smooth and tantalizing rather than demanding, but his breathing swiftly grew ragged, his desire too strong to contain. Fully aroused, he brushed her hand aside so he could move atop her to end the fiery torment her caress had created within his loins. He wound his fingers in her tangled curls to hold her still, his tongue plundering her mouth as he plunged deep within her, his thrusts rapid as he sought to give her in this narrow bunk the same splendid rapture they'd shared in her oversized bed. Her beauty was remarkable, but so was her delight in his affection; and soon he felt her joy pulsating deep within her. He shuddered violently, unable to hold back the ecstasy which burst from within him to fill her graceful body with the essence of his love. The beauty of that moment sent its boundless joy coursing down his spine and through his limbs; yet even when his passion was finally spent, he did not withdraw, but lay cradled between her thighs, too content in her embrace to move away.

Bianca lifted her hands to comb the soft curls at Evan's nape, her worries about the uncertainty of her future dispelled by the richness of the pleasure they'd again shared. Despite his size and strength, he was a surprisingly gentle man, his touch always tender, and she did not mind that he still held her enfolded in his arms. The motion of the ship, a slow, steady rocking, was soothing, and had he not spoken to her, she might have again drifted off to sleep.

Evan raised up on an elbow, his delight in Bianca shining brightly from the depth of his golden gaze. "I did not mean to make love to you again without the benefit of marriage, but your beauty is impossible to resist."

"I did not think it was my beauty you found so exciting, but my touch," Bianca teased as she let her fingertips wander down his back to again caress his bare hips.

Evan began to chuckle, then buried his face in her golden curls. Her scent is delicious too, he realized, as luscious as the taste of her kiss. "Did you remember to bring your perfume?" he asked softly as he nuzzled the elegant curve of her throat.

"Of course, a lady never goes anywhere without her perfume," Bianca replied seductively, "least of all to America."

"You'll be a sensation in Virginia, but I warn you, I'll make a jealous husband who'll tolerate no competition for your affection." He'd deliberately planted that idea in her mind. He wanted her to believe he'd fight the man who came after her out of jealous rage, not out of the lust for revenge. When he leaned back to gauge her reaction to his remark he was sorry to see by her puzzled expression that he'd only confused her.

"If you think so little of me, why have you asked me to be your wife?" Bianca asked in a breathless whisper, frightened that he might have changed his mind about binding their romantic alliance with a legal tie.

Evan leaned down to kiss her flushed cheeks sweetly before he replied in a far softer tone. "I have not accused you of being unfaithful to me, my dearest. I am merely letting you know if I have a fault, it is jealousy. I want no arguments about the fact that you belong to me."

"Surely it will not be my fault if other men wish to argue about it since I will not encourage them. Are Americans so lacking in manners they feel it proper to court another man's wife?" the high-spirited beauty asked pointedly.

"Americans are no different from men anywhere, Bianca. You will soon learn that." Evan moved slowly then, with a sensuous grace, allowing the desire which still enflamed his blood free rein. He ended her questions with long, deep kisses as he allowed the delicious warmth of her slender body to flood his loins with new strength so they could again become as one. She seemed to have been created solely to pleasure him, and he took his time, enjoying each nuance of her affection until the madness of ecstasy made such care impossible. She was the most exciting woman it had ever been his pleasure to meet, and that she had become his so easily was a bit of good fortune he'd not treat lightly. He continued to hold and kiss her, to speak sweetly to her and to cuddle her slender body in his arms until, no longer able to delay their wedding, he reluctantly had to leave her side.

"My cabin boy is named Timothy Stewart," Evan

explained as he pulled on his breeches. "I gave him strict orders never to disturb us, but before I go to Will's cabin to dress, I'll tell him to fetch the tub and hot water for your bath."

Pleased that he was so thoughtful of her comfort, Bianca smiled with genuine delight. He was as pleasant in his manners as he was in his appearance, which she found fascinating. His body was every bit as perfect as the statues to which she'd compared him, but when he turned to look at her, she was happy to see that the curiosity in her glance had not embarrassed him. "A bath would be wonderful. Then I must find someplace to store my things. I do not want them to be in your way."

She'd brought far more than he'd thought necessary, but since the voyage would be a long one, he had wanted her to have all she'd need.

"That can wait until tomorrow. Just bathe and dress so we can be married within the hour."

Bianca swung her legs over the side of his bunk, certain her possessions deserved more care than he seemed to believe necessary. "Perhaps Timothy can help me sort out my things. You'll want your cabin to be neat for the ceremony."

Evan pulled his shirt on over his head, thinking he was well enough dressed for the moment. "We're not going to be married in here, my pet, but out on deck where my crew, that is, Will's crew, can be witnesses."

Appalled by that thought, Bianca leapt to her feet and began to argue. "Since none of my family are here to complain about those arrangements, I must do so myself. I've no desire to put on a public spectacle. Can't we just be married here with a witness or two? Why must we entertain the crew? The ceremony would be far more dignified if held in private."

Since dignity was the last of Evan's concerns, he swept her protests aside. "I want no doubt that we are married,

Bianca, and with the entire crew to witness the event, there can be no argument," he replied firmly. "It is a glorious day so we'll be married on deck where we can take advantage of its beauty. This cabin is scarcely the proper setting."

Bianca looked around the oak-paneled room, thinking the compact design of his quarters not only functional but handsome as well. "This is no chapel, that is true, but I'd much prefer to be married here."

Evan gathered up the clothes he wished to wear along with his razor before going to the door. "I've told you my reasons for wanting to be married on deck, and I'll not change that plan. I'll send Timothy with the tub and hot water. Put on your cloak if you don't want him to see you in your chemise."

Bianca's expression registered chagrin as she glanced down at the badly wrinkled garment. When her soon-to-be husband left, still chuckling at her request for a dignified ceremony, she could barely summon the self-control to stifle the shrill scream of frustration which filled her throat. "He is a worse tyrant than Paolo!" she finally whispered angrily. "My concerns mean nothing to him!" Evan's desire to parade her on deck was demeaning and ridiculous in her view, but she had asked in the most polite manner she knew how to be married in the privacy of his cabin and her request had fallen upon deaf ears. Not wanting the cabin boy to suspect what they'd been doing, she made up the bunk quickly, donned her cloak, and sat down at the table with a book she'd grabbed from the adjacent shelf. When Timothy knocked at the door, she hoped she looked as though she'd spent the afternoon reading. The lad appeared to be no more than ten and seemed even more embarrassed than she was, however. She smiled, hoping to put him at ease as he brought in first a small copper tub and then several buckets of warm water, soap, and a towel. "Thank you so much, Timothy.

Will you come back in a half an hour or so to remove the tub?"

"Yes, ma'am," the shy boy responded readily. "I'll wait just outside."

"Thank you. I'll call you when I'm finished." Since he seemed so eager to please, Bianca took the precaution of locking the door so he'd not be tempted to enter before she was ready, and tossing her rumpled chemise upon a chair, she stepped into the steaming tub. The warmth of the water felt very soothing in her troubled mood so she waited until it had begun to chill before she picked up the bar of soap. It was not nearly so fine as the perfumed soap she habitually used, and she was sorry she'd not thought to bring several bars of her own. "The first of many such oversights, I'm sure," she chided herself. Nonetheless, she was determined to make do with what Evan had handy at the moment, for surely there would be ample time to go shopping at the *Phoenix*'s next port of call. That thought brought a contented smile to her lips because it was apparent to her now that Evan was as rich a man as he'd boasted. His ship was a fine one, and since he built such splendid vessels she was certain he owned a few more. He was so liberal with his affection, she knew he would be a generous husband in all respects, and pleased by that prospect, she decided she'd be smart not to offer any further protests over where he'd insisted they have the wedding. She stepped from the tub, confident their marriage would be a happy one despite the haste of their courtship, and began to dress rapidly so Evan would not think her overly concerned with her appearance. She swiftly realized, however, that while she could undress by herself quite easily, it was impossible for her to lace her corset up the back and she had no choice but to await Evan's return. She again donned her cloak and had Timothy remove the tub, but she didn't think it would be wise to ask the shy boy to assist her in so personal a task as getting dressed regardless of what duties he performed for Evan.

Thinking it only polite to introduce William to his future bride before the ceremony, Evan wanted to first make certain the striking Bianca was fully dressed before he summoned the former mate. When he found her wearing no more than a fresh chemise and several layers of petticoats his expression grew stern. "I would like to make you my wife before nightfall, Bianca. What have you been doing all this time?" Since she was surrounded by heaps of clothing, he thought perhaps she had had some difficulty selecting a gown. "Wear whatever you like. You will look beautiful no matter what you choose."

"Thank you," Bianca responded sweetly as she reached up to give him a kiss. "I know exactly what I wish to wear, and while I do not want to be a nuisance I need help to dress."

"Of course, I should have thought of that," Evan apologized. He could not recall ever having to serve as a lady's maid, but he thought the task would certainly prove amusing. "What must I do first, help you attach your stockings, or style your hair?" he asked as he made a gentlemanly bow.

"Neither!" Bianca giggled at his teasing, and picking up her corset she slipped it on and turned her back toward him. "All you need do is lace this up for me. I can manage the rest myself."

"You are so slender. Why do you bother wearing a corset at all?" Evan joked as he began to tighten the laces on the heavy linen garment stiffened with whalebone. "You should have just gotten dressed without it."

"My waist is small enough that is true," Bianca agreed. When he was finished she turned to face him. "But wearing a corset has other advantages." She had no need to explain that it served to lift and enhance her bosom since that was where his gaze was firmly fixed. She waited a moment for his glance to drift up to meet hers and then continued in a casual tone. "I have gowns whose skirts must be attached to the loops at the waist of the corset so you see, going without it is quite impossible."

"I had not realized a lady's undergarments could prove so fascinating, or so practical," Evan confided, but his glance again swept over her slowly, the soft swells of her figure still his most obvious interest. Her beauty was as bewitching as her lively charm, but he forced away the wave of desire her mere presence brought and gestured toward her gowns. "I'd appreciate it if you dressed promptly since everyone is waiting and I want you to have a moment to speak with the captain first."

Bianca had already chosen a gown of pale pink satin delicately embroidered with rosebuds, and after shaking it out began to dress with the haste Evan seemed to think necessary. "What will the man wish to say to me?" she asked nervously. "Are there questions of some sort I must answer correctly? If so, please tell me the proper answers so I will not disappoint him."

"Questions?" Evan asked with a puzzled frown. "He'll have no questions. I merely wanted him to meet you, that's all. There is no test you must pass before we wed."

"Oh, I see." Bianca continued to don the pretty gown, finally adjusting the fullness of the skirt and the lace trim at the neckline and at the ends of the sleeves. "Do you think I should comb my hair into a different style? I thought this one very nice."

Her golden curls were so attractively arranged Evan did no more than shake his head before leaning down to kiss her lips lightly. "No. I was merely teasing you when I offered to style your hair. You are a very lovely bride, Bianca. I'll go and fetch Will. Give me just a moment."

While he had expected the man to be impressed by Bianca's beauty, he'd not thought she'd be so taken with him that she'd wish to begin a lengthy conversation, but she asked Will so many polite questions about the voyage and then about America that he found himself growing most impatient. He had had ample warning that she liked the company of young men, but he'd not expected her to flirt so openly with his friend. Slipping his arm around her waist, he attempted to sound merely anxious to wed rather than furious that she was so friendly. "You'll have more than enough time to hear Will's whole life story before we reach Virginia, my pet. We've far more important business to attend to right now."

Completely enchanted, William Summer found it difficult to take his eyes from the vivacious blonde bride's delightful smile, but at last he forced himself to do so. "I would like a word with you first, sir. In private," he added forcefully.

Exasperated by the continual delays, Evan begged Bianca's forgiveness, then nearly pushed Will out the cabin door. "What problem can possibly have arisen in the last few minutes? Has a ship giving pursuit been sighted?"

"No," Will responded quickly. "It is the wedding. I did not expect Miss Antonelli to be so, well, so fine a lady. Her English is perfect. She does not seem a bit foreign as I thought she would, but like one of our own. This scheme of yours is simply not fair to her and I can not condone it."

Evan's eyes narrowed only slightly as he clasped his hands behind his back, and his voice low, he replied. "I am pleased you like Bianca, but as it is impossible for her to return to her home, what do you think would become of her if I did not marry her today?"

"Why is it impossible for her to return to her parents?" William asked in a hoarse whisper. "Surely she'll not want to stay with you after she watches you kill Charles's murderer in cold blood, for her ties to the man must be close."

That was a possibility Evan had not even considered, and he was silent a moment. "Since I do not know how long it will be before the man overtakes us, I am hoping that Bianca will think of herself as my wife by the time he does. It will then be far too late to send her back to her parents, Will. Indeed, it is already too late now."

Appalled by that announcement, William began to swear, then caught himself abruptly. He knew Evan Sinclair far too well to be surprised that he'd placed loyalty to his deceased brother above respect for a young woman, but still he was shocked by what he'd done. "She is little more than a beautiful child!" he protested angrily.

"Go on, say it," Evan dared with icy calm. "I've taken advantage of her, used her to further my own goals. If she hates me for it, so be it, but she will at least have the advantage of being my wife. I will not use that lovely creature, treat her as a whore, and then send her home carrying my bastard. This marriage is for her protection, certainly not mine. If you are truly concerned about the girl, then you must be able to see marriage is my only honorable choice."

As usual Evan had been blunt, but his argument was so compelling William knew he had no real choice but to agree to perform the ceremony he'd requested. He took a deep breath and then exhaled slowly. "All right then. Let's get it over with promptly."

Evan's smile was a wicked leer. "That has been my hope all afternoon. Assemble the men, and I'll bring Bianca."

William stared up at the taller man whose courage he'd so often admired. "Every man on board knows why we went to Venice. She's bound to hear the gossip soon."

"Captain Summer, should any man be so foolish as to whisper my brother's name within Bianca's hearing, he will have spoken his own death sentence. See that none do."

While William had never known Evan to be needlessly cruel, there was not the slightest doubt in his mind that the man had never issued an idle threat either. "I will see to that immediately," he responded, and after he'd given the order to assemble, he made certain all those under his command knew how highly Evan prized the woman who would soon become his bride.

Chapter V

Partially shielded from the brisk wind by the foremast and the crush of men who surrounded them, Bianca nonetheless found the deck of the *Phoenix* a most unsuitable place to be wed. Evan was in such high spirits she'd given no further thought to dissuading him from marrying out in the open, surrounded by the ship's crew, but being the only woman among so many men did nothing to ease her anxiety. She clung to his arm with both hands, so intent upon ignoring the many pairs of eyes focused upon her that she was paying scant attention to William Summer's solemn reading of the marriage ceremony. Although she could not understand why, the men's stares did not strike her as being merely curious; rather, to a man, they were regarding her with an insulting intensity. Perhaps they were a superstitious lot and disliked having her aboard simply because she was a female. What other reason could there be? Americans might have all sorts of peculiar customs about which she knew nothing, but she was grateful that Evan obviously did not share the crew's apparent prejudice against her.

She'd worn her cloak and covered her hair with the hood; still, the wind whipped the curls around her face, stinging her eyes and blurring her vision. From the first instant she'd seen Evan Sinclair striding across Paolo's crowded ballroom, her life had been in constant turmoil, but this hastily planned wedding was so far from the ceremony she'd one day expected that she did not even notice when William paused for her to respond. When Evan patted her hand lightly, she realized such inattention had been most inappropriate, but truly she hadn't heard the question and was uncertain what her reply should be.

When Bianca did not respond as promptly as he had, Evan whispered softly, "You must say, I do."

Bianca looked up at him then, her smile a shy one. "I do," she announced with surprising calm for once she knew the correct response she had no trouble reciting it. She paid strict attention then as Evan spoke his vows and she recited her own clearly, but the stares of the men were still so unfriendly as to be almost hostile and she began to wonder what Evan had said about her. Whatever could he have said when they'd known each other so brief a time? Even to simple seamen she knew this marriage must seem ill advised, but she prayed that truly it wasn't and that they'd find the same lasting happiness together she knew her mother and father had always enjoyed. How her parents could still be happy after what she'd done she didn't know, but she hoped in time they would forgive her for following her heart rather than obeying their stern command to marry Paolo for reasons other than love.

When asked for a ring, Evan pulled the gold signet ring from the little finger of his right hand. It was too large to fit Bianca but he winked slyly, silently promising she'd soon have a ring of her own. He then held her hand tightly so she'd not lose it before the brief ceremony was over. William Summer pronounced them man and wife, and read the appropriate blessing, but when Evan bent down to give her a light kiss, Bianca found it difficult to believe they were truly married.

"May I be the first to wish you every happiness, Mrs. Sinclair." William then offered his congratulations to Evan with what he hoped would pass for sincerity, for despite his apprehension, he did not want to make this beautiful blonde woman aware of his fears.

As the members of the crew filed by to offer their best wishes, Bianca attempted to appear pleased, but she could not recall ever meeting any men such as these. They were all as young as William and Evan, deeply tanned, muscular of build, and extremely fit. Sailors to be sure, but they reminded her of mercenaries for they were a fierce-looking lot, each armed with a pistol or a wicked knife at his belt, and a few had both. Her curiosity as well as her fear aroused, Bianca's agile mind was posing many questions, but she could do no more than smile and thank the rugged-looking men for their kind wishes. She was grateful when Evan ordered an extra ration of rum to be distributed to the crew, then escorted her back to the privacy of the cabin they now shared. She first tossed her cloak upon the heap of her still-unsorted belongings and then turned to face her new husband. "Just how well do you know this man Summer?" she asked breathlessly.

"Very well." Thinking the occasion of their marriage deserved something in the way of celebration for them too, he searched through his store of liqueurs for a fine brandy he thought she'd like. Pouring a small amount into a silver goblet, he handed it to her then poured himself a far more generous portion. "I would like to propose a toast: to us, my beauty, and to a long and fruitful marriage."

Bianca touched the rim of her goblet against Evan's, but knowing her mother had produced no more than one child despite her devotion to her father, she hoped he did not want too many children. Thinking that a matter better left undiscussed for the present, she asked a more pressing question. "Venice is a heavily trafficked commercial port so I have seen a good many sailors through the years. Does the crew Captain Summer has assembled not seem unusual to you?"

Not understanding her interest in the crew when he wanted to celebrate, Evan shrugged impatiently. "No, but I had no idea you were interested in ordinary seamen." He'd been annoyed by her friendliness toward Will, but he'd not considered that her tastes in young men might extend to the rest of those on board as well! She was so charming a creature he could easily understand how his brother had fallen in love with her without ever realizing the flattering attention she must have paid him was nothing unusual. The awareness that he'd just made such a flirt his bride was not at all pleasing so he took another deep drink of his brandy.

Not having meant to upset him, Bianca smiled prettily. "You have warned me you are the jealous sort, but you need have no worries. None of the men is as handsome as you, and I doubt any is even half so bright and charming." When his expression softened slightly at that compliment, she continued in a more serious tone. "I found the roughness of the crew very troubling. They appear to be a gang of cutthroats, and I wonder if we are safe with them. Is America filled with such tough-looking young men?"

Finally understanding that she thought his men frightening rather than attractive, Evan was so relieved he laughed aloud at her choice of words. "The *Phoenix* does indeed have a crew of America's finest, and you think they look like cutthroats?" When her lovely blonde head nodded and he saw that she was not amused by his teasing, he tried to reassure her. "In 1776, when the Colonies declared themselves independent of Great Britain, we had no navy. Men who owned ships were commissioned to serve as officers aboard their own vessels until warships could be built. Most of the men you describe as cutthroats served with me aboard this very ship for the better part of the war. Now that it is over and won, they are merchant seamen again. I know them to be a courageous lot, and I like to think they look it, rather than villainous."

"Well I did not mean to insult them, but they all looked at me so strangely, Evan. Not the way a man looks at a pretty woman, but differently. I really don't know how to describe it if you did not notice it too."

Evan knew exactly how his men regarded her, as dangerous. She was at least partially responsible for Charles's death, and they did not want her to be responsible for their own. Since such an explanation was impossible to give, he promptly made up another. "Frankly, I believe the men are all jealous of my good fortune, and thinking of their own wives and sweethearts at home has naturally depressed them. The extra rum will lift their spirits, you needn't worry about them any further."

Bianca thought loneliness an absurd reason for the men to dislike her, but she kept that thought to herself, thinking perhaps in time they would become more friendly. "I saw them only briefly," she explained apologetically. "Perhaps when I know them each by name, I'll be able to form a better opinion of them."

"That won't be necessary," Evan reminded her. "I plan to keep you amused myself."

"Of course, but quite naturally during the course of the voyage I'll be able to learn the men's names." Bianca began to pace restlessly as she sipped her brandy, for regardless of how highly Evan might regard Captain Summer's crew, she thought them a peculiar lot still.

"I doubt you'll have such an opportunity, Bianca, because whenever you are out on deck, I'll be with you, and none of the men would dare call on you here." Thinking their conversation nearing dangerous ground, Evan tossed down the last of his brandy and, setting his goblet aside, changed the subject abruptly. "I should have had Timothy bring you something to eat after your nap. Please forgive my lack of manners. He'll bring our supper in just a moment."

"I have not thought of food once," Bianca admitted frankly, and indeed her mind had been far too preoccupied with the preparations for their wedding for her to feel hungry. All too conscious of the power of Evan's steady glance, she turned toward the clothing she'd brought. "If you'll just tell me where I might store my things, I'll put them away."

"Bianca," Evan called softly, "they can wait."

She tossed her blonde hair as she looked around. "No, they can't. Your cabin was so neat before I arrived, and I know you must hate the mess I've made even more than I do."

Since they had already made love several times, Evan knew that prospect could not possibly be troubling her, but something else definitely was. He crossed the small distance between them, took her goblet, and placed it upon the table. Then he took her hand. "Come here," he invited, favoring her with a ready grin, and seating himself on the nearest chair, he pulled her down across his lap. He nuzzled her throat with teasing kisses and then paused. "The voyage home will be a long one so there is no rush to do anything, least of all put away your belongings when there are other pasttimes which are so much more diverting."

While Bianca understood his meaning readily, it seemed an inopportune time to make love if Timothy were about to join them. She twisted his ring nervously, finally removing it and placing it in his palm. "I'll only lose this, you should keep it."

"I'll buy whatever you like, rubies, emeralds, sapphires, diamonds. What is your preference?" Evan slipped the ring back on his finger without arguing, for it had been his father's and he didn't want to see it lost either.

"Surprise me," Bianca suggested distractedly, her pose still stiff as she sat perched upon his knee.

"All right, I will." With a delighted chuckle, Evan raised his hand to her nape to hold her still while he kissed her. He was gentle, not demanding, but several seconds passed before she relaxed against him so he could deepen his kiss to the point they both enjoyed it. "There that's better. I don't want you to worry, Bianca. Everything will turn out all right for us; I promised you that."

"I know." Yet she did not feel as though anything had gone right, not the way they'd left her home with the stealth of thieves before dawn, or the hurried way they'd been married with only strangers to wish them well. Perhaps the men weren't strangers to Evan, but they certainly were to her and it sounded as though they'd remain as such. Rather than begin a litany of complaints, however, she chose only one to share. "It is only that I have never disobeyed my parents, and in this matter I have disregarded their wishes so completely I know they will never forgive me."

"You no longer have any need for parents, Bianca. You are now my wife and your happiness is my responsibility," Evan reassured her proudly.

"I did not mean to insult you." Bianca was dreadfully afraid that no matter how she chose to describe her torment it would sound like criticism to him. "If only you'd help me to put away my belongings, then—"

Disappointed that his lovely young bride had not responded to his affection as he'd hoped, Evan placed her lightly upon her feet and then rose. "I see. I shall not have a moment's peace until you have attended to that chore. Since I have ample storage space for my clothing, let me just organize it better and then you may put all your things away." Why Bianca was so set upon keeping his cabin neat he didn't know, but he was fast becoming as nervous as she so he welcomed the task. They'd been at sea nearly twelve hours. How long would it take Charles's murderer to load a ship with provisions and set out after them? "What do you think of my ship?" he called over his shoulder. "She is a type known as a Baltimore Clipper, a vessel built for beauty and for speed."

"She certainly seems very fast," Bianca replied, "but does she carry enough cargo to make such a long and dangerous voyage worthwhile?"

His shirts refolded to take up less space, Evan moved over to the next drawer, his choice of conversation had been calculated, and he'd not expected her to be so sharp in her observations. "There are times when speed is a greater asset than cargo space."

"In time of war you mean?"

"Precisely," Evan agreed.

"How many guns does the *Phoenix* carry?"

"Only twelve, but the crew makes every shot count. Despite the roughness of their appearance, they are well disciplined." Seeing no point in expounding further on exploits of his men, he changed the subject slightly. "What sort of ships does your father own?" he asked nonchalantly.

"Ships?" Bianca sat down to watch Evan work, but her pose was still tense. "Our family fortune was made in the spice trade. Although my father is still involved in it to some extent, he is a wholesale merchant who buys from others and then sells at a profit. As an advisor to the Doge, he is more involved in politics than anything else. Other than our gondolas, he owns no ships of his own. But what about you, to whom do you expect to sell the

Venetian glass you bought? Will you sell it directly to the public, or to someone else who has a ready market for it?"

"I had no idea you were so skilled in the art of commerce, Bianca." Indeed, Evan found it difficult to stay ahead of this young woman, but he needed far more information than she'd yet revealed so he continued. "As I told you, I build ships for a living and make an occasional cruise. However, my stepfather supplies stores throughout Virginia, stores which carry fine merchandise, and we are partners in this venture. What sort of ships does the Doge own?"

At that question Bianca's expression brightened noticeably. "Well there is the *Bucentauro,* of course. It is a fabulous galley. The wood of the barge has been covered with gold leaf so it shines in the sunlight as though it were made of pure gold, and the canopies on deck are crimson and gold with heavy fringe. It is rowed out into the lagoon when the Doge marries the sea each year in a special ceremony. He tosses out a ring and proclaims the union between Venice and the sea will last forever. It is very exciting. I've seen the ceremony several times."

Evan tried not to show his impatience. Although Bianca's story was interesting, it was not the one he wanted to hear. "What an extraordinary custom. This ship, the *Bucentauro,* it is rowed you say?"

"Yes. Why it must take nearly one hundred men to row her, but it is a magnificent ship."

"What else does the Doge own?"

"Gondolas, of course. I doubt he has need for anything more since he does not leave Venice."

"What about Paolo?" Having emptied two drawers for her use, Evan turned back to face his bride.

"Paolo's family produces crystal. I thought that's why you went to his party, so Marco could introduce you to him. Didn't you go out to Murano to watch the glass blowers at work?"

Evan was having no success in keeping the young woman on the subject he wanted to discuss: the ships which might be at that very moment giving pursuit. "Yes. It was a fascinating process to observe, but tell me, does Paolo not own ships in which to transport his wares?"

"No. Like you, those wishing to buy Venetian glass come to Venice," Bianca explained matter-of-factly.

"I see." Evan grew thoughtful, aware that the murderer was unlikely to have a ship at his immediate disposal and would require a day or two to begin the chase.

Evan's expression was so dark his thoughts were impossible to comprehend so Bianca did not disturb him. Instead she rose and carefully folded her garments, arranging them neatly in the space he'd cleared. "There. Now your cabin is neat again, and I will make every effort to see that it remains that way."

"I have never shared my quarters with a woman, but I am pleased to find you are such a neat one." As Evan lowered his lips to hers he heard a firm knock upon the door and drew away. "That will be Timothy."

"Oh, good. I am hungry after all." Rather than wait for Evan to do it, Bianca crossed to the door and let the cabin boy enter. He carried a silver tray bearing several covered dishes from which a savory aroma escaped. She recognized the tantalizing fragrance of roast chicken as the boy carefully covered the round table with a linen cloth, and set two places with silver. Evan helped her to be seated, and she found it difficult to wait while Timothy served them. The moment the lad left them alone she picked up her fork and took a bite. "This is delicious!" Bianca exclaimed happily.

Evan stared at the obviously famished young woman and slowly shook his head. "Your family did not say grace before meals?" he inquired curiously.

Horribly embarrassed by that question, Bianca placed her fork beside her plate and folded her hands primly in her lap. "I'm so sorry. You must think me totally lacking in manners."

"On the contrary, I think I should have provided something for you to eat hours ago. Please don't wait for Timothy to arrive with our meals. If you are ever hungry, just tell me so and I'll see that something is prepared immediately. If there is anything you need, please ask and I'll see to it."

"Well thank you, but my requirements are few." Bianca reached out to touch his hand lightly, for he had been very kind to her. He took her hand as he bowed his head and asked God to bless not only their supper but their marriage as well. Meanwhile Bianca blushed with shame for she'd not even thought he might wish to do so. When he released her hand, she apologized once more. "Really, I am sorry."

"Bianca, just eat your meal before you faint from hunger," Evan replied with a chuckle. Then he filled their goblets with wine before he began to eat with the obvious enjoyment she had shown. He could afford to relax for the time being, since it was highly unlikely they'd be overtaken before dawn. His curiosity was intense, however, for he was praying it would be Paolo who came after her, not her father or men sent by the Doge.

"Don't you usually dine with the captain?" Bianca wondered aloud.

Since he was accustomed to serving as the captain of the *Phoenix* himself, it took Evan a moment to realize why Bianca would ask such a question. "Yes, but I doubt Will expects to have my company on our wedding night," he replied with a crafty wink. "However, should we grow bored with each other, I suppose I could go and find him."

Bianca's cheeks turned nearly as deep a red as her wine, for she'd not even thought of the evening in those terms. "I, that is, I was not talking about tonight, but of your usual custom."

"Oh, I see." Evan took another bite of chicken, pretending not to notice how badly he'd embarrassed the pretty young woman. He seemed to do that rather often, and though he enjoyed teasing her, he thought he'd be wise to be more careful in expressing his sense of humor in the future. "You needn't worry about Captain Summer. He'll have plenty of company for meals, and I think you and I will get along very nicely by ourselves."

"Yes, I hope so," Bianca agreed, but while she continued to enjoy the succulent roast chicken, questions occurred to her. "You apparently have confidence in Summer and his crew, but how often has he sailed the Mediterranean?"

"This is the first voyage for all of us, why?" Evan poured himself more wine, but he gave her no more than a drop to replace the single sip she'd taken.

"The perils are many, not due to difficulties in navigation but to the thieving pirates who abound in the waters off the Barbary Coast. They would not attack an American ship entering the Mediterranean, but it will be more difficult to escape them as we leave."

"You needn't concern yourself with pirates, Bianca. We're far too swift for them," Evan boasted proudly. He had made plans for fighting a battle all right, but certainly not with pirates!

"The *Phoenix* might easily be able to escape a ship or two, but they often hunt in packs. They have absolutely nothing to fear you see, for the rulers of Algiers, Morocco, Tunis, and Tripoli have lived by piracy for hundreds of years."

Since his bride apparently had an abundance of

knowledge on this subject, Evan encouraged her to share it. "Well, in the unlikely event that we should be attacked and captured by pirates, what would our fate be?"

Bianca took another sip of wine, and after a thoughtful pause, she replied, "Well it would all depend upon whose pirates we happened to meet. The Bey of Algiers is a greedy soul. He would enslave the crew, sell the cargo, add the *Phoenix* to his own fleet, and most likely try to get a high ransom for me once he learned who I am."

"I see. And exactly what would happen to me? Do I end up as a slave or would you insist that your husband be ransomed with you?"

Her meal finished, Bianca placed her knife and fork across her plate. She could tell by the merry sparkle in her husband's eyes that he was teasing her again, but she replied seriously. "I am afraid we would both end up as slaves since there is no one to pay my ransom. My parents will consider me dead for marrying you, and so will all their friends. Were the Bey to send someone to Venice to demand a ransom for my return, he would be sent away empty-handed, and I doubt anyone would be sent all the way to America to ask for gold to set you free."

Evan nodded thoughtfully. "That's not a pleasant prospect, my dear, but surely your parents would not refuse to pay your ransom."

"They most certainly would!" Bianca insisted firmly. "Don't you have any idea what I've done? My parents had arranged a marriage with Paolo Sammarese. Not only did I refuse to honor that promise, but I have run away with you. How can you doubt that I will be disowned for such disobedience? Are American parents so liberal they would not do the same thing with their daughters?"

"The ways to become disgraced are nearly endless in my country too, Bianca, but I doubt parents would leave their daughter in the dungeon of the Bey. At least I hope they wouldn't."

"Well, I hope Captain Summer's crew is as fierce as they look, that's all." Bianca's delicate features were set in a petulant frown, for she feared he was not taking her seriously on this matter of grave importance.

"Pirates are the least of our worries, Bianca, the very least." Evan was trying to reassure her. He could well imagine how furious her parents would be with him for eloping with her, but if her father had killed Charles, he'd neither let her go without a fight, nor allow her to spend her life in what would undoubtedly be the Bey's harem, not his dungeon. Indeed, he was hoping that Paolo would not let her go either. "How did we ever chance upon so gruesome a topic?"

"As you have said, this voyage will be a long one, and it's only natural that we'll want to discuss its perils, isn't it? It wouldn't be gruesome to plot a strategy to escape the pirates' clutches, in fact it would simply be stupid not to do so," Bianca pointed out logically.

"I can't argue with you on that. I'll tell you what, I will speak with Captain Summer about it myself, first thing in the morning. You need have no further worries for our safety; he and I will take care of it. I'm confident Barbary pirates can be no more difficult to defeat than British warships."

At the mention of the British, Bianca couldn't suppress the thought which came instantly to her mind. "Oh, do you suppose that's it? Do the men dislike me because my mother is British? When we were first introduced, I thought you'd not forgive me for it."

Surprised by her question, Evan tried to think of an appropriate answer. "First of all, they believe you to be a Venetian. Only Will knows you are half English. Secondly, we were all British subjects ourselves until a few years ago so our own heritage is British, and no one would hate you for possessing blood he also shares."

"I suppose that is true," Bianca responded. She tried to think of some more diverting subject. However, the day had been such a trying one she found that task impossible. She simply smiled at Evan and hoped he'd think of something for them to discuss, but he sat silently watching her, his smile a pleasant if teasing, one.

"Would you like something more to eat, some tea perhaps?" he finally offered.

"No. The meal was delicious, but I can't eat another bite." She took several sips of wine and then set her goblet aside, suddenly self-conscious about what she was certain he'd suggest next but he surprised her again.

Evan shoved his plate aside and then rose to his feet. "Get your cloak. Let's go up on deck for a stroll. It's far too early to go to bed, even tonight."

"All right."

Bianca soon found herself clinging to Evan's arm for support as they traversed the deck of the elegant vessel. The last rays of the setting sun shaded the white canvas sails with a deep golden hue endowing the ship with new beauty as she sped through the shimmering waters of the Adriatic Sea. They did not really try to walk around the deck but stood at the rail, watching the close of the day and the appearance of the first stars of the night. The last time she'd gazed up at the heavens and wished for adventure, she had not dreamed how exciting her life would suddenly become. She looked up at her husband then, her eyes filled with affection. "I love you, Evan," she said suddenly, and though her voice was lost in the wind, he understood her message clearly and drew her into his arms, not caring that they were creating a spectacle until he drew away and saw her bright blush. He turned her around then, placing her back against his chest and wrapping his arms around her to keep her warm as he watched the beauty of the night enfold.

He bent down to speak softly in her ear. "This is my

favorite time of day. This and dawn."

"I feel that way too," Bianca declared, reflecting that at dusk the deep blues of the sky and sea blended together to create a magic that was entirely new. She relaxed in her husband's arms, her hands over his, his warmth every bit as enchanting as the night's beauty.

After spending a few minutes watching the couple he'd married, William Summer had to turn away. He had never felt so guilty about anything he'd done, but he felt that in marrying Bianca Antonelli and Evan Sinclair he'd committed some terrible wrong. That they appeared to be so ecstatically happy together only added to his sense of foreboding. Evan was handsome; it was no wonder Bianca had accepted his proposal. And she was as beautiful a young woman as he'd ever seen, so he was certain Evan's affection would seem genuine to her. It was undoubtedly as genuine as any his friend had ever shown a woman, but William knew Evan too well to believe he had married the girl to protect her reputation. If only Charles had not come to Venice alone! . . . William knew it was useless to waste time in regret, but he could not change the way he felt. At least Evan had left Venice in good health, he was thankful for that. Now all they need do was return to Newport News unscathed. While Evan and Bianca watched the stars overhead, Summer kept his glance focused upon the wake of the *Phoenix*, hoping, like Evan, that the trap baited with the delectable Bianca Antonelli would swiftly be sprung and Charles's murderer slain before the tension of the wait became any more unbearable.

While it was very pleasant holding his bride in his arms, Evan soon found her nearness impossibly distracting, and wanting to again sample her charms, he escorted her back to his cabin. "I don't want you to become chilled, and the temperature drops suddenly once the sun has set."

"Yes, I know." Bianca folded her cloak over a chair and looked around his compact quarters, hoping to find something interesting she'd not noticed. She was tired, but not sleepy, still too excited by their elopement to hide the nervousness she'd displayed all day. During the day, the cabin was brightly lit by the sun which shone through the skylights overhead, but now it was dimly illuminated by lanterns. Their rosy glow, though romantic, simply embarrassed her.

Evan was far too perceptive a man not to observe Bianca's discomfort, but his need for her loyalty did not permit him to allow her to brood in solitude over the way she'd left her home. Thinking she would appreciate some privacy in which to disrobe, however, he crossed to the door. "I need to speak with Will one last time. Prepare for bed and I'll be back in a few minutes."

When Bianca turned, he had already gone. Not knowing how long he'd be away, she hastened to remove and put away her clothing, and to don her nightgown before he returned. The soft linen gown was new, the bodice, sleeves, and hem trimmed with tiny tucks and decorated with wide bands of lace. She'd thought it almost too pretty to wear to bed, but surely on her wedding night a bride should have the prettiest of gowns to wear. That thought made her laugh, for she knew no respectable bride looking forward to her wedding night had the knowledge she now possessed.

"Oh, Bianca, what a scandal your marriage will have caused!" She sat down upon Evan's bunk to brush out her hair thinking it was a good thing she was not overly dependent upon the attentions of a maid as were some of the girls she knew. She'd always preferred to take care of herself rather than stand quietly to be dressed or have her hair groomed. Her father had often teased her about her independence, but it would serve her well now. When she was satisfied that her long golden curls were thoroughly brushed, she took out the brandy Evan had shared with her before supper and placed it upon his table with two goblets. It was foolish to worry about what tomorrow might bring when she wanted to make this a night her new husband would always remember.

Evan had had every intention of allowing William Summer to assume command of the *Phoenix,* but that was proving difficult when their opinions differed so greatly upon the methods he'd chosen to accomplish the task at hand. Will did see the merit in posting additional men on watch, however, and grateful that they'd not had to argue the point, Evan left him and returned to his cabin. He'd not expected to find Bianca attired in so fetching a gown, and he was delighted she'd thought he might enjoy another brandy. She was proving to be such a surprisingly attentive wife that he had to force himself to remove his coat without ungentlemanly haste.

"I have never seen a more beautiful gown. I know the women of Venice are famous for their lace, and regret that I did not buy some for my mother."

Bianca took his navy blue coat and hung it over the back of a chair. For their wedding, he'd worn the same clothing he'd had on the day she'd met him in the Piazza San Marco, but she'd yet to see him in any garb she didn't regard as handsome. "You mentioned your stepfather this afternoon, and now your mother. Do you have brothers and sisters?" she inquired politely.

"No." Evan had no intention of mentioning Charles yet, so he let her assume incorrectly that he was an only child. When she came forward to unbutton his waistcoat and shirt, he was surprised that she'd wish to help him undress, but he found the lightness of her touch too pleasant to offer a complaint. Before she could step away, he pulled her into his arms and kissed her lightly, thinking he should take his time with her that night, but her brandy-flavored kiss was so delicious he couldn't bear to pull away. His hands moved slowly down her spine, finally pressing her hips firmly against his as his tongue sought to know her mouth as well as his own.

Far from being distressed by the ease with which she'd aroused him, Bianca wrapped her arms around Evan's waist and moved her whole body against him with a seductive caress. Her motions were not the least bit subtle, but demanded the same fiery response she'd elicited that afternoon. Graceful and alluring, she was a temptress of the most exotic sort, her soft blonde curls brushing against his bare chest as she punctuated their deep kisses with playful nibbles.

His mind clouded with the warm smoke of desire, Evan at last forced himself to step back. He'd never made love to a woman without removing his boots, but Bianca was damned close to becoming the first. He sat down at his table, took a long sip of the brandy she'd poured for him, and then reached for his right boot. "You are the most affectionate young woman I have ever had the pleasure of meeting, my dear, but you must allow me a few minutes to remove my clothes before we consummate our wedding vows."

"You think me too forward?" Bianca asked with a wide innocent gaze. "My parents are a very romantic pair, but perhaps yours are not."

Evan thought her naïveté charming. He did not rely upon observations of his parents for knowledge of how a man and woman who enjoyed each other's company should behave. She was quite young, however, and he could expect her to know only what her mother had taught her.

"Just how old are you, Bianca?" He tossed his right boot aside and quickly reached for his left, but his appreciative glance did not leave her face.

"I am sixteen. How old are you?" the startled young woman countered.

"Thirty-two, exactly twice your age," Evan replied with a teasing smile.

"And you have never been married?" Bianca asked hesitantly.

Evan laughed at that question, and after tossing his left boot aside, he rose to face her. "It is a bit late to ask that. Would you object to being my second wife, or the third?"

Bianca bit her lower lip nervously, uncertain what to say. "You shouldn't ask me that unless there's a reason. If you have been married before just say so, but don't tease me about it."

He had not forgotten her temper, he'd only forgotten not to arouse it, and as he peeled off his clothing he spoke in a soothing tone to reassure her. "I have never been married before, Bianca, but I did not realize it would upset you so badly if I had." He could see tears sparkling upon her long lashes so he continued. "We promised today to love each other from this day forward; isn't that enough for you?"

Bianca sat down upon his bunk as she considered his question, not realizing her pose was a most enticing one. "Because you are a man and somewhat older than me, you do not have the right to tease me constantly. I wish you would stop it."

Despite his best efforts not to do so, Evan began to laugh, he could not help himself. When the green of her eyes began to glow even more brightly with the fire of anger, he took the time to finish his brandy before he apologized. "I think it is you who are the tease here, Mrs. Sinclair." Moving to her side, he sat down and brought her left palm to his lips. "I find you here, dressed for bed in a seductive gown and sipping brandy. You help me out of my clothes, return my kisses with an enthusiasm for which any man would be grateful, and now you wish to pick a fight with me over the number of wives I've had when you are the first. How am I to describe you in any terms save that of a tease?"

"I am no tease!" Bianca protested sharply, but Evan's glance was so inviting she could not take her eyes from his as he again raised her hand to his lips. In the dim light, his glance was filled with the golden gleam she loved, and she was fascinated by him still. "I wanted only to please you, but I do not want to have to stand in line to do it," she explained.

"Beloved, were I to have had fifteen other wives, you would never have to stand in line. Now, come here." Although the buttons on her nightgown were tiny, he unfastened them swiftly to expose her marvelous figure to his view. He longed to taste the soft pink tips of her breasts, to kiss her pale skin until he set her desire aflame. He wanted to know her beautiful body, and her lively mind. He wanted to enjoy her totally, to savor every particle of her being, and he paused only long enough to toss his breeches aside before he leaned across her, forcing her down upon his bunk.

Bianca combed Evan's auburn curls away from his face as his tongued caressed her breast. She held him close, delighted with his sweetness, her argumentativeness dispelled by the magic of his affection. He was a lover of great skill. His touch was so soft, so gentle, as it moved down her stomach that she felt she was truly precious to him. She breathed deeply as she enjoyed the rush of pleasure which swelled from deep within her slender body, setting every inch of her fair skin to tingling with anticipation. His embrace was tender, his kisses lavish, and when he turned her gently to separate her thighs she felt like purring as she moved against him. His mouth tickled as his tongue flicked over the soft flesh of her stomach, and she could not suppress a throaty giggle which made him stop for only an instant to return her loving gaze. His hands locked firmly around her waist then, capturing her in a pose she couldn't change as he began to nuzzle the golden triangle of curls between her thighs.

Although she could scarcely draw in breath, Bianca called his name, but Evan was enjoying the loving game he'd begun too greatly to end it at that moment. His tongue parted her flesh to conquer all resistance to the intimacy he'd initiated; then he slowly teased her senses until she was writhing in his arms, too lost in the torrent of ecstasy he'd created to want him to stop. He felt the very same rapture she enjoyed as he spread playful kisses down her thighs before his eager mouth returned to the hot, moist center of her being, his tongue finally plunging deeply to savor the inner recess of her body. He was seeking to bind her to him with pleasure, but joy this rich was meant to be shared and he could no longer deny his own need. When he released her, she made no move to escape him and his mouth swiftly sought hers, eager for the moment their bodies would be joined as one. She enfolded him in a loving embrace, matching his driving thrusts with a graceful intensity that thrilled him anew. She was an enchantress, but as the climax of their union burst from within him, his thirst for revenge haunted him still. Fate had given him a bride like no other, and as he would in battle, he vowed to use such a splendid gift to his own best advantage.

Chapter VI

Evan lay with Bianca cradled tenderly in his arms, her head nestled lightly upon his left shoulder as he lazily combed the strands of her golden hair with his fingers. He knew she was no closer to sleep than he, but his thoughts were bitter, filled with violence, while he was certain hers were charmingly innocent and sweet. Since the hour he'd learned of his younger brother's death, he had been consumed with the desire for revenge. Bianca's unique charms were a delightful diversion, but he'd not lost sight of the true reason he'd married her. Wealthy men had always arranged the finest possible marriages for their daughters in order to further their own goals, but he seriously doubted Francesco Antonelli would have had Charles killed. He understood the way the man behaved now. He'd merely have forced Bianca to marry Paolo, and by that clever act he would have given her new husband the problem of dealing with an amorous young American. Paolo, driven mad by jealousy, must have plotted the murder. With Bianca gone, the arrogant Venetian would be forced to come after her himself, to reclaim her for his own and, more importantly, to win glory for her rescue. A slow smile curved Evan's lips. Paolo Sammarese might think himself clever, but Evan knew he himself was a damned sight more cunning. He'd kill the bastard before the Venetian had time to do anything more than hail the *Phoenix*. Paolo was as good as dead, and finding that certainty deeply satisfying, Evan was content to, again, give his full attention to his lovely bride. He turned upon his left side now, supporting her head upon his outstretched arm.

"I can't seem to control my passions where you are concerned, but there is so much I want to teach you. I know I am far too impatient, and I should have been more thoughtful," he whispered softly, his warm breath caressing her ear.

The lanterns had been turned down low so the light in the cabin was too dim for him to see the blush which darkened her cheeks, but Bianca could feel its heat. She doubted there was an inch of her body he had not caressed or kissed since they'd first made love. She had not dreamed their intimacy would be so complete, but she was afraid he might have found her awkward in her attempts to return his affection. "I'm sorry. What must I learn to please you?" she asked hesitantly.

Evan chuckled as he gave her an enthusiastic hug. "Nothing, I am very pleased with you already. What I meant was there are all sorts of marvelous ways to make love, and I want us to enjoy them all. There will be plenty of time, though. I did not mean to rush you so, or to take more than you were ready to give."

Bianca was quiet for a moment, uncertain how to reply. He had shocked her deeply, that was certainly true, for she'd had only the vaguest idea of how a man and a woman made love before she'd been with him. Although he was a passionate man, he had always treated her tenderly. His kiss and touch were gentle, endlessly tantalizing, no matter how bold his actions. He made making love so wonderfully pleasant, she knew no words fine enough in either of the languages she spoke to describe it. She did not think he needed to apologize to her, and she said so. "Evan, you are the most fascinating man I have ever met, and undoubtedly the best of lovers. I know I am untutored in the ways to give you pleasure, but you have never asked for more than I have wanted to give."

"But I did not bother to ask," Evan teased playfully, too wise to remind her she'd not found the first kiss he'd stolen from her in a darkened gondola enjoyable enough to return. Truly, he thought her talent for making love a natural gift which only he had been fortunate enough to discover. Meaning to have her again, he lowered his mouth to hers. His kiss was unhurried, slow and sweet, as his right hand moved gently over the smooth swell of her breasts. His fingertips alternately circled the pale pink tips until they were firm peaks; then he slid his hand over her hip to draw her near. He was in so relaxed a mood he felt no urgency now, simply the longing to possess her lithe body, her remarkable beauty. He had never been with a woman who hadn't expected something from him in return, yet Bianca responded solely to his affection as though that were her right as his wife. *Wife.* The word echoed in his mind with a hollow ring, for their bond was too new for him to fully comprehend how it could have grown so deep. Her fingertips were now tracing slow swirls down his spine as she returned his kisses, distracting him from any thought deeper than how he wished to take her this time.

Bianca could tell by the increasingly unsteady rhythm of Evan's breathing that he liked her to touch him, and his body was so splendid she found it enjoyable to explore. Slowly she brought her hand over his hip, resting it there lightly for a moment before proceeding to a caress far more intimate in nature. His flesh was smooth, yet hard, throbbing, as her fingers closed around him. All the power his sleek body possessed seemed concentrated in the shaft which had first pierced her body, bringing pain then pleasure so rich it had seared her soul to his. Consumed by the heat of desire Bianca enflamed his magnificent bronze body with the unquenchable fire of passion. Their spirits were one now as she willingly gave her body to him.

His need for her affection overwhelmed Evan once more, and he slid his arm around Bianca's left thigh to rest her leg upon his hip. Then, sliding his right leg between hers, he waited for her to mesh their bodies. He made love to her this time with a languid ease, letting the beauty of the feelings which flowed so easily between them build to a peak of nearly unbearable rapture before he quickened his motions to bring them to the ecstasy of a perfectly timed union. She was such a gracious young woman, unsparing with her love, and he found pleasing her so delightful a pastime that his own pleasure was all the more rich. The more he lost himself in her, the greater his own satisfaction became. This was something so new he could not even begin to understand how she worked such magic, but he did know he'd never tire of being under her spell. His passion for her sated for the moment, he lay cradling her gently, their arms and legs still entwined. Their mood too blissful to inspire conversation, they continued to exchange sleepy kisses until sleep overtook them.

When she awakened late the next morning, Bianca covered a wide yawn and then turned to look for Evan, only to find she was the cabin's sole occupant. Her husband had thoughtfully folded her nightgown and laid it upon the foot of the bed. A basket of oranges and another of biscuits rested on the table. She hoped he'd brought them rather than Timothy, but she felt too marvelous that morning to care if the cabin boy had seen her sleeping. There was a pitcher of water on the washstand so she bathed and hurriedly slipped on clean lingerie, not wanting to be teased about being a sleepyhead. However, she had to sit down and wait for Evan to come and help her dress. Wearing a corset was a nuisance without the attentions of a maid, but what was she to do? While she could tighten the laces herself, she could not tie them securely enough to finish dressing alone. Too frustrated to wait any longer for Evan, when Timothy came to her door with a pot of tea, she considered her predicament resolved and turning her back toward him, asked for his help. "I need you to tie my laces in bows, Timothy, will you do that please?"

The boy's dark eyes grew wide at the impropriety of that request, but he knew better than to refuse it. "Captain Sinclair told me I was to be of service, ma'am," he declared. Then he placed the teapot upon the table, and after wiping his hands on his breeches, he grabbed the silken cords and tied them in secure, if clumsy bows.

Intrigued by his comment, Bianca smiled prettily as she hastened to dress. "Thank you for your help, but why do you refer to my husband as Captain Sinclair? Isn't William Summer the captain of the *Phoenix*?"

Timothy blushed deeply, certain he'd just made an awful blunder. "Yes, ma'am, he is, but I worked first for Captain Sinclair and I do not know what else to call him."

"You must ask him then, Timothy, for I am certain the *Phoenix* should not have two captains."

"Yes, ma'am."

Seeing she'd embarrassed him, Bianca attempted to put him at ease. "When did you first go to sea, Timothy?"

The shy boy frowned slightly as he tried to come up with the correct answer. "At the war's end. My pa sailed on the *Phoenix* but he was killed by the British. I've got three little brothers so my ma was happy when I was offered this job."

Bianca buttoned up her bodice quickly, certain she

shouldn't be keeping the young boy, but she was still curious and wanted to ask him a few more questions before she dismissed him. "It was my husband who hired you, not Summer?"

"Yes, ma'am. He looks after my family now. Says he owes my pa that much since he was a good hand."

Impressed by her husband's generosity, Bianca hoped to learn still more about him. "I'm certain your family is a deserving one. Does my husband see that in addition to your job you have some schooling?"

Timothy shook his head as he answered proudly. "I've been to school, but I'm learning better things now."

"Yes, I can just imagine that you are." Bianca's glance swept his uncombed hair before straying to his frayed shirt and worn breeches. The lad looked as though he'd been plucked from the gutter, certainly not the way she thought a cabin boy aboard such a fine ship should be groomed and dressed. Since he was too young to be responsible for his own attire, she decided she'd speak to Evan about him that very morning. Her husband claimed to have so much free time, why hadn't he spared a moment to see that Timothy was properly groomed and clothed? Or was that rightly William Summer's job? "Tell me, how long has Summer been captain of the *Phoenix*?" she asked suddenly, not wanting to accuse the wrong man of being derelict in his duties toward the child.

Horrified by that question, Timothy backed away, inching toward the door as he stuttered nervously, "Not, not long!" Unable to stammer more than that hasty reply, he bolted out of the cabin.

"Timothy!" Bianca called after him, but he did not return. She stood at the door, perplexed by his hasty flight. She'd not meant to frighten him. Evan spoke about William Summer with such confidence, but it was plain Timothy didn't want to talk about the man. Why was that? Now having numerous questions only her husband could answer, she decided to let breakfast wait while she went to find him.

She raced up the steps, then halted abruptly and took a deep breath as she reminded herself she was now a married woman and should behave like a lady. She turned toward the stern, where she saw a group of men huddled together, and seeing Evan in their midst, she knew better than to disturb him. He was clearly leading a discussion to which the other men were paying close attention. His voice was lost in the wind which whipped through the sails overhead, but she could tell by the intensity of his expression that the subject was a very serious one. William Summer was standing to Evan's left, frowning sullenly, but as Bianca watched, he remained silent. Whatever her husband's point of view, it appeared to be a compelling one for the others were all nodding in agreement.

As Evan stood with members of the crew, Bianca could not help but notice the striking difference between her husband and the others. It was not simply his fine clothing which set him apart. He was the tallest, and while all the men were muscular, his build was easily the most powerful. Standing upon the deck, his legs apart to give him perfect balance despite the constant motion of the ship, he exuded the confidence born of long experience. An imposing sight. Bianca did not doubt for an instant that despite William Summer's title it was Evan who was in command of the *Phoenix*. He was such a joy to watch she decided to remain where she was, partially hidden by the wooden rail of the companionway, until he finished talking so she could speak with him privately.

Expanding upon an idea Bianca had supplied, Evan was refining his plans. "My bride warned me to be on the lookout for pirates, and I will tell her the cannon drills we hold daily are for that purpose. A Venetian ship may overtake us today, or perhaps not until tomorrow or the next day, but it will come soon and I want us to be fully prepared for it. We will respond in a friendly fashion, make no effort to escape it; but as soon as I ascertain the identity of those on board, I'll give the order to blast the cursed vessel right out of the water."

At that announcement, William could no longer hold his temper or his tongue. "Since it is one man you want dead, not a hundred, would it not be better to lure him aboard where you can challenge him face to face?"

Since they had often plotted strategy as a group during the war, Evan did not regard such a question as insubordination. "That was my original plan as you know, but I am trying to think instead of what is best for Bianca, as you suggested I do, Will." There was only a slight trace of sarcasm in his voice. "I do not want her to blame herself for Paolo Sammarese's death when in fact, she'll have nothing to do with it." When his explanation met with no further objection, he continued. "At the first sign of the Venetian ship I'll take her below and tell her to stay there, lock her in my cabin if I must. She'll not see anything that happens, and I'll tell her we've rid the seas of one less pirate ship. Pirates are what she fears so she'll believe me readily enough. I'll not invite Sammarese aboard for as soon as I'd killed him his ship would undoubtedly fire on us. No, it is the element of surprise which is crucial here, and I'll not give them any advantage. Besides, those who sail with Sammarese will be his friends, and as such they deserve no mercy from us since any one of them may have held the knife which killed Charles. Now give the order to begin today's drill." Having prepared no alternative plan of his own, William Summer promptly gave that command, and it was swiftly relayed to the gun deck. The six twenty-four-pound cannon on the starboard side fired a thunderous volley which was followed by a blast from the six guns on the port side. Reloading in slightly under a minute's time, each gun crew then fired a second round.

Satisfied that his men had lost none of their speed, Evan called a halt to the drill, and at that precise moment he noticed a white-faced Bianca watching them. Caught off guard, his hate-filled glance met hers and held for a second too long. Following his gaze, the crewmen turned, and she was shocked by the combined fury directed toward her. As if it were a tangible force it sent her reeling backward, and she stumbled down the steps. She'd not expected the crew to like her until she'd had an opportunity to win their respect, but her husband's hostility was so plain in the evil light in his gaze that she could barely find the strength to swallow the scream which filled her throat. She raced for the safety of Evan's cabin as swiftly as her feet would carry her pain-numbed body. Inside it, she slammed the door and then fumbled for the key, but the one she'd used the previous day was missing from the lock. Terrified, she backed away, scurrying behind one of the heavy chairs for protection.

Evan lost no time in pursuing his bride. Though he was positive she hadn't overheard his remarks, he knew she'd been frightened unnecessarily, and he'd not meant to do that. As he entered his cabin, he saw the tears streaming down Bianca's cheeks so he spoke in a reassuring tone. "I'm so sorry. Captain Summer wanted to have a gun drill. I should have had the sense to come and tell you that the men were only practicing. There's no need for you to be frightened."

In the time it took Bianca to find her voice, she could only marvel at the dramatic change in her husband's manner. His smile was charming, but she couldn't forget the way he'd looked at her only moments before, with a glance that spoke more eloquently of hatred than of love. She'd seen exactly who'd been giving the orders for the drill, so she knew he was lying by mentioning Summer in his apology. She could only speculate as to why. "I was too naïve, too stupid obviously, to understand why you were questioning me about ships yesterday. You expect someone to come after me don't you, and it's obvious you mean to attack them when they arrive!"

Since that accusation was impossible to deny, Evan tried another approach. "Bianca, why would you think such a thing? You're not making any sense at all." He remained by the door, his expression still a disarming one. He had no intention of revealing his true plans to her, but he cursed himself for not realizing how swiftly she'd jump to the correct conclusion when the cannons were fired. "Recall yesterday's conversation and your concern that we might be attacked by pirates. Summer is no fool. He's well aware of the dangers involved in sailing the Mediterranean, and he keeps his crew well prepared to meet them. Should your father wish to pursue us or Paolo, or even the Doge for that matter, I would welcome him." With a welcome the man will not live to forget, Evan swore to himself.

Bianca wiped away her tears. She was still frightened, but not too confused by the logic of Evan's comments to counter them well. "I told you, no one will come after me. My family will consider me dead, Paolo must surely despise me, the Doge would have no interest in interfering in such a private matter. But why would you have asked me about their ships if you weren't expecting to have to fight them?"

Evan shrugged as if he were perplexed by her question, and continued to speak his lies smoothly. "I build ships and will apologize if I discuss them too frequently for your tastes, but I had no evil intentions."

Bianca's knuckles grew white as her hands tightened upon the back of the chair she'd grabbed for protection. "I don't believe you! You admitted what you were to me yourself. There's little difference between a pirate and a privateer, but whatever you are plotting, it is a waste of time because no one will come after me!"

"This argument is totally ridiculous, Bianca. My only concern is for your safety in what you yourself told me are pirate-infested waters. You seem to think I am planning to attack a ship you are positive will never set sail. Doesn't this situation strike you as being completely absurd?" Evan asked with a deep chuckle. Sensing someone behind him, he turned to find Timothy approaching and sent the lad on his way. "Please bring us a fresh pot of tea to enjoy with breakfast, and be quick about it."

Bianca was scarcely reassured, but when Evan explained their dilemma in such ludicrous terms, she had to admit her fears sounded silly. She was positive no one would come after her, so no matter what desperate action her dashing young husband planned, he'd have no opportunity to carry it out. She relaxed only a bit, but a faint trace of a smile brightened her expression. She knew she'd seen something in her husband's glance that he hadn't meant her to see, but perhaps he'd been so intent upon his discussion of pirates with his men, he'd not truly seen her for a second or two. That explanation was a plausible one and she tried to make herself believe it, but she still felt uneasy. "What I say is true, Evan. After what I've done, no one in Venice will care whether I am alive or dead."

That she actually seemed to believe such a sad thing pained Evan deeply, but he hastened to offer reassurance of his own. "Your welfare is now my responsibility, Bianca, as it should be. Why don't you sit down and enjoy your breakfast. I'd like to join you if you don't mind."

Bianca hesitated a moment, afraid she'd behaved like a

frightened child when she was now a married woman and should be able to converse with her husband on any subject without losing her composure. Then, recalling the elegant example her mother had always set, she smiled and sat down in the chair she'd been gripping so tightly. "This is your cabin; how can I object to your company?"

"I hope you don't wish to." Before Evan could pull up a chair and sit down opposite his bride Timothy reappeared. He dismissed the boy again, however, preferring to pour their tea himself. Since Bianca's mood now seemed more agreeable, he dared to ask her a teasing question. "You are bright, my pet, but also very imaginative. Do you really consider me no better than a pirate?"

Bianca took an orange and began to peel it rather than return his inquisitive stare. Her hands were trembling so badly she could barely hold onto the fruit, but she concentrated upon that task rather than her husband's mocking smile. "I know very little about you, Evan, but I think you're capable of accomplishing whatever you desire, be it good *or* evil." He certainly had in her case, but she knew he must realize their courtship had been shockingly brief.

Evan took a sip of tea, grateful he'd been able to calm this volatile beauty so easily, yet he knew he'd have to be far more careful of her feelings in the future. "I only hope to take you home and make you happy. Those do not seem like sinister goals to me, my pet."

"Nor to me either." Bianca had to agree, but she was still curious. "Even though I know no one will bother to come after us, what would you tell my father if he did?"

"First, I hope you would introduce me to him," Evan began, a wicked grin on his face. "Then I'd tell him how pleased I was to meet him and to have married his beautiful daughter, after which I'd send him on his way."

"If he had gone to the trouble of coming after me, I doubt he'd simply shake your hand and leave," Bianca offered softly, afraid to raise her voice or gaze directly at him.

"I said I'd keep you amused for this voyage, but is this what you like to do, make up imaginary dilemmas and then propose solutions?"

"In this case, yes," Bianca admitted frankly.

Evan sighed wearily, but he didn't really mind catering to her whims. "All right then. I would tell your father I enjoy having you as my bride and I intend to keep you with me. What would he be likely to do then? You know him and I don't, so you will have to tell me."

Bianca frowned slightly as she responded. "I'm afraid to consider what might happen, but I am positive he no longer feels he has a daughter so you are safe."

"I am safe?" Evan scoffed, highly amused by that remark. "Do you actually think he could harm me?"

"Yes." Bianca looked up then, the pretty green of her eyes veiled by a mist of tears. "I think if he wanted to kill you he could do it quite easily."

Evan sat back in his chair, stunned by the confidence with which Bianca spoke that threat. Damn, he wished he could ask her what she knew about Charles's death, but he dared not reveal who he was or what his mission to Venice had really been. He'd been convinced that Paolo Sammarese was the killer, but had it actually been her father? He'd know soon, he realized. A Venetian ship might be sighted within the hour. "I'd assumed, as an advisor to the Doge, your father's talents would lie in the field of diplomacy. Was I wrong?"

"No. He is a skilled diplomat, but we were talking about what he'd be likely to do about you and me, not what he'd do in a matter concerning all of Venice."

"Oh, yes. Of course. Well, if you don't mind, I'd just as soon discuss something else, anything else, rather than your father's desire to see me dead."

"I'd never let him kill you, Evan. Don't be silly!" Bianca replied, indulging in her first real smile of the day. "Besides, I'm certain he has disowned me so he'd have no reason to care whether I became a widow or not."

"Let's hope that you never do, my dear." Evan finished his tea in one gulp for he was eager to get back up on deck, but he sat with his bride until she had finished an orange and two biscuits. "In the future, it would be best if you waited here for me. I don't want you wandering around the deck alone. You might trip and fall, or be injured in a dozen other ways, and you are far too precious for me to allow that to happen. If I awaken before you, I'll come back to check on you frequently so I can escort you up on deck myself. It is another splendid day, and I know you don't want to sit in here all alone."

Bianca placed the teacups upon Timothy's tray and then rose to fetch her cloak. "Yes, I'd like to spend my time on deck with you if I won't be in your way."

"Never," Evan replied with a deep chuckle, and pleased that he'd been able to distract her from her too-perceptive questions he bent down to give her a kiss before he took her arm.

Knowing the noise of the wind might make conversation on deck difficult, Bianca lay her hand upon Evan's sleeve to stay his impatience. "I wish to speak with you about Timothy for a moment."

"What about him?" Evan asked with a puzzled frown.

"Since you were not here, I had to ask him to assist me in getting dressed this morning. I hope you will not consider that improper. I had no idea when you might return." Before Evan could make any comment on that revelation, she continued. "He told me you support his widowed mother and his little brothers, is that true?"

More embarrassed about what she had found out than about Timothy having seen her in her lingerie, Evan nevertheless admitted that it was, indeed, the truth. "I do what I can for them. I'll not allow the families of the men who died while serving under my command to beg on the streets."

"There are others then?" Bianca asked with a growing sense of pride.

Although Evan preferred to keep such matters to himself, since she'd learned of the Stewarts, he knew she'd undoubtedly find out about the others. "Yes, there are, but I am a wealthy man, Bianca, and I do not mind sharing my good fortune with widows and orphans."

"No, you wouldn't. But who is responsible for Timothy's welfare now? Is it you or Captain Summer?"

In a split second Evan made his choice and responded confidently. "I am, why?"

"He needs a new suit of clothes, that's why. He should have a haircut too. Furthermore, I doubt he has mastered all he should in the way of schooling, and you need to provide him with a tutor if he hasn't."

Evan stared down at the lovely young woman before him, his amusement evident in his rakish grin. "Is your desire for children so strong you've decided to adopt Timothy as your own?"

Bianca's cheeks flooded with color. When she could formulate a coherent response to his taunt, she replied heatedly, "No! That's not it at all, but surely you do not want your cabin boy to dress in rags and to be unable to read and write!"

"Timothy has other clothes, Bianca, but I believe he was helping the cook scour the galley this morning and did not want to ruin his best attire. He was well dressed last night when he served our supper. Didn't you notice him then?"

She'd had far too much on her mind to notice the boy's clothes at suppertime, but she hated to admit it. "If I did, it has slipped my mind. I'm pleased to hear he has adequate clothing, however. How are his reading and his math?"

Evan shrugged. "I really don't know. I do not wish to serve as his tutor if he needs help, do you?"

"I would not mind that chore. He is a likable lad and seems smart. He can not be a cabin boy forever."

"No. But he can sail with me for as long as he likes."

"With you?" Bianca asked with an inquisitive glance.

"Yes, with me," Evan replied, not understanding her question.

Seizing the advantage she was certain she now had, Bianca asked calmly, "Why did you tell me William Summer is the captain of this ship when it is obvious you are in command?"

The warm golden brown of Evan's eyes grew as dark as his expression. Bianca Antonelli was a great beauty, but she was also far too bright for her own good. She wanted the truth, but so did he. For an instant he was tempted to grab her elegant white shoulders and shake it out of her. She knew the answer to the mystery he'd gone to Venice to solve, to the murder he sought to avenge, he was positive of it, but he didn't want her to know anything more about him than she already did. As he opened the cabin door, he clasped her arm firmly and his voice low, he offered the best explanation he could provide. "I own the *Phoenix*, beloved, so it is quite natural that Summer and the rest of the crew show me the respect I deserve. Now, the day is far too fine to waste. Let's go."

Bianca did not argue, nor did she ask what had become of the key. Indeed, she was far too frightened to refuse his invitation or to ask any more questions about William Summer, for the fierce light in Evan's eyes had warned her that doing so would have unfortunate consequences. Her husband had a temper, and apparently it was as bad as hers. He'd admitted to being jealous too. Dear God, she prayed silently, what sort of man have I married? He was so handsome it almost hurt to look at him, but she wondered what terrible secrets he might have hidden in his heart.

Chapter VII

They had been at sea for ten days, and William Summer was at his wit's end. He might now have the title of captain, but he still felt as though he were Evan's mate, regardless of the fact that he had been given full responsibility for the *Phoenix.* Keeping the sleek vessel afloat was a matter of slight consequence, however, when all aboard were consumed with the same lust for revenge as her owner, and were so alert he had only to whisper an order to have it immediately obeyed. The same gut-wrenching tension which had plagued their days during the war held them all in a merciless grip. All except Evan's stunning bride, Will reminded himself. Still an object of considerable curiosity among the crew, the young woman spent the day at her husband's side, apparently as eager as he for the freedom of movement the deck provided. He could not recall ever meeting such a beautiful woman, but she was also the most restless of individuals. Although she had to take two steps for each of her husband's, she seemed never to tire of walking by his side, and even when Evan relaxed against the stern rail, she was never still but constantly paced this way and that as they talked, her steps so dainty she appeared to be dancing. What they had to discuss in such detail he could only guess.

Will pulled his hat lower down upon his forehead to shade his eyes as he continued to observe the attractive couple. He'd seen Evan charm women often enough to know the man was damned good at it, but he also knew how quickly his handsome employer tired of his conquests. Perhaps it was only that he was at sea and there were no other women about, but Evan seemed to be fascinated by his lovely wife, though Will knew the attention he paid her was simply part of the elaborate ruse in which they'd all become involved. He doubted Evan was capable of love, but if he were he'd certainly not fall for the woman whose beauty and charm had cost his brother his life. He and Charles had been too close, the younger man admiring his elder brother with a devotion that was almost embarrassing to behold. Charles had had a natural talent for commerce and had joined his father's firm, but he'd often stated that he envied Evan his ability to command a ship with such masterful ease.

That was how much the young man knew, Will scoffed to himself. Charles's parents had kept him out of the war in which Evan had proven himself to be one of the most vicious adversaries the men of the British Royal Navy ever had to face. Sinclair had had the devil's own cunning plus the speed of the *Phoenix* which he'd used to every advantage, appearing with the first rays of dawn to strike without warning, inflicting heavy damage upon enemy ships and then disappearing in his own cannons' smoke only to reappear from the opposite direction firing another deadly barrage. They'd sunk many a ship twice their size before her captain had had time to fire, let alone reload his guns. Evan was a born killer, utterly ruthless, but Charles had never seen that side of his brother. Will had. He knew what was coming and he wanted it over as quickly as possible. The whole crew were as thirsty for blood as Evan, as eager for the battle which was sure to come, for what man alive would let Bianca Antonelli go without a fight to the death?

Will had tried in vain to think of Bianca as Evan referred to her: irresistible bait for the trap in which to catch his brother's murderer. She was simply too pretty to be tainted with evil, far too sweet in her manner to inspire any response save admiration. That Evan would use her so badly pained him more by the hour, yet when he saw them together, his friend treated his bride with such courtesy he dared not complain about her situation. Nonetheless, he failed to see how they could sink Paolo Sammarese's ship without her knowing exactly what had happened, for she seemed far too bright to be content to remain below while Evan told her they were fighting pirates. As a boy Will had learned from bitter experience that one lie always led to another, and he often wondered if Evan had ever spoken a true word to Bianca. That thought made him feel bad too, for he knew she deserved far better from her husband. Sick with guilt over his part in fooling her, his eyes aching from the effort to continually scan the horizon for Paolo's ship, Will went to his cabin to rest, hoping that sleep would put their deadly mission out of his mind for an hour or two at least. But images of the lovely Bianca Antonelli danced through his dreams, adding to his torment.

Evan leaned back, resting his elbows upon the rail, content to gaze down at Bianca's enchanting smile for the moment. He found her endlessly entertaining; she was so full of life, never quiet nor still. "So you have not ridden a horse, not even once?" he asked skeptically.

"You have been to Venice; we had no need for horses there. Why would I ride when I could travel more easily by gondola?"

"The countryside is pretty, but you never left your

city of islands?"

Bianca licked her lips thoughtfully, wondering how best to defend the only life she'd ever known. "Venice may seem small to you, but we did not lack for anything."

"You've just admitted you had no horse!" Evan teased playfully.

"Only because I did not need one!" Bianca laughed with him then, and when he extended his arms she went to him willingly, putting her arms around his waist to hold him tight. She had carefully studied every nuance of his expression in order to better understand his moods, and he never laughed unless he was truly amused so she could not help but be happy too. They'd seen no sign of pirates, nor of any other ships, and she hoped they never would. She loved standing at his side while the sea breeze dampened their hair and the sun brightened their cheeks. She had grown up at the edge of a lagoon, but the charming canals which crisscrossed the crowded city of Venice provided no wide vistas such as these. She adored the openness of the high seas. The whole world seemed to stretch out before them, theirs for the taking, and she could think of nothing more exciting than being with Evan on the deck of the *Phoenix,* except of course, lying in his arms. They made love often, and just as he'd boasted, she doubted any woman had had a more attentive husband. She'd taken great care not to provoke his anger again. Instead she flattered his vanity as her mother flattered her father's, and he'd been so wonderfully sweet she'd not once regretted her decision to marry him. The life they'd begun was very pleasant.

With Bianca snuggled against him, Evan found serious contemplation of any sort difficult, but he was deeply troubled all the same. He was skilled in the art of attack, not retreat, and he'd been certain the battle to avenge his brother's death would have been fought and won by now. With each passing hour he grew more confused, for had

Bianca been wrenched from his embrace, he would not have wasted even one precious second in organizing a pursuit. He kissed the top of her glossy curls and gave her another affectionate squeeze. What could be keeping Paolo, or her father for that matter, from coming after them? They were following the most heavily trafficked course so the *Phoenix* could be easily pursued, but he had no idea what to do if a Venetian ship did not soon appear. The wait was pure torture. Although he had Bianca to help him pass the days and she made the nights splendorous, he did not want to sail all the way home under the threat of an attack. He wanted the battle to be waged and won before the sun set, if not sooner, but when he turned to glance back at their wake, the horizon revealed no approaching sails and he cursed angrily to himself. He could scarcely return to Venice and challenge all who cared to fight him. He must think of a viable alternative. He needed to talk with Will and some of the others, but with Bianca as his constant companion, he had no opportunity to plot a strategy. Seeing Timothy leave the galley to spend a few minutes on deck, he realized Bianca had provided the answer to his dilemma.

"I have neglected to follow your advice about Timothy, my pet. I really must see that he be tutored in the subjects mastered by a boy his age."

Bianca had not dared to mention the boy again because their last conversation about Timothy had so infuriated Evan. "I'm certain you know far more about the education of cabin boys than I do, but I did volunteer to be his tutor should he need one and truly I would not mind."

"Let's not upset the lad. I'll ask him to bring a pot of tea to our cabin, and after he's served it, I'll simply hand him a book. If he can read it well, I'll dismiss him and tomorrow I'll check on his sums. If he stumbles over the words or the numbers, then you'll have a pupil, but I doubt either of you can spare more than an hour a day for lessons."

"What will you do while I tutor Timothy?" Bianca asked with a sultry glance.

"I will make myself useful somehow, my love. Do not fear that I will become bored." Evan was sincere in that promise for he was certain an hour a day would be sufficient to plot his revenge.

When Timothy proved to have no talent for reading or math, Evan was delighted. Bianca decided that the hour after breakfast was the best time for the lessons and her husband agreed. But he suggested she start the lad's lessons immediately, and leaving her in his cabin with Timothy, he went to find Will, elated to have the opportunity to speak with him alone.

When he was seated in Will's cabin, Evan stretched out his legs and grinned happily. "Although it is early, I'd not refuse a drink if you offered one."

Will brought out the bottle of whiskey he kept handy and poured a generous amount into two battered pewter mugs. After they had each taken a swallow, he asked the most obvious question. "Where is your charming bride this morning, still asleep?"

"No. She convinced me I'd been negligent in providing for Timothy's education, and she's taken on the task of tutoring him herself for an hour each morning. I only hope he does not prove to be too apt a pupil for I need some time to myself."

"You've grown bored with her already?" Will tossed down the rest of the fiery whiskey in one gulp, sorry to see that the inevitable had happened so soon. Had he ever the good fortune to find such a woman he would never tire of her company, no matter how much time they spent together. Eternity would seem too brief.

Evan observed his former mate's disgusted expression and instantly became defensive. "Whether or not I'm bored with Bianca is not the issue. I went to Venice to find Charles's murderer and to make him pay dearly for what he'd done. I thought my attentions to Bianca would inspire him to come after me as swiftly as he'd gone after Charles, but when I found her locked in her room, weeping pathetically over being forced into marrying Paolo, I had no choice but to change my plans and bring her with us. I thought the killer would come after her as soon as he could commandeer a vessel, and neither her father nor Paòlo Sammarese would have had any difficulty doing that. I can't imagine what can be keeping them, but it's plain we can't reverse our course and head back toward Venice." His problem clearly described, Evan picked up Will's bottle and replenished both their mugs.

Will shook his head. "None of us wants to see Charles's murderer go unpunished, but if the bastard has not fallen for your trap, what can we do? If a woman as lovely as Bianca is not enough to lure the beast from his lair, nothing will do it."

The two young men continued to drink as they tried to decide how best to avenge a murder when they had failed to flush the culprit out into the open. They had numerous ideas, which became increasingly bizarre. Finally Evan was disgusted.

"I swear I would have killed him with my bare hands had he approached me in Venice."

"But he did not," Will reminded him sadly. "Perhaps, had you remained another day or two, things would have worked out differently."

Evan didn't bother to explain that such a delay had been impossible after he'd made love to Bianca in her own bed. Finally, after a long sullen silence, he slammed his empty mug down upon Will's desk and got unsteadily to his feet. "Well at least I have Bianca and the man who murdered Charles doesn't. I have that satisfaction. It is a fine one, but I want still more."

His mind no longer all that clear, Will nevertheless had a sudden thought. "What if you were wrong? What if neither Paolo nor her father is the killer?"

"Blast it all!" Evan shouted. "It doesn't matter who the man is; Bianca is still the key! Charles's infatuation with her is what cost him his life, that much is more than plain!"

Will had to nod in agreement. "Then the killer will come after her. He must. Perhaps in another day or two."

"A few more days, or weeks, perhaps a month, or a year! Christ almighty! I do not want to wait my entire life for the bastard to arrive!" With that bitter oath Evan opened Will's door and moved toward the ladder, certain he should go up on deck for some air before rejoining his bride, but more than an hour had gone by and she was already waiting at the rail for him.

Since he had no reasonable excuse to offer for being quite drunk before noon, Evan hoped Bianca would not notice his state. However, her shocked expression revealed that she had taken in his unsteady gait. Taking his place at her side, he leaned against the rail and looked away, knowing the chill ocean breeze would readily restore his sobriety. He'd never made excuses to anyone and he did not intend to make them to her. If he wanted to drink himself into a stupor early in the day, he didn't want his wife nagging him about it, but he doubted Bianca would hold her tongue. "When I told you not to come up on deck alone I expected you to obey me. It is much too dangerous," he remarked suddenly, offering a complaint of his own before she could voice hers.

Bianca simply stared at Evan, too astonished to see him in such a sorry condition to object to his rebuke. Although he drank wine with their meals, she'd never seen him the least bit affected by it. Whatever had he been doing? While she'd busied herself tutoring Timothy, he'd wiled away his time by getting drunk. What would have prompted him to do such a stupid thing? If something was wrong and he'd taken to drink because of it, she wanted to know what the problem was. Laying her hand upon his sleeve, she called his name shyly. "Evan?"

"What?" He growled his response, still not turning to face her.

Bianca had no wish to fight with her husband in front of the crew so, hiding her hurt at his rudeness, she left him alone but as she reached the companionway she met William Summer who also seemed far from sober. "Surely the captain of a vessel, if you are indeed the captain of the *Phoenix,* ought to set a better example, sir!" With that bit of hostile advice she swept past him, hurried down the steps, and ran to her husband's cabin. What is the matter with everyone? she wondered. Oh, she knew men liked to drink, and some more than others, but she'd not suspected Evan or Will to be so weak. She flung her cloak over a chair and began to pace the cabin with a fluid, though somewhat agitated stride. Evan had been so nice to her the last few days and she knew she'd done nothing to upset him, but somethng had happened. Why wouldn't he confide in her? When he did not join her at noon, she ate the meal Timothy brought, then remained in the cabin rather than go up on deck alone again since Evan had obviously been annoyed with her for doing that although she knew her way around the *Phoenix* now and doubted she'd be hurt. As she saw it, her husband had gotten drunk and had been unforgivably rude. He owed her an apology and she'd make him come to her to give it.

A properly rigged ship sails itself, and the crew of the *Phoenix* were so skilled in trimming the sails to take every advantage of the wind, she was a joy to command even when her captain was not at his best. Since Will could scarcely be critical, he kept Evan company until they were both quite sober and realized how foolish they'd been to get so drunk when at any moment they might be called upon to fight. Their lives would depend upon the coolness of their minds and the steadiness of their hands, assets both men usually possessed.

When the afternoon arrived and Bianca did not reappear, Evan was too proud to go and fetch her, but the longer he had to think about the curt way he'd spoken to her, the more ashamed he became and that feeling was such an unusual one for him he was overcome with remorse. However, thinking a few hours on their own would do them both good, he waited until time for supper to return to his cabin. Once there, he found Bianca's hostile stare difficult to return. He knew then that delaying his apology had made it no easier to give, but he tried his best to sound sincere.

"I'm sorry I've done such a poor job of keeping you amused today. Will and I got to reminiscing about the war and—"

"Is that your usual pastime?" Bianca interrupted quickly. "To boast of your victories and get so drunk you can not even be civil to your own wife? If so, then please tell me the next time you're in such a disagreeable mood and I'll make it a point to stay out of your way!"

As usual his perceptive bride had a damned good point, and Evan didn't bother to argue. "All right, I will do that. Now please come and join me. The cook has prepared a fine meal for us, and I do not want it to go to waste." As he helped her to her chair he leaned down to kiss her cheek lightly, but her pose was such a stiff one he knew she was still in no mood to enjoy his affection. After seating himself, he reached for her hand. "I have not had the privilege of having my wife on board until now, and if occasionally I slip back into the habits of my bachelor days, I hope you will forgive me."

"Well, just who is next in line to assume the command

of the *Phoenix* when you and Will become so fond of reminiscing you can not tell the bow from the stern?" Bianca asked crossly.

"This ship is filled with capable men, Bianca, but I am the only one you need to know." Evan tried to force back his temper, but the wench had such a ready wit and sharp tongue that he found his anger impossible to control. With a sullen frown he poured their wine and began to eat, giving up on conversation since she'd refused to accept his apology graciously. An apology he'd not be tempted to repeat!

Bianca toyed with her food. She'd spent most of the day feeling unbearably lonely and she'd no wish to spend the same sort of miserable night. They'd had far too fast a courtship, followed by what had to have been one of the most informal wedding ceremonies ever performed. Yet despite the haste with which they'd been married, she'd done her best to please her husband and had thought things were going well for them until he'd used his first spare moment to get drunk.

"This is no way to begin a marriage," she finally said softly, more to herself than to him.

"I beg your pardon?" Evan swallowed hastily, so lost in his own thoughts he'd not heard her clearly.

Bianca straightened her shoulders proudly, hoping she could say what must be said without dissolving in a flood of tears. "I have tried to be the best wife to you I know how to be. If you're so unhappy you get drunk at your first opportunity, I think perhaps we'd both be better off if you put me ashore when we reach the coast of Spain. I trust since you take great pride in your wealth you'll give me sufficient funds upon which to live. We can simply forget we ever met, let alone that we were married."

"You're not serious!" Evan gasped, and beginning to choke, he grabbed for his napkin to cover his mouth as he coughed.

Bianca waited for Evan to catch his breath and then replied calmly. "I have never been more serious in my life. I've no wish to be married to a drunk, and you obviously find my company objectionable so why should we stay together?"

"In the first place I am not a drunk, which I think you should know by now. I've explained what happened this morning, and I can assure you it won't happen again. I find your company delightful in every respect. Furthermore, I'd never set a beauty like you ashore with no more than gold to keep her safe. That idea is absurd!" The more he thought about her suggestion, the more infuriated he became. "When I made you my wife I meant to keep you, damn it! Not to kiss you good-bye after no more than a few weeks' time. Are you certain you're not the one who is bored? I know you enjoy the attentions of men, plenty of them. Am I not enough for you?"

Bianca leapt to her feet as she cried, "Get out! Get out of here and don't ever come back! I'll not listen to my own husband call me a whore!"

Evan stared up at the hysterical beauty, certain he'd not called her that despite her accusation. "I don't want to be called a drunk either," he reminded her sternly. "Now sit down and stop acting like a child."

"I will not!" Bianca screamed defiantly.

"You won't what?" Evan asked with menacing logic. "Sit down or stop acting like a child?"

The green of Bianca's eyes burned with a savage glow as she responded in a threatening whisper. "This is all some sort of a joke to you, isn't it? Do you enjoy teasing me so greatly you can not see how badly your behavior today hurt me? Or is it that you simply do not care?" Without waiting for him to respond with what she knew would be another sarcastic comment, Bianca grabbed her cloak and left his cabin. At least on deck she would have the comfort of the sea breeze. Her husband certainly provided nothing in the way of understanding. She tore up the steps, then stopped to make certain she'd not be in anyone's way before she crossed to the rail. The night was going to be another clear one, with stars that seemed close enough to touch. Bianca concentrated on the beauty of the heavens rather than the unhappiness which filled her heart.

When Will noticed Bianca standing alone, he scanned the deck for Evan and finding his friend nowhere about, he approached the pretty young woman. "Good evening, Mrs. Sinclair," he said politely, but the look she turned upon him was scarcely welcoming.

"Good evening." Bianca replied coolly, tempted to again tell William Summer exactly what she thought of him. However, knowing she had no friends on board, she thought better of insulting the captain twice in one day.

Will leaned back against the rail, determined to make up for the kind of day he was certain she'd had. "None of us is used to having a lady on board. If sometimes we forget and behave thoughtlessly, I hope you will forgive us."

"If you are trying to apologize by telling me my husband will be prone to forgetting he has a wife, that is not a comforting thought!" Bianca turned her back on him, their conversation over in her view.

"Mrs. Sinclair," William complained hoarsely. "I was not making apologies for Evan, but for myself!"

In no mood to chat with the man, Bianca was thoroughly annoyed because he didn't have the sense to see that. She wanted only to be left alone, not to continue the argument she'd had with Evan with someone else. When Will did not speak again but remained by her side, she finally grew calm enough to realize he was not going to leave her so she turned back to face him. "I haven't known my husband for nearly as long as you, but if he should chance to forget me again, I would appreciate it if you would remind him I exist. If you'll do that, I will be happy to forgive you for today."

Will considered her bargain briefly then agreed. "Evan did not forget you for a minute, it wasn't that at all, but I'll remind him of his duties to you if ever that is necessary." As indeed he had already done on several occasions, he thought, all to no avail. "It's growing cold, I think I should escort you back to your cabin."

"Thank you, but that's the last place I'd like to be." Where she'd sleep she didn't know, but Bianca had no desire to share her husband's bed that night. If one of them had behaved childishly she was certain it was he for he'd teased her again rather than regarding her as an adult with views which merited serious reflection and needs which deserved courteous attention. If he truly loved her, he'd not have gotten drunk and then ignored her the whole day. She felt justified in remaining angry since his apology had obviously been insincere.

William swallowed nervously, uncertain what to suggest since there was still no sign of Evan. Clearly the beautiful young woman was his responsibility for the present, but he had no idea what to say to improve her mood. The times they had spoken together Evan had been with them, and she'd been so pleasant and full of questions he'd not felt a bit awkward. Now he shuffled his feet nervously and racked his brain for some neutral topic to inspire polite conversation. "Have you traveled much?" he finally asked.

"No, not at all," Bianca admitted, surprised that he'd ask such an irrelevant question.

Disappointed she'd offered so little by way of reply, William said the only thing which came to his mind. "I'm surprised to hear that. You seem so at home on deck I had no idea this was your first voyage."

"We Venetians are as much at home on the water as the land. I've spent far too much time in a gondola to become seasick aboard the *Phoenix.*" Indeed the very idea was so amusing she had to laugh, the musical tones of her voice relaxing the tension between them. "I know this is your first voyage to the Mediterranean, but where else have you been?"

William shrugged. "I've sailed the coast of America from north to south as well as the Caribbean. I hope to see more of Europe, though, now that I've had a taste of it."

"What is our next port? Is it to be French or Spanish?"

"We've yet to decide," William responded truthfully. They'd been far too absorbed in maintaining battle-ready alertness to consider putting in at any port, but he'd not admit that. "Since our provisions are plentiful, I imagine it will be Spanish."

"Who's going to make that decision, you or my husband?"

"Mrs. Sinclair, you made a remark to me this morning, about my not really being the captain of the *Phoenix.* Let me assure you that I am most definitely the captain of this vessel, but with her owner aboard, naturally I expect him to give me his opinions and I'd not ignore them."

"Why not? Would Evan relieve you of your command if you did?" Bianca asked curiously.

"He'd have that right." The moonlight made the lively blonde's glorious curls gleam like a halo, and Will was tempted to reach out and touch her hair though he knew such an intimate gesture was unthinkable. She was smiling slightly now, all trace of impatience gone from her voice, and he found himself again searching for something clever to say. Unlike Evan, he'd little experience conversing with fine ladies, and was embarrassed she'd think him a fool.

Bianca could not help but notice Will's pained expression, and thinking perhaps he had other duties to which to attend, she bid him good night. "I did not mean to keep you, Captain Summer. I'll be all right here alone."

Certain she was bored with him then, Will still would not leave her side. "No. It would be most improper of me to leave you without an escort. If you're not ready to return to your cabin, I must stay with you."

"That won't be necessary. I don't want you to regard me as a nuisance the way my husband does."

"But that's simply not true!" Will protested, but he knew his friend's motivation for marriage. He could not excuse that or the casual disregard he'd shown for his wife's feelings that day. The man had been a fool not to seek Bianca's company earlier, but to ignore her at night was unforgivable in Will's view. "Your husband is a proud man, Mrs. Sinclair, but you are so charming that—"

"That what? I need have no pride of my own?" Bianca asked, close to tears once again.

"Of course you are entitled to your own pride," Will agreed with an exasperated sigh, annoyed he'd unintentionally insulted the pretty young woman. "But I can not allow you to spend the entire night on deck. If you'll not return to your husband's cabin, then I'd be pleased to offer mine."

Knowing Evan thought her a flirt, if not far worse, Bianca dared not accept that invitation. "Thank you, but no. I would prefer to remain here."

"I must insist, Mrs. Sinclair. Believe me, you'll find my cabin far more comfortable than spending the night under the stars."

"I won't argue with that, Captain, but what you suggest is impossible."

Since the wind had already turned cold and would grow colder still, Will decided to simply bide his time, thinking the chill of the night would soon convince her of the wisdom of his offer even if his words hadn't. "All right, if that is your decision, but should you change your mind just let me know and I'll place my cabin at your disposal."

"My wife will have no need for your cabin or for anything else you can provide, Will, not tonight, not ever." Evan spoke in a menacing whisper as he stepped from the shadows, but he gave no indication of how long he had been listening to their conversation.

Certain his offer had been misunderstood, Will dared not leave before he'd made things clear. "If ever your bride has need of me, I shall be more than happy to render assistance. Surely you can not wish me to do otherwise."

"Except in the unlikely event of my death, I can not imagine why Bianca would have any need of you. Good night, Captain."

Rather than make a difficult situation worse, Will turned to go but before he could take his first step Bianca reached for his hand giving his fingers an affectionate, if brief, squeeze. Pleased that she understood his concern for her welfare was genuine even if her husband didn't, the young man strode off to speak with the men on watch, his smile a wide one.

Chapter VIII

Before Bianca could utter a single word of protest, Evan swept her up into his arms and carried her below to his cabin. He kicked the door closed behind them, walked to his bunk, and sat down with her draped across his lap. He began to kiss her then, very softly and sweetly, his tenderness surprising her so greatly she hesitated an instant before wrapping her arms around his neck to return his generous affection. She'd expected him to direct the same bitter sarcasm toward her he'd shown to William Summer, and had been ready to defend herself again, but his wine-flavored kisses were so sweet she swiftly forgot why they'd spent the day apart. His tongue was teasing as it first parted her lips, but when she responded readily his kiss grew demanding and she liked that better still. She accepted this sign of devotion though he'd made no spoken apology, and she made no move to escape his confining embrace.

Evan chose each of his moves with care, for he was sorry he'd forgotten Bianca was a woman who could be reached quite easily through her emotions. His pride had made him arrogant, and when he'd spoken sharply to her that had only served to enrage her. He vowed never to make that foolish mistake again. He wanted her always to be the dear maiden he'd first seduced rather than the willful vixen she'd been when they'd first met. He vowed that he would treat her with kindness because each of them suffered too greatly when he did not, and indeed her kisses were so pleasant he delayed seeking more, contenting himself with the task of removing her hairpins to release a cascade of golden curls until she unbuttoned his shirt and began to run her fingertips over his bare chest. Evan found her caresses delightful, yet he waited a long while before leaning back to remove his coat. Then he slipped her cloak from her shoulders, making the first move to help her disrobe. He wanted to take her slowly, if need be to spend hours demonstrating his affection for her, and to finally dispel any thought she might have of defying him again.

The table had been cleared, the lanterns turned low, and the cozy cabin was filled with a relaxing warmth. He'd taken great care to create this romantic setting, and he meant to use it to every advantage. Having gained considerable experience by helping Bianca dress each morning, Evan removed each of her garments with practiced ease. He slipped off her shoes then unfastened her stockings, allowing his fingertips to savor the smoothness of her calf before he tossed the silken hose aside. Next he removed the bodice of her gown, lowering his lips to the soft swell of her bosom before he reached for her skirt, taking his time with each of the hooks which held the many yards of satin in place at her waist. He knew her lithe body well now, yet doubted he'd ever tire of enjoying such heavenly perfection. The laces securing her corset came loose easily and casting that confining garment aside, he slipped his hand under her camisole to caress her breast, content for a long while to tease the pale pink tip between his fingers while his tongue returned to enjoy the sweetness of her mouth. If it took until dawn to accomplish what he'd set out to do, he'd not complain. There was no urgency in his kiss or caress, only a lavish tenderness which molded her spirit as well as the subtle curves of her body to his will.

Cradled in Evan's arms, Bianca lifted her hand to his nape to slip her fingers through his thick auburn curls. She cared little about what had made his mood so loving, she wanted only to savor these moments, and she returned his deep kisses with unabashed delight. As he peeled away the layers of her lingerie, she snuggled against the hard muscles of his chest, certain his pleasure was as great as her own. His deeply tanned skin was flushed with the heat of desire, and when she slipped his shirt from his shoulders, he shook it off quickly without even lifting his mouth from hers. She reached for his belt buckle next, intent upon helping him cast off his clothing, but he shoved her hands aside as he gripped her waist, setting her on her feet momentarily while he stripped away the last of her lace-trimmed apparel.

"I think we'll find my bunk more comfortable now," he whispered hoarsely as he pulled back the covers so she could climb in. Sitting down on the edge, he quickly flung his boots aside, then rose briefly to remove his breeches before joining her in the narrow bed. He drew her into his arms, trailing light kisses along her throat until he felt her shiver with anticipation at the delights to come. He lowered his mouth to the tip of her breast then, his tongue tracing hot circles upon her cool white skin. She provided endless pleasure to his senses, for her graceful body was scented with a delicate fragrance he found every bit as enchanting as the taste of her creamy smooth flesh. He'd never grow bored with a young woman so delectable as she, and he chuckled to himself as he recalled Will's question. No. Bianca Antonelli was going to be his woman forever.

The flushed skin of her breasts tingling with excitement from her husband's sensuous touch, Bianca slid her hands over his broad shoulders to press him close, but he was like the warmth of the wind, impossible to hold. Tremors of pleasure then filled her loins with a luscious warmth as his fingertips began to explore her body with a tantalizing caress. "I love you, Evan, I love you so," she whispered softly, and his lips returned to hers for kisses so ardent she was breathless when he again tore his mouth away to taste the fullness of her breasts and then caress the softness of her stomach before straying up the insides of her thighs with light teasing nibbles. As the tip of his tongue invaded the last recess of her being, she closed her eyes, intent only upon savoring the rapture of his exotic loving. His slow, sweet kiss flooded her senses with an ecstasy so complete it grew to a shattering peak, filling her slender body with a searing heat which gradually diffused to a blissful warmth. He moved over her then, lacing his fingers in her tangled curls and covering her flushed cheeks with kisses as he began to seek his own pleasure, tempering the power of his thrusts with a graceful rhythm until they were truly one. This was all he'd longed to have, her total surrender, and the rapture which swept through him crested within her, leaving them as close as any husband and wife can ever hope to be. A long while passed before he broke the silence which enhanced the warm bond he'd created between them.

"I know you were reluctant to accept my apology before, but are you still?" he whispered softly.

Bianca found Evan's shoulder a comfortable pillow, but she raised up on her elbow to study what she could see of his expression in the dim light. "No. But when we can find such happiness together, you must be able to understand why it hurt me so deeply when you preferred getting drunk with Captain Summer to being with me."

That he'd made her jealous had not even occurred to Evan, and he was quite puzzled as how best to respond.

"He and I are friends, Bianca, and enjoy being together, but I'll know better than to neglect you so shamefully ever again." With that promise, he pulled her back into his arms, smothering with kisses any other complaint she might care to make until he was certain she'd forgotten them all.

When it was time for Bianca to tutor Timothy the next morning, Evan sat down on his bunk with a book. He stretched out and crossed his legs to get comfortable. He'd planned to read for an hour, but he soon found his wife's instruction so interesting he covered no more than one paragraph. Having noted the errors the boy had made when first they'd asked him to read, she was patiently helping him learn the rules of phonics which he'd missed. They spent the rest of the time on improving his knowledge of addition and subtraction, dealing with the essential facts as though they were playing a memory game. Bianca had so engaging a manner that the hour sped by quickly, and when Timothy left, it was plain he'd thought his lessons were fun rather than trying.

Impressed by her skill, Evan paid his bride a sincere compliment. "You are a born teacher, my pet. I can see our children are going to be very bright indeed."

Bianca looked away, too embarrassed to respond for a moment. "I hope so too," she finally replied.

Evan chuckled to himself as he slid off his bunk. He found her shyness appealing, but he did not tease her about it. "Do you mind if I stay to observe your lesson again tomorrow?" he asked instead.

"No, not at all, but if you have other things to do please don't think you must." Bianca knew he'd wanted to reassure her with his presence, but she didn't want him to think she wouldn't trust him out of her sight. "There are other times we can be together."

Evan bent down to nuzzle her throat playfully as he helped her to don her cloak. "Then I will come and go as I please, but I'll take care not to disturb either you or your pupil. Now let's go up on deck and see what sort of a day we have."

Pleased that his mood was again so charming, Bianca nearly danced along beside him as they strolled around the deck. She'd grown accustomed to the stares of the deck hands, and they had gradually become more friendly in their manner. "Do you own other ships, Evan? I've never thought to ask."

"Yes. I have others, but they are merchant vessels and not nearly so fine as this. I prefer to build ships for other men to sail. That is my main interest now. You've not married a man devoted to the sea who'll be gone for months at a time. I'll not leave you on your own, Bianca. Was that your real concern?" he asked with a rakish grin.

"No. I have no worries at all. I was merely curious," she replied with a saucy toss of her lovely blonde curls. Then she took his arm, happiness again complete.

Inspired by his bride's ebullient mood, Evan searched his mind for ways to insure that her happiness was not fleeting. Finally deciding that he'd not provided her with a wide enough variety of activities, he challenged her to a game of cards that very afternoon. To his delight he found the lively young woman to be an excellent player, no matter what game he chose to teach her. They soon learned each others' strategies, but that made the games no less fun. Bianca had such enthusiasm she was difficult to beat despite his skill; yet she refused to play for money or for any other reward except affection, and so no matter who won the game, they both enjoyed the payoff too greatly to feel one of them had lost. As an added diversion, Evan then suggested they read to each other before bedtime, for he had books of poems and plays which were amusing to share. In such ways, he made certain Bianca's days were full despite the close confines of the *Phoenix*, and he'd thought she was happy until one day she became unnaturally quiet and, asking to be excused, returned to their cabin in the afternoon, leaving him to stroll the deck alone. It was so unlike her to seek her own company he was greatly perplexed, but respecting her wishes he left her alone until it was nearly time for supper. When he then found her weeping as though she'd suffered the greatest of tragedies, he was both shocked and alarmed.

Sitting down upon the side of the bunk, he pulled her into his arms, smoothing her tawny curls with tender pats as he tried to ascertain what could have upset her so. "Beloved, whatever can be the matter? I told you that should you ever lack for anything I would willingly provide it. Now please tell me what is wrong. Is it merely homesickness? I can't bear to see you so unhappy."

Bianca choked on her tears, too embarrassed to reveal the real cause of her sorrow, but Evan continued to make sympathetic comments, persisting in his attempts to gain her confidence until finally she grew calm enough to explain. Summoning all her courage, she hoped he'd not think her impossibly silly, but she feared he'd be as disappointed as she when she told him what was wrong. "You have mentioned your desire for children so often that I was hoping, well I truly wanted . . ."

As she again dissolved in a torrent of tears, Evan quickly counted the days since their wedding and made what he was certain was an accurate guess as to the cause of her despair. Lifting her chin he kissed her tear-soaked lashes sweetly before he explained, "Not every couple has a child nine months after they are wed, Bianca. If we do not have one for several years I will not be troubled, now cease to worry. I understand how women are made and when it is inconvenient for you to make love all you need do is tell me. Now please do not do this to yourself ever again. I don't want you crying over something which can't be helped. If you are unhappy, no matter what the cause, I insist that you tell me or I will think you're unhappy with me."

Bianca wiped away her tears with her fingertips, afraid to believe what he said was true. "But I don't understand why it did not happen, Evan, when we have been together so often." Her expression was still downcast, for because she had not yet become pregnant, she feared she never would and she couldn't bear to think she might be unable to give Evan the sons she was certain he wanted.

"My pet, sixteen is very young to become a mother. It is undoubtedly to our advantage that you have not conceived so soon. What more can I say to lift your spirits to their usual heights? I am used to your being a lively companion, and that's the young woman I want to see. Now, smile for me." Evan hugged her warmly, sorry that she'd given the conception of a child so much thought. "If we do not become parents until next year, or the next, or the year after that, I will never complain, and I do not want you to worry over the matter either."

"Is that really the truth?" Bianca inquired shyly, thinking he might simply be saying what he thought she'd want to hear.

Certain that while he'd no intention of ever revealing his true plans to her, he'd not lied, Evan swallowed hard before he replied. "Of course," he finally said with a disarming chuckle. "Now wash your face so you'll look pretty for supper and we'll forget you ever shed a tear."

But as Bianca slept contentedly in his arms that night, Evan was disgusted with himself for losing all track of the time. He'd been so intent upon keeping his new bride amused he'd not realized how many days they'd been at sea. He'd never failed in anything in his entire life. He'd never found any goal impossible to attain, nor had he once doubted his ability to avenge his brother's murder. That he'd not succeeded in his aim was simply due to lack of opportunity, not cowardice, but his frustration was just as great. Bianca would find Barcelona entertaining, he'd no doubt of that, but he'd make damned certain when they replenished their stores that they had gunpowder in abundance. Perhaps the murderer was more clever than he'd thought. Perhaps he'd set a course which would intersect theirs later, closer to Gibraltar where the sinking of the *Phoenix* could be attributed to pirates. As he lay in the darkness he realized such a plan would be a good one. Perhaps in focusing attention on their wake they'd made a grave error. Maybe the killer's ship lay not behind but ahead.

The next morning while Bianca tutored Timothy, Evan went to Will's cabin, saying only he wanted to study the navigational charts of the Mediterranean. However, once these were spread out, he told his former mate of his latest thought.

"Yes, that would be a clever plan as we've naturally expected to be overtaken by a ship giving pursuit. If instead the villain has plans to meet us head-on, at a location he's chosen, he'll think we can be taken by surprise. Nothing could be further from the truth." Will straightened up then, his usually pleasant expression aglow with a fiery determination. "You're right about our having become complacent. We have grown less vigilant since there's been no sign of pursuit, but I'll see we don't persist in such a mistake again since it could well prove fatal."

Evan knew the man was as good as his word. "We'll take on supplies in Barcelona, but give the men no more than a night's liberty. I'll be busy sightseeing with Bianca so you see to what's needed in the way of provisions."

"Oh, dear God!" Will shouted suddenly. "What if the scoundrel has beaten us to Spain? He may already be waiting in Barcelona. The instant you leave the ship with Bianca he could have you surrounded. You'd be as dead as your brother, and he'd have Bianca to boot."

That prospect was so unsettling Evan needed a moment to fully appreciate it, and then his temper exploded in a colorful string of violent curses. Disgusted by his own lack of foresight, he at last grew calm enough to compliment his friend. "You're right of course. We've been expecting an attack upon the high seas, but it could more easily come in port." He slumped down into the chair at Will's desk and covered his eyes with his hand for a moment. "What would you do if you were he, Will? The bastard's a coward, we already know that, so what will his next move be?"

The fair-haired young man pursed his lips thoughtfully. "He'd not have the experience you possess at sea, Evan. You have every advantage on the water and he must know that. If he sailed straight for Barcelona, thinking we'd surely stop there, then he may tell the authorities some story, perhaps that Bianca was kidnapped, and we'll be welcomed with a barrage of bullets if not cannon fire."

Evan swore again. "Damn it all! Who knows what that butcher might do, but I'll not walk into any trap he might have set. We'll not go near Barcelona. We'll put in down the coast at Valencia instead. It is a sizable city and should be able to supply all our needs."

Will still wasn't satisfied. "That will outfox him for sure, but bring him no closer to his reward."

"He must have calculated our speed down to the last second, else he'd not have a moment to spare. When we don't arrive in Barcelona within the week, he'll have no other choice but to come after us. On the other hand, if he is waiting near Gibraltar, the extra day or two we make him wait will work to our advantage."

Will rolled up the charts they had been using and put them away. He knew his navigational skills were second rate compared to Evan's, but after Bianca's arrival the charts had all been moved to his quarters so he could compute their course himself. He still took the precaution of having Evan check his calculations, however. "The gun drills have kept the men sharp in their skills. Don't worry. We'll be able to sink whatever hostile vessel we encounter. I'm sure of it."

"So am I." Evan rose to his feet, his expression deadly serious. "I've not mentioned any port to Bianca, so the choice of Valencia shouldn't arouse her curiosity."

Will had seen how happy Evan's vivacious blonde bride had seemed in recent days, but he was still concerned about her. "I've not ever heard her voice a single complaint, have you?"

"No, but in so many ways she is still a child, Will. She has a woman's beauty, remarkable intelligence, and endless charm, but there are times she is truly more child than adult." That she'd had her heart set upon giving him an heir so swiftly was not a confidence he'd share, however. He laughed as he feigned a blow to his friend's shoulder. "I mean to keep her in my cabin rather than yours though!"

Will was not nearly so amused as Evan, but he merely shrugged. "My offer still stands."

"As it should, but truly it is not needed." Evan left Summer then to fetch Bianca, his zest for her company not in the least bit dulled by talk of battle. He scanned the horizon that morning with fresh enthusiasm, as eager for revenge as ever, and the fact that his young wife would be by his side made the prospect of victory all the more sweet.

Bianca found the city of Valencia very charming. In the crowded and noisy port Evan rented a carriage to take her into town, where he delighted her by buying everything which caught her eye. When the shops began to close for siesta and the breeze was scented with the sweet fragrance of orange blossoms, she was more than ready to return to the *Phoenix*. Their carriage was overloaded with parcels containing new silk lingerie, several bolts of fine fabrics, ten yards of delicate lace, a half-dozen exquisite fans, and a dozen bars of perfumed soap for her bath. Evan had wanted no more for himself than several place settings of heavy Spanish silver which he insisted would be practical for use on the *Phoenix*, but when he'd seen swords and knives of the finest Toledo steel, he had been unable to resist them. It took several trips to unload the carriage, but when everything had been carried to his cabin, he looked around in dismay.

"I fear some of these things will have to be stored in the hold, my pet, for we can scarcely walk from my bunk to the table now."

"We could simply remain in your bunk then," Bianca suggested with a teasing purr but, she ducked out of his reach when he made a grab for her, her laughter as bright as his.

"At least you could thank me properly for all these presents," Evan teased, moving to block the doorway so she could not flee.

Bianca giggled as she shook her head. "You'll have to catch me!" She was quick, but loved him too dearly to avoid his clutches for more than a moment. As they collapsed across the bunk she whispered a seductive invitation. "What do you suppose the Spanish do each afternoon when they are supposed to be sleeping?"

"Probably this," Evan replied, a devilish gleam turning the warm brown of his eyes to burnished gold. Without bothering to remove more than his belt he pushed her skirts aside, tore away her undergarments and dropping down between her legs he began with a powerful staccato rhythm to satisfy both her curiosity and her passion.

Her initial surprise at her husband's unrestrained approach to making love was swiftly dispelled, and Bianca clung to him, her fingers digging into his broad shoulders, her lips trembling beneath his as the magnificent pleasure they shared soared to a rapturous peak. Floating upon clouds of ecstasy she had no thought save that of pleasing him. Her graceful motions kept perfect time with his until, fully satisfied, he found blissful relaxation in her arms. When at last she opened her eyes she was also in a state of perfect peace until she saw the clear blue sky through the skylight above and recalled they were in port. Men were roaming the decks as they stowed away the provisions and at any second one might chance to glance down at them. "Evan!" she cried hoarsely, her voice frantice in his ear. "Someone might see us!"

His lips nestled tenderly against the smoothness of her throat, Evan deemed that a slight problem as he murmured, "There is not a man aboard who would be shocked to learn I make love to you often, Bianca. Now hush."

"I'll not hush!" Bianca responded, and gave him an emphatic shove. "Get off me!" He was far too heavy for her efforts to be effective, however.

Evan shook his head sadly as he leaned back. "Will you make up your mind, woman! You're the one who started this, not I."

His accusation was so ridiculous Bianca's anger lasted only an instant before she was convulsed with laughter. She reached up to pull him back into her arms. "It is not our fault if we are so passionate a pair, is it, Evan?"

"I've not complained," he reminded her, his mouth stilling any further protest before she could speak it.

He found her charms irresistible and continued to do his best to make the afternoon in Valencia one she'd not soon forget, but when they left port on the morning tide, his passion was once again focused solely upon defeating an enemy who was maddeningly elusive.

Bianca noted the difference in her husband's mood, for it was sharp rather than subtle. He conferred often with William Summer, and the entire crew gave off an almost tangible tension, their voices strident as they called to one another from their perches in the rigging. If they were to be attacked by pirates it would be now as they neared the narrow Strait of Gibraltar, and Bianca was grateful that her warning had been taken seriously. The *Phoenix* was well armed and skillfully manned, but she doubted they could escape unscathed from an attack by pirates.

The sun was already high overhead on the morning three Tripolitan ketches appeared on the southern horizon. Their single triangular sails lateen rigged, they kept their distance for more than an hour, then gradually began to close in, stalking the *Phoenix* with deadly precision. Bianca remained at her husband's side, certain he could win any fight against rabble such as these cowardly pirates who attacked in packs, but he had no intention of allowing her to witness a battle of any sort.

Evan took his bride's arm and directed her toward the companionway. "I want you to remain in our cabin. The deck will be far too dangerous for you."

Bianca walked down the ladder ahead of her husband, but she argued at every step. "I could load pistols or care for the wounded, but I can't do anything down here!"

"Is my peace of mind worth nothing to you?" Evan opened the door to his cabin and ushered her inside. "Now just stay put until I come for you." Not giving her any more time to object to his order he closed the door and locked it, pocketing the key before he returned to the deck.

That he'd dared to lock her in infuriated Bianca and she kicked the door soundly, but that only hurt her toes, and made her feel no less abused. Crossing to the table she climbed onto a chair, but discovered she still couldn't see the deck through the skylight. Then, remembering the time she'd been locked in her room at home, she pulled a hairpin from her golden curls and, jumping down off the table, went over to the door. She'd seen Evan unlock her bedroom door in a matter of seconds, but she had to struggle with the highly polished brass lock for more than half an hour before she had the same success. Knowing her husband would be furious with her, she remained at the bottom of the ladder, hoping to hear enough of the action taking place above to have a clear idea of what was happening.

The *Phoenix* remained on course, sailing smoothly through the blue-green of the Mediterranean as though her captain had taken no note of the three ships giving pursuit. The gun crews were standing by, however, cannons loaded and ready to fire the instant the word was given. Evan and Will stood side by side, waiting only for the Tripolitan Ketches to come within firing range. "Let them come a little closer, Will," Evan whispered softly. "I want to be certain we've only pirates here rather than someone else."

"Since it will make no difference who the hell it is, I think they are close enough!" Will had always admired Evan's courage, but he doubted he'd ever understand how the man managed to turn from good-natured friend to cold-blooded killer at the blink of an eye. His fists were clenched at his sides, sweat pouring down his back as he waited, not daring to draw a deep breath as the ketches, separated now, each boat setting its own course, moved to surround the *Phoenix*. "Blast 'em now, or they'll be too far apart!"

Evan held the spyglass, searching the bearded faces of the crews of the approaching boats for someone he would recognize. Finding no such person aboard the ketches, he waited no more than a split second before announcing with icy calm, "Give the order to fire."

Bianca heard him speak clearly, instantly recognizing her husband's voice before Will relayed the order and the port cannons erupted with a shattering burst of flame. The roar was deafening, and smoke filled the air, burning her eyes. She choked on the acrid fumes, but since she could ascertain nothing from where she stood she threw caution aside and raced up the ladder. She paused only a moment, then dashed to the rail from which she could see two of the pirate vessels engulfed in flames, gaping holes in their hulls at the water line. The third had veered out of the path of the cannons' fire. She watched in horror then, as fire began to belch from the undamaged boat's cannon, its target the rigging directly above her head. She realized that the pirates would want only to disable the *Phoenix* so they could board her, but she knew Evan would never allow that. As the second volley was fired she heard one of the *Phoenix*'s men scream as he lost his hold upon the rigging. That piercing shriek was followed by a sickening thud. The sailor's body had landed not a yard from where she stood, splattering her skirts with blood. It lay in a twisted heap. Obviously the man was dead, but Bianca could do no more than stare at the grisly mound which had once been a vital young man. She was thrown off balance then, as the *Phoenix* came about, and was badly shaken but not knocked off her feet. The starboard cannon were as accurate as those on the port side, their fire now ripping through the hull of the lone attacker. The *Phoenix*'s crew was well practiced in the deadly art of gunnery. Bianca had to cling to the rail for support, but she was fascinated by the sight of the burning ships. The pirates were leaping into the sea, their clothes aflame, still she could not turn away. The blazing skeletons of their vessels were rocking precariously, offering no salvation, and Bianca was horrified when the pistol fire began. Stunned that the crew of the *Phoenix* would be so bloodthirsty as to shoot at men in such dire circumstances, she dashed along the rail until she came to her husband's side.

"Stop them!" she screamed. "They're firing on men who are as good as dead!"

Evan's expression was a taunting leer as he looked down at his disheveled bride. He did not seem particularly surprised to see her, but he was, nevertheless, displeased that she'd disregarded his wishes so boldly. "This is no time for compassion, Bianca. An enemy spared today could return tomorrow to kill us all, and I'll not be so careless with our lives. Now, go below before you see anything else that's not meant for your eyes."

Thoroughly sickened to find her husband a far more brutal man than she'd ever suspected, Bianca turned away, the solace his cabin offered now most welcome, but when she saw Timothy sobbing dejectedly by the dead man's side she went to offer what comfort she could. She knelt down by the boy, placed her arms around his shoulders and said the only thing which seemed appropriate. "He died very quickly. I'm certain he did not suffer."

Timothy, however, cared little that his friend's death had been mercifully sudden; he knew only that someone he'd liked was gone. He took great care to straighten out the man's grotesquely broken legs and crossed his arms over his chest before he looked up at Bianca. "Stay with him, will you, while I get some canvas to wrap his body?"

Although the sight of the dead man made her sick, Bianca nodded. She looked away, glad that if one of their number had to die it hadn't been little Timothy, or Evan, or Will. By coming up on deck she had placed herself in as grave danger as the men, but that didn't occur to her.

When Timothy returned she helped him lay his friend's body on the canvas. The lad then carefully folded the heavy fabric over the dead crewman before he went for a needle and thread to make the shroud secure. When Bianca stood up, sorry the boy had such a grim task but offering no objection for he'd taken it upon himself, she noticed the others gathered about her, admiration lighting their eyes. Knowing she'd done nothing of which to be proud, she lifted her blood-stained skirts and went below to her husband's cabin, where in privacy she gave in to the nausea which overwhelmed her at the thought of such a hideous death.

Chapter IX

More than an hour had passed before Bianca heard a light tapping upon the door. There had been no sound of gunfire for a long while, and thinking it must be Timothy with warm water for a bath, she remained seated upon the bunk as she called out, "Yes, come in."

William Summer opened the door only slightly, and seeing Bianca looking every bit as distracted as when she'd left the deck, he hesitated a moment before extending his invitation. Her pose was a casual one. She was hugging her knees, resting one cheek on her forearms. Her long golden curls fell about her shoulders in wild disarray, but despite the sorry state of her dress she was so beautiful it took his breath away. "I am going to read the burial service for Nathan, I thought you might wish to join us."

Since the unfortunate man's blood still stained her clothes, Bianca shook her head emphatically. "I'd rather stay here if you don't mind. I'm not properly dressed for a funeral."

"The service will be brief. Your attire won't matter to the men."

Bianca closed her eyes slowly as though she were

overcome with fatigue, her long thick lashes making violet shadows upon her pale cheeks before she looked up again. "Did my husband send you to fetch me?"

"No. This was my idea entirely," Will admitted readily.

Bianca didn't know what would be best, or what Evan would wish. She'd seen more than she'd wanted to, far more. He'd been right about that, but did she want to add to that misfortune by participating in a burial at sea?

Will leaned back against the doorjamb, longing to go to the pretty young woman and take her into his arms, to make her forget the horrors she'd seen. Instead, he could do no more than speak to her in a soothing tone. "Evan tried to keep you here, away from the danger. Why didn't you stay where you'd be safe instead of joining us?"

Bianca lifted her chin proudly as she replied, "I wanted to know what was happening, that's all. There was no reason to shut me in here like a naughty child."

Since Will considered that a matter she should take up with her husband, he wisely returned to his original question. "Everyone is ready. Since you were so curious before, don't you want to see this too? Unfortunately it is the end of far too many battles."

Bianca swung her legs over the side of the bunk and slipped on her soft kid shoes. "Does my husband ever take prisoners, Will, ever?"

"No one makes prisoners of pirates, Bianca. They know it as well as we," the young man replied with an unfamiliar note of impatience in his voice. She was backing him into a corner. He could see what was coming, and he didn't like defending Evan one bit.

"And during the war? Did he make prisoners of the British?" She came toward the young man, her walk a slow seductive sway, yet she was totally unaware of the wildly erotic effect she had upon him.

"No, he did not," Will replied hoarsely. He tried to

look only at the pretty young woman's face, but it was impossible to ignore the loveliness of her figure. He kept telling himself she was his best friend's wife, but that proved to be totally ineffective in cooling the desire her closeness created.

Bianca studied Will's pained expression for a moment, not understanding why he seemed so ill at ease but certain he'd always tell her the truth. "I see. Would that be your policy too?" she inquired politely.

"In a war, yes," Will responded confidently. "It is difficult enough to wage a battle without stepping over men in chains."

"So you simply sunk the British warships, then shot their crews before they could drown. Is that what you did?"

"It is not an uncommon practice, Mrs. Sinclair, and truly far more humane than the British policy of putting a man aboard a filthy prison ship and providing him with such meager rations he starves to death. Now I must insist you hurry if you wish to come with me."

Startled by the hostility of his tone, Bianca simply stared at him a long while before asking, "Why are you calling me Mrs. Sinclair again when just moments ago you called me by my first name?" To her amazement, Will began to blush as though she'd caught him doing something truly wicked. This was such an unexpected reaction to her question she could not help but laugh. "Call me whatever pleases you, Captain Summer; I'll not cause you any further embarrassment." She walked out the door ahead of him then, not bothering to don her cloak.

Evan had not realized Will had gone to fetch his wife, but he was greatly annoyed that the man hadn't first asked his permission. Obviously what she'd witnessed had upset her badly, and he didn't want to add to her grief. He moved to her side, taking her hand in his as he listened to Will read the words they all knew by heart. To have suffered even one casualty pained him greatly, but rather than question God's will, he simply resigned himself to the loss. When the poignant service ended and the canvas-wrapped body was consigned to the sea, he paused only long enough to send Timothy to fetch warm water so Bianca could bathe. Then he led her away. When they reached their cabin, he handed her the key to the door.

"Since I myself taught you how to open the door without this, I'll give it back to you to save you the trouble of picking the lock again. Perhaps the next time I ask you to stay below you'll give my wishes more thoughtful consideration."

Bianca turned away, sorry he'd chosen to take such a belligerent tone. "I was worried about you, about all of you. How could you have expected me to stay down here and listen to the gunfire, not knowing whose it was or what was to become of us?"

"The danger to us was slight, Bianca." Evan had assumed his usual sarcastic tone.

"Somehow I doubt Nathan would agree with that!" the feisty young woman responded sharply.

Since he was certain that remark didn't merit a reply, Evan turned and walked out of the cabin, thoroughly disgusted with his beautiful bride. Women were a damned bother aboard ship, he decided, but there was nothing he could do about the nuisance Bianca presented now.

When Timothy arrived with the tub and warm water, Bianca asked him to wait a moment. "I want to give you these clothes. They're ruined and might as well be tossed over the side. Will you do that for me?"

"Yes, ma'am." Timothy shuffled his feet nervously, ashamed she'd seen him crying like some baby. "I'm sorry about before," he mumbled, so softly she barely heard his apology.

"Sorry about what, Timothy?" Bianca was mystified. "I don't know what you mean." She removed her skirt quickly and handed it to him before peeling off her bodice. Both garments were splattered with Nathan's blood, but she was relieved to see that none of the gory red stains marred the snowy whiteness of her lingerie.

Timothy didn't look up. "About . . . about crying," he stammered.

"But you said Nathan was your friend. Surely you weren't the only one who cried for him."

"No, but I was the only one who let it show."

"Oh, I see. Well I think you were very brave, Timothy. When Nathan fell you didn't think of yourself, only of him. You could have been hit by the pirates' fire too."

"You think I'm brave?" Timothy's face lit up with a bright glow of pleasure at her compliment. "Really?"

Bianca put her hand around the boy's shoulders to lead him toward the door. "I most certainly do. Now take care of those things for me, please."

"Yes, ma'am. Then I'll see to your supper." Timothy was still beaming from ear to ear as she closed the door behind him. Thrilled by her praise, he walked away, his chest puffed out with pride.

After her bath, Bianca chose to don her nightgown rather than dress again. Her cloak would provide sufficient cover if Evan wished to go up on deck, but somehow she doubted either of them would be in the mood for a moonlit stroll that night. She'd already washed her hair and brushed out the damp curls so she sat down at the table and began to thumb through the book of poetry they'd been reading. Although beautifully written, none of the poems seemed to fit her mood, however, and she soon tired of them. By the time Evan appeared, followed by Timothy bearing their supper tray, she was too happy to have his company to want to continue their argument. Nonetheless, she had no intention of apologizing, and she could tell by the firm set of his jaw that he'd not beg for her forgiveness either. Once they'd taken their places at the table, she waited until Timothy had served them and left before she spoke. "I hope we see no more of those hateful bandits from the Barbary Coast."

Surprised that she'd dared to mention them, Evan nonetheless agreed. "So do I. We were fortunate to meet only three ships, but I doubt we'll see more now. We're too near to Gibraltar for them to have the courage to chase us."

Bianca was grateful he'd followed her example and been civil. She continued in a casual tone. "Does it not strike you as strange that Gibraltar is a British fortress rather than a Spanish one?" she asked absently.

"Not at all, since the British have an insatiable appetite for territory. The Spanish fought for possession of it from 1779 to 1783, losing two thousand men in their final attempt to regain what is really no more than a fortified hunk of gray marble." Evan looked up then, startled to realize he and Bianca frequently discussed subjects it had never occurred to him women would enjoy. "Perhaps you heard about it."

"Of course," Bianca readily admitted. "The Spanish had hoped the British would be too preoccupied with their efforts to suppress rebellion in the American Colonies to be able to defend the fortress. Unfortunately for them, they were wrong."

"Bianca, who taught you about such things? That conflict was over two years ago when you would have been no more than fourteen. Why would a war waged between Spain and Britain over a rocky fortress have interested you?"

Bianca laid her knife and fork across her plate before she replied, for she was greatly annoyed that he'd ask such an insulting question. "Need I remind you of my mother's heritage? Besides, the siege of Gibraltar affected shipping in the Mediterranean, and you know how greatly Venice relies upon the sea for trade. Why wouldn't I have known what was happening? Do the young women in Virginia know nothing of events taking place in the world?"

"Damn little I'm afraid," Evan answered with a rueful grin. "But I'll see you don't fall behind in your knowledge of world affairs since you are so well versed in them now."

Bianca straightened her shoulders proudly. "Are you making fun of me again?" she asked pointedly.

"No! Of course not!" Evan assured her almost too promptly. "It simply had not occurred to me how different you are from the women I've known, that's all."

Bianca found that statement worthy of pursuit. Lifting one well-shaped brow quizzically, she said in an encouraging tone, "In what way?"

"Well, I suppose we expect women to be attractive and charming, to be faithful wives and devoted mothers, but not to be interested in events such as foreign wars, which men find so intriguing."

"I'll not pretend I'm stupid, Evan." She shook her lovely blonde head in wonder. "How do the women in Virginia stand it?"

Evan sat back and began to laugh, his amusement quite genuine. "I don't believe they feel in the least bit slighted, Bianca, but they have no European background, nor have they led a life as exciting as yours."

"The War for Independence did not affect them?" she asked quickly.

"Of course. It affected everyone. Many people thought we were wrong to want our freedom from the Crown, so we not only battled with the British but with our own citizens as well. Friendships of long standing came to an abrupt end. Families sometimes found their loyalties divided. Some people simply left, fled to the Caribbean or returned to England. But the matter is settled. We are at peace, and prospects for it to continue are excellent. We've all picked up the lives we set aside to fight the war. You'll find Virginia a delightful place to live in all respects." He finished the last bites of his supper, trying to think how best to approach a most delicate matter. Stalling as long as he could, he waited until Timothy had returned to clear the table. Then he poured Bianca only a few drops of brandy since he doubted she'd drink more, but he was far more generous with himself. Evan sipped his brandy slowly, aware the silence between them was becoming awkward.

"Bianca, you are very bright as well as incredibly beautiful," he began.

"Well, thank you," she replied with an innocent smile. She was surprised that he'd wish to pay her such a lavish compliment.

Evan nodded, sorry she'd interrupted his train of thought. "You're welcome. What I'm trying to say is that I want you to be happy with me, to enjoy my home and friends as greatly as I do. I would like us to live in harmony, but I wish you would consider the fact that I possess considerable intelligence as well as you. Therefore when I ask you to do something, I'm not at all pleased if you disobey me."

While Bianca knew exactly what her husband was talking about, she was nevertheless deeply offended. "I am your wife, and I'll not allow you to order me about like one of the crew!"

"Have I ever treated you in so insulting a fashion?" Evan asked skeptically. "Have I not tried to make your life with me a most pleasant one?"

Bianca squirmed nervously in her chair. Evan looked so calm, so in control of himself, while she felt trapped.

Hating such a helpless feeling, she rose and paced the cabin with a short, hurried step. "You are the best of husbands, Evan. I've told you so many times. I know you are disappointed in me for being so willful, but truly I can not behave differently."

Evan frowned in frustration, uncertain how to respond to such a candid admission. He needed her complete trust, and while he felt he was close to winning that, he needed her obedience as well. "That you were not severely injured today when Nathan was killed is nothing less than a miracle, Bianca. I'll not allow you to risk your life so thoughtlessly ever again. We still have a long way to go before we reach my home. Should we encounter any other unexpected peril, foul weather or more pirates,"—or the murderer who wouldn't rest until he'd taken her from him—"if I tell you to go below, I want you to remain here where you'll be safe. If I give you any directions at all, I want them followed because you are precious to me and I've no wish to lose you."

While it would have been a simple matter to agree and then disobey him later, Bianca could not bring herself to lie. She bit her lower lip nervously as she continued to pace, her lack of resolve very clear. "I understand what you want me to promise, Evan, but how can I agree when I don't know how I'll feel later? Perhaps what you ask seems only proper to you. Nonetheless, it might be impossible for me, and if I've promised to obey you and then do not, you'll be twice as angry with me."

As she moved the decorative folds of her soft linen gown accented the superb contours of her lush figure while her bright golden curls framed her face with an enchanting glow. She was so distracting a sight that Evan sighed wearily, his hunger for her love too strong to permit him to continue such an argument, especially when he feared she was telling him the truth and any promise she might give him now she'd not keep. He reached out, grabbed her hand, and pulled her down upon his knee. "When it upset you so greatly to disobey your parents, why do you give my wishes so little thought? I have only your best interests at heart, nothing more, my dearest."

Bianca put her arms around his neck and laid her cheek against his as she hugged him tightly. "I love you, Evan, but—"

"You love your freedom more?" Evan asked solemnly. "I'll keep you in chains if I must, but I'll not allow you on deck ever again if I know you'll be in the slightest bit of danger."

Horrified by that threat, Bianca leaned back slightly so she could meet his gaze. Finding his dark eyes smoldering with a fierce light rather than a warm glow of love, she was truly frightened. "You wouldn't put me in chains, you wouldn't!"

"Oh, yes I would," Evan assured her, but he found the softness of her supple form so incredibly alluring he laced his fingers in her curls and used a searing kiss rather than logic to silence her protests. Lifting the hem of her nightgown, he ran his hand slowly up and over her thigh, caressing the smooth pale flesh lightly before his fingertips reached their true goal and he felt all resistance to his forceful affections fade as she relaxed in his arms. That he found her defiance as heady an aphrodisiac as her charm was a weakness on his part, but he had no desire to fight such a failing. She had as little will power as he, and when they were together, nothing mattered but the joy they found in each other. His breathing already ragged, Evan found the sweet warmth he'd created within her far too enticing to delay taking his passion for her to the limit. After a quick tug to release his belt buckle and free himself from the constraints of his breeches, he spread Bianca's slender thighs and pulled her across his lap. Holding her tiny waist tightly he eased her slowly down upon himself until their bodies came together with an eagerness which shocked and yet pleased them both. As always his strength was the perfect complement to her grace. Their arms entwined, they clung to each other, their kisses wild, both driven by an insatiable hunger as the blazing rapture of their love consumed their bodies in a fierce, throbbing heat. A delicious spiral of sensation sent their spirits soaring to the heights of pleasure and then let them drift gently back down into a peaceful state which lingered long after the fires of their passion had been quenched. Their kisses sweet, they continued to languidly enjoy each other, their bodies still joined, for neither could bear to pull away and render them into two separate souls again.

When Evan awoke the next morning, he found Bianca comfortably supported by her pillow as she lay quietly observing him. A faintly amused smile graced her delicate features, and it stirred a strange feeling of unease within him. Sitting up to face her, he was quick to ask, "What do you find so funny at this early hour?"

She shrugged nonchalantly. "Only you. Do you realize all I need do is raise my voice to you and you'll make love to me? Do you think I'm so easily distracted as that, Mr. Sinclair? Or since you are so insistent I follow your orders, would you prefer to be called Captain?"

"Evan will do." The handsome young man combed his hair back from his eyes with his fingers as he tried to think how best to counter such an accusation, since it was true. "Is it my fault I find you as exciting when you are mad as I do when you are deliberately trying to charm me?"

"When did I ever have to try to charm you?" Bianca saucily flipped her golden curls. "Never that I recall."

With a throaty chuckle Evan dived for her, catching her in an eager embrace. "You're doing it now! Admit it!"

Bianca batted her long eyelashes coyly as she

responded teasingly, "It is your vanity which makes it appear so, sir. Nothing more."

Evan pushed her down into the pillows, the stubble of his beard tickling her throat and making her laugh. "You are a flirt, Bianca, but as long as you flirt only with me I'll not complain."

At that comment, the fair beauty's laughter ceased, and growing serious, she lifted her hand to his temple to sift his shiny dark hair through her fingertips. Indoors, its deep auburn shade seemed merely dark brown, but she knew when he stepped out into the sunlight its reddish cast would come alive with a vibrant sheen. "The problem is, we finish every argument in bed, my love, and I do not think that is a wise habit."

That she saw through his efforts to dominate her so easily infuriated Evan, but he dared not let his anger show for that would be admitting she was right. He flashed his most disarming grin and teased her instead. "Shall I make an appointment with you to argue each day after you've tutored Timothy? Would you like that better?"

"No, of course not. I don't want to argue with you at all."

"Then all you need do is devote your energy to pleasing me as greatly out of this bed as you do in it!" With a playful swat to her hip, Evan left the bed before she could take the subject of their recent argument any further. He'd continued to dress in Will's cabin to give her the privacy she needed to prepare for the new day, and he was glad doing so provided an excuse for escaping her presence swiftly that morning.

Needing still more time alone after he'd dressed, he went up on deck. There he could let his bitterness show. He gripped the rail as he scanned the horizon for approaching sails, devastated by his failure to give Charles's murderer what he deserved. He dared not make

Bianca more suspicious, and he knew she was far too perceptive a young woman to continue to be fooled. When William Summer came up beside him, Evan's expression was filled with rage. "What in God's name am I to tell my stepfather, Will? He was depending upon me to set things right."

"You've done your best. We'll all tell him that."

"It is not character references I need, but results, damn it!" Evan struck the rail so hard he bruised the heel of his hand, but he didn't even flinch. "Every time I look at Bianca I'm reminded of Charles and of how I've let him down. It's as if I see his smile in hers. He was so very much like her. He had the same lively wit, the zest. Why I didn't realize that before today I don't know. It's no wonder he loved her so."

"And what about you?" Will asked in a voice so low it was lost on the morning breeze.

Evan shot his old friend a glance so darkly threatening it sent a chill clear through Will. "I've made her my wife and that is tribute enough to her beauty. I'll not give her my heart to wear on a chain as well."

"How can you not love a creature as endearing as Bianca?" Will forced himself to ask.

Evan turned away, that subject so painful he'd not discuss it. His best had always been good enough before, but it certainly wasn't this time. Bianca's love was both a treasure and a curse, but he had no hope of escaping her exotic spell when to be free was the last thing he'd ever want. By the time he reached home he knew he must find some way to ease his conscience, but without killing Charles's murderer he was damned if he knew how.

As the *Phoenix* entered the Atlantic, Bianca continued to pass the days by tutoring Timothy, strolling the deck, and playing cards with her handsome husband; but Evan was often so lost in his own thoughts that she knew he preferred to be alone though he was too polite to say so.

Yet, while he might often be tense and distant all day, he never failed to be a tender and ardent lover each night. She found herself dismissing his moodiness as the result of boredom, for the voyage was a long one and she enjoyed his affection in the evenings far too greatly to complain because he was not always the best of company during the day. She hoped only that once they'd returned to Newport News and he could again devote himself to building ships, his temperament would become more even. To her great delight he never seemed bored with her, and she hoped he never would. She was both a patient and devoted wife, and she'd not given him the slightest cause for grief since the day they'd met the pirates. Still, she hoped their first child would be conceived during the voyage, and she was deeply disappointed because that had not yet happened.

William Summer had more than enough to do in his new capacity as captain, but whenever he chanced to find Bianca on deck, he made an excuse to speak with her. He'd never known a young woman so spirited or so lovely. He was completely captivated by her, but he hoped she'd think his interest only that of a polite friend.

Although Bianca had attempted to tame the wisp of hair which blew across her eyes, it had escaped her hairdo so frequently, she had finally given up the effort. The wind was brisk and she was glad for Will's attentive company since Evan had been silent most of the morning. "How did you and my husband happen to meet, Captain Summer?"

Will looked over at Evan, not certain his friend would want him to relate the tale, but hearing no objection, he cleared his throat and tried to make his account as brief as possible. "I suffered the dire misfortune of being captured by the British and sent to a prison ship along with several others from my crew. The conditions were too abysmal to describe to a lady, but we were all dying, a slow hideous death, when Evan took it upon himself to set us free."

Bianca turned to look at her husband, but his glance was fixed on the horizon and she doubted he'd heard anything Will had said. "Evan rescued you?" she asked with growing excitement.

"Oh, yes. The whole lot of us. It was a very daring thing to do. He and some of his men sneaked aboard after midnight. They overpowered the guards, tossed them over the side, and then sailed that cursed ship down the coast. After setting us all free, they torched the vessel so it could never again be used for such a vile purpose. Most of the prisoners were too weak to join Evan's crew, but those of us who could were eager to do so."

Bianca took her husband's arm, making certain she caught his full attention before she spoke. "Why did you never tell me the story of how you rescued Will, since it is such an exciting one?"

Evan shrugged as if being considered a hero was a slight honor. "That raid naturally impressed Will far more than it did me. I'd almost forgotten it."

Will laughed at that show of modesty. "If you find Evan reluctant to recount his adventures, I'll be happy to tell you about some we shared."

"Oh no," Evan protested quickly. "I have other means to keep Bianca amused and I require no help from you."

Her cheeks turning a deep rose hue at that boast, Bianca gave Evan's arm an impatient squeeze. "Hush! I know how greatly men enjoy exchanging war stories, and I don't mind listening to them either although I'll not get drunk with you two!"

Evan shot Will a warning glance to insure his silence. "Will and I have learned our lesson, Bianca. If you want us to regale you with tales of the war, we'll do so over a pot of tea and nothing stronger."

Thoroughly confused, Will continued to smile. When he and Evan were alone they often discussed the part Bianca played in their plans, never their experiences in the war they'd fought so hard to win. That was where they'd gone wrong, he realized with a sudden flash of insight. Evan had pursued his brother's murderer with the same fierce zeal he'd shown in attacking his wartime enemy. He'd thought he could identify the villain and kill him as easily as he'd once sighted British ships and destroyed them. Men weren't ships, however, and it might take months of clever detective work to ferret out a murderer, hardly the week Evan had allowed. Will was as unhappy as his friend to be returning home without having gained the satisfaction they'd sought. Yet, as he returned Bianca's warm smile, he was not sorry they'd gone on such a quest when it had brought such a woman into their lives.

Chapter X

"The waters of the James River merge with those of the Nansemond and the Elizabeth near the mouth of the Chesapeake Bay forming a superb natural harbor known as Hampton Roads. 'Roads' is the maritime term for a safe anchorage." Evan's attention appeared to be focused upon the chart he'd rolled out upon his table, and neither his warm gaze nor his soft tone revealed the depth of his inner turmoil. In a few hours' time they'd be home and he had no excuse for failing to get the revenge he'd sought in Venice. There would be a handsome profit on the sale of the exquisite crystalware which filled the hold of the *Phoenix*, but that would provide scant consolation to his parents for the loss of their son. To have been so close and to have failed to bring Charles's murderer to justice was not a defeat a man as proud as Evan could accept, let alone gracefully. As he looked up at his bride, he found Bianca's eager enthusiasm to reach his home difficult to share, but he did his best to do so. "Newport News is located on the James River side of the peninsula. It's the perfect location for shipbuilding and dry docks. My family home is farther up the river. We own far more land than anyone had in Venice, of course, but you will again live at the water's edge. I hope that will make

Virginia seem less strange to you."

"It sounds lovely, Evan, truly it does. I can not wait to meet your mother and stepfather," Bianca exclaimed excitedly. "What will they say when you tell them we are married? Will they be thrilled, or shocked," Bianca hesitated for a fraction of a second before speaking her fears aloud, "or perhaps disappointed that you did not marry the daughter of one of their friends."

Evan rolled up the chart as he replied in the best humor he could affect. "As a matter of fact, before I left for Venice my stepfather spoke to me in a rather stern fashion, hoping to inspire me to marry promptly upon my return. He can't complain when I've already followed his suggestion and taken so beautiful a bride." Indeed, he found Bianca's loveliness more appealing with each new day, but his conscience seldom let him forget that her beauty had enticed Charles to his death. As he'd come to know her more fully, his appreciation of this remarkable young woman had deepened, and he could not now imagine himself content in the company of any other. He'd also made the painful decision that her connection with Charles's death would have to be a closely guarded secret or he feared she would never be accepted by his family and friends. He'd been so confident that marrying her would bring him the man he sought he'd never once considered how she'd be regarded by his relatives should he fail. Were they to know she'd been the object of Charles's affection, her presence would be a constant reminder that the young man's killer had escaped punishment and a constant reminder of the part she'd unwittingly played in the young man's death. He had never blamed her for being so bewitching a female, for merely being herself, but he doubted the others who'd loved Charles would be so generous. It was a complex dilemma, one he'd considered often. As a result he had vowed to keep certain information to himself. "As soon as we dock this afternoon I'll send Timothy to my stepfather's office with a message to let him know we've arrived. I'd like to meet with him alone first, to give him the news of our marriage and a brief account of our voyage and cargo. That will save you the bother of sitting through a tiresome meeting."

"But I don't mind listening to you two discuss business, Evan, really I don't. I'll be happy to come with you," Bianca instantly declared.

Drawing her into his arms, Evan kissed his charming bride's forehead. "If you don't mind, I really do want to speak with him alone first. I'll not embarrass you by making you listen to me describe your many virtues to the man."

"Virtues?" Bianca was far too bright to accept that explanation, and taking immediate exception to his term, she said impatiently, "You are afraid he'll object to me, aren't you? Well it is far too late now if he does!"

Evan had to laugh at that show of indignation, for like all of her moods he found this one appealing. "Let me explain something. My father was twenty years older than my mother. When she was widowed she was in her early twenties. Then she married Lewis. He and she were both twenty-six. He is only sixteen years my senior and while he did his best to be a father to me when I was young, once I was grown and chose to take charge of my father's shipbuilding concern rather than to go into partnership with him, he made no further attempt to influence my decisions. He'll not object to you; I would simply like to tell him about our marriage privately. I'm certain Lewis will rush right home to see that a welcoming feast is prepared and that my mother is ready to receive us. Bianca, your welcome to our home will be a gracious one."

Embarrassed that she'd thought otherwise, Bianca drew away with a remorseful frown. "I'm sorry. Of course you would want time to tell your parents about me so they can appear to be happy rather than merely surprised. I do so want them to like me, Evan. I will try my very best to impress them favorably tonight."

"Only tonight?" Evan teased playfully.

"Of course not only tonight!" Bianca knew he wanted to make her smile again, but his explanation of the relationship he had with his stepfather brought another question to her mind. "Was your mother only sixteen when you were born?"

"Yes." Evan readily understood her interest, but he quickly dismissed it. "Bianca, we do not need a babe to distract us from each other. Undoubtedly some of my mother's friends will inquire as to why we have no child on the way, but I hope you'll tell them that is our own business and we choose to live our lives without their interference."

Shocked by that bit of advice, Bianca quickly rejected it. "But, Evan, that would be a terribly rude thing to say!"

"Why? It is the truth. Now let's go up on deck. There's a lot to see as we near the port, and I don't want you to miss any of it. In 1607 the first permanent English colony in the New World was settled on a site thirty miles up the James River, Jamestown it was called, after King James I. The three ships which brought those first settlers were under the command of Captain Christopher Newport. Newport News is named for him."

"Is Jamestown an interesting place to visit?"

"I'm afraid there's little left to see there. The colony was abandoned after the capital was moved to Williamsburg, so I'll take you there instead. We'll pass Hampton as we enter the harbor. It was founded in 1610 by settlers from Jamestown, so it is one of our oldest towns if you are interested in our history, though I'm afraid our past is a very recent one compared to that of Europe. How old is the city of Venice, for example?"

"It was founded in the fifth century by refugees who fled from the mainland to the Venetian lagoon after the city of Aquileia was destroyed by Attila the Hun," Bianca stated, matter-of-factly repeating the story she'd learned as a child. She quickly tied the bow on her cloak and took her husband's hand, still eager to see whatever he wished to show her. "But because your country is such a young one, it is all the more interesting to me, Evan. I want to see everything now that we're finally here. There were days when I thought this voyage would never end, but since it is over I know I will always remember these first months we've spent together very fondly."

Evan swept her through the door, his smile wide for he took her remark as a compliment. "I'll do my best to see that you recall all the time we share fondly." Even as he spoke, however, he hoped a happy future would not be as impossible to arrange as the successful completion of his mission to Venice.

As soon as the *Phoenix* entered its berth at the Sinclair docks in Newport News, Timothy ran all the way to the warehouse which supplied Lewis Grey's shops, only to find the man had not come into the city that day. Uncertain how to reach his house, he dashed back to the *Phoenix* to get the directions.

"It's much too far, son. You needn't bother with it. Just go on home and tell your mother I'll be by to see her later in the week." Evan tipped the boy handsomely for running the errand, then dismissed him.

Timothy nodded, but didn't turn to go. "I want to thank you, Mrs. Sinclair, for teaching me so much. My mom will want to thank you too."

"It was a pleasure, Timothy. Tell your mother I'll look forward to meeting her." Gracefully, Bianca bent down to give the shy boy a kiss upon the cheek and then she waved to him as he ran down the gangplank. "He should be in school, Evan. See that he goes now, won't you?"

"Yes, ma'am," Evan replied with exaggerated politeness. "I'll see to it right away."

"Is this how you intend to behave now that we're home, Evan Sinclair? Do you just plan to tease me constantly?" Not amused, Bianca put her hands on her hips, the green of her eyes glowing brightly with warning fire. At times Evan complimented her upon the intelligence of her remarks, but often his mood was so teasing he seemed not to respect anything she said. That she could still not tell what to expect from him from moment to moment annoyed her terribly.

"No, but I can't resist doing so when you give me orders. However, this time you're right. I'll not be needing Timothy as my cabin boy any longer so he should be enrolled in school. Now is there anything else you're afraid I might neglect to do?" Evan put his hands behind him and rocked back on his heels. His casual pose and slight smile revealing none of the bitter disappointment he felt at knowing he'd have no opportunity to speak alone with Lewis Grey before introducing Bianca to him. While it shouldn't have surprised Evan that even this small detail of his plan had been impossible to implement, it did. When, in response, Bianca simply tossed her curls, obviously more peeved than angry, he took her hand and led her to the rail where she'd have the clearest view. "Will you excuse me a moment? Since I can't speak to Lewis, I would like to send a message home to let everyone know we've arrived. We're way ahead of schedule so they won't be expecting us yet. I'll just be a minute."

"I'll be fine," Bianca assured him, certain she'd not be bored. Although the cargo would not be unloaded until the following morning, there was still plenty of activity on board the *Phoenix*, and when William Summer came to her side she greeted him warmly. "How long will you be in port before your next voyage, Captain?"

Will had been hoping he'd have an opportunity to tell Bianca good-bye, but he moaned in mock horror at her question. "After so many weeks at sea, that's not something I'll ask for a few days if you don't mind. I'm too glad to be at home."

Readily understanding his reluctance to discuss that subject, the blonde beauty pursued another which she hoped he'd find more enjoyable. She was so delighted to have arrived in Virginia that her mood was a festive one, and she could see by Will's charming grin that he, too, was elated. "I know you have no wife, but is there someone special who's been awaiting your return?"

Will gave a rueful laugh as he shook his head. "Unfortunately no, Bianca, but I'll do my best to find an agreeable feminine companion to help me celebrate my homecoming."

Bianca's long dark lashes nearly swept her brows; she was so shocked that he'd make such a suggestive comment to her. She'd meant only to be friendly, not to encourage such a confidence. Still, he'd made her curious. "Is that what you and Evan used to do, just find a couple of women and—"

Sorry he'd been so tactless in his remarks, Will interrupted before she could finish her question in a fashion he was certain he didn't want to hear. "No. Evan and I move in entirely different circles here in Newport News. We have our own friends." That was more or less the truth, but he'd not reveal that her husband's tastes were far more expensive than he could afford.

"We won't be seeing much of you then?" Bianca asked with genuine regret.

Will's clear blue gaze swept longingly over the lovely young woman before he replied. "No, but when I'm here I live at an inn called the River's End. They keep my mail when I'm away too, so you can always leave a message for me there should you ever need me."

Again Bianca scarcely knew how to respond. He'd always spoken to her in such a respectful tone, but when he'd mentioned finding a feminine companion she was certain he'd meant a whore; and as if that weren't bad enough he'd now been so bold as to suggest she leave him notes at his hotel! "I doubt that I shall have any need to contact you, Captain, but I'll suggest Evan invite you to come to our home for dinner so the three of us might continue our friendship." Hoping that would put him in his place, she was startled when he reached for her hand.

"I am serious, Bianca. Should you ever have the slightest need for a friend, do not hesitate to call upon me. You'll meet many people here, the city's finest citizens, but I'd like to think you'll still think of me as one of your best friends no matter how many more you make."

His manner was suddenly so intense the blonde beauty grew frightened and pulled her hand from his. He had been good company on the voyage, but surely married women could not cultivate the friendship of single men here without risking the worst gossip. Bianca had no desire to embarrass her husband or his family with such behavior. That Will admired her so highly was flattering, but she could not encourage his attentions. "Timothy is a fine boy. Do you know his mother?" she said suddenly.

Taken aback by such an irrelevant question, Will shrugged helplessly. "Well, yes I do, but—"

"Since she is a widow with small children, perhaps she would appreciate your friendship more than I. And surely there are other respectable women in the city whom you would not have to pay to help you 'celebrate' your return home. I really can't allow you to hope that we will ever share more than this voyage, Captain."

Will knew he'd been clumsy, and certain that Evan would return in a matter of minutes, he knew he had no hope of impressing her unless he could do it quickly. "I will pursue every respectable lass in Newport News if that will please you, Bianca, but it is you I am worried about, not me. Even though you doubt it now, someday you may have need of me. The River's End isn't elegant, but you can ask for me at the desk without fear you'll be accosted by rowdy sailors. Just promise to remember where you can find me, that's all I ask."

If for no other reason than to send him on his way, Bianca swiftly agreed. "I'll not forget, Captain Summer." but she added quickly, "However, when we do meet again, I'm certain it will be in my husband's home."

"I'll look forward to it." Will gave up in frustration then, certain Bianca thought him a rake when all he'd wanted to do was offer her friendship he was sorely afraid she might desperately need. Evan was so impulsive a man Will doubted he'd considered what people would think of his Venetian bride, but hoping her life would be a good one regardless of the reason for the marriage, Will wished her well and then returned to his duties, disgusted because he'd made such a poor job of impressing her with his sincerity.

Since he had absolutely no choice, Evan sent the most diplomatically worded note he could compose to his stepfather, saying only that he'd married a young woman he'd met while in Venice and that he and his bride would be home for supper. He hired a carriage, had it loaded with all their belongings and purchases, and prayed in the months he'd been away that time had lessened his parents' grief. Since he'd left his mother still weeping for Charles, he hoped she'd had time to accept his brother's death, and would forgive him for failing to avenge it. As they left Newport News to make their way north to his home, he tried to put Bianca's mind at ease, but he could tell by her restless pose and anxious glance that she was as nervous as he. In the afternoon sun the blue-green waters of the James River sparkled brilliantly, while the lush grass which grew along the riverbank swayed, with a soft rustle, in the gentle breeze. As they passed the homes of his neighbors he pointed them out, hoping to distract himself as well as his nervous bride.

Bianca thought the stately Georgian mansions magnificent, but she found the delightful openness of the countryside most appealing. "This is like living in some beautiful park, Evan, or like a king's estate. The forest is so beautiful. It would be wonderful to be able to ride. Will you please teach me how so we can go riding together soon?"

"Of course," Evan promised agreeably. "We own riding horses as well as animals trained to pull a carriage. I'll find you a gentle mount, and we'll have my mother's dressmaker make you a habit so you'll be able to ride in comfort and in style."

Bianca gripped her husband's hand more tightly as she flirted quite openly with him. "When I think of some of the other amusements you've taught me, to ride a horse should be a simple matter."

Evan laughed with her, delighted as always that her wit was so quick. He'd simply not reveal she was the woman Charles had loved since he was convinced she was blameless in the matter of his death. Only his immediate family and the men aboard the *Phoenix* knew why he'd gone to Venice, and there was no reason to spread the tale now. The impossibility of his plan did not occur to him until Lewis rushed out to the carriage to meet them and he saw his stepfather's enthusiastic grin turn swiftly to an expression of utter horror. The startled man took no more than one brief glance at Evan's striking blonde wife before looking up at his stepson with an expression of total disbelief. To avert what he felt would be an unpleasant confrontation, the young man hugged Lewis tightly, drawing him aside as he whispered a desperate command. "I'll explain everything later. Say nothing to Bianca!" When he released his stepfather, he glanced toward his home and was surprised at how ill kept it appeared. The flower beds which flanked the steps leading to the impressive two-story brick dwelling were choked with weeds. Although the day had been warm, the drapes at the first-floor windows were all drawn, while the shutters on the second floor were closed, giving the once-gracious home an abandoned look that saddened Evan terribly for he'd hoped to return to the happy atmosphere he'd always known, not the obvious sorrow of a family still in deep mourning. He presented Bianca to his stepparent, but before the man could speak more than a brief greeting, he inquired about his mother.

Lewis was so appalled by Evan's choice of bride he scarcely knew how to respond. "She has not been at all well, I'm afraid. I've stayed home with her frequently, but my presence does not seem to provide the comfort she craves. I hope you have news which will ease her mind." His glance gave the distinct impression he thought that unlikely, however.

Evan saw the unspoken question in his stepfather's eyes, but before he could respond with another plea for silence they were surrounded by a rush of chattering servants, eager to welcome them home. He busied himself directing the unloading of the carriage, then escorted Bianca to his room where he politely excused himself to allow her the opportunity to bathe and dress for supper. Hoping to find his mother's health not nearly so delicate as Lewis had reported, he started toward her room but found his stepfather blocking the door.

Without speaking, Lewis motioned for Evan to follow him across the hall, to a bedroom used solely for guests. The older man took the precaution of locking the door and then spoke in a hoarse whisper so the subject of their conversation could not be overheard. "First, I want you to tell me where you got the audacity to bring that woman here, and then I'll decide if the story's fit to tell your mother!"

Evan took a deep breath. He was sorry that Lewis had found their arrival so unsettling but determined to make his explanation brief. "As you know, I went to Venice with the single intention of finding Charles's murderer and making him pay the ultimate price for his crime. I considered it vital that I locate the 'golden-haired goddess' who'd bewitched him so. I had few clues but Bianca's maiden name is Antonelli, which accounts for her handkerchief being embroidered with the letter *A* while her remarkable beauty speaks for itself." He paused then, knowing no matter what else he said, his tale would have the same sorry ending. "I used myself as bait, fully expecting my interest in her would enrage the killer sufficiently to inspire an attempt upon my life. I planned to see that such a move resulted in the murderer's death, not mine. Unfortunately, things were far more complicated than I had anticipated. When I realized Bianca was the one who would suffer because of my plot, not Charles's murderer, I left Venice and took her with me. We were married aboard the *Phoenix*. She doesn't even know I'm Charles's brother, nor does she suspect that I was merely using her in an attempt to avenge his death."

Thoroughly confused, Lewis took out his handkerchief and mopped his perspiring brow. "Don't you think you should have told her the truth, Evan? My God, man, the woman is your wife and she has no idea as to the reason why?"

"She is more than merely beautiful, when I said I had fallen in love with her she believed me."

Unable to make any response for a moment, Lewis simply regarded his stepson with an incredulous glare. Finally he uttered a bitter accusation. "How could you have married the woman who is responsible for your own brother's death?"

"That's a lie!" Evan snarled hoarsely. "She is as innocent as you in the matter and I'll not have her reputation tainted by that despicable crime! If you can not promise to treat her with the respect she deserves, I'll simply make my home elsewhere!"

Appalled by that threat, Lewis shook his head emphatically. "No. Your mother has suffered too greatly from your brother's loss; you can't leave her too."

Evan straightened his shoulders proudly, though he regretted that his homecoming had been anything but a joyful one. "Then the choice seems clear. You must accept Bianca as my wife."

Lewis's frown deepened as he considered the few alternatives he had. "Your mother didn't read Charles's journal. At first her sorrow was so deep I did not even suggest she do so. Then you needed it for your trip. It would mean a great deal to me if you would return it now."

"Of course. You may have it, but if Mother never read Charles's glowing descriptions of the woman with whom he fell in love, she'll not recognize Bianca as you did. Her mother is British, her English is flawless, she'll not strike anyone as foreign." Elated by that realization, Evan rushed on. "Don't you see, no one need ever know Bianca was involved with Charles's death if you do not tell them, for I certainly never will."

Lewis nodded thoughtfully. "It seems I have no choice but to agree. I will give you my word that I'll keep this secret but as soon as someone mentions his name, won't Bianca become suspicious?"

"I know that is bound to happen sooner or later, but I'd prefer not to face that problem until I must."

"That's no solution, Evan," Lewis responded angrily. "You must tell your wife about your brother tonight, before she meets your mother, or it will be too late. Marion is sure to speak of him and to mention that he died in Venice under mysterious circumstances."

Evan felt sick to his stomach, but he couldn't deny the truth of his stepfather's words. "You're right, of course. I'll have to find some way to tell her about Charles without making her suspicious of my reasons for marrying her. I don't want her to learn my original intention. Such knowledge would destroy our marriage, and it's been a happy one for us both."

Lewis reached for the key to unlock the door. "I'd hoped your voyage to Venice would ease our grief; instead, you've only compounded the anguish of Charles's death by taking his love as your bride. What can you possibly tell your mother about your trip that won't break what little is left of her heart?"

"Do you want me to lie to her?" Evan asked softly. "To tell her I succeeded in slaying Charles's murderer? Is that what you want me to do?"

Lewis turned back to face his stepson, his gaze as troubled as his conscience. "You'll have to make that decision for yourself, Evan. We've already decided to lie to her about Bianca; perhaps it would be best to tell her the truth whenever you can."

Evan lifted one eyebrow quizzically, no longer certain what would be best for his mother or himself. "Perhaps if I simply tell her I am home that will ease her mind sufficiently for one day."

"Let us hope that it does." Lewis opened the door, but was wise enough to allow Evan the opportunity to speak with his mother alone.

Marion Grey's golden brown eyes lit with excitement as her handsome son came through the door. "I heard all the commotion outside, but I dared not even hope it would be you!" She offered her cheek for Evan to kiss and hugged him tightly. "I would have gotten up to meet you. I'm sorry you've found me here in bed. I don't know why I've been so tired lately, but now that you're home I know I'll feel much better."

Evan sat down upon the edge of the massive fourposter and took his mother's hands, determined to try to provide the reassurance he was certain she expected. Her fair skin was still unlined but she seemed far more frail than he'd recalled. Her white lace cap and delicately embroidered nightgown were freshly laundered as were the bed linens, and there was a vase of pink rosebuds on the nightstand. He was pleased to see that though she hadn't been well she'd not been neglected. The sweet lavender fragrance she used assailed his senses, evoking bittersweet memories of his childhood, and he leaned down to kiss her again before beginning his tale. He could not remember ever having been reluctant to speak with her before, they'd always been close, but now his mouth had grown so dry he doubted he could bring forth any words, let alone reveal how badly he'd failed her.

"Evan? What's wrong, dear?" Marion inquired softly.

Taking the most optimistic tone he could, Evan forced himself to smile as he gave an account of his good news first. "I've taken a wife, Mother. A delightful young woman I met in Venice. I've brought her home with me, and she's as anxious to meet you as I am certain you must be to meet her."

Deeply shocked by such an unexpected announcement, Marion leaned forward, her grip upon her son's hands now as frantic as her expression. "I care nothing about your wife! It is Charles's murderer I want dead. That's why you went to Venice, not to chase after women! What can you tell me of the man who murdered Charles? You killed him, didn't you? Well, didn't you?"

That his mother's grief had turned to such bitter hatred horrified Evan. She'd always been so gentle he felt he scarcely recognized her in her present mood, but though it would have been easy to lie, he couldn't bring himself to do it. Clearing his throat, he gave the only reply he could. "I did my best to find the man, Mother, but I could not."

Marion began to shriek then, all semblance of sanity gone from her. "Then why have you come home? Why have you come home if the murderer still lives? Why?"

Upon hearing his wife's shrill cries, Lewis Grey rushed into the room. He'd understood immediately what Evan had told her, but even knowing his wife's fragile mental state he'd not expected so terrible a reaction as this. "Just leave us, Evan. I will take care of her. Just go!"

"No!" Marion screamed. "Don't make him go!" Tears rolled down her pale cheeks as she clutched her husband's sleeve. "He has too much to explain!"

Lewis took Evan's place at Marion's side, and he pressed her face to his chest to muffle the sound of her pitiful cries. "You can speak with Evan again later, sweetheart. Now I want you to take some of your medicine and rest."

Evan backed away, uncertain why Lewis thought their conversation would progress any more smoothly later. The truth had obviously sent his mother into hysterics;

nevertheless, he was sick of lies. He hesitated at the door, but she was still sobbing so dejectedly he doubted she would hear anything he might say. Praying the scene he'd now have to play with his wife would not end so badly, he left the room, closing the door softly behind him.

Chapter XI

If Bianca had learned anything from her mother, it was that servants could always be counted upon to know all the family gossip, and to spread it at every opportunity. Mattie, the pretty dark-skinned girl who'd helped her to unpack, was no exception. She'd begun to talk the minute Evan had left them, and she did not cease her animated conversation until Bianca, having finished bathing, dismissed her. The young bride wanted time alone to think about all the maid had told her before she saw her husband again, if for no other reason than to attempt to avoid flying into a rage when she confronted Evan.

She sat at one of the windows she'd opened, dressed only in a chemise, as she brushed out her still-damp hair with furious strokes. The paneling which adorned the walls of the large room was painted pale green, but she found that restful shade not at all soothing. Bianca had noted that the furnishings of the spacious home revealed superb craftsmanship. They were not nearly so ornate as those of Venetian homes, of course, but that was to be expected of Georgian style. That the mansion was staffed by African slaves had shocked her at first, but the servants had been so friendly she'd soon overcome her fears.

Now, as she sat alone, Mattie's tales filled her thoughts. Evan had said he was an only child, but she'd just been told he'd had a half brother, a man of considerable intelligence and charm, whose death had sent the household into mourning so deep they had yet to resume a normal way of life although nearly a year had passed since the young man had died. Why did Evan lie to me about having a brother? she wondered. But when he finally entered the room one glance at his troubled expression told her she'd be a fool to pester him with questions. Setting her brush aside she leapt to her feet and ran to him. "What's wrong, Evan? How did you find your mother?"

The late afternoon sunlight streamed through the windows, giving Bianca's golden blond hair a fiery luster, but the cool green of her eyes was filled with a concern so genuine that Evan found it difficult to begin the explanation he knew she deserved to hear. Taking her hand he led her back to the window seat, and after she'd taken her place, he sat down beside her.

"I've so much to tell you, but I'm not certain where I should begin." He looked out at the James River then, recalling the hours he'd spent as a child, staring at the water in fascinated silence and dreaming of the day he'd be old enough to go to sea. "Do you like this room?" he asked absently.

Dismayed by that question, Bianca nevertheless replied sweetly, "Why yes, it is very handsome, just like you." That the wardrobe was so filled with his garments there had been little room for hers she didn't bother to add. There would be plenty of time later to make room for her things, and she was far too curious about what he wanted to tell her to issue any complaints about his home.

"Thank you," Evan responded and he smiled slightly.

He brought her palm to his lips for a gentle kiss and then apologized. "There's something I've not told you about my family, Bianca. We've suffered a terrible tragedy, the pain of which I'd hoped would have faded by the time we arrived home. Now that we're here you're sure to hear of it, and I should be the one to tell you first."

"What tragedy, Evan?" Bianca thought it best not to let him know Mattie had already told her a great deal about his family.

Hoping to end this ordeal swiftly, Evan took a deep breath and began his tale. "This was my father's home. When Lewis and my mother were married, he moved in here with us. He was an ambitious young man from a good family, albeit one of modest means, and my mother had great faith in him, which has been well rewarded. Through her contacts and influence Lewis became successful in business. He's an importer mainly. He supplies luxury goods to retailers in northern cities, but he also owns several stores here in Virginia—in Richmond, Alexandria, and Williamsburg—in addition to shops on the other side of the bay in Portsmouth and Norfolk. He's always been very devoted to my mother, not merely out of gratitude for her assistance in helping him get his start, but out of love." Evan paused a moment, sifting carefully through the facts at hand so he might relate most of the truth if not all of it. "They had one son who was quite handsome, tall and well built, but blond and blue eyed like Lewis rather than dark like me. He was an ambitious lad, brash, but so charming he was enormously popular with men as well as young ladies. It's possible you may have met him when he was in Venice last fall. His name was Charles Grey." Evan watched Bianca's expression closely for some sign of the shock he was certain she'd feel at that announcement, but to his dismay she merely shook her head.

"No. I'm sorry to say I didn't. I rarely met foreigners,

Evan. Had you not been invited to Paolo's home, or to the other Carnival parties, I'd not have met you," Bianca explained simply.

Astonishing as that statement seemed, Evan could see by the innocence of her expression that Bianca was telling him the truth. Yet how could Charles have been so deeply in love with her if he'd done no more than gaze longingly at her from a distance? Was it possible they'd met only briefly and she didn't recall his name? The only portrait of Charles was hung in his mother's room, and he dared not take Bianca there to view it now. Confused, he was debating how to continue when Bianca prompted him.

"What sort of tragedy befell Charles?" she inquired sympathetically.

"He was murdered, set upon by thieves according to the authorities." Evan found that lie a convenient one to tell. "My mother has not been herself since his ship arrived home bearing his body and we were given an account of what little is known about his death."

At the mention of the ship, Bianca could not suppress a startled gasp. "Evan, your brother wasn't murdered in Venice was he?" She was horrified by that possibility and her expression became as pained as her husband's.

"Yes, he was." Evan waited a moment, thinking perhaps Bianca would now realize who Charles had been, but her concern was an entirely different one.

"Oh, how dreadful! What must your parents think of me then? Will they hate me because their son was killed in Venice? Is that likely?" Tears welled up in her eyes, spilling over her thick lashes to roll down her cheeks in two slippery trails.

Evan's own eyes filled with tears at that sight, and he pulled his weeping bride into his arms to offer the only reassurance he could. "Of course not, my dearest. They will love you as I do. It is only that my mother has been dwelling on Charles's death, and her heart is so filled with anguish she can think of nothing else. She is a wonderful woman, truly she is, and now that we're home I hope we'll be able to ease her grief." He combed Bianca's damp curls away from her face with his fingers, then brushed the curve of her throat with his lips, sorry the happiness she'd felt that morning at their homecoming had been so brief. He was thoroughly depressed as well, but with his wife in his arms his thoughts turned swiftly from sorrow to desire. He'd often used her charms to block his own pain, but whatever his reason for making love to her now, he knew the richness of their pleasure would be the same.

Lifting her lithe beauty into his arms, he carried Bianca to his bed, placing her gently upon the white spread before he stepped over to the door to turn the key in the lock. Her glance was confused for only an instant, but as he began to rapidly discard his clothing she sat up to turn back the covers. After brushing away her tears, she unbuttoned her chemise, obviously having no objection to what he wished to do. She had never refused him, he realized with a heady satisfaction. They were a well-matched pair in many respects, especially so in bed. He joined her then, pulling her into his arms with a savage grace, too hungry for the delicious taste of her kiss to waste a second on unnecessary motion. The lush curves of her figure were so splendid he never tired of tracing them with his fingertips and lips, but now his need for her was too great to permit him to indulge in the lazy teasing they often enjoyed. He wanted to fill his soul with the ecstasy of her passion, to ease his tormented mind with the rapture of her love. Doing so provided the ultimate escape, and as his caresses became more intimate the warmth of his expert touch inspired in his lovely mate a longing as deep as his own. Yet her pale flesh was cool, while he was engulfed with a fiery heat as he entered her, so forcefully their bodies shuddered as they came together. It was a union of the most primitive sort, swift yet bringing pleasure of such shattering intensity its energy was soon spent. It left them both shaken to the very marrow by the power of the erotic celebration they'd shared, and their compelling need for each other sated, they remained together, too lost in the beauty of their love to want to part.

Evan lay nestled so contentedly in Bianca's arms that she thought he might have fallen asleep, and truly she would not have minded if he had. He had exhausted her with his strength, taken all she'd had to give, and then demanded even more. He fascinated her still, even more so, it seemed, as the bond between them grew stronger. She now knew he'd kept the secret of his brother's death from her out of kindness, not to exclude her from his life. She'd wondered so often about the darkness of his moods that it was a relief to understand their cause. Slowly she was gaining his trust, and she hoped soon their separate beings would merge, not simply when they made love, but at other times when they were together. She let her fingertips move slowly over the powerful muscles of his shoulders, caressing the auburn curls at his nape before her hands strayed down his deeply tanned back and over his narrow hips. "That first time I saw you without your mask, I thought you the handsomest man I'd ever seen. You confused me very badly that night, and I think perhaps I'm just beginning to know you."

Evan raised up on an elbow, his expression now a relaxed one. "All I thought when I saw you was how much I wanted us to share this." He leaned down to kiss her, his mouth slowly enjoying hers until he again felt tremors of desire flicker through the length of her elegantly proportioned body. It took so little for her to arouse him, no more than a seductive glance or a softly whispered invitation, but he knew his affect upon her was just as profound. He felt her need for him now as it grew from deep within, enflaming his passions anew, and he made love to her this time with tantalizing slowness, delaying their ultimate pleasure until his body, no longer his own, was totally hers to command.

That night, when they joined Lewis for supper, Bianca paid close attention to the man's remarks and she found him a most charming host. He'd be forty-eight she realized, slightly older than her father but just as attractive and fit. She was certain his son must have been a handsome man indeed, and she was sorry Charles had met with such a tragic fate; but Evan had issued a stern warning. She was not to mention Charles's name, and she respected her husband's request. The men's conversation consisted mainly of tales of Virginia's early history, which she found an entertaining, though somewhat unusual, choice since she had nothing in the way of knowledge to contribute. When the dishes from their last course had been cleared away, she thought the two men might wish to speak alone, but Lewis surprised her by asking to be excused.

"I usually dine with Marion in her room," he offered by way of an apology. "She was sleeping so soundly when I came downstairs I didn't want to wake her, but I must go up and see if she needs me now. I know this is your first night here, my dear, and I hope you'll excuse my wife for not joining us. She hasn't been well for several months. Please don't consider her rude. I will introduce you to her the minute she feels up to it."

"I shall be happy to help you in any way I can, Mr. Grey, to read to your wife, or to simply sit with her and be company. I'd like to do whatever I can." As Marion's new daughter-in-law, Bianca thought such a gesture only proper.

Lewis glanced over at Evan, hoping for assistance of some sort, but receiving none, he made his excuses himself. "You are very generous, Bianca, but at the present what Marion needs is simply rest." In spite of his earlier doubts, he'd found the young woman extraordinarily attractive, and very bright and pleasant as well. That she had such charming manners pleased him too, but since she was a Venetian, he feared she was the last person his wife would permit at her bedside. He could understand why Evan had overlooked Bianca's part in Charles's death, he intended to try to do the same, but he knew his wife would not. There was little he could do to make his daughter-in-law feel welcome, but he offered the only courtesy he could. "I'm so sorry we didn't have your room ready for your arrival. Perhaps tomorrow we can discuss how you'd like it redecorated and furnished. It's rather uninteresting now, but we can have it redone to please you in just a few weeks' time."

"I'll see to it," Evan volunteered readily. He was not about to admit that his bride had simply taken up residence in his room for the time being. "Since Mother has been resting so comfortably, I'll not come in to tell her good night unless you send for me."

Lewis nodded in agreement, thinking that decision a wise one. Then, after making another brief apology, he left them to see to his wife's comfort. As soon as Evan had showed her into the parlor, Bianca attempted to stifle a throaty giggle. "Just where is my room supposed to be? At least Lewis did not ask me if I liked the color so I didn't have to admit I'd not seen it."

Evan chuckled as he poured them each a brandy. "It's the room next to mine, of course. I sometimes used it as a study but it does have a bed if you'd like to try it."

Bianca took a small sip of her brandy, certain he was teasing her. "I don't want to try it; I want to sleep with you as I always have. A lady is expected to have her own room, of course, and I'll see that mine is made so attractive I'll not ever be lonely."

"You are all that will be needed to make the room

exceedingly attractive, my pet. Come and sit down here beside me." He led her over to the sofa and when she was seated he took the place at her side. They had survived the first day in his home, and while it had not gone as smoothly as he'd hoped, it hadn't gone as poorly as he'd feared it might. At least Lewis had proved reasonable, though his mother hadn't. "Tomorrow I'm going to speak with our doctor and find out exactly what's wrong with my mother. If it is no more than grief, I'll encourage her to get out of bed and start living again. She has many lovely friends who'll want to meet you, and that's reason enough for her to begin entertaining again."

"Your stepfather is very kind, Evan, but won't he be upset if you question the way he's been caring for your mother?"

"Probably not. He's so concerned about her he won't object to me trying to help." As Evan spoke, he realized that since his voyage to Venice had not brought his mother the peace of mind she craved, he'd simply have to provide it in another fashion. If Charles's death could not be avenged for the time being, it could at least be accepted. That thought didn't make the pain of his failure any less intense, but he vowed to handle that in his own way. Surely he could do something to raise his mother's spirits if he put his mind to it. "Let's give my mother a few days to adjust to my return, and our marriage. Then I'll see if I can interest her in helping you redecorate your room and in shopping for new things. She knows all the best shops and has excellent taste."

"Let's not expect too much, Evan. It might be awhile before she wants to leave her home on such frivolous errands. I won't be insulted if I have to take care of everything on my own. My taste is very fine too."

Pleased that Bianca was not only clever but understanding, Evan slyly grinned and rose to his feet. He offered her his hand. "I don't recall ever having spent such an exhausting afternoon. I'm going up to bed. Would you care to join me?"

Taking his hand, his spirited blonde wife offered a jest of her own. "Of course. If you're so terribly tired, I suppose I can always find something to read for an hour or two."

Evan finished his brandy and set their glasses aside. "The night you read yourself to sleep in my bed will be a sorry one indeed." The warm golden glow in his eyes left no doubt in her mind as to how he planned to finish the evening. "We have the luxury of a sizable bed for a change instead of a cramped bunk, and I plan to see we make good use of it."

"Evan," Bianca cautioned in an embarrassed whisper, "must you speak so loudly everyone in the entire house will hear you?" Since she already knew Mattie liked to gossip, she was certain the other servants did so as well.

To silence her protests, Evan picked up the startled young woman and carried her up the stairs to his bed, positive everyone already knew what they'd be doing that night without his having to tell them.

Having posted a sufficient number of men on watch to guard the cargo, William Summer left the *Phoenix* for the evening. Until the ship was unloaded, he'd be living on board, but that didn't mean he couldn't visit several of his usual hangouts and enjoy himself. Old friends were anxious to congratulate him on his promotion to the rank of captain, but he would be expected to buy the next round of drinks and he knew he'd soon grow tired of celebrating when it proved too costly. In no mood to gamble, he nonetheless strolled over to an establishment run by a flamboyant woman named Fanny Burke. Her place featured not only games of chance, but attractive young women as well, several of whom greeted him by name as he entered. But he was looking for someone special that night, someone young and pretty, and he wanted her to be blonde. He knew exactly what he was doing, but he didn't care. He wanted to drive thoughts of Bianca Antonelli from his mind for one night, and when he saw an attactive blonde moving toward him, he broke into a wide grin.

Lily had learned how to smile seductively without revealing one of her front teeth which was badly chipped. She was pretty, even without the exotic makeup sailors usually found so appealing, and she liked the looks of this sandy-haired young man. He was well dressed, which meant he'd have plenty of money, and when he seemed undecided, she wasted no time. She didn't want one of the other girls to approach him. "My name is Lily," she announced in an inviting whisper. "I don't believe we've met."

"William Summer, Captain William Summer," he said with a chuckle of pride. "But I'll answer to Will."

"You're the captain of your own ship?" Lily asked hopefully, slipping her arm through his so he'd not move away.

While he hated to disappoint her, Will replied truthfully. "The *Phoenix* is owned by Evan Sinclair, but I am her captain."

"Aren't you very young to have so much responsibility?" Lily asked, giving him a coquettish glance, then moving closer still and pressing the full length of her body against his.

This young woman's eyes were a soft clear blue, not green, and the curls she'd swept atop her head were fair, but not a glorious golden blond. Her figure was slender, yet it lacked the sultry allure he'd found so distracting in Bianca. Nonetheless, Will was in a forgiving mood, and he decided she'd suit his purpose for the night. "Do you really want to discuss merchant ships?" he asked slyly. "Wouldn't you rather just take me upstairs to your room?"

"I beg your pardon?" Lily whispered hoarsely, her eyes wide with astonishment. Some men didn't bother to discuss anything but her price, while others seemed to like a bit of polite conversation first. She liked the talkers ever so much better for they let her pretend, albeit briefly, that she was a lady. She'd mistaken this man for the latter type and was sorry to find that he was not.

Now Will was puzzled. "The last time I was here, this parlor was used for no more than introductions. Has the routine been changed?"

"Of course not," Lily assured him, and taking his hand she led him up the stairs to a room at the very end of the dimly lit hall. It was far from the most elegantly furnished rooms in the house, but she was new and had been given the only space available. "What is it you want?" she asked flippantly as she locked the door, no longer bothering to lower her voice to a pleasing level. Her dress was striped satin in a soft apricot shade, new though not particularly pretty, and she now began to remove the bodice with hasty tugs. "Well, what is it you like?" she demanded impatiently.

Will looked around the room, glad to see it was neatly kept though it was sparsely furnished. He didn't understand why Lily's mood had changed so abruptly. "Did I offend you somehow?"

Lily laughed at his question. "You can't insult a whore. Don't you know that?" She continued to disrobe, peeling away the layers of her clothing with surprising haste. She wanted only to take the man's money as quickly as she could now and then get him out of her room. It was late. With luck, she'd have no more customers that night and she could then go to bed alone.

Will sat down on the edge of the mattress and pulled off his boots. Lily was not what he wanted at all, he realized, but since he'd gone this far it was too late to walk out of her room and look over the others. Still, he didn't like her attitude, and he began to argue with her.

"Well I'm sorry if I insulted you, Lily, but I didn't call you a whore. Come here. I'll help you undress."

While she was surprised by that request, Lily moved over to the bed. She didn't bother wearing a corset so there was little for him to remove, but he stopped when he reached her chemise. Not understanding why, she loosened the drawstring at the neck herself. The undergarment slipped to her feet, revealing high firm breasts above a narrow waist and slender hips. Her legs were long and perfectly shaped if a trifle thin. She knew her figure was more boyish than womanly. Nonetheless, she struck a provocative pose, then waited for him to reach out and touch her; but he began unbuttoning his shirt instead.

"Why don't you wash off that makeup? I'll bet you're far prettier without it."

"Look, it's late. I'd like to please you, but I haven't the time to take off my makeup and then put it back on for the next man who'll walk through the front door." She reached for the covers to pull them back, but Will caught her wrist in a firm grip and turned her toward the washstand.

"I'll pay for the rest of the night so you've no one to please but me. Now go wash your face."

"Aye, aye, Captain," Lily responded sarcastically, but as she lathered up her washcloth she saw him watching her in the mirror and she wished he'd been as nice as she'd expected him to be. Her eyes filled with tears at that thought, and she looked down so he'd not see.

"How old are you, Lily?"

"Old enough," was her only reply.

The girls seemed to be getting younger each year, but Will thought perhaps that was because he was getting older. He stripped off the last of his clothes, got into the bed, and was pleased to find it was very comfortable. Fanny knew how to run a house efficiently; as always the linens had been freshly changed. The setting wasn't the best, but Will considered it adequate, and when Lily came to join him, he was shocked to find her much prettier than he'd thought and so young he had to know the truth. "I mean it, just exactly how old are you?"

Lily slipped under the covers and, caring little for his topic of conversation, she reached out to touch him with a slow, tantalizing caress. He responded, immediately becoming hard, which pleased her, but he laced his fingers in hers to stop her play.

"There's no need to hurry when we have all night," Will explained simply. Why he felt he needed to talk with her he couldn't imagine, but he knew it was important that he try. "Answer my question," he insisted firmly.

Lily sighed unhappily. She was afraid he was going to spend the whole night talking so she'd never get any sleep. "I'm nineteen," she announced proudly.

"The hell you are." Will leaned across her as he spoke, forcing her into the softness of the feather pillows. She'd not bothered to turn down the lamp, and he could plainly see the sparkle of tears in her eyes. He didn't understand what he'd done to upset her, but he kissed her lips softly, hoping to entice the truth from her with affection.

Men seldom took the time to kiss her and never so sweetly as Will. In a few seconds Lily relaxed sufficiently to smile in the way she thought was most flattering. "Eighteen?"

Thinking that was at least a start, Will kissed her again, letting his mouth linger upon hers until he hoped he'd restored her initial good humor. "I want the truth, Lily."

After a long silence, the slender blonde admitted grudgingly, "I'm seventeen. Now I suppose you'll want to know my whole life story."

"Not unless you want to listen to mine." Yet Will was intrigued by the girl's defiance. He'd never bothered to wonder why women chose such a life, but a desperate need for money seemed the most likely reason. Thinking her story might possibly prove interesting he asked, "Do you want to talk now or later?"

When she didn't answer, he released her hand and lowered his mouth to the tip of her breast. Her fair skin held the fresh clean scent of soap, which made her youth seem all the more poignant. Drawing away slightly, he said, "The choice is yours."

"Later," Lily replied softly, hoping he'd soon be too tired to want to chat. When he again lowered his mouth to her breast, she stroked his soft curls lightly, her touch far more bashful than his. He hadn't told her what he liked, but she didn't ask again. She simply waited for him to tell or show her what he wanted to do. When he pulled her close; his fingertips straying along her inner thighs before slipping through the soft triangle of tawny curls nestled between them, she ceased to care. He was one of the nice ones after all, the nicest yet, and she closed her eyes to shut out the sight of the dreary room. She'd been there just two weeks, but they seemed more like two years or two lifetimes.

Will felt her leave him. The instant she turned her mind away from him he knew what she'd done and drew back. "Lily?" he called softly. "I want this to be good for you too."

Startled by the sound of his voice, Lily opened her eyes, her cool blue glance curious. "Why?"

"Why?" That question struck Will as being so wildly funny he could not help but laugh. "I'll be damned if I know, but I do." He stretched out on his back and propped his head on his hands. "I wanted tonight to be special, but maybe that's impossible."

"Special? Like what?"

"I was doing my best to show you," Will responded, chuckling. He'd wanted to take a beautiful woman to bed, and here he was with this surly kid who was providing no more than a body. He should have known there wasn't another woman like Bianca, not in the whole world.

Lily propped herself up on her elbow so she could study his expression. She thought him very good-looking, and he'd been gentle; most of the men certainly weren't. "So why did you stop?"

"I didn't stop, you did," Will explained matter-of-factly.

"What is it you want me to do, Captain? To make love? Really make love?" Lily asked incredulously.

"Is that so surprising a request?"

"Well, it's the first time I've heard it," she replied. Nevertheless, she leaned over to kiss him, and this time when he wrapped her in a warm embrace she let the sweetness of his affection warm her clear through. Her need for love was far greater than his, and if he wanted to pretend they were lovers, truly lovers, then she wanted to do that too. A long while later she fell asleep, still cradled in his arms, but when he left the bed and began to get dressed she awakened abruptly. "I thought we were going to talk," she complained sleepily.

"It's nearly dawn and I've got to get back to my ship. We'll talk another time." Will adjusted the collar of his coat, and after checking his appearance in the mirror, he strode toward the door. He'd left her a generous tip, but he was strangely reluctant to leave. "Thank you," he called softly, but when there was no reply he assumed she'd fallen asleep and let himself out the door. He felt no different than when he'd arrived several hours earlier, he realized. In fact, he felt far worse. Lily was just a kid, probably a scared one, and he wasn't proud of the way he'd used her. He just wanted to forget the whole night, but when he reached the parlor he found Fanny Burke and a girl he knew as Rosemarie trying to revive a man who'd obviously had far too much to drink.

At the sight of the powerfully built young man, Fanny gave a cry of delight. "Help us here, luv. Nigel has drunk himself into a stupor again, and Rosie and I can't get him outside to the carriage. Even if we could Jacob's too damn frail to lift him."

"Is this Nigel Blanchard?" Will asked as he bent down to haul the expensively dressed man to his feet.

"The very same. Do you know where he lives?" Fanny was still a striking brunette, though she was now in her forties. She liked to dress in the bright ruffled garb of a gypsy, and she wore so many bangle bracelets she jingled as her hands fluttered over her disheveled customer.

"Yes, he's a friend of Evan's so I'd better see him home."

Nigel was so limp Will simply tossed him over his shoulder to carry him outside. After shoving him into the backseat of the carriage, he climbed up beside Jacob and waved to Fanny as they set off. He didn't see the pale figure standing at a window and watching him with tear-filled eyes until he disappeared from sight.

"I know the way," Jacob mumbled softly. "I ought to by now."

"I'm sure you do." As Will leaned back to get comfortable, he tried to recall what Evan had told him about Nigel Blanchard. The Blanchard fortune was derived from banking, but it certainly didn't look as though Nigel would be at his desk that morning. It was his twin sister Evan knew best, but Will had only seen Sheila a time or two himself. The Blanchard twins were an elegant pair, but he'd never met them formally.

Taking Nigel home when he was too drunk to walk out of Fanny Burke's could scarcely be called a proper introduction.

The road curved along the bank of the James River, but the Blanchard's house was nearer to town than the Sinclair place. It was an imposing brick structure, but there were no lights glowing in any of the windows when they arrived. Since Will didn't think it would be a good idea to leave young Mr. Blanchard lying on the front steps for someone to discover at dawn, he leapt down from the carriage and went up to the front door, but he'd knocked no more than twice before it swung open.

Sheila Blanchard was livid, her rage lighting the soft ivory shade of her fair skin with a deep blush. A fierce light glowed in her brown eyes, and her jet black curls flew about her shoulders as she stormed out the door. "You needn't wake the entire house with that incessant knocking! Just get him upstairs to bed and be quick about it!"

Will forced back the anger which rose in his throat, but he was sorely tempted to tell this shrew exactly what he thought of her and of her brother. Deciding it would be easier to lug the man up the stairs than it would to put this bitch in her place, he went back to the carriage, and after exchanging disgusted glances with Jacob he opened the door and pulled out their passenger. Again lifting Nigel over his shoulder, he marched back toward the house and followed Sheila up the stairs. Her white linen gown was trimmed with so much lace it was nearly transparent, which made the climb far more interesting than he'd anticipated for her figure was a very good one, but when she thrust some coins into his hand after he'd placed Nigel on his bed Will finally had to object. "I don't want your money, Miss Blanchard. I did this as a favor for a friend."

"You're not one of Mrs. Burke's men?" Sheila asked in surprise. "I know that's her carriage and driver."

"That might be true, but I'm just along for the ride." Will turned to go, having no wish to continue their discussion. When Sheila followed him downstairs to the front door he thought she meant only to lock it behind him, but she reached out to catch his sleeve.

"Wait a minute. I do know you from somewhere, don't I? At least give me your name so I can tell my brother he owes you a favor."

"I did the favor for Fanny Burke, not your brother, so he doesn't owe me a thing but my name's William Summer."

Sheila frowned slightly. He was an attractive man in a rugged sort of way, but it took her a few seconds to place him. "Oh, now I remember. You're Evan's mate, aren't you?"

"I was, now I'm the captain of the *Phoenix.*" Will backed away, determined to be on his way, but again the fiery brunette followed him.

"Is Evan home?" she asked quickly, her excitement plain.

"Yes he is. The *Phoenix* docked yesterday afternoon." Will climbed back up beside Jacob trying his best to hide his smile.

"Well, you tell him I expect him to come see me by this afternoon at the very latest!" Sheila ordered sharply. "It's been months since he was home and I've almost forgotten what he looks like."

"I'd advise you to do just that, Miss Blanchard, because his wife is a very beautiful woman and he'll have no reason to call here again."

Sheila's pretty skin went as pale as her gown. "His wife!" she shrieked hoarsely. "Where did he get a wife?"

"Mrs. Sinclair is a native of Venice. Now, if you'll

excuse me, I've got a ship to unload." Will tipped his hat and gave Jacob a firm nudge in the ribs to inspire him to start the team. He didn't glance back as they drove away, but he laughed to himself as he tried to remember how stricken Sheila had looked at his news. He wanted to describe her reaction to Evan.

Chapter XII

Bianca lay across the foot of the bed, watching Evan draw the blade of his razor slowly up his throat. She'd never known him to cut himself, but he handled the sharp instrument with a touch so light she feared he might someday be careless. She never tired of looking at him, even when his task was a mundane one, and she always enjoyed his company, especially when they were relaxing together in a private moment they shared with no others. He planned to go back to the *Phoenix* and then on to his shipyard, but she was so full of questions she doubted he'd be able to leave on time.

"Should I ask if your mother is feeling well enough to see me, or do you really want me to wait until you can introduce me to her yourself?"

"Please wait. I doubt she'll be up before I leave, but give me the chance to talk with her again tonight. Seeing me just upset her yesterday, and I want to make certain that doesn't happen again today."

"Why would she be upset with you, Evan?" Bianca sat up and smoothed out the folds of her skirt. Already fully dressed, she was waiting for him to escort her to breakfast.

"She was just surprised to see me, that's all." Evan

told her that lie because he had no time to think up a more plausible excuse. "I'm certain she can't help but think of Charles when she looks at me, and naturally that made her sad." He knew *sad* wasn't a strong enough term to describe his mother's reaction, but it would have to do. Setting his razor aside, Evan rinsed the remains of the shaving soap from his face and picked up a towel to dry off. "I hope you aren't bored while I'm gone. You won't get lost if you go for a walk and stay on one of the paths, or you might tour the house and see if there are any furnishings you'd like to have moved into your room. Think about a color scheme, that sort of thing; then you'll have something to discuss with my mother when you do meet her. Mattie will take care of the laundry and do anything else you require of her."

Uncertain as to whether or not she should speak about the servants, Bianca hesitated a long moment before mentioning what was on her mind. "I've never owned a slave, and though Mattie seems very pleasant, I'm afraid I don't quite know how to treat her."

"Mattie isn't a slave." Evan turned to face her as he picked up his shirt. "There are many influential people here who oppose slavery, Bianca. Thomas Jefferson, George Washington, and Alexander Hamilton to name just a few. I believe as they do that slavery is abhorrent, completely inconsistent with the ideals of the Declaration of Independence for which I spent a good many years fighting. We have Negro servants here, that's true, and their ancestors were brought here as slaves, but I freed them all years ago."

Relieved and very favorably impressed, Bianca smiled more brightly. "Can you do that? Just tell the people they are free?"

Happy to discuss a subject other than his mother's mood, Evan broke into a charming grin. "Yes, slaves are simply regarded as property. I inherited twelve when my father died. They were all household servants. We do not raise tobacco or cotton like some of my neighbors who own dozens of slaves that work their land. When I freed them three left to seek lives of their own elsewhere, but the others stayed on and are now paid a salary. Our housekeeper, Viola, is Mattie's mother, while Nathan, who cares for the stables and grounds, is her father. You'll get the names of the other six straight eventually. Please treat them all as politely as you would have treated your own servants at home."

"Oh, yes, I shall." Bianca looked up at her husband, once again amazed by the complexity of the man. "May I send for the dressmaker you mentioned?"

"If you like." Evan was pleased to think Bianca was so resourceful, for he wanted her to be too busy to have time to wonder about his mother's opinion of her. "Show her the fabrics we bought in Spain, or choose something she suggests if you like it better."

"I will not be expected to wear black, will I? I don't wish to appear disrespectful to Charles's memory, so if you think I should I will have a few black dresses made."

Evan had no desire to see Bianca dressed in mourning for Charles, that thought was simply macabre. "No, I want to see you in the colorful silks and satins you've always worn. Since you brought so few garments with you, select whatever you need: lingerie, ball gowns. Oh yes, don't forget the riding habit. The cost is of no consequence." He kept up a polite stream of conversation while they shared their morning meal, then confident that she'd spend a pleasant day he kissed her good-bye and left for town.

Eager to take a walk and explore, Bianca went back upstairs to fetch her cloak, but as she passed Marion's door she heard the unmistakable sounds of an argument. She recognized the soothing tones of Lewis's deep voice, but the replies were shrill, certainly not the sounds she had expected from a woman who was reportedly far from well. Not wishing to eavesdrop, she walked straight to Evan's room and picked up her cloak, but as she retraced her steps to return to the stairs she heard crying so pitiful she was tempted to knock at Marion's door and offer her assistance. To wait for Evan to present her formally to his mother seemed a mistake when the woman was suffering so terribly, but she'd given her word so she decided to wait at least a day or two before attempting to see Marion on her own.

Since the entire cargo was to go to Lewis Grey's warehouse, Will found the unloading a simple yet tedious matter to supervise. He was not usually so restless after a long voyage, but he was finding it difficult to keep his mind focused on seeing that the Venetian crystal Evan had purchased had the proper handling. There were magnificent chandeliers in addition to fine crystal vases and glassware, and he didn't want to see a single item broken due to carelessness. He moved back and forth along the dock with a slow even stride, the force of his presence giving the men reason to take care, though all too often he found himself thinking of the slip of a girl with whom he'd spent the night. She was so different from the other women he'd met at Fanny's that he found their brief encounter impossible to forget. He'd wanted only an evening's amusement, but Lily had provided far more. The girl had been very friendly at first, then maddeningly aloof, and finally she'd come into his arms so sweetly her touch had been as soft as an angel's wing. That was the sensation which stayed in his mind and flooded his body with longing. He'd gone looking for just any woman since he couldn't have the one he truly wanted, but he'd found something so unique he wondered if perhaps last night had been no more than a dream. If he went back to Fanny's would Lily be happy to see him again? Hell, would she even recognize him? It would be better never to go back than to return and find Lily less than he remembered. She's just a feisty kid with hardly any figure, he told himself over and over again, but the more he thought about her, the more he felt that dismissing her from his life so hastily might be a grave mistake.

By nightfall Will had changed his mind so often he didn't know what he really wanted to do. He ate supper aboard ship then went for a long walk, hoping to clear his mind. He had two choices, he decided. He could go back to Fanny's and see if Lily still fascinated him after a few moments of conversation, he had promised they'd have another opportunity to talk, or he could go elsewhere and see if he met another young woman who interested him more. As if that were possible, he thought angrily. He'd known plenty of women. He liked the pretty creatures when they were nice to him, but he'd never enjoyed anything deeper than a casual friendship with any of them except Bianca. He'd promised her he'd find himself a respectable lass, but what woman from a fine family would be interested in him? Oh, he was a captain now, of course, and that would bring him good money, but he'd be home so seldom no decent woman would want to waste her time waiting for him. He gave the dirt of the path a savage kick, depressed for he'd found Lily so confusing a creature he could not decide what to do about her. If he went back to see her that night it would only make her all the more conceited and difficult. She'd think him smitten with her and a man would be a damned fool to fall for her when she was a . . . He could not even bring himself to say the word. He was so ashamed of nearly calling her that. "Damn!" he shouted to anyone who cared to listen. He walked clear to the outskirts of town before he returned to the *Phoenix* and stretched out on his bunk, and a long while passed before he realized if he didn't go back to Fanny's, Lily would just spend the night with someone else. Maybe even someone he knew. That sorry fact was enough to jolt him into making up his mind, but he took the time to clean up and change his clothes before leaving the ship to go see her.

Will saw the crowd milling around Fanny's front steps the minute he turned the corner of her street. She didn't allow her customers to annoy the other residents of the neighborhood, so, curious as to what had caused such a commotion, he quickened his step. When he spotted a sailor from the *Phoenix* he walked over to him.

"What's going on, Rich?"

"Nothing you'd want to see. Some guy from Hampton got drunk, went wild and beat up one of the girls. Tore up the whole place when they tried to throw him out. The house is such a mess Fanny's closed it for the night. Guess I'll go on over to Mabel's. Want to come along?" Then, remembering Will was now the captain of his ship rather than simply the mate, he rephrased his question in more respectful terms. "I mean, would you like to come along, sir."

"No, thanks. Which girl was it?" Will asked apprehensively.

"I don't know her name, a pretty little blonde. At least she was pretty before that brute got to her."

That was all Will needed to hear. He pushed his way through the crowd, cursing his pride for not allowing him to come to Fanny's earlier that evening. The front door was nearly torn off its hinges, and two of the establishment's many maids were busy sweeping up debris in what had once been the rather garishly furnished parlor. Red roses from a shattered vase lay strewn about the carpet as though they'd been tossed upon a grave, but Will didn't bother to step around them as he spoke to the maids. "Which girl was hurt?"

The taller of the two women looked up from her task to reply nonchalantly, "The place is closed, sir, you'll have to leave."

"Damn it! I'll not go until I know who was hurt! Was it Lily?"

"Yes. But you'll still have to go away like the others, Fanny said so."

Will's heart lurched, and disregarding the maid's directions, he quickly raced up the stairs. The hall was filled with half-clothed girls lounging in the open doorways and complaining about losing a night's pay, but he paid no attention to their giggles and seductive invitations as he hurried to the last room. He flung open the door but Fanny sprang from the bed and came forward to scold him crossly.

"Lily's in no mood for company tonight, Will Summer, so just take yourself elsewhere," she ordered firmly.

Will stared past the brightly made-up madame to the small figure huddled on the bed. That she'd been badly beaten was obvious for her features were so bruised and swollen he scarcely recognized her, and the room was a shambles. The mirror above the washstand was shattered, the single chair was a heap of splinters, and the doors of the wardrobe had been kicked in. Ignoring Fanny's command, Will snarled, "Where is the man who did this?"

Fanny put her hands on Will's chest, but her attempt to shove him back out the door proved futile. "He met with a nasty accident on his way home, so you needn't concern yourself with him."

Will could well imagine what had happened to the fool. He was probably at the bottom of the James River by now, or he soon would be. "How'd the maniac get in here in the first place?"

Fanny gestured helplessly, making the dozens of

bracelets she wore jingle noisily. "I make mistakes sometimes. We all do. But I've no time to chat; I've got to take care of Lily."

"Have you sent for a doctor?" Will's eyes hadn't left the girl on the bed. She'd covered her face with her hands when she'd recognized him, but he'd seen enough to know she needed medical attention.

"Honey, the doctors in this town don't care to make house calls here. I can take care of her myself. I've tended worse in fact."

Will was afraid he was going to be sick, but he brushed the woman aside. "I have too. I'll take care of her myself."

As he started for the bed, however, Fanny grabbed his arm. "That's not a good idea, Will."

Will didn't argue, but the look he gave the woman was so threatening she dropped her hand and backed away. "All right, suit yourself. There's water and clean towels by the bed. Just ask if you need anything else." Shaking her head at the stubbornness of the man, Fanny walked out and closed the door.

"Lily?" Will reached out to touch her hair, then drew his hand back when he realized it was covered with blood. "Dear God, Lily, what happened?"

Lily peeked through her fingers, too embarrassed to let him see her face. "Not all men are nice like you, Will. Some are mean, but only a few are this cruel." Her teeth had cut the inside of her lower lip, and she wasn't sure she could speak clearly enough to be understood.

Will dipped the end of one of the towels in the bowl of water Fanny had brought, but he didn't even know where to begin. Thinking the gash in her head was the most serious of her injuries, he sat down on the edge of the bed and pressed the damp towel to it. "I should have been here earlier; then this wouldn't have happened."

"It happens all the time," Lily whispered softly.

"Tonight, tomorrow, next week, whenever, all the time. You don't have to stay."

"Yes I do." Will insisted, still fighting the nausea that filled his throat. He had tended men who'd been horribly injured in the war so wiping away blood was nothing new to him, but he'd never seen a beautiful young woman this badly hurt. Her condition pained him greatly. The bodice of her dress was torn, her stockings were ripped, and he suddenly feared all her wounds might not be visible ones. "Did the bastard rape you too?" he asked hoarsely.

"You can't rape a whore," Lily mumbled dejectedly. "Nobody would believe that."

"Well, I'd believe it. Did he do it or not?"

Surprised by the anger in his voice, Lily lowered her hands in order to see him better and was surprised by the glimmer of tears in his eyes. This man was actually crying because of what had happened to her. She couldn't take that. "You go on home. I can take care of myself." She tried to raise herself up on an elbow, but the pain in her head was so bad she had to lie back down again. "Just go away."

"Lily, answer me. Did the bastard rape you or not?"

"You ask too many questions."

"Oh, dear God." Will knew he was going to be sick, he just knew it. Some help he was when he felt worse than she looked. He got up, walked over to the window, and opened it wide, hoping some fresh air might help to settle his stomach. "Fanny said she took care of the man. If she didn't I will."

"I don't belong to you," Lily pointed out sarcastically. "Stay out of this."

Will leaned back against the window sill, thinking her point well taken, but he realized he did care what happened to this stubborn child and he wouldn't deny it. "This room's a mess. I'd like to take you over to my hotel. I'll help you clean up first and then we'll go."

Lily just wanted him to go away. "Look, if I leave Fanny will give this room to someone else and then I'll have nowhere to go."

"You won't have to go anywhere. I'll pay for your room at the hotel and for everything you need." Will didn't believe his own ears, but he knew he couldn't leave Lily with Fanny now that this awful thing had happened to her. It had happened once and it could happen again, and again. He'd not risk that. Even though she'd not admit it, he was certain she'd been raped and that hurt him all the more. He went back to the bed, sat down, and dampened a fresh towel to wash her face. She hadn't said yes or no to his offer so he decided he'd just carry her over to the hotel since he doubted she'd have the strength to resist. "Look, I'll provide a room for you, and in a few days we can decide what you want to do."

"You want me to be your mistress, is that it? To sleep only with you?" Lily clearly thought that idea preposterous.

To Will, a mistress was something only a rich man kept, but he didn't know how else to describe what he was offering. "I just don't want to see you hurt like this again, Lily. I'll do whatever I must to stop that from happening."

Although amazed by the sincerity of his tone, Lily found it difficult to believe he'd be so noble. "Why?" she asked curiously.

"Why?" Will lifted her chin gently so he'd not hurt her bruised lips as he cleaned away the blood which had dropped down her cheek from the scalp wound. When he caught a glimpse of her chipped tooth he exclaimed unhappily, "Oh, no. He broke your tooth."

"That happened years ago, but don't change the subject. Tell my why you're so concerned about me."

Will shook his head. "Now you're the one asking too many questions, Lily." He didn't really understand his need to take care of her, and he knew he'd never be able to explain it to her. "Have you got something else to wear?"

"You'll have to look and see." Suddenly very tired, Lily closed her eyes. She ached all over from the savage beating she'd suffered, and she didn't think she could summon the energy to change her clothes.

By the time Will had gotten clean garments laid out, Lily was sound asleep. He'd stopped the bleeding from the scalp wound and she didn't seem to be in pain, but Will hesitated to wake her after what she'd been through. He didn't want to leave her alone either. Thinking he'd be smart to tell Fanny what he wanted to do before he carried one of her girls out the front door, he went downstairs to find her. She was in her office, seated at her desk and sipping a brandy. Will refused the one she offered him.

"Lily looks so awful she'll be of no use to you for some time. I'd like to take her over to the River's End where I can look after her. I know you're far too busy to do it."

Fanny gave the young man a long, hard look before she decided to offer some motherly advice. "You don't really want to do that, Will. Oh, you might think you do tonight, but I can guarantee by tomorrow morning you'll be sorry. Lily's as common as they come. She's a pretty little thing, but she'll only break your heart. I know you'll take good care of her because you're a nice man, but she'll just repay your kindness with the worst kind of trouble. Do yourself a favor and go on home. Lily will be able to work again in a week or two, and you can see her as often as you like then."

Fanny's comments made Will so angry he could scarcely see for the second time that night. "Just because you think Lily isn't worth my trouble doesn't mean I have to agree. I plan to take her and keep her. If you want me to pay you something to make up for the money she'll not earn for you, I'll gladly do it."

Fanny was surprised by the hostility in his voice, and she became strictly professional as she challenged him. "I see. This is to be a simple business transaction, is it?" She waited a moment and then made an extravagant demand. "I've spent quite a bit on the girl for clothes, makeup, perfumes, everything she needed. She had nothing when she came to me, and she's only been here a couple of weeks but already she's quite popular. I think a thousand dollars might cover my losses, however. How soon can you give me the money?"

"A thousand dollars?" Will was stunned by the large sum, and his shock showed clearly in his pained expression.

Fanny sat back in her chair, and after getting comfortable she adjusted her ruffled skirt to reveal her slim legs which were only a hint of the many charms she still used to every advantage. "It looks like you've failed to consider what your interest in Lily will cost. To keep a mistress isn't cheap, Will. This thousand dollars is merely the beginning. If you haven't got that, then maybe you'd better just take my advice and pay for Lily's favors when you can afford to visit her here."

"No," Will insisted emphatically as he rose to his feet. "I'll get the money, and I'll pay you tomorrow. I still want to stay with Lily tonight though. I don't want her to be alone if she wakes up in pain."

Fanny shrugged, sorry he'd not seen the truth of her words. "You'll have to carry one of my chairs upstairs so you'll have a place to sit."

Will thought that idea as ridiculous as her other ones. "The bed is big enough for us both. I'll be fine." But as he left the madam to finish tallying her day's receipts, he was not nearly so confident as he'd sounded. He'd have to go to Evan and ask for an advance on his salary, and that would leave him with little to pay for his own living expenses, to say nothing of Lily's.

She was still sleeping soundly, and since he didn't want her to wake up in the morning wearing the torn dress, he carefully removed what was left of it. He peeled away her stockings and found her feet to be as dainty as those of a princess. She had lovely hands too, delicate with long shapely nails, although she'd broken several trying to fight off her assailant. Nothing about the girl was common except her attitude, and he was certain he could change that. He undressed quietly, then slipped under the covers. He dared not put his arms around her for fear of hurting her, but he cuddled up close, and after praying Evan would give him the money to set her free, he fell into a troubled sleep.

When he awoke before dawn the next morning, Will realized it would be cruel of him to tell Lily she would soon be leaving Fanny's before he was certain he could raise the money to make that possible. She was still sleeping soundly so he took great care not to wake her as he got dressed. He sprinted all the way to the *Phoenix* in order to have time to bathe and dress properly for his meeting with Evan. Since the man had stopped by the previous morning on his way to his office, Will was certain he would again and he wasn't disappointed.

"We've got almost everything unloaded. We'll finish by noon." Will was proud of that fact. He drew Evan aside. "I'd like to speak to you in my cabin before you go."

Evan shot his friend a quizzical glance, then agreed. "Of course. Let's go below." Once they were seated in Will's cabin, Evan looked around the cramped quarters and made a suggestion. "Move your things into my old cabin. I've no plans to set sail again in the near future."

"I'll do that then." Thinking it only polite to inquire about Evan's problems before mentioning his own, Will began with a question. "Did your conversation with your mother go any better last night than your first meeting with her did?"

"Unfortunately no," Evan admitted with a weary sigh. "She just took one look at me and started weeping over Charles again. I've not been able to introduce Bianca to her yet for fear Mother will create a scene. She doesn't understand how I could have married rather than avenge my brother's death."

"But you didn't!" Will argued. "You only married Bianca so she'd lead the killer to you."

"Well I can hardly tell my mother that, now can I?" Evan pointed out sharply.

"No, of course not," Will admitted. "Well, how is Bianca getting along?"

"Very well actually. She's begun to rearrange several rooms of furniture so she can have what she wants in her own room, as soon as it's painted in the shade she insists upon. And she's had the flower beds weeded, the riding trails cleared, the horses groomed, the carriages washed, and oh yes, today she's meeting again with the dressmaker to choose some fabric for new gowns. In one day my wife managed to direct more activity than my mother has in the last year. I'd always known her to have a high level of energy, but she amazed even me with all her accomplishments. Thank God there is still plenty to keep her busy and out of my mother's way."

"She'll make a wonderful mother herself." Will was certain of it, although the thought of Bianca with Evan's babe in her arms was a surprisingly painful one and he looked away to hide his discomfort.

"Yes indeed. But that's not likely to happen for quite a while. Now what did you need to see me about this morning?"

"I need an advance on my salary," Will explained simply. "I've expenses I hadn't expected."

Will was too good a friend for Evan to argue over a

small sum of money. "How much do you need?" he asked helpfully.

Since he had several months' back pay coming, Will asked only for what he'd have to pay Fanny. "A thousand dollars."

"Good Lord, Will, that's nearly a year's wages!" Now Evan didn't know what to think. "Look, if you've gambling debts, whatever, I'll just cover them for you and you can pay me back a little bit each month. We needn't call it an advance on your salary. Whom do you owe? We can walk over to the bank, and I'll get you the money so you can pay him off now."

Will got to his feet and thrust his hands into his pockets. "I've no debts. There's a new girl at Fanny Burke's who just doesn't belong there. She got beat up pretty badly last night, and I've offered to take care of her. Fanny wants the money to let her go."

Evan stared at his friend for a moment, thinking surely he must be telling some sort of ridiculous joke, but Will's expression was a deadly earnest one. "Are you serious? You want to buy one of the girls from Fanny?" he asked incredulously.

"No. I'm not buying her." Will tried to explain the situation calmly, but his voice began to rise in spite of his intention to plead his cause in a logical manner. "Fanny just wants the money to cover the loss in Lily's earnings and for her expenses. You needn't just hand it to me; I want it to be an advance."

"The problem with advancing you your salary, Will, is that eventually that money will be spent. Then you'll have no money coming in to cover new expenses, and you'll be forced to request another advance, then another. You'll never be able to get even. If you've become so attached to this Lily after being home only two days, she must be very special indeed. I'll gladly give you the money and you may pay it back whenever you're able. There's no hurry."

"Do you have time to visit the bank now?" Will asked anxiously. "Thank you. I should have said that first, but can you give me the money now?"

"Of course." Evan rose to his feet and slapped Will warmly on the back. "I owe you quite a bit more too. Let me pay you that amount while we're at it."

"Thank you again." Will reached out to catch his friend's sleeve. "Please don't tell Bianca about this. She wouldn't understand about Lily, and I wouldn't want to upset her."

Evan's smile vanished at the mention of his wife's name. "I'm sure Bianca knows of such women, Will, and if you want to look after the welfare of one, why should it upset her? She is after all my wife and not yours."

"You misunderstood me," Will pointed out quickly. "I meant only that Bianca is a very fine lady, and I would not wish to shock her with the knowledge that I have a companion who would not be considered fit company for her."

"Well, whether or not she'd be shocked is a moot question. This is a matter between you and me, and she has no need to learn of it. Will that soothe your conscience sufficiently where Bianca is concerned?"

Will nodded gratefully. "Yes it will. Thank you."

"You've thanked me enough for one morning, now let's go get your money."

Nigel Blanchard welcomed Evan in his most charming fashion, but despite the fact that Will had delivered him to his bed the day before, he didn't recognize him that morning. "My sister tells me you've brought home a bride. Naturally we're all anxious to meet her. Would a dinner invitation some evening next week be convenient?"

Evan had things to do, and spending the morning chatting with Nigel wasn't one of them. He knew there were lots of people who'd be eager to entertain Bianca, but he also knew his own mother should meet his wife before her friends did. "We've just returned from a lengthy voyage, Nigel. Give us a couple of weeks to get rested and settled, won't you? That way we'll be able to repay your hospitality more promptly."

Nigel knew that answer wouldn't please Sheila, but he had no choice but to agree. He took care of Evan's withdrawal, noting the young man did no more than count the money to be certain he'd received the correct amount before handing it over to his friend.

"I'd like to open an account with part of this," Will announced proudly. Evan paid him a more than generous salary, and he hoped he'd be earning enough to make Lily's life comfortable for some time to come.

"Of course, we are always happy to welcome new depositors," Nigel assured him with another of his ingratiating smiles.

Having taken care of his errand, Evan went on his way, and as soon as Will had signed the papers necessary for opening his account, he left hurriedly too. Nigel realized he'd gotten no information about the new Mrs. Sinclair, which displeased him greatly since he knew Sheila would be annoyed with him for not learning something about the Venetian woman. His sister would have been able to pry the minutest details from Evan, while he'd simply been brushed aside as though he were no more than an insignificant clerk, rather than one of the owners of the bank. It would do no good to complain, he told himself angrily. Evan Sinclair had enormous wealth, and the bank needed his money too badly. He put on his brightest smile in order to greet his next customer, a prominent woman he'd never liked either, but he'd give her no reason to suspect she was not considered one of his dearest friends.

Chapter XIII

When Will came through the door, Lily didn't even glance up from the cup of soup she was trying to sip without having it dribble down her chin. Her lips were still too swollen to permit her to eat without mishap, and she was embarrassed to be seen making such an awful mess. Hiding her excitement, she blotted her mouth on a napkin before she spoke in a sullen tone. "I thought you'd changed your mind about me."

In the clear light of the new day the deep purple bruises which marred Lily's fair skin looked even more ugly than Will had remembered. Her left eye was now swollen shut by the worst black eye he'd ever seen, while her right eye was swollen due to the affect of her tears. Her mouth was a sorry sight but at least her nose hadn't been broken. She had a very sweet little nose he realized, almost as perfect as Bianca's. The maids had cleaned up the room, and had helped her bathe and dress in a pretty nightgown, but she still looked so forlorn he could not help but be worried about her. "I'd not change my mind about you," he responded with a ready grin, hoping to lift her spirits. "But I did have a shipload of crystal to finish unloading and a few errands to run before I came to get you this morning. It wouldn't have been very helpful of me if I'd taken you over to the hotel and we'd found they had no rooms available."

"But they do?" Lily asked hesitantly.

"Yes, and I reserved one of their best for you."

"Just for me?" the battered girl asked suspiciously. "Where will you be?"

"In the room next door. That way if you need me I'll be close by."

Lily thought him foolish for going to the expense of renting two rooms. "Wouldn't one room be enough for us?"

Will leaned back against the side of the bed and crossed his arms over his chest as he attempted to explain what he'd had in mind. "Look, Lily, I just want you out of this place. If something happens between us two, then it happens; if not, you'll still be out of here and better off."

Lily wasn't so certain. "What do I have to do so something does happen between us?" she asked curiously.

Will hated to look at her when her appearance depressed him so greatly, but he wanted to be positive she understood his offer had no strings attached. "You don't have to do anything special, Lily. Just be yourself and we'll get along real well."

The fragile blonde thought that prospect highly unlikely. "How old are you?" she asked suddenly. "I should have asked you that question last night."

"I'm twenty-eight, why?"

Lily shrugged, having had no reason other than curiosity for wanting to know. She tried to take another sip of soup but gave up the effort and set the cup aside when she was unable to swallow the savory broth because it oozed all over her lower lip. "You have a wife? Children?"

"Of course not!" Will responded with a disgusted

frown. "I'd not have come here in the first place if I'd had a family."

Lily laughed at his indignation. "We get lots of married men here, lots of them. Just ask Fanny if you don't believe me."

His expression growing dark, Will replied in an emphatic tone, "I'd rather discuss something other than Fanny's clientele if you don't mind. If you're finished eating, I'll take you on over to the River's End."

Lily still hadn't made up her mind about what she wanted to do. Will was nice, but if he soon tired of her, then what would she do? Fanny most likely wouldn't take her back, and she'd heard Mabel Longstreet was a bitch. Maybe she should just stay put. Looking up at his serious face, she made up her mind quickly. "It's not gonna work, Will, not if you're gonna pretend I'm something I'm not. I've been taking care of myself too long to let you start watching out for me. I think I'll just stay here."

"The matter is already settled, Lily. You're coming with me." Will wasted no time in arguing over the matter. He walked over to the wardrobe and began to remove her clothes from it, rapidly folding them into a neat bundle. "Rachel Kelly owns the hotel. I told her you'd be moving in this morning, and that's just what you'll do. You won't even need to dress. Just put on your cloak, and I'll carry you up the back stairs so you won't be seen."

"You ashamed to be seen with me?" Lily asked accusingly.

Exasperated because she seemed to misunderstand everything he said, Will forced himself to speak in a low even tone instead of following his first impulse and shouting. "No, of course not. It's you I'm thinking about, Lily. I don't want you to be embarrassed by the way you look. I didn't know your last name; just tell me and I'll sign the register for you."

"I know how to read and write," Lily announced proudly.

"I'm sure you do, but it would be easier if I did it for you since you're not looking your best. Now what's your full name?"

"Lilith Easton," the little blonde replied softly.

"That's a lovely name."

"You really like it?" Lily asked demurely. "I chose it myself."

Will shook his head in disbelief. "You mean you just made it up? What's your real name?"

"It doesn't matter anymore. I'm no heiress you can take home to collect a fat reward." Lily began to laugh at her own joke, but finding that too painful for her battered face, she stopped abruptly.

Will swore to himself he'd learn everything there was to know about Miss Lilith Easton, most especially the truth; but he knew he'd never win her trust until he got her out of Fanny's and showed her exactly how well he meant to treat her. He walked over to the window and waved to Jacob, who was waiting in the alley below with the carriage. "Let's go," he said, and before she could protest, he'd placed her cloak around her shoulders and had lifted her into his arms.

"Wait. My clothes!" Lily cried out in alarm.

"I'll come back up for them," Will assured her graciously. "I'll search the entire room, and I'll not miss a single thing, not even a hairpin." He strode down the hall, scarcely feeling Lily's slight weight. The few girls who were up at that hour laughed and waved good-bye as they passed, but true to his word, Will saw that Lily was comfortably seated in the carriage and then he dashed back up the stairs two at a time and gathered up all her belongings, leaving nothing behind except the half-eaten cup of soup.

It was the accusing gleam in his mother's eyes that haunted Evan. She despised the man who'd murdered Charles, and totally consumed by that loathing, she'd turned her hatred upon her surviving son for having failed to avenge his brother's death. Each time Evan entered her room she simply stared at him coldly, her anger too bitter to voice. She refused to accept his presents and she ignored his polite attempts at conversation. It was obvious she'd not forgive him until he brought her the news that Charles's murderer was dead. Lewis tried his best, but could not make her see how wrong she was to blame her son for adding to her grief when he'd done his best to ease it.

As Evan closed his mother's door, he was overcome with sorrow. She was no longer the dear woman he'd always loved but a vicious stranger. He'd been home a week, but she'd not shown the slightest interest in him or his bride. It was as if she'd fed on her grief until there was no room in her heart for the love she'd once felt for him. That he was alive and eager to please her meant nothing. Evan had been sick of lies, but he now doubted the wisdom of telling her his mission to Venice had been a failure. It had been a complete and utter disaster, but he'd not allow that sorry fact to ruin the happiness he'd found with Bianca. She was a continual delight to everyone. She'd charmed Lewis so sweetly he regarded her as his daughter, while the servants had found her enthusiasm for filling their home with beauty a refreshing change from the gloomy atmosphere his mother had created. Everywhere Evan looked there was evidence of Bianca's hand. The house had been so thoroughly cleaned every last speck of dust had been swept away. The curtains had been washed and ironed, the rugs beaten, the silver highly polished, and now his wife's room had been freshly painted in the soft pink shade she'd wanted so badly. By exchanging pieces of furniture with the guest bedrooms, she'd managed to create the perfect room for herself, a sweetly feminine boudoir of which she was very proud. As he walked toward her room Evan wondered what tale he could spin to excuse his mother's continued rudeness toward her new daughter-in-law, but he was sick at heart for the truth was something he could never tell.

In the months they'd been together Bianca had learned to respect her husband's moods, yet she saw far more than he seemed to realize. She doubted that his mother's illness was physical and thought it far more likely it was mental in nature. Whether it was due to the horrible tragedy of Charles's death or to some other cause Bianca didn't really care. What mattered to her was that Evan was miserable when she wanted him to be as happy as she was. The house was very beautiful, his stepfather was a dear man, the servants were friendly and industrious, and she would have considered her life idyllic had it not been for his mother's illness. More than once she'd gone to the woman's door, intent upon introducing herself since Evan had not done so, but she'd done no more than touch the knob when she'd been overcome with such a strong feeling of foreboding that she'd not dared to knock, let alone enter unannounced. When Evan came through the door, she could tell instantly that the conversation he'd just had with his mother had gone no better than his others, but she inquired thoughtfully, "How is your mother feeling this evening?"

Bianca was already dressed for bed, her golden curls framing her delicate features with an angelic sweetness, and Evan simply wanted to make love to her to forget the wretched guilt with which his mother's bitterness had filled him. The doctor had said he could find nothing physically wrong with her, but each time Evan spoke with her she'd been more distant and his hopes for her recovery had become more faint. Her hatred was slowly killing her, yet he was powerless to end her despair. Charles's killer will have two victims, he thought bitterly, two lives he could neither save nor avenge. He sank down on the edge of the bed and pulled off his boots with weary tugs. "No better, I'm afraid." The vagueness of that comment was in itself a lie in Evan's view, for he actually thought his mother's condition was more grim.

Bianca moved across the bed, and kneeling behind her husband, she put her arms around his waist, then lay her cheek against his shoulder. "Sometimes nothing can be done, Evan, and one must accept a sad situation."

"I've been unable to convince my mother of that, unfortunately," Evan admitted remorsefully. "Charles's death is apparently impossible for her to accept."

"It has been only a year," Bianca reminded him softly. "Perhaps—"

"No, the passage of time will make no difference to her." Evan was the only one who could have made a difference, and he'd failed. The pain of that knowledge held him in a merciless grip. He'd lost his only brother, and now it seemed he might soon lose his mother as well. As he put his hands over Bianca's, his tension slowly melted into desire, and he forced himself to think of more pleasant thoughts for her sake. "This room is perfection. I didn't think you could do it without buying anything new, but you have."

Puzzled by his abrupt change of subject, Bianca nonetheless understood that his mother's poor health pained Evan too greatly for him to want to discuss it any further. "I'm glad you like it. Shall we redo your room next?" she whispered teasingly as she raised up to nibble his earlobe.

"I may never go in there again if you stay in here," Evan responded with a rakish grin. God, how he needed this dear creature. He needed her thoughtfulness and love more each day, and he turned to pull her into his arms, the passion of his kiss unmistakable evidence of the depth of his desire.

Bianca's lips never left Evan's as she helped him peel off his shirt. She loved the muscular curves of his body, the angular planes, and her hands moved over his broad shoulders with an appreciative caress. Then her fingertips combed through the dark curls which covered his chest, tracing a pattern of lazy circles until she felt his breathing quicken. He was the most exciting of men, so handsome and strong, and she never tired of exploring his magnificent body with her hands and lips. He could make love with an easy grace, or a thrilling wildness which made the beat of her heart throb with the same primitive rhythm that inspired his deep thrusts. She wanted his strength now, not his tenderness, and she tossed her nightgown aside, her mood one of total abandon. Bianca understood exactly what her husband craved, release from the torture which plagued his mind, and she came into his arms whispering an invitation so delicious he saw no reason not to accept it immediately. His lips lingered first at her breasts, savoring the taste of her lightly perfumed skin before his kisses left a quivering trail across the flatness of her stomach as he sought the soft triangle of blond curls which veiled his true goal. He loved the sweetness of her flesh, the hidden recesses only he had enjoyed; and the quick motions of his tongue teased her senses until he'd set her soul aflame with desire. He moved over her then, slowly caressing the length of her slender body until, with a swift plunge, he made them one. His motions were far from subtle as he sought the bright haze of ecstasy their union always created. He wanted it even more now, so he kept his passion in check until he felt her pleasure swell to a throbbing peak. Then, wanting to share that rapture, he allowed it to overwhelm him like a cresting wave at last bringing the blessing of a dreamless oblivion. Within moments, he slept soundly, still cradled in her loving embrace, so bathed in love the sorrow of his cares no longer filled his soul with pain.

When Will brought Lily a delicious supper he'd thoughtfully cut into bite-sized pieces and then conversed politely while she ate, she began to think perhaps she'd been smart to come with him. Her hotel room was far nicer than the one she'd had at Fanny's, and from the glimpse she'd had of his through the doorway, his accommodations were fine too. After he kissed her cheek lightly and bid her goodnight, she expected him to return to share her bed, but he did not, which left her feeling puzzled and inexplicably sad. She realized she was far from pretty and decided that was the cause of his lack of desire. Consequently she was pleased when she looked in the mirror the next morning and found her features looked far more normal even though her bruises had barely begun to fade. She asked the maid to prepare a bath, and was busy washing her hair when Will came into her room. Embarrassed, he turned to go, but she saw no reason for him to leave and called to him with a teasing laugh. "You needn't be so shy with me, Will. We've already slept together so we've no secrets left to share."

Will turned back slowly, amazed by that comment. "We hardly know each other, Lily. I'd say the number of secrets we have to share is nearly endless."

Lily shrugged and continued to massage the soapy lather through her fair curls. "Want to help me rinse my hair?" she asked in an inviting whisper. She'd not been a mistress before, but she was certain he'd expect her to amuse him in every possible way. When he came over to the tub, she ran her wet fingertips up the firm muscles of his thigh. "It is a shame this tub is not big enough for both of us. If you built a house for me, then we could have a larger one though, couldn't we?"

Will's breath caught in his throat, but whether it was because of the boldness of her gesture or because of her outrageous suggestion he didn't know. "You want me to build you a house?" he asked hoarsely. Such an expense was completely beyond his means for the present, but he'd not admit that to her. "I'm home too seldom to need a house, Lily, and you'll be fine here in the hotel."

The little blonde frowned petulantly. "Just what am I supposed to do here in this room all day when you are away? If I had a nice house I could tend the garden, grow pretty flowers, learn how to cook you delicious meals. What can I do here except keep your bed warm while I await your return?"

That she might grow very bored without him was a problem Will had not even considered. He wanted to handle one difficulty at a time, and first he wanted to make certain she was feeling well. Although he tried to avert his eyes as he poured the bucket of warm water over her hair he could not help but notice the long dark bruise which marred the fair skin of her left side just below her breast. She must have gotten that when she'd fallen, and recalling she'd cut her head he admonished her sternly. "I don't think you should have washed your hair so soon, Lily. That scalp wound was deep and it can't possibly be healed."

"You worry too much, you know that?" Lily stood up then and let the water drip off the slight swells of her body while she patted her hair dry. Being nude in front of him bothered her not at all, but she could see by his bright blush that it certainly bothered him. "You've not lived with a woman before have you?" she asked perceptively.

Will hesitated a moment before answering, trying to still the pounding of the blood which rushed through his ears. Despite her bruises he found her boyish figure appealing, but his concern was for her comfort, not merely to satisfy his own lusts. "No, but I'll get used to it soon enough," he promised with far more confidence than he felt.

"I sure hope so." Lily smiled as best she could, hoping her swollen lips were not too unattractive, but Will left the room with two brisk strides, leaving her wondering again why he'd been so adamant about bringing her to the hotel if he planned to ignore her.

Just as Fanny had predicted, in a week's time Lily's injuries were no longer apparent beneath a light layer of makeup and she was thoroughly bored with the life of leisure Will had provided. Although she tried she hid her frustration poorly. He'd brought her books to read, but they were classics, far more difficult than the light romances she was used to, and she had to struggle to make sense out of them although she didn't admit that to him. She pretended to love the stories he'd brought and made certain she had at least one book open at her side at all times so that when he chanced to enter her room he'd think she'd been reading. He'd bought her a piece of needlepoint, a bouquet of roses in several shades of pink on a background of green, which would make a pretty pillow, but she found the delicate handwork tedious and made minimal progress on it. Newport News was a small town with few amusements, which was why Fanny Burke did such a good business, however, while Lily craved the excitement of the life she'd known, she had no wish to return to it. All the girls knew it was better to be kept by one man, to be his mistress than to be the whore of any man who had the price. Somehow she'd thought making that change would make her happy but it hadn't. She felt lost and alone, and Will continued to be so polite and aloof she was out of patience with him. She still recalled the night they'd spent together in vivid detail. He'd known exactly what he'd wanted from her then, and she knew she'd pleased him too. So what was the matter now?

Will spent his days seeing that all necessary repairs were made to the *Phoenix*. She was Evan's pride and he wanted to make certain the sleek ship didn't suffer any neglect under his command. He'd been to the shipyard too, but neither he nor Evan seemed in the mood to laugh together as they once had. Impressed by the methods employed at the Arsenale in Venice, Evan was busy trying to implement improvements which would allow him to build ships at a faster rate than his competition in the North. The secret lay in having all the various sections completed and ready to assemble so that once the keel was laid a ship could be put together in a rapid sequence instead of by crafting the vessel one piece at a time. The Venetian approach had made sense to Will when his friend had first explained it to him, but the old-timers, who'd been building ships since before Evan was born, thought his ideas absurd. That they had been successful in Venice for six centuries impressed them not one bit. That aggravation was not something Evan tolerated well since his problems at home were so acute, and Will was perceptive enough to realize his visits were not enjoyable, but were merely a distraction.

Will had no idea what other women did with their time, but when he returned to the River's End in the evenings he could tell Lily had made little use of hers and he didn't know what more to suggest. Maybe a house of her own was the best idea, but he didn't see any way he could afford such a luxury. He'd hoped when she was fully recovered from her injuries they'd be able to talk about her future, but she seemed to have no interest in planning any activities beyond those to fill the next hour. She was as Fanny had described, a very pretty girl but one without Bianca's complex personality and fine education, and he felt badly each time he compared her to the Venetian beauty, knowing it was not Lily's fault that she had not had that wealthy young woman's many advantages. She knew how to smile and flirt, but serious conversation with her proved nearly impossible for she always gave flippant replies rather than thoughtful ones. Why she had such an aversion to the truth he couldn't guess, but he was sorry she still lacked the confidence in him to reveal it. He went to bed alone each night, telling himself he'd not rush things between them. He found that arrangement no more satisfactory than Lily, however, and depressed, he did not know what else to do. He slept badly and awoke each morning in a more downcast mood.

While she appreciated all William Summer had done for her, Lily sensed she'd disappointed him in ways she didn't even understand. There was only one thing she did well, but he seemed to have no interest in sharing her bed. He did not denounce her past as immoral, but she knew something was wrong and she was tired of waiting for him to explain what it was. She'd made a point of finishing one of his books, never complaining how badly it bored her, but when he'd wanted to discuss it she'd realized instantly it was all too obvious she hadn't understood what she'd read. Being far too proud to admit that, she had simply argued with him about his interpretation, a ridiculous confrontation neither of them had enjoyed. She'd completed one whole rose on the needlepoint, but her stitches were uneven so she knew he'd not compliment her on it. It was a pretty piece, yet she did not have the patience to do it well and that frustrated her greatly. She feared she lacked not only the temperament but the skills to be a lady, and therefore she would never please him. When he again wished her good night and remained in his own room, she gave up all pretense of understanding his moods. After he'd put out his lamp, she waited a few minutes to be certain he'd be in bed; then she removed her clothes and opened the door which connected their rooms.

There was no moon, but Will heard rather than saw her standing in the doorway. "What is it, Lily?" he asked softly, doubting they'd have anything more to say to each other that night.

Having no questions she thought he'd answer, Lily came forward and sat down on the edge of his bed. She reached out to touch his hair lightly, combing the thick strands between her fingers. She thought him quite handsome now that she saw him so frequently. "You're a fine-looking man, Will," she said simply. When he didn't push her hand away, she lowered it to play with the soft curls which covered his chest. Certain he slept nude she drew back the covers slightly then let her fingers stray down his stomach, her caress growing far more bold when she found him fully aroused.

"Lily!" Will exclaimed hoarsely. He grabbed her wrist in a vicelike grip, but with a lilting giggle she simply leaned over to encircle the tip of his throbbing shaft with her lips. Her tongue filling him with a pleasure far too rich to deny, he made no further effort to resist her playful affection but he released her hand so he could slide his fingers through her curls to hold her face close. Their many problems faded like ripples widening in a pond as she worked her magic on him, creating within his loins a fiery heat which melted all resistance to her well-practiced charms. He was young, his body well muscled, and she enjoyed providing him with this sensual pleasure since she had failed to bring him joy by any other means. She was an expert at her trade, highly skilled at giving men rapture, but that thought didn't enter Will's mind. He knew only that what she was doing to him was too good to stop, and he lay back, enjoying it until his whole body shook with a rush of ecstasy he could no longer contain. If this were all he could expect from her, in that instant he vowed it would be enough.

When Will caught her in his arms Lily was surprised to think he might want more of her, but he wanted something far different. He enfolded her in a tender embrace, cradling her head against his shoulder as he whispered softly. "I wish I knew your real name. I'd tell no one, but I'd like to be able to use it at times like this."

Lily rested her arm across his stomach, her pose relaxed even though she'd grown wary. He was very sweet, but she'd made the mistake of falling in love once and had paid too high a price to ever repeat that mistake. "Call me whatever you like, Will. My name isn't important."

Will cleared his throat, about to tell her a name meant a great deal since it carried its owner's reputation, but he realized that was a totally inappropriate argument to use with her. "If you'll not tell me, then I'll simply call you Lily for you are like that beautiful flower in so many ways."

"What ways?" Lily asked in disbelief, not understanding that his compliment was sincere.

Will had not meant to confuse her, and he searched his mind for some way to impress her since that always seemed to be nearly impossible. "You are fair, pretty, graceful, as lovely as a flower," he explained slowly, hoping this time his point would be clear. The fragrance she wore was a subtle one, and he added, "You smell as sweet as a lily too."

"Oh, I see," Lily responded softly. Tears welled up in her eyes to spill over her lashes and splash down upon his chest before she could catch them. She was embarrassed to weep in front of him but no one had ever said such a sweet thing to her and she was touched.

"Lily?" Will shifted his position to look down at the fragile blonde, but the room was so dark he could see nothing. He could feel her tears, however, and leaned down to kiss them away. The sweetest of longings filled him then, and he covered her face with tender kisses before lowering his mouth to her breast. He wanted it to be as perfect as it had been with them before, to be like making love, truly making love, and as she wrapped him tenderly in her arms, it suddenly was.

Chapter XIV

Wanting to give Bianca a nice present, Evan bought a gentle dapple-gray mare for her. She named the pretty little horse Moonbeam, and as soon as her new riding habit had been delivered they began her lessons. While she was an enthusiastic student, she had so little experience with horses she was easily frightened. Evan, therefore, took great care to see that she was never in danger of being thrown, and he made the tone of his instruction entertaining rather than strict. He was very patient with her, content to simply wander the trails which crisscrossed their land until she had the necessary skills in horsemanship to allow him to take her on more adventuresome rides. Encouraged by his easy affection and helpful manner, Bianca made steady progress toward becoming a good rider. She liked the path near the river best, thinking the view enchanting, and while Evan knew that trail well he never grew bored when her company was so enjoyable. Not until the afternoon they met Sheila and Nigel Blanchard did he realize he'd been keeping his lovely bride all to himself.

It was not mere coincidence that had brought the Blanchard twins to the riverbank that day. Sheila had sent one of her servants over to request a recipe from Viola, having given the woman very clear instructions that she was to return before noon with every scrap of information it was possible to gather about the new Mrs. Sinclair. Nothing gleaned from that ruse had pleased the haughty brunette, however, for she doubted any young woman could be as attractive and charming as the young Venetian woman was reported to be. She enlisted her brother as her escort and went out for a ride, knowing it would be a simple matter to overtake Evan and Bianca since she'd been told they frequently liked to travel the path nearest the river.

At first Nigel had been reluctant, but he'd become as curious about Evan's bride as his sister so he finally agreed to accompany her out of real interest rather than a tiresome sense of duty. They made their way to the James River and tried to appear genuinely surprised when they happened upon Evan and Bianca just beginning their ride.

Bianca's light woolen habit was well tailored, and its soft forest green shade provided a superb complement to the deep emerald hue of her eyes and the bright sheen of her golden hair. The wide brim of her stylishly beribboned hat shielded her fair skin from the rays of the sun while hiding none of her beauty. She smiled as Evan introduced his friends, but she found Sheila Blanchard's comments so forward, she was tempted to reply to them in a far from gracious manner. The young woman was clearly the more bold of the two, but she supposed in any set of twins one would quite naturally be the leader. With their dark glossy hair and flashing brown eyes, the Blanchards were an attractive pair, Bianca realized. Sheila was quite pretty, and her brother Nigel was handsome, if a bit shy. Nonetheless, she hoped Evan was not overly fond of them because after only a few minutes she grew very weary of their company.

Sheila's inquisitive glance raked over Bianca's face and figure searching for the flaws she was certain must be present, but she could discern none, which infuriated her. Noting the blonde's tiny waist, she took satisfaction in the fact that the young woman didn't appear to be pregnant. Evan had obviously not had to marry her, but Sheila was devastated that he had. "I am so pleased to meet you, Mrs. Sinclair. It's wonderful that you speak enough English to be understood," she said with scant enthusiasm, and then, turning toward Evan, she addressed the rest of her conversation to him, her tone and gestures now openly flirtatious. "I thought surely by now your mother and stepfather would have had a reception to introduce your bride to everyone, Evan. I hope we didn't miss it."

"There will be plenty of time for parties, Sheila, since Bianca and I will be married for a lifetime," Evan responded confidently, apparently not at all concerned about their lack of a social life.

Taken aback by that noncommittal reply, Sheila insisted some sort of reception was definitely in order. "I haven't seen your mother at church since early last spring. If she's not been well, I'll be glad to take over the burden of planning the party to help her. She used to entertain so lavishly, everyone has been awaiting an invitation from her. Surely she wants to honor your bride, but if for some reason she's unwilling to do it, we'd be happy to host a reception, wouldn't we, Nigel?"

"Of course," the young man offered agreeably, breaking into the warm grin he used so effectively with the bank's customers for he'd found Bianca's fair beauty most appealing. Her English was as proficient as his own and while he understood his sister's reasons for disliking her, he certainly didn't share Sheila's attitude. If Sheila wanted an opportunity to see Evan, Nigel was quite willing to help her. At the same time, however, he'd do his best to see that Bianca wasn't neglected. "Would a week from Saturday give you enough time to issue all the invitations?"

Shocked that the twins would assume he'd agree to their ridiculous offer to host a reception for them, Evan replied curtly, "We aren't even distantly related so there's no reason for you two to host such a gathering. I'll introduce Bianca to my family and friends in time. You needn't concern yourself any further with the matter."

Sheila laughed at his sternly worded refusal, tossing her raven-hued tresses and obviously thinking him impossibly naïve. "Oh, Evan, don't you know anything about human nature? You must introduce your bride soon or everyone will think you're ashamed of her because she's foreign. You wouldn't want your friends to gossip about her, would you?"

"None of my friends is ever going to spread rumors about Bianca, Sheila, most assuredly not you." While Evan's threat was only an implied one, its meaning was more than clear in the hostility of his gaze. "Now if you'll excuse us, we'd like to continue our ride."

As he turned his mount back toward the path, however, Sheila deftly edged her horse between his and Bianca's so she could be at Evan's side. Nigel readily took up a position next to Sinclair's wife.

"We'll ride a ways with you," the brunette offered brightly, swiftly changing the subject before Evan could refuse her company. "I've not been invited to view the crystal you brought home from Venice. Isn't it any good?"

"It is more than merely good, it is excellent." Evan looked back at Bianca and saw by her perplexed expression that she was as pained as he to have the Blanchard's company on what had begun as a very pleasant but private ride. "Lewis hasn't finished cataloging and pricing it all, but I'm certain he'd allow you first choice if there's something you'd like."

Sheila licked her lips provocatively. "Why, Evan," she purred softly, "you already know what I like."

Evan shot the crafty wench a fierce glance in the hopes of silencing her outrageous comments before they got any more out of hand. She didn't own him, she never had, and he'd not allow her to pretend there had been anything more between them than a casual flirtation. He knew she enjoyed playing the tease while at the same time demanding the respect due a young lady from a fine family, but he had no patience with her antics that day. "What you like doesn't interest me in the least," he told her sharply. "Make your request to Lewis, and he'll give you an appointment to select whatever you'd like to buy."

Seeing his sister lean over to whisper something to Evan, Nigel reached out to give Bianca's hand a comforting pat. "You must forgive Sheila," he advised softly. "She'd always expected to marry Evan herself, and I'm afraid she's dreadfully disappointed she's lost him."

"Oh, really?" For some reason Bianca did not find that news at all surprising, nor did it inspire any sympathy. "What a shame," she remarked casually, as if he'd made a remark about a subject no more important than the weather.

"Yes, isn't it?" Nigel agreed with a laugh, and for once his delighted smile was genuine. Most women lacked the courage to stand up to his sister, and he was glad to find Bianca had no such lack of spunk. It is no wonder Evan married her, he thought. She is a beauty, and very bright as well.

That he thought his sister's plight amusing made the young man far more appealing to Bianca. Perhaps Nigel was nothing like the outspoken young woman she'd found it so easy to dislike. She decided he did not deserve to be dismissed too quickly. "Are you an old friend of my husband's too?"

"You might say we all grew up together, although my sister and I were closer to Charles in age than Evan, who barely tolerated our tagging along after him. His brother was one thing you see, he felt responsible for him, but I do believe he regarded us as simply a nuisance."

Bianca nodded thoughtfully, understanding how that might easily have been the case. "Tell me something about Charles," she said with an inviting smile. "Evan is quite naturally reluctant to talk about his brother, but I'd like to know more about him."

Nigel frowned momentarily for trying to find a way to adequately describe that young man was difficult. "Well, let me see," he began hesitantly. "Charles resembled his father in that he was blond and blue eyed, but his features weren't all that different from Evan's. He was tall and well built, and all the young ladies found him enormously attractive, a happy fact he appreciated to the fullest. He was always in high spirits and wonderfully popular. How he could have met with such a ghastly death I can't imagine since he'd led such a charmed life. We all miss him terribly, and I think we always will."

Bianca smiled prettily, grateful for his comments. "If Charles were so dashing a figure, why did Sheila prefer Evan?"

Nigel chuckled at that question. "Don't you think your husband is dashing too?"

"Yes, of course I do," Bianca readily replied. "But I asked about your sister."

"Well then, perhaps it was simply a matter of taste. Evan is a far more serious man than Charles ever was; I think that's why he appealed to her more. Quite frankly, I really don't know Evan as well as I did his younger brother. He and I have never been close, although I do handle his accounts at our family's bank."

Since she had seen little of Newport News other than

the port and Evan's home, Bianca was curious about the town. "Is banking a profitable business here?"

"Everything is profitable in the cities surrounding Hampton Roads, Mrs. Sinclair. Norfolk, which is located on the southern shore, is a much larger city than ours, but it was a stronghold of the Tories and was destroyed during the War for Independence. It's still in the process of being rebuilt, and a building boom requires a great number of large loans which I am more than happy to provide. There is an element of risk, of course, but the opportunities for profit far outweigh them."

Nigel's expression grew far more animated when the subject turned to banking, and Bianca thought him like the young men of Venice in that respect. He could be charming company, but his heart was obviously committed to commerce, not romance. Since Evan was the only man she'd ever love, she forgave Nigel that fault and continued to encourage him to tell her more about Hampton Roads since he was so knowledgeable.

When Evan again glanced back over his shoulder, he was annoyed to find Bianca talking so easily with Nigel. He realized that he should have known his lovely wife could charm any male and Nigel Blanchard would be no exception. He'd had more than enough of Sheila, however, so at the first opportunity he turned his horse toward a path which led back to his home. "I'm sorry, but we'd planned only a brief ride today," he announced firmly, "and it's time we returned home."

Disappointed because Evan had been so maddeningly aloof, Sheila bid him a curt good-bye, then deliberately wheeled her bay gelding around in so sharp a turn that Bianca's little mare was forced off the path. Moonbeam slid, stumbling as she tried to find firm footing on the rocky incline at the river's edge, and Bianca would surely have been thrown had Nigel not quickly reached out to grab the dapple-gray's bridle and urge her back onto the level ground of the path. The dangerous incident was over in a matter of seconds, but Sheila had already ridden away, apparently completely unaware of the havoc she'd created. Badly shaken, Bianca gripped Moonbeam's reins tightly, trying to smile bravely as she thanked Nigel for his timely assistance, but Evan simply cursed loudly.

"You know Sheila is often thoughtless," Nigel explained in an apologetic tone. "I'm certain she meant your wife no harm."

"That's a damned lie and you know it!" Evan responded heatedly. He was furious with the willful Sheila for endangering his bride's safety.

Thinking that it might have been her own lack of experience rather than Sheila's carelessness which had presented the problem, however, Bianca attempted to soothe her husband's volatile temper. "I'm fine, Evan, truly I am, so you needn't make such an awful fuss. Thank you again, Nigel, for being so helpful. I'll look forward to seeing you again sometime soon." That she'd not included his sister's name in her good-bye was no oversight and she could tell by the width of Nigel's smile that he understood.

Pleased to find Bianca Sinclair so delightful a young woman, Nigel Blanchard bid her good day, and urging his mount into a brisk canter, he followed his sister's trail.

"I'll strangle that bitch if she ever tries to harm you again, even with a cross word!" Evan vowed hoarsely. "That was no accident, and you know it as well as I do. She was hoping you'd fall and be badly hurt."

That Sheila's pettiness had upset him so badly troubled Bianca, for it seemed likely she and Evan had been very close at one time when he had such strong feelings about her. Not wanting to get into the middle of an argument between her husband and the hostile young woman, however, she again tried to persuade him the matter was of no consequence. "I doubt it was an accident either, but I wasn't harmed. The next time we meet I'll be more cautious, and should we be on horseback I'll promptly dismount," she promised, her enchanting smile melting his anger.

Since Bianca could laugh at Sheila's jealousy, Evan felt foolish for continuing to be so angry about it. "You are a remarkable woman, my love, and I'll trust you to put Sheila in her place. Now, I've no reason to get back early. I just wanted to be alone with you. What did you and Nigel find so interesting to discuss?"

As he brought his horse back upon the trail, Bianca gave Moonbeam a slight nudge with her heels to set her in motion. She'd not admit to being curious about Charles since that was too likely to upset him. "He told me about the marvelous business opportunities in and around Hampton Roads. Actually, it was like talking with Paolo Sammarese, only the geography was different."

At the mention of Paolo's name, Evan's expression darkened to a menacing scowl. He'd taken an instant dislike to the arrogant Venetian, and he wished for the thousandth time that he'd found proof of the man's guilt and had punished him.

Alarmed by the sudden darkness of his mood, Bianca inquired sweetly, "Evan, what's wrong?"

"Nothing," he replied with a shrug. "I'm sorry. I should have asked if you've ridden long enough. Perhaps you'd like to return home."

Bianca was doing her best to become a proficient rider, determined that since Sheila was obviously highly skilled, she'd not quit just because she'd had a bad scare. "No, it's a lovely day, let's enjoy it."

"As you wish."

While they followed the riverbank Evan offered little in the way of conversation, for his mind was preoccupied with thoughts of Venice. It distressed him to know that Paolo Sammarese was still alive and well while his brother was dead, and by the time they returned home he knew there would be only one way to clear his mind of the memories which haunted him. As always, Bianca came into his arms with a passion so uniquely her own she swiftly turned the remainder of the afternoon into a glorious preview of paradise.

The scene at the Blanchard estate was a far different one, however. Nigel thought his sister's behavior unbelievably rude and stupid as well, and he lost no time in telling her so. "Sinclair seems perfectly happy with his little blonde wife, and you'll only make him all the more protective by threatening her life so recklessly. You'd be far more wise to cultivate Bianca's friendship." As I intend to do, Nigel thought.

Sheila's pretty features were contorted in a stubborn pout as she paced the parlor. "I'll never be that woman's friend, never! Evan was mine, everyone knew he was mine!" Suddenly she shrieked pitifully, "How could he have married someone else?"

Nigel poured a double shot of whiskey into a glass and made himself comfortable on the sofa. Then he let her rant and rave for a full half hour before he spoke again. She reminded him of their mother, a strikingly beautiful woman who had died far too young. Now that their father was also deceased, Nigel was doing his best to act as the head of the family, but Sheila made it impossible for him to enjoy that role at times.

"It seems everyone must have known Evan was 'yours' but the man himself. Just consider your options for a moment. If you pretend to be Bianca's friend, you will be able to see Evan frequently. Should there be any problems in their marriage, you'll be able to take swift advantage of them by appearing to be sympathetic to them both, while in reality you'll be doing your best to drive a wedge between them. If you continue to be so hostile toward Bianca, you'll never see Evan. Now which is the wisest choice?"

Sheila glared defiantly at her brother, fuming still. "Be nice to her? How can I possibly do that when the mere sight of them together makes me ill?"

"I liked your suggestion of a party," Nigel offered shrewdly. "That would be a good place to start."

"But you heard Evan refuse my offer to host a reception. He'll not change his mind either. You know he won't."

"That's true, he's every bit as stubborn as you are, sister dear, but if we gave a party simply to begin the social season, he'd have to come and bring his bride. If he didn't, your prediction of gossip about the young woman would prove all too true and he'd dare not risk that. I say we give a party a week from Saturday. Send out the invitations tomorrow."

An evil smile slowly curled Sheila's lips as she nodded slowly in agreement. "Brilliant, Nigel. That's absolutely brilliant. Can I count on you to stay sober for that evening, or is that too much to ask?"

Nigel rose to refill his glass. "I'll be sober; you needn't worry about me. That party is going to be too much fun to miss."

Evan was away the morning the Blanchards' invitation was delivered, and Bianca tapped the cream-colored envelope impatiently against her well-manicured nails, knowing precisely what it would contain without breaking the seal. While she had no admiration for Sheila, she knew the young woman was correct in predicting their absence from such a social gathering would cause considerable comment. She'd still not met Evan's mother, and perhaps due to her illness, none of Marion's friends had come to call. She had no idea who Evan's friends were since he never mentioned their names. Except for the members of their household, she'd been completely isolated since her arrival in Virginia. This was a sorry fact she could no longer ignore, yet she knew Evan wouldn't want to attend the Blanchards' party. She was certain he'd provide an excuse, and while she couldn't blame him when Sheila was so obnoxious, she was certain he had other friends who were nice people and whom she'd enjoy getting to know if she were just given the chance.

She'd been too passive, she realized. She'd waited for Evan to choose the time to introduce her to his mother and his friends, but surely that had been a mistake for he was much too preoccupied with his own problems to devote any more time to her amusement than he did. At the very least she should have insisted he escort her to church, and she doubted that his mother was so terribly ill she wouldn't survive a few minutes of her daughter-in-law's company. She'd been waiting for the woman to have a good day, but what if she never did? How long would Evan expect her to be content to live in her mother-in-law's house as a stranger? He was wonderfully attentive in the evenings, but his ships occupied his days while hers were spent in a home which was not even her own.

The invitation still clutched tightly in her hand, she walked out to the kitchen to speak with Viola about the noon meal. Since Lewis was away Bianca was aware that Mattie would be sent upstairs with a tray for Marion, and knowing her situation was unlikely to change unless she seized the initiative herself, she decided it was high time she did. "Viola, I'll take Mrs. Grey's lunch tray up to her. We need to have a little talk." Before the startled housekeeper could do more than gape, Bianca picked up the silver tray which had already been prepared and left the kitchen to return to the main house. She carried it carefully up the stairs and straight into Marion's bedroom as though it were her usual duty to serve her mother-in-law's meals.

"Good afternoon, I'm Bianca. How are you feeling today?"

Marion knew exactly who the attractive blonde was, but she had no interest in chatting with her. "Take that away, I'm not hungry," she ordered crossly.

"Whatever you wish," Bianca agreed politely. "May I bring you something else instead?" That Evan had his mother's golden brown eyes surprised her, for she'd believed her husband's unusual coloring to be unique. Marion's hair was hidden beneath a frilly lace cap, but she was certain it would still be a glossy auburn shade. In no hurry to leave, Bianca balanced the heavy tray on her left hip as she waited for the woman to reply.

"All I want is my son," Marion whispered sadly.

"Evan isn't home, but I'll tell him you asked for him the minute he returns."

"No!" Marion shrieked hoarsely. "I want to see Charles!"

"Charles is dead," Bianca reminded her calmly. "But I'll be happy to stay with you until your husband and Evan come home."

Momentarily distracted by her visitor's offer, the grief-stricken woman eyed Bianca suspiciously. "You are much too young for Evan," she finally announced.

Smiling at that opinion, Bianca disagreed. "He doesn't think so, and neither do I."

"Well I do!" Marion shouted. "Now get out of my room and stay out!" To emphasize that order, she grabbed the vase on her nightstand and hurled it toward her daughter-in-law who, burdened with the heavy tray, couldn't avoid being hit. The silver tray clattered to the floor, dishes shattering, as the vase struck Bianca in the upper arm, a sharp edge creating a long gash. The young woman's sleeve was soon soaked with the blood which ran down her arm and then began to drip off the fingers of her left hand. Horrified by that gory sight, she turned to flee but found Evan blocking the doorway.

"What in God's name are you doing in here?" he shouted to his wife. He looked in dismay at the food and flowers scattered upon the floor before he realized Bianca had been badly hurt. Without taking the time to reprimand his mother, he reached for his wife's hand and, yanking her along beside him, strode down the hall to her room. "Sit down!" he ordered sharply. He quickly removed her blood-soaked bodice and tossed it aside. "This cut's a bad one. How did it happen?"

Bianca watched as her husband tried to stem the flow of blood with pressure from his hands, but several minutes passed before he was successful. Her face was ashen, her whole body trembling from shock. "I thought if I took your mother's lunch up to her it would give us a chance to become acquainted. I didn't imagine that she would, well, that she would become so upset with me."

Evan swore under his breath. "I thought you understood that my mother is too ill to be disturbed. What did you say to upset her so?"

Feeling guilty, Bianca looked away, unwilling to answer that question.

"What did you say?" Evan asked once again.

"Nothing," Bianca lied. "I merely offered to stay with her until Lewis came home. She told me to get out but gave me no time to leave."

Disgusted because she'd not followed his orders where his mother was concerned, Evan nevertheless was too worried about her arm to scold her. He dropped his hands and stepped back. Noting that no more blood was seeping from the nasty wound, he turned away to rinse his hands at the washstand. "I'll have to go and ask Viola for some linen to use as a bandage. Sit still. I don't want that to start bleeding again."

Bianca nodded, her eyes filling with tears of anger rather than pain. "I was only trying to help, Evan. This is my home too, or at least I thought it was."

Although outraged because she'd brought such an injury on herself, Evan was moved by her sorrowful expression, and he leaned down to kiss her lips tenderly. "Just sit still. I'll be right back and we can discuss everything then."

When Evan returned with the clean linen, he was also holding the Blanchards' invitation, which he'd opened. "Did you tell my mother about this party?" he asked accusingly.

"Why no. I'd not even opened the envelope. I must have dropped it when I dropped the tray," Bianca explained nervously, certain he'd not take her to the party now.

Evan tossed the invitation on the bed as he began to tear the linen into narrow strips. "Well my mother is hysterical thanks to you, but I'm going to let Viola worry about her. That cut is long but not deep, and since the edges are clean if I bind it up tightly the scar will be slight. There's no point in sending for a physician. He'd make no better job of this. I've had plenty of practice in dressing wounds, unfortunately."

Bianca sat without murmuring a single complaint as her husband took care of her arm. He did seem to know what he was doing, but she reflected that the sleeves of her gowns would cover whatever scar she might have. The pain didn't disturb her half as much as the knowledge that her effort to meet her mother-in-law had ended so disastrously.

"I'm sorry," she finally whispered. "I thought I could do something to help. I've little to do here, and I was hoping your mother and I could become friends."

Evan tied the ends of the bandage in a knot, and after again washing his hands, he bent down to remove

Bianca's slippers. "I want you to take a nap, a long one. This whole unfortunate mess is better forgotten, but I want you to promise me you'll not try to speak with my mother again unless I am there with you. She is a wonderful woman, the best of mothers, but since she lost Charles, she's no longer herself and I'll not risk having you hurt again."

Bianca stood up so he could unhook her skirt and unlace her corset. Then picking up the Blanchards' envelope, she handed it to him before she lay down on the bed. "I didn't mention that invitation to her, really I didn't."

Evan read the handwritten note again quickly, then shoved it into his pocket. "The party's not until next weekend so you should be well enough by then to attend, but I want you to keep what happened today a secret. You must never tell anyone my mother attacked you."

"Of course I'd never tell, but are we really going to the Blanchards'?" Bianca asked excitedly, her joy clearly revealed in the sparkle of her pretty green eyes.

"We'll go. I'm sorry I've been so remiss in introducing you to my friends. They'll all love you, but none so dearly as I."

When Evan bent down to kiss her lips lightly, she reached up to hold his mouth to hers for a deep kiss which set his heart pounding with desire, and while Bianca spent the afternoon in bed as he'd intended, she wasn't alone.

Chapter XV

Lewis Grey was outraged when he learned what had taken place that afternoon. "Viola gave Marion so much laudanum she'll be asleep for days! How could you have allowed her to be so careless?"

Evan had no intention of admitting he'd been making love to his wife after he'd left Viola to tend to his mother. "Need I remind you Bianca got the worst of it? She'll stay away from Mother now, but she meant no harm by visiting her today."

"Don't you think I know that?" Lewis snapped angrily. "She is so sweet I did not doubt her motives; it is only that her presence here is damn awkward and something like this was bound to happen sooner or later. I dare not hope this will be the last time either."

Evan straightened up to his full height, giving himself the clear advantage in every respect. He'd offered to leave once, and was ready to make good on that threat now if Lewis didn't back down. "Bianca is my wife, and this is my home. If she is not welcome here, neither am I," he pointed out with fierce logic.

Lewis threw up his hands in disgust. "You see what she's done? She's put us all on edge. I never thought I'd ever hear you raise your voice to me, let alone threaten to move out, and it's all because of her."

"I'll raise more than my voice in another minute," Evan threatened hoarsely. "Mother's grief for Charles is an obsession which is consuming us all. God help me, but she'd be better off dead when she's so filled with hatred she'd hurt a gentle creature like Bianca, someone who's done nothing whatever to harm her."

"Nothing? Blast it all, Evan, your brother is dead because of her! That she's now your wife doesn't change that fact; it only makes it all the more painful!"

Rather than ram his fist into his stepfather's face, Evan left the parlor. He then strode out the front door and kept on walking until he reached the river. Taking the path leading toward town, he walked with his head down, his hands jammed deep in his pockets. He was so lost in thought he barely had time to leap out of the way as Sheila came riding around the bend in the trail. She quickly reined in her horse, as shocked to come upon him as he was to see her.

"Why, Evan, what a delightful surprise! I hope you were on your way to see us to accept our invitation." She greeted him excitedly, her pleasure at their chance meeting undisguised.

Evan was in no mood for company, especially hers. "We'll be there, of course. I might have known you'd find some excuse for a party even if it isn't to be a reception honoring us."

Sheila licked her lips slowly, hoping he'd remember how sweet her kisses had been. "Nonsense. Nigel and I had been discussing this party for weeks. I'm so happy you and your bride will be there. She's a lovely girl, Evan, truly she is; and I know everyone will like her as much as my brother and I do."

Evan doubted Sheila could possibly be sincere, but he had no desire to get into another argument that day. "My wife is remarkable in every respect, and I'm sure everyone will find her charming. I'll tell her you are looking forward to seeing her again. Now, if you'll excuse me, I must be getting back home."

"Wait!" Sheila tossed her dark hair as she called out to him. "Why don't you climb up behind me and we can ride double to your house. Do you remember how you used to carry me behind you?"

Evan scowled angrily, remembering that whenever he'd been foolish enough to allow her to ride double with him she'd used that as an excuse to put her hands all over him. He was angry with himself over the few times he'd been foolish enough to kiss her. Since he'd never cared for her demanding kind of affection, he felt he should have been wise enough not to respond to her, no matter how slightly. "No, thanks. I came out for a walk because I wanted the exercise. Good day to you." Evan waved as he turned away again, his long stride carrying him back toward his home at a brisk clip. At least his destination was clear, even if he still had no idea how to restore happiness to his family once he arrived there.

Sheila watched him until he was lost from view then she raced home, eager to tell her brother she'd found Evan Sinclair walking by himself down by the river.

"Do you believe he'd simply be out for a stroll? Have you ever known Evan to waste a minute of his time?"

"Never," Nigel agreed. "He must have had something on his mind that he wished to ponder it alone, or perhaps his reason for wandering about the countryside was nothing more than a desire to escape his wife's company. You see, I told you to bide your time. Just be pleasant whenever you meet him, and you may have another chance at Evan yet." Recalling Bianca's question, he mused thoughtfully. "I have never bothered to ask, but why did you always prefer Evan over Charles? Charles was more your type, really, far more fun loving and carefree."

"That's certainly true enough." Sheila was far too clever to admit how close she and Charles had actually been. That was a secret she'd never reveal. While Evan had always been her favorite, she'd enjoyed flirting with Charles too, and thinking she might one day have to settle for him, she didn't want him to suspect he'd been her second choice. Now he was dead, and Evan was married to another. "What a silly question. Isn't the reason for my choice obvious? Evan is the one with the wealth. Oh, I know Lewis Grey has some money, but Charles's inheritance would never have equaled Evan's fortune."

"I had no idea you were so practical, sister dear. Are you certain you'd not like to come to work for me at the bank?" That his sister had such a mercenary streak disgusted Nigel completely even though he knew her other faults well.

"Don't be ridiculous!" Sheila scoffed. "You do well enough for us both. Now I want you and your friends to keep Bianca occupied at our party so that I'll have a chance to talk with Evan alone. Can you manage that?"

"It will be a pleasure," Nigel assured her with a deep bow, his plans for the evening as selfish as hers.

"Evan, will William Summer be there tonight?" Bianca was dressed in an exquisite gown of pale blue satin. The Spanish lace which adorned the sleeves hid all trace of the long slash on her arm and as she turned in front of the full-length mirror she was very pleased with what she saw.

"I doubt it," Evan replied with a broad smile, for though he was not overly pleased to be attending the Blanchards' party, he was delighted to be escorting his lovely bride.

"But he's a captain now, doesn't that give him some status here in Newport News?"

"Of course it does, but Sheila and Nigel will never concern themselves with newly gained status when there is so much old wealth to consider."

"Is your wealth very old?" Bianca came forward to rest her fingertips upon his chest. He was dressed in a blue velvet coat elaborately embroidered with silver thread. His red vest was also embroidered with silver, and there were highly polished silver buttons where his red breeches ended at the calf. He wore white stockings and, rather than boots, black shoes with heavy silver buckles. The wide ruffles of his white shirt sleeves fell over the backs of his hands, but the elegance of his clothing enhanced his rugged masculinity rather than detracting from it.

"When he was a young man, my grandfather came from England as a bond servant so it's no older than that," Evan replied with a chuckle. "All we Sinclairs needed was the opportunity this country provided. We've done very well for ourselves."

"You certainly have," Bianca agreed, but her gaze grew distant as memories of her home overwhelmed her. "It is difficult in Venice to become wealthy if one isn't born into a fine family. The opportunities to improve one's lot are very few."

"Well, I'm certain if anyone wishes to know something of Venice tonight, it will not be how your society functions, but how you manage to make your way about in boats. That will intrigue people most."

"Really? I shall be happy to discuss travel by gondola for as long as they like." Bianca gave him a bewitching smile as she took his arm, eager for the evening to begin.

* * *

Sheila was also dressed in blue, and she regretted that choice the instant she saw Bianca come through the door. Pale blue complemented the blonde's delicate coloring far better than it did her own dark beauty. Aware of this, Sheila belatedly thought no matter how fashionable the color might be, she should have worn something more vivid.

"Smile," Nigel whispered softly. "Evan will never leave her side if he senses the least bit of hostility. You know how to be a gracious hostess, now do it." He left her then to greet their guests, his smile one of his most charming.

Evan was pleased to find that while all present were openly curious about his bride, she was so friendly in her manner they quickly forgot she was a stranger. When the dancing began, she was a popular partner, but despite the loving smiles she directed his way, he could not help feeling jealous. He didn't like sharing her with other men even for so little as a dance, yet he now realized he should have introduced her to his friends immediately since she enjoyed people so. He'd been very selfish, and he promised himself he'd never again get so involved in his own problems that he neglected her needs. She was far too lively a young woman to be content to sit at home waiting for him to arrive in the evening, and he was glad to see that the women present seemed to like her as well as the men did. Now if only his mother would. . . .

"Evan, why are you scowling like that?" Sheila took his arm and pressed close as she asked her question. "You used to love parties as greatly as I do."

Evan looked down at the dark-eyed young woman, amazed by the way she'd managed to wrap herself snugly around his arm in a matter of seconds. In more ways than one she reminded him of a serpent, and he began to laugh, his mood instantly a good one. "You would like the parties in Venice, Sheila. Before Lent they have elaborate costume balls which last until dawn. Perhaps one spring Bianca and I will give one."

For an instant Sheila was certain her brother was wrong, and being sweet to Evan and his bride wasn't going to get her anywhere, but when she realized he hadn't stepped back to avoid her touch, she thought perhaps Nigel may have been right. They continued to chat amicably as he told her about the lavish costumes worn in Venice, and greatly intrigued, she suggested they plan a masked ball before spring. "Why wait so long, Evan? It would be great fun to host such a fabulous party during the holidays. You've plenty of time to plan it and I hope you will."

Evan shook his head. "Bianca is the one who should do that, not me." He was grateful for Sheila's suggestion, for he knew how much Bianca would enjoy entertaining his friends. Nonetheless he was aware that his mother's delicate health would prevent any such gathering in his home in the near future. In many ways, his father's house was no longer the place for him and Bianca. He'd have to do something about that soon, but he'd not share those thoughts with his hostess. "This is a very enjoyable evening, Sheila. Thank you for inviting us," he said instead.

As Bianca glanced toward her husband she was shocked to find him and Sheila standing in so intimate a pose. What they were discussing she couldn't guess, but to see him talking so attentively with the stunning brunette both surprised and disappointed her. Nigel had said his sister had expected to marry Evan. Had her husband encouraged that hope? She turned back to her partner and tried to smile, but suddenly all the excitement had gone out of the dance.

Nigel had been watching Bianca all evening, waiting for the opportunity to make the most of their new friendship. He saw her frown as she glanced toward her husband and his sister, and smiled to himself. When the music ended he made certain he was close at hand so he might escort her off the dance floor. When he gave her a cup of punch from the bowl heavily laced with spirits, she made a face as she tasted it, but he only laughed. "Don't you like it? That's one of my favorite recipes, and our other guests seem to enjoy it."

"It is a bit strong, don't you think?" Bianca inquired politely. Wondering why Nigel Blanchard would wish to see her drunk, she set the cup aside, certain she'd want no more.

"I have brandy in my study, would you prefer that?"

"No thank you. I'm really not thirsty." She remarked absently, her eyes never leaving the raven-haired woman at her husband's side.

Since he'd obviously failed to impress her, Nigel took another tack. "I can not help but notice how interested you are in your husband. If you would prefer his company to mine, I'll be happy to escort you to his side."

Embarrassed to be so transparent in her emotions, Bianca was also sorry she'd hurt Nigel's feelings. Tapping his chest lightly with her fan, she hastened to disagree. "We are no longer newlyweds, Mr. Blanchard. You and your friends have all been so charming, I've had no time to worry that Evan might be lonely."

"Good, because nothing would please my sister more than to think you are jealous of her," Nigel advised her slyly, pretending to have her best interests in mind rather than Sheila's and his own.

"Jealous?" Bianca spread her fan coyly as she scoffed at that idea. Although she was seething with anger, she knew better than to display her true feelings in front of a roomful of strangers. She'd smile all evening, no matter how little she felt like doing so. "I've no reason to be jealous of your sister, or of anyone else."

"That's the spirit! Now if you'd like to dance again, I

would love to be your partner."

Since Evan still showed no sign of growing bored with Sheila, Bianca placed her hand on Nigel's sleeve, determined to make the best of an evening which certainly wasn't turning out to be as enjoyable as she'd hoped. "You have a lovely home, perfect for entertaining."

"Thank you. Don't you think Evan's home is equally well suited for it?" he remarked nonchalantly.

"I, that is, his mother has not been well so we've been unable to entertain as yet," Bianca admitted hesitantly, certain Marion's poor health was not a secret, even if the nature of her illness was.

Nigel seized upon that remark to make a suggestion he hoped would create considerable strife between Evan and his bride. "What a pity," he declared sympathetically, "that you do not have a home of your very own. Oh, I realize that house is Evan's rather than Lewis Grey's, but it's been his mother's and stepfather's home for so long I doubt he recalls that he owns it. Perhaps he does not know that Sarah Marshall passed away while he was gone. She was an elderly widow, childless, and left her property to her church, but they've asked me to try to sell it. The congregation needs funds rather than a house too far from town to serve as the rectory. It is a lovely place, not too distant from your present home. Would you like me to approach Evan about it?"

It took Bianca a moment to realize that Nigel was serious, but of course he'd be serious, she reminded herself, for he was discussing a business proposition. Although she tried not to let her feelings show, her delight at the prospect of having her own home was impossible to hide. "I don't believe my husband would appreciate such a suggestion from me, Mr. Blanchard."

"Please call me Nigel," he requested warmly. "I will be happy to approach him with the matter if you'd rather I did. Perhaps he'd be interested in the property simply as an investment."

"What you wish to discuss with my husband is your own business. If he is offered a piece of investment property I don't know whether he will be interested or not, but please do not mention my name if you do talk with Evan about it."

"In banking, Bianca, and in my personal dealings as well, you will find me wonderfully discreet," he assured her softly, his mouth so close to her ear his warm breath caressed her cheek.

Bianca was afraid the man had misunderstood her, but she wanted nothing to do with buying a house if it meant Nigel would expect favors from her in return for handling the matter. She was tempted to slap his face and then leave him standing alone in the middle of the dance floor. However, before she could voice an objection to his seductively worded promise, Evan was at her side, his expression shockingly fierce.

"I realize it will be hours yet before you run out of partners, my love, but I'd like to dance with you myself for a while." He dismissed Nigel Blanchard with no more than a curt nod and pulled her into his arms. He was a very fine dancer, so graceful he made the intricate steps she'd had difficulty following with Nigel seem simple, yet his manner had never been less charming. When the musicians had finished playing that number, he took her hand and led her off the floor.

"I thought you wished to dance," Bianca whispered softly, afraid he was angry with her and might create a scene. That was ridiculous of course, as she'd done nothing more than dance while he'd been flirting quite openly with Sheila.

Evan looked down into his bride's clear green eyes, but he saw neither conceit nor guilt in their luminous depths. Instead he recognized the sorrow in her expression, and confused by it, he drew her near as he lowered his voice to a husky whisper. "I think you've met everyone. I'm ready to go now if you are."

"I don't think we should be the first to leave, Evan. Since I am new, our departure would only spark gossip and I'd rather not inspire any if you don't mind." Actually she had no more interest in remaining at the party than he, and she stood stiffly at his side wondering how long such a gathering usually lasted.

Evan now felt he'd made a mistake in seeking out Bianca, but damn it all, he was tired of making aimless conversation with the other guests when he'd much rather be with her. She was so lovely he found it difficult to take his eyes off her, and he found it only natural that he preferred her company to that of the other women present. None of them had ever inspired the slightest bit of devotion in his heart, but she was his wife! He was so disappointed in her reaction to his suggestion they go home, he was tempted to just walk away, to try and ignore her until she finally decided they could safely leave without causing comment. Hell, he could walk home, and later she could return in his carriage. He thought of several alternatives, all equally insulting to his pretty bride, but he couldn't bring himself to actually choose one and carry it out.

After five minutes of the most awkward silence she'd ever endured, Bianca looked up at her husband and apologized. "That was silly of me, wasn't it? There's no reason for anyone to gossip about me so it shouldn't matter at what time we leave. If you're ready to go, I am too."

"Thank you," Evan offered tersely, uncertain whether he'd won that argument or not. Bianca's beauty and vivacious personality would always make her popular. Wherever he took her, her reception would be a warm one so he knew he might as well get used to that and cease to worry. She was his wife, and he knew without question she would never give him cause to regret marrying her. To act like a jealous ass was stupid and he was ashamed of himself for being so overbearing. "I've changed my mind, though. Come dance with me again." The music had just begun, a spirited piece danced in a large circle, each woman progressing to a new partner at the end of each chorus. Bianca looked back toward him frequently, her glance questioning, but he smiled and winked, determined they'd have as good a time as everyone else that evening.

Sheila came up to her brother, her voice a vicious whisper as she complained to him. "Just look at them! Have you ever seen a more disgustingly happy couple? They make me sick!"

Nigel turned his back to the dancers so he'd not be overheard. "Just be patient. They'll soon be at each other's throats, I'm sure of it." If he failed to create a sufficient amount of discord over the Marshall property, he'd simply move on to something else. He was certain he could spark an argument between Bianca and Evan eventually; then he'd need only fan the flames. "Patience, Sheila, is a virtue you simply must cultivate."

Before she could tell her brother just what she thought of such advice, they were joined by two of his friends and the opportunity was lost. But she reflected that she'd been too patient where Evan was concerned and she'd not make that same mistake twice.

By the time they reached home, Bianca was so confused she didn't know what to make of her husband's behavior. He'd danced with every woman at the party, shared jokes with all the men, and had ended the evening in such high spirits she wondered why she'd ever thought of him as being too reserved to enjoy parties. They'd been one of the last couples to leave too, a fact which had forced her to hide her repeated yawns behind her fan.

Had the musicians not insisted they could play no longer, she feared she might have fallen asleep standing up. It had been a wonderful party, and she had been sincere in her praise when she'd bid Sheila and Nigel good night. However, she truly didn't know what to expect from her husband now that the hour was so late.

Evan's plans were quite definite, however, and he followed Bianca into her bedroom, tossing his clothing this way and that as he pulled it off. When she came forward to pick it up, however, he reached down to do it himself. "I'd tell you to leave these things until morning, but I can see you'd not do it."

"That suit is far too handsome to be laying on the floor, Evan." Bianca smiled as she scolded him, wondering what had made him so careless, but when he grabbed her around the waist and drew her near she understood.

"The next time we are invited to a party, I will make love to you all afternoon before we go. Then I won't suffer as badly as I did tonight." He covered her face with lavish kisses before finally capturing her mouth in a far more intense display of affection, and plucking the pins from her hair, he ran his fingers through her golden curls, his hunger for her love unrestrained now that they were alone. Realizing she would never be able to disrobe in such a tight embrace, he stepped back so she might slip off her gown, but when she moved slowly in order not to damage the new satin dress he could barely stand the delay. No woman had ever set his blood aflame as she continually did, and the second she tossed her blue gown across a chair he spun her around to unlace her corset, his hands shaking he was so eager to possess her.

"Evan!" Bianca giggled excitedly, thinking his haste greatly amusing. "Stop and take a deep breath, or I'm afraid you'll tear my lingerie."

"I'll buy you more," Evan vowed hoarsely, but he took

care not to rip her delicate undergarments as he stripped her slender figure bare. He bent down to kiss the fullness of her breasts, and finding her perfumed skin delicious, he dropped to his knees, his hands holding her tightly around the waist so she'd not escape his deep searching kisses as his probing tongue forced her thighs apart so he could savor the uniqueness of her femininity more fully.

A willing captive in his exotic embrace, Bianca slipped her fingers through Evan's glossy auburn curls, freeing them of the confining ribbon at his nape. She leaned against him then, lost in the warmth of his affection. He knew so many wonderful ways to give pleasure, and she enjoyed them all. Her whole body came alive with tiny tremors of delight, which made him all the more eager to please her. Only when she thought she would surely faint from the joy of his loving did he carry her to the bed to finish what he'd begun, and as the fiery heat of her passion enveloped him he was as lost in pleasure as she. Their motions were perfectly timed, rushing them toward the peak of rapture, where they remained suspended for what seemed like an eternity before drifting slowly back to reality.

Bianca hugged her husband tightly as she whispered in his ear. "Just when I think our love can never be more complete, you bring us closer still."

Evan's kiss was no less hungry now. He adored his wife and would never have enough of the love she lavished upon him so unsparingly, but their closeness was shattered by a piercing shriek which echoed down the hall like the wail of a banshee. Badly frightened Bianca clutched the sheet to her bosom as Evan leapt from the bed and hastily pulled on his breeches. "Is that your mother?" she asked shakily.

"I'm afraid so. I hope it is no more than a nightmare, but if Lewis needs help I should be there to give it. You just go to sleep."

Bianca didn't argue as Evan sped from the room, but she knew she'd never be able to fall asleep after such a terrible fright and she was much too curious to remain in bed. After waiting a few minutes, she got up and tiptoed down the hall. Being smart enough not to intrude, however, she stayed hidden in the shadows outside her mother-in-law's door. She could hear Marion weeping, then voices she recognized as belonging to Lewis and Evan, but what they were saying she couldn't quite catch. Surely they were only trying to calm the distraught woman so they'd all be able to sleep, she thought, and ashamed of herself for trying to eavesdrop, she returned to bed, hoping her husband would soon join her.

Nearly an hour passed before Evan returned to Bianca's room. Grateful to find her still awake, he tossed his breeches aside and, climbing into bed, pulled her into a close embrace. But as his fingertips moved slowly down the silken smoothness of her arm he felt the new scar, and saddened by it, he drew away. His features were a mask of sorrow as he explained, "I wanted you to be happy here, to know only the joy of my loving, not to find pain." As his lips traced the length of the thin scar lightly, he wished his kiss could make it fade.

They had not talked about his mother since the dreadful day Bianca had met the woman, and she knew instinctively that Evan did not want to talk about her now. Whether Marion had had a nightmare, or had become hysterical really didn't matter. What Evan was talking about was the love they shared and the life he'd hoped to give her. "I am happy with you, Evan, truly I am."

How she could possibly be happy when the whole house was continually in turmoil due to the depth of his mother's grief Evan didn't know. It was no longer a home, but an asylum. Suddenly he wanted desperately to take her away, and his voice was filled with excitement as he said, "Let's go up the river to Richmond for a few days, just get away from this house. What do you say? Let's go tomorrow."

"Can you leave on such short notice? I know you've been very busy at the shipyard and—"

"The shipyard functions quite well without me being there, and if it didn't I wouldn't care. I just want to get away. Please say you'll come with me."

Bianca lifted her arms to encircle his neck, as eager for his deep kisses as he was to give them. She was far too wise to think they would find anything changed when they returned home, but she wanted too greatly to please him to say no. Sensing her acceptance in her kiss, Evan shifted his position, bringing them together in one graceful motion. He moved slowly, deliberately creating the sweetest of tensions until he felt the ecstasy of their union shudder deep within his slender bride. Having pleased her, he buried his face in her tangled curls, and let the beauty of her boundless love flood his powerful body with pleasure and fill his tormented mind with peace.

Chapter XVI

William Summer read through the list of duties he'd been given. When Evan had appeared at his door, he'd been afraid it was to announce a voyage. He was so relieved to find he wouldn't have to leave Lily alone, he'd quickly agreed to performing a few favors. His friend had spent no more than ten minutes telling him what had to be done in his absence, and although Will would have been happy to take care of it all without pay, Evan had insisted upon rewarding him handsomely for his time. Will was to check with Lewis each day to see if there was any service he might perform. The next item on the list involved contacting the foreman at the shipyard occasionally. Should an emergency of any sort arise he was to send for Evan immediately. Then there were the families Evan supported. Will had known about Tim's mother, of course, but the lad was now in school and Evan wanted a report on his progress. As for the other widows whose names and addresses he'd been given, Will was to visit them and see that their expenses were paid, but that would take no more than half a day to accomplish. Actually the chores would provide more of a diversion than work, and Will looked forward to them.

Lily peeked through the door to be certain Will's visitor had left. "Are you alone?" she inquired softly.

"Yes, come in. You needn't have hidden like that, Lily. I'd gladly have introduced you to Evan Sinclair. He's my good friend as well as my employer."

Lily had been certain Will would be embarrassed by her presence in his room, but she kept that to herself. She crossed to the window and looked out, hoping to see Evan as he left the hotel. "Is he the well-dressed gentleman across the way? The tall one with the reddish hair?"

Will quickly moved to her side, and finding she'd spotted his friend, he agreed. "Yes, that's Evan." Seeing the admiration in her glance, he felt a bitter pang of jealousy for Sinclair was not only handsome, but rich as well. He was also quite happily married, Will reminded himself, and ashamed of his thoughts, he made his tone casual as he explained, "He married a young woman he met while we were in Venice, and now he wants to show her something of Virginia. He's asked me to take care of a few things for him while they're away."

"Will you have to leave Newport News too?" the slender blonde asked apprehensively. Her greatest fear was that at any moment Will would come to his senses and send her packing.

"No. All the tasks involve Evan's interests here." Will saw the relief in Lily's eyes, and he hastened to reassure her. "Look, if ever I am called out of town I'll not leave you stranded here at River's End. I'll see that you have sufficient funds to cover your expenses while I'm away."

Money had not been the cause of her concern, however. It had derived from her growing regard for him. She would miss him terribly were he to leave her, even for a day. She turned away, disappointed that he thought her expenses were more important to her than his company. "What sort of woman did your friend marry? You said you weren't in Venice long, how could he have had time to fall in love?"

Finding that question impossible to answer with the truth, Will laughed rather than reveal Evan's actual motives. "Surely love is not something which can be measured in hours, Lily. Bianca is very lovely, a lady any man would be proud to call his wife."

"That's nice," Lily remarked absently, trying desperately not to think that the life she'd led had left her totally unfit for marriage.

While Will knew his companion seldom pursued any topic in depth, he was surprised that she'd lost interest in talking about love so quickly. "Evan asked me to run some errands. Get your cloak and come with me. It's a pretty day for a walk."

They often went out for a stroll in the evening, but Lily was reluctant to appear on the street with him in broad daylight. "Why don't you go on by yourself? I'd just be in your way," she said graciously, certain that's what he'd really prefer.

"Just what have you got to do that's so important you don't have the time to come with me?" Will asked impatiently, upset because she'd not thought his idea a good one.

"Nothing really," Lily admitted reluctantly. "I just thought you'd rather go alone."

"Well, I wouldn't. Now fetch your cloak and let's go." As they left the hotel, he took her left hand and placed it upon his arm. "We needn't stop by the shipyard or Lewis Grey's warehouse today, but we can visit the widows Evan supports and make certain they have no problems which require his attention."

"Widows? Of what concern are such women to him?" Lily asked curiously.

"I suppose it does seem like a strange interest, but it's not so unusual for a wealthy man to look after others who are less fortunate. I told you we fought together during the war. Evan looks after the widows and orphans of the men who were killed while serving aboard the *Phoenix*."

Deeply touched by such kindness, Lily was unable to suppress the tears that came to her eyes so she turned away, pretending an interest in the merchandise displayed in the shop windows they passed instead of commenting upon Evan's generosity. However, she was often quiet in Will's company, and he did not complain about her silence as they strolled along in the sunshine. She tried not to notice the curious glances directed her way, but she recognized more than one man she'd known at Fanny Burke's. Horribly embarrassed by those memories, she wished Will had allowed her to remain back at the hotel.

The darkness of Lily's mood wasn't lost on Will, and he rightly guessed its cause. A few of the men they'd passed had obviously been surprised to see her; several others had averted their eyes quickly as though they were afraid she might speak to them. He knew quite well what Lily had been, but until that very instant he'd not realized escorting her about in public would cause such a stir. He'd been at sea too many years to worry about what the citizens of Newport News thought about him. That city was only a tiny portion of the world, and he'd seen too many exciting places to care what a few farmers thought of his woman. Suddenly he chuckled for he knew why the men they passed appeared to be so nervous. They were the ones who couldn't afford to have their lives touched by scandal, while he had no such concern.

The first home they visited was a noisy place filled with small children. Their mother, a good-natured woman, invited Will and Lily in for tea, and chatted easily with them while they sipped it. Timothy's mother was far more reserved, but the boy had done well in school and she was pleased to be able to send that news to Evan. By the time they'd visited all the homes on the list they were both tired. The day was far too fine to return to the hotel, however, so taking Lily's hand, Will led her down to the river. When they came to a peaceful spot a good distance from town, he sat on the grass and pulled her down beside him with a playful tug.

"That wasn't such a terrible ordeal, was it?" he asked with an easy grin. "I'm sure a couple of the women were disappointed to see us rather than Evan, but none of them seems to have any great difficulty at present."

"But Mr. Sinclair wouldn't fail to help them if they had some sort of problem?" Lily asked, wonder in her voice.

"Of course not, he works very hard to earn his money, but he is generous with it, not miserly. When I become successful, I hope I'll remember his example."

"I think you're successful now, Will," Lily remarked sweetly. "You are captain of a fine ship, doesn't that make you proud?" He'd given her a tour of the *Phoenix*, and she'd thought it the most magnificent ship afloat.

"Yes, it does," Will admitted. "All I ever wanted to do was go to sea. It never occurred to me I'd become a captain one day, but Evan made certain I was prepared for the job."

"He sounds like a wonderful friend. How long will he be away?"

"A couple of weeks." Will stretched out on his back to enjoy the softness of the grass more fully. He was in a lazy mood, and thought perhaps they'd stay by the river's edge all afternoon.

Lily held her breath, she wanted to know how much longer she could expect him to be in Newport News, but she was afraid of what his answer might be. "Do you think you might be leaving when he returns?" she asked in a breathless whisper.

"A voyage to the Caribbean is a possibility, but that's a brief trip. We'll not be going back to Europe so late in the year. Why?"

"I just wondered." Lily hugged her knees, grateful that he had no plans to leave in the near future. She'd failed miserably in her attempt to think only of the security he provided. Each day his kindness touched her more deeply, and while she knew it was an impossible dream, she couldn't help but hope he'd never tire of her company. She'd be hurt when he left her, badly. She knew it was stupid to care for a man, any man, not just one as dear as Will, but she'd not been able to help herself in his case.

"Lily?" Will had frequently tried to encourage the young woman to tell him about her past, and today their mood was such a relaxed one he hoped he might, at last, be successful. "I've long wondered about something too."

"About what?" Lily asked nonchalantly.

"I want to know how you came to be working for Fanny Burke. You know I won't criticize you for it, I'd just like to know why."

"What difference does it make?" Lily responded sullenly. "I'm not working for her anymore."

Will looked up at the pattern of clouds passing by overhead and tried not to sound overly curious. "You're a pretty girl, a very nice one too, although you try to hide it by acting tough. I simply don't understand why you would have chosen such a life and I wish you'd tell me why you did."

Lily laughed at the irony of his words. "It wasn't my choice, Will. The truth is, I had no choice about it."

"But you must have!" Will insisted.

Lily just shook her head and remained silent. When several minutes had passed, during which Will had made no effort to coax her into telling him about herself, she glanced over at him. Seeing by his befuddled expression that she'd simply hurt and confused him, she decided perhaps he did have a right to know something more about her. "I grew up in North Carolina, in a little town on the coast, the name of it doesn't matter. It wasn't all that different from Newport News. Some men earned their living by being farmers, some as merchants. Others went to sea. The war was no harder on us than on others."

Will sat up, certain that since Lily had finally decided to tell him something about herself the tale deserved his full attention. He leaned forward slightly and took her hand to lend her the courage he sensed she'd need.

"My father owned a tavern, a rowdy place which catered to sailors as well as men from town. While he expected me to wait on tables, he let everyone who walked in the front door know I was his daughter and he'd allow no disrespect. He was very strict, jealous too, although my mother never gave him any cause. He criticized her constantly and always had his eye on me as if he knew I'd disgrace him the first chance I got." Lily withdrew her hand from Will's to wipe a tear from the corner of her eye. "There was a boy I liked real well, a farmer's son. His name was David, and he was different from the rest. He'd bring me flowers, sometimes write me sweet little poems. He wanted to marry me, but my father said he wasn't good enough for me, that he lacked ambition." Lily hesitated a long while before speaking again, her story clearly a difficult one to tell. "My father caught us together one afternoon. He beat David something awful; then he started on me. He called me a whore and grabbed my hair so I couldn't get away while he hit me. He's the one who broke my tooth."

Will began to swear, unable to understand how Lily's own father could have abused her so cruelly. He pulled her into his arms and hugged her tightly, furious that he'd not been there to protect her. "It's all right, Lily. I understand now."

Lily pulled away from his embrace as she disagreed. "No you don't." She began to sob pathetically then, the horror of her memories almost too great to bear. "When finally he grew tired of beating us, he threw what was left of me in the back of the wagon and took me to a whorehouse on the edge of town. He told the madam that was where I belonged, and she was kind enough to take me in to save me from him. When I was well enough to work, she dressed me up like a little girl so men would pay more for me." Lily's gaze was bright with tears as she asked defiantly, "Now do you still think I had a choice about my life?"

Her story had sickened Will, but thinking solely of Lily's anguish, he pulled her back into his arms and kissed away her tears until she at last grew calm. "You heard nothing from your mother, or David?" he finally asked. "Neither came to get you?"

"My mother was too terrified to try to save me. She thought my father would do the same thing to her if she defied him. David came to see me once, but he paid just like everyone else. He didn't even talk to me, let alone say he loved me, so I guess my dad was right about him being weak. That was when I decided it was time to move on. I've been in half a dozen places just like Fanny Burke's, and the men were all the same."

"Lily, I don't want to hear anymore." Will covered her damp cheeks with kisses, his pain as great as hers. He knew she'd been treated horribly by men, and that knowledge tore his very soul in two. The spot he'd chosen for them was secluded so when Lily's response was the predictable one, he didn't push her hands away. Wanting her too badly to explain that she need not repay his sympathy in such an intimate fashion, he shoved her skirts and petticoats aside so he might take her swiftly. Yet, as always, his need was tempered by the tenderness which filled his heart.

Lily clung to her lover with savage abandon, for only with him did she allow herself the freedom to accept the love he was so eager to give. The power of her long-suppressed emotions swirled within her, taking her swiftly to the shattering climax which left her languidly resting in his embrace, sated by pleasure, cleansed by tears. He had taught her more than the most imaginative of madams ever had, but she knew his fascination with her wouldn't last. It couldn't, not when he was so fine a man and she was no more than trash her father had thrown out.

The beauty of the autumn day filled Evan with hope and he brought Bianca's fingertips to his lips for a playful nibble. "We'll spend the night at an inn in Williamsburg, several nights if you like. I have acquaintances there who'll be delighted to entertain us even though I've given them no notice of our arrival."

Bianca had not thought leaving his home could make such a difference in her mood, but her spirits were as high as her husband's. Their luggage had been loaded in the carriage by the time he'd returned from town and the vehicle's slow rocking motion provided so comforting a rhythm her thoughts rapidly became romantic. "I'd rather simply be alone with you, Evan. Would your friends be insulted if we did not call on them?"

A sly smile curved across Evan's lips as he contemplated the full import of her question. "We've not had a real honeymoon yet, have we?" While their display of affection had been lavish on the voyage home, his mind had been so frequently occupied with plotting revenge that his mood had often been too dark for his company to have been truly enjoyable. Now he wanted to devote himself fully to giving her pleasure. The golden gleam of his eyes held a taunting fire as his glance traveled slowly over her delicate features before straying to the swell of her bosom. His mother's dressmaker was a talented woman who'd supplied a new wardrobe as stunning as Bianca's Venetian garb had been. For travel she'd chosen a simple dress of light gray linsey-woolsey, but the pretty blush in her cheeks provided all she needed in the way of color.

"I disagree, I think we've had a perpetual honeymoon." Bianca reached out to touch Evan's cheek with a fond caress. "At least you've always made me feel loved, and I hope you'll never doubt my affection for you."

While her words brought a stab of guilt, Evan refused to give in to it. He'd wanted only to make her *feel* loved in the beginning, but when had the ruse become reality? When had the lure of her beauty been surpassed by the need to capture her heart? He did not know. Do you love her? Will had asked that question once. Evan could no longer recall his reply, but he knew it had not been yes. Her lips were far too inviting to resist, and he leaned over to kiss her gently. "I love you, Bianca. With all my heart and soul, I love you."

Delighted by his words, the blonde beauty threw her arms around his neck to return his kiss with a far more enthusiastic one of her own. His fingertips moved tenderly over her breast, and she was sorry they were in his carriage rather than her bed. When at last she could bear to draw away, she asked in a teasing whisper, "Is this road frequently traveled, or may we assume it will be deserted save for us?"

"I have ridden upon it many times and not passed another soul for hours. Were you hoping for company to help while away the time?" Despite his words, Evan was certain he knew exactly what she had in mind.

"The only company I crave is yours, sir." Bianca reached for the hooks on her bodice, her motions deliberately enticing. "This gown is a trifle warm. Do you mind if I loosen it a bit?"

"Not at all," Evan replied with a chuckle, thinking again he was the luckiest of men to have found such an affectionate bride. "In fact, I find the weather rather warm myself." He removed his coat, and began to unbutton his shirt with one hand while he kept his eyes upon her. He knew the smoothness of her creamy complexion extended down her throat and over her breasts to the softness of her stomach, the curve of her hip, the elegant line of her legs, all the way to the pink tips of her toes. Had her figure been carved in ivory by a master it could be no more perfect, and lost in her exquisite beauty, he pulled her into his arms, his dream of love happily within his grasp.

They were a nimble couple with few inhibitions, and despite the close confines of the carriage, they found the lack of space an exhilarating rather than an insurmountable problem. Once their clothes were tossed aside Evan pulled Bianca astride him, eagerly enfolding her in a tight embrace. His hips rose to meet hers as she moved upon him with lively grace, forcing his thrusts deep within her until he could no longer hold back the raging ecstasy of his passion and it exploded from deep within him, filling her again with his seed. He twisted his fingers in her golden curls to force her head down upon his shoulder so he could enjoy their closeness in perfect peace, not once recalling the terrible tragedy which had prompted him to marry this vibrant creature he loved so dearly and made love to so often.

It was nightfall by the time they reached the outskirts of Williamsburg, but Evan knew the city well and directed their driver to his favorite inn, the Ralegh Tavern, where the proprietor provided a gracious welcome, a hearty meal, and several jugs of flavorful wine. In a lazy mood, they retired early, but it was a long while before they fell asleep.

Awakening before Evan, Bianca lay snuggled against him, too content to rise. She propped her head on her hand and, in that comfortable pose, watched him sleep, fascinated as always by the handsomeness of his auburn hair and finely drawn features. If anything she thought him even better looking than when they'd met, for now he meant so very much more to her. When he at last opened his golden brown eyes, she leaned down to give him a light kiss upon the cheek. At home he was always the first one awake, and she thought perhaps it was the strangeness of their surroundings which had made her so restless. "Good morning, husband. What would you like to do today?"

Evan caught her in a joyous hug. "Exactly what we did yesterday," he replied with a hearty chuckle. "That was a perfect day."

His enthusiasm was delightful, and Bianca did not pull away but rested languidly in his arms. "Can we just keep on going, Evan? Travel all the way to Maryland, and then keep on going if we like?"

Evan frowned slightly as he leaned back to look down at his lovely bride. At times she still had an innocence which completely concealed the wonderfully passionate nature he knew her to possess. "What is it you really wish to do? Travel, or merely keep me amused in the carriage?"

"Can't I do both?" Bianca asked coyly.

"I don't mind the carriage for a short trip such as the one we made yesterday, but if you really wish to see more of the country, I'd prefer to sail up the coast and put in at the major ports. That would be far more swift, and much more comfortable."

Bianca readily agreed. "I see. But we could be away for months. Can you afford to take an extended vacation now?"

"Not really, but if that is what you want to do, we'll do it," Evan promised agreeably.

Bianca thought a moment, then shook her head. "No. This is holiday enough. Now tell me something more of Williamsburg while I dress."

Evan pretended scant interest in her activities, but as always he was fascinated by the easy grace which made each of her motions as enchanting to observe as the steps of the most intricate dance. "I told you about Jamestown. When that city was destroyed by fire in 1699 the colonial capital was moved here. It was moved again to Richmond in 1780, but Williamsburg is still a flourishing community even if it is not one of the major trading centers. The plantations in this region raise tobacco. It's a profitable crop, and the landowners can afford to come here to buy items they can't make on their own. The College of William and Mary is here. It was founded in 1693, and provides a fine education. As for the town, it is a lovely one, in which most of the buildings are made of brightly painted wood rather than brick. We can just stroll around this morning, and if you see anything you like I'll be happy to buy it for you."

"Anything?" Bianca asked with a seductive glance.

"Yes, anything. Is there something in particular you'd like to have?"

Bianca brushed the tangles from her long curls as she gave that question some serious thought. "Do they have perfume here?"

"Of course. It's imported from France as I recall."

"Why, Evan, when did you ever have reason to purchase perfume? Was it a gift for a lady?"

"Yes," Evan admitted with a sly grin. "But I've completely forgotten who she was."

Bianca turned toward the bed. Clad only in her lace-trimmed chemise, she didn't realize that the early morning sunlight streaming in through the windows outlined the lush curves of her slender figure with a provocative splendor. "I hope that she stays forgotten."

Evan barely heard that remark; he was so entranced by his wife's beauty. He extended his hand to draw her near as he called her name softly. "Bianca. Come here please."

His young wife hesitated a moment, mystified by his sudden change of mood for she had merely been teasing. Since he was so handsome a man, he'd undoubtedly courted many lovely young women before meeting her. She was the one he'd married, however, and that was all that mattered to her. She smiled as she came forward to take his hand, certain that whatever he requested, she'd be happy to grant it. "Yes, my love?"

Now that her hand rested lightly in his, Evan was uncertain what he'd wanted to say other than how deeply he loved her. She was as bewitching in her beauty as the magnificent fall day promised to be, for she was also an example of the perfection only the brilliance of nature can create. "I've not been much of a husband to you thus far, Bianca. First it was the strain of a long voyage, then the problems I encountered at home: my mother's illness and the resistance to my ideas at the shipyard. I've allowed too many things to distract me when your love is all I really want, all I'll ever need, to be happy. I'll promise you now not to neglect you again."

"Evan, when have you ever neglected me?" Bianca inquired with a mystified glance. It was true his mood was often a solemn one, but he never failed to provide love in abundance each and every night. She climbed up on the bed and curled up beside him. "My father had many interests. He was always involved in one intrigue or another, some related to business and others purely political. Yet at night, when we were all together, he gave my mother and me his full attention, so no matter how busy his day might have been, we never felt neglected. You are just as thoughtful a man. When we are together you give me not only your undivided attention, but your love as well. I do not expect you to spend all your time with me. I'd never ask that. All I ask is that the hours we share are the best they can be."

At the mention of her father a tight hard knot formed in Evan's throat, and only by great effort was he able to force it away. He drew Bianca close, desperate to feel the sweetness of her lissome body. He had to forget the tragedy which had brought her to him; he had to or he'd soon be as consumed with hatred as his mother. "I love you, Bianca," he whispered hoarsely. "God, how I love you."

While she understood the sudden darkness of his mood no better than before, Bianca returned Evan's eager kisses without questioning his motives. She loved him too dearly to wonder what had inspired this sudden burst of passion when she wanted only to enjoy it.

It was nearly noon by the time the handsome young couple left the inn to stroll down the wide main street named for the Duke of Gloucester. With the college at the west end of the boulevard and the Capitol at the east, there was an imposing view in either direction. Since Lewis Grey owned a shop there, Evan took Bianca to that one first, and when he escorted her through the door, they were welcomed enthusiastically by an elegantly dressed woman in her early thirties who rushed forward to greet them.

"Mr. Sinclair, what a wonderful surprise. It has been more than a year since you were last in Williamsburg."

Since the woman's interest in her husband seemed a bit too keen, Bianca gripped his arm more tightly as she wondered what his relationship to her had been. It was not surprising that he'd be recognized in a shop owned by his stepfather, but that he'd be welcomed with such unabashed delight shocked her.

"I believe you're right, Mrs. Maguire, but it looks as though things are still going very well here. I wanted my wife to see the town, and of course we'd not pass by your shop without dropping in to say hello."

"Your wife?" Rachel Maguire had barely noticed the blonde at his side, but Bianca had her rapt attention now. "How do you do, Mrs. Sinclair," she managed to say, but her smile was faint.

"I'm very well, thank you, Mrs. Maguire," Bianca replied politely, and since there was something she wished to buy she saw no reason to try to make polite conversation. "My husband told me you carried French perfume. May I see your selection please?"

"Of course." Rachel gestured toward the counter as she looked up at Evan with a quizzical glance. She'd not thought he'd ever marry. That he had wed so young and charming a creature as this lovely blonde surprised her all the more.

Evan immediately sensed the tension between the two women and tried to hide his smile. Rachel was a widow, and although she was a very attractive one, he never combined his stepfather's business with his own pleasure. He knew her slightly, that was true, but only in her capacity as manager of this shop. As Bianca sampled the various scents, he lounged against the counter, and when she placed a drop of one on her wrists he reached out to catch her hand so he could judge its fragrance for himself. "This one is very nice."

"We'll take it then, Mrs. Maguire," Bianca declared. Then she spent another half-hour looking at the merchandise before she was ready to leave. Everything was appealing, imported and expensive; yet several other customers came in to make purchases so it appeared to be a thriving business as well as a fashionable shop.

When they were on the walkway, she again took Evan's arm. "Are all of Lewis' shops as popular as that one appears to be?"

"Yes, they all do well since he provides quality goods at fair prices. I should really have taken you to his warehouse though. It doesn't have the showcases or friendly clerks, but it contains all the items he sells. I'm sorry I didn't do that, Bianca."

"There's nothing I lack, Evan." Seeing that his expression was again downcast as though he'd failed her in some important way, she went on. "You provided me with a complete new wardrobe. Truly, a small bottle of perfume is all I needed, and now I have that." When he began to smile, she hugged his arm with an affectionate squeeze. "Mrs. Maguire seemed very disappointed to hear I was your wife. I can't imagine why."

When Bianca raised an overly innocent gaze to his, Evan burst out laughing. "I can't imagine why either except for a widow's natural interest in a wealthy man. You'll forgive her that, won't you?"

"Is that all I should forgive?" His lovely blonde wife asked in a teasing whisper.

Evan nodded. "That's all."

"Good." Certain he was telling her the truth, Bianca turned her attention to the well-dressed people on the street. She'd seldom had the opportunity to shop since she'd left home, and suddenly she longed for the familiar sights of Venice. Williamsburg was a charming place, Evan's description had been accurate, but there were no canals, no sleek gondolas to take them where they wished to go. Suddenly the awareness that she would never again see her dear parents was too much to bear. She was a stranger in a foreign land, and despite the excitement of being with her handsome husband in such an enchanting place, she longed for the exotic sights of the home to which she'd never return.

When they reached a shop owned by a fine jeweler, Evan stopped abruptly. "Bianca, I have never bought you a ring!" he declared. She had brought her own jewelry with her and wore it often so her fingers were seldom unadorned, but he'd not until that very moment realized he'd still not provided her with a wedding ring. "Let's see what this fellow has to offer."

His enthusiasm so brightened her mood that Bianca reached up to kiss his cheek lightly. "You are so dear, Evan, but please, the ring need only be a simple one."

Evan shook his head. "Let's not argue, my love. You'll wear what I buy you and that will be that." He quickly ushered her through the door, introduced himself, and asked to see an emerald ring since he wanted jewels to match the vivid hue of Bianca's eyes. The proprietor was wise enough to know a wealthy man when he saw one, and he opened his safe to display his most expensive wares. He had a few emeralds already set, and other stones they might choose from as well.

Bianca eyed the glittering jewels, certain they must be very costly. She thought one ring far prettier than the rest. It held a sparkling deep green stone surrounded by small diamonds. "May I try on this one please?" The instant Evan had slipped it on her finger, she knew it was the one she wanted, but didn't wish to appear extravagant in her tastes. "What do you think of this one?" she asked shyly.

"I think it was made just for your hand. It's by far the prettiest ring too." Evan waited a moment until he was certain she'd not change her mind. "We'll take that one please."

The balding jeweler was so delighted to have made such a wonderful sale that he nearly sang as he asked if there was anything else the couple might like to see, but Evan assured him the ring was all they needed for the moment. As they left the shop, he slipped his arm around

Bianca's narrow waist and pulled her close. "I don't know how I could have forgotten so important an item as your ring. The next time I make such a stupid error, tell me about it."

"I have given the matter no thought myself, Evan You needn't apologize any further." She held her left hand out so the sparkling stones of her new ring would reflect the sun's fiery light. "This is lovely. Thank you."

"You are very welcome." Before Evan could take another step, he heard someone call his name. He turned and saw a heavyset man racing down the walk, waving and yelling as he hurried to overtake them. "It's Tom Nicholson, and there will be no escaping him." He whispered softly, but his smile let her know he wasn't too annoyed.

"I was just speaking to Rachel Maguire, and when she mentioned you were in town I hoped I'd be able to find you." Tom took several deep breaths before continuing in an excited rush. "We're having a party tonight. It's just luck that I discovered you were here, but I insist you and your lady attend. You simply must come. There will be dancing and plenty to eat and drink. You'll know all the other guests."

"Bianca, I'd like to present one of my oldest friends, Thomas Nicholson, a man I met during my brief stay at William and Mary. Bianca is not merely my lady, Tom; she's far more. She is my wife."

"Your wife?" Tom asked in dismay. "Why wasn't I asked to your wedding?"

"We were married at sea, Mr. Nicholson, with no guests except for Evan's crew," Bianca explained sweetly as she took the man's pudgy hand in hers. He had seemed shocked to find Evan wed, but she did not want him to feel insulted as well. She looked up at her husband, her eyes bright with anticipation. "Do we have time to attend the party?"

Evan had been delighted when Bianca had suggested they avoid his friends in Williamsburg as he'd wanted to keep her all to himself. Now he realized that to accomplish that goal he should simply have taken her aboard the *Phoenix* and sailed well out into the Atlantic Ocean before dropping anchor. He knew she loved the gaiety of parties and the fun of meeting new people, and despite her request for privacy the previous day, she'd obviously forgotten it the moment Tom had spoken his invitation. He'd not deny her any happiness. "We will make the time," he promised with an easy grin, but he knew he'd spend the entire evening anxiously awaiting their return to the inn where he could again savor his bride's incredible gift for love.

Chapter XVII

As their carriage creaked slowly over the ruts in the road Bianca raised her hand to cover a wide yawn. She was sleepy, that was true, but also blissfully happy. They'd spent a delightful two weeks as guests of the Nicholsons. Patricia was as stout of figure as her husband Tom, but she was a wonderful hostess who had insisted they move from the Ralegh Tavern into her home where they'd been constantly entertained. Now that they were returning to their own home Bianca hoped the euphoric mood of their brief holiday would continue indefinitely.

Seeing his wife's pretty smile, Evan tightened his embrace into a warm hug. "I don't have to ask if you enjoyed our stay in Williamsburg; I can see that you did."

"I'm afraid I'll recall only a few of the names, we met so many people, but I'll remember all their faces when I see them again. The Nicholsons were so charming I hope we'll be able to repay their hospitality sometime soon."

Evan nodded in agreement. "I'd like that too. My mother was known for her parties, but unfortunately now it is impossible for her to entertain."

Bianca considered her next comment thoughtfully before voicing it. "I know that, Evan, but we've got to have a life of our own. Your mother's illness might make entertaining more difficult, but it shouldn't be impossible for us."

Evan tried not to let his true feelings show in his expression, but he was far more disappointed than she that his home had become such a dreary place. "I'm sure everyone understands our circumstances. We won't be criticized for not entertaining for a while."

Bianca didn't argue, but she was determined to improve their situation even if he was reluctant to make the changes she thought necessary. While Evan's days at William and Mary had, indeed, been few due to a far keener interest in designing and building ships than in purely academic subjects, he'd made many friends in Williamsburg, like the Nicholsons who remembered him still. She was certain he had numerous friends in the communities surrounding Hampton Roads too. She'd met a few at the party they'd attended at the Blanchards, but she'd seen none since. Now that autumn had arrived, they could expect to receive more invitations, and she'd not be content simply to visit other people's homes without issuing them invitations to her own. She glanced up at her husband, and was sorry to see that his gaze had darkened. When he was happy, his brown eyes were alight with a golden sparkle, but that charming glow was completely absent now. He was pretending an interest in the passing scenery, but she doubted he'd even noticed its beauty. His mood had been lighthearted since the moment they'd decided to visit Williamsburg, and she was sorry that as they were returning home he was again preoccupied with the problems they'd left behind. "Evan?" she called softly.

"Yes, my love?"

"I think we should finish this trip as it began, don't you?" She slid her fingers lightly over his before tickling his palm playfully. "The day is warm, the road seldom traveled." She was delighted to see him smile, and she covered his face with kisses as she reached for the buttons on his shirt. If she could bring a smile to his lips so easily with affection, she was certain she could find a way to again fill his home with joy.

If Marion Grey's health had not improved significantly whie they were away, at least she was no worse and Evan was grateful for that. He was ashamed at how easily he'd put his mother out of his mind, but now that they were home he had to force himself to walk into her room, though he knew remaining with her for any length of time would be impossible. He crossed the room quickly and bent down to give the troubled woman a light kiss upon the cheek, planning to make his visit brief.

"Sit down, Evan. I want to talk with you," Marion ordered coldly. She pointed to a chair and waited while her son brought it forward and made himself comfortable. Without bothering to inquire as to his trip, she immediately began a fiercely worded accusation. "Why have you lied to me all this time? Why didn't you tell me the truth about that woman when you first brought her home?"

Evan gestured helplessly. He did not know what wild idea had seized his mother's tormented mind now. "If you are referring to Bianca, I've told you all there is to tell. She's a delightful creature, and I'm sorry you've not made her feel welcome here. She wants very much to be your friend as well as your daughter-in-law."

Without speaking, Marion reached under her pillow and withdrew Charles's journal. She tapped the black leather cover lightly with her index finger as her golden eyes narrowed to menacing slits, her silent rebuttal of his words crushing.

"Did Lewis give you that?" Evan asked hoarsely. If she'd read Charles's last entries she would know exactly who Bianca was, and he could scarcely imagine how brutal her rage was going to be.

Marion continued to eye her handsome son with a chilling glance. "My husband is as great a liar as you. He thought he'd hidden this book well, but I found it. That slut you call your wife murdered Charles! How dare you bring her here and tell me his murderer went free? How dare you!" In contrast to the violent scenes she'd staged in the past, Marion took great care to speak in a whisper which would attract no one to her room. "It seems I lost not one son, but two, to that Venetian whore!"

Evan slowly rose to his feet and placed the chair near the wall, stalling for time as he struggled to think of some coherent reply, but she'd pushed him way past the limit of his patience. Finally he turned back to face her, his voice as tightly controlled as hers. "Bianca does not even recognize Charles's name. I won't deny that he fell in love with her, that much is obvious from reading his diary, but his infatuation was entirely one-sided. Bianca can not be blamed for his death."

"I want her out of this house, Evan. Tonight!" Marion insisted with an evil sneer, her whole body tense with hatred.

"Aren't you forgetting that my father left this house to me? You and Lewis live here as my guests; Bianca and I are not yours. Now put that book back where you found it, and the next time you call my wife anything other than a lady I'll slap your face. I don't care if you are my mother; you'll not go unpunished if you insult Bianca again." With that calmly worded threat, Evan turned on his heel and left the room, but he walked down the stairs and out the front door into the night rather than join Bianca in her room for he knew she could tell at a glance how poorly his conversation with his mother had gone. The woman was completely mad, but he'd not allow her to inflict her pain upon Bianca. At least Marion remained in her own room, and he was certain his wife would never risk visiting her there again. Still, his mother's discovey of Charles's journal had complicated things considerably. "Damn!" He swore loudly, cursing the day his younger brother had set sail for Venice. The sorry results of that ill-fated voyage kept compounding, and unlike a battle fought during wartime, the enemy was his own mother's relentless hatred which couldn't be defeated with cunning or strength. When he reached the river, he started to turn toward town, but remembering his last encounter with Sheila Blanchard, he quickly chose the path leading in the opposite direction and walked with a long purposeful stride until he'd finally exhausted his body as well as his mind.

Bianca did not inquire as to where her husband had been when he finally came to her bed. His skin was so cold she was afraid he'd caught a chill so she pulled him close to share her own warmth. As always her generous affection provided the cure for his pain, and his anguish quickly became passion. It was not until much later, when he'd fallen asleep still cradled in her embrace, that she began to worry. She feared that someday her love might not be enough to sustain him.

By the time they'd been home a week, Bianca felt as though they'd never been away. Despite her best efforts to be cheerful, the atmosphere in the elegantly furnished house was one of gloom since both her husband and father-in-law were constantly concerned over Marion's perpetually dark moods. While Evan spent little time in his mother's company, Lewis seldom left her side. When he began taking all his meals upstairs with his wife, Bianca decided it was time she made a suggestion to her husband. "I know it would be impossible for us to hold a lavish ball, but I'd like to invite a few of your friends here for dinner. We should repay the Blanchards' hospitality and—"

Evan shoved away his half-eaten dinner. "No, not

yet." The idea of sitting through any meal with Sheila was more than he could bear to contemplate. She'd spend all her time flirting with him and making innuendos Bianca would surely mistake for the truth. He wanted no part of any intimate dinner party Sheila would attend. "You must simply be more patient, my love, we'll be able to entertain as lavishly as you'd like one day. I'm sure of it."

"Are you suggesting we simply wait for your mother to die before we begin to live?" Bianca asked in a sudden fit of temper. She was sick to death of having to respect her mother-in-law's feelings when the woman apparently took great delight in making them all miserable.

"Bianca!" Evan exclaimed in a shocked gasp. Shaken because she'd read his mind so easily, he nonetheless refused to admit how accurate she'd been. "I didn't mean that at all." He tossed his napkin on the table and swiftly left the dining room, intending to take one of his long walks. He'd become accustomed to them, and they provided a release for the nervous energy which would have made sleep impossible.

Bianca rose gracefully, as though she were accustomed to dealing with such rudeness as her husband had just displayed. She went to her room to prepare for bed and seriously considered locking her door. Finally deciding that would only enrage Evan, she discarded that idea when another more appealing thought suddenly came to her. Nigel Blanchard had mentioned a house, a nice one. Surely he'd be willing to show it to her, and if it was truly as good a buy as he'd claimed, she'd do her best to convince Evan that they needed a home of their own, a place where they'd not constantly have to worry about his mother. Pleased with that plan, she prepared for bed, but curled up on the pillows with a book instead of going to sleep. When Evan came home, she heard him climb the stairs. His steps only hesitated at her door as he passed by so she slid off the bed and went into his room to invite him to join her as he always did.

"If you think I'm angry with you for behaving so rudely, you're wrong because I've already decided to forgive you," she told him with an enchanting smile. "I am not a patient person, but if I must cultivate that trait to please you then I will do my best to do so."

Evan relaxed immediately, charmed by her sweet smile and loving glance. "No. I am the one who is impatient, Bianca. The situation here is totally beyond my control, and while I can do little but accept it for the present, I find that impossible."

As Bianca came forward, she was tempted to ask Evan about the house Nigel had mentioned, but she decided to wait until she'd seen it for herself. She slipped her arms around his waist and snuggled close, delighted by his body's ready response to her embrace. She'd advised him herself that acceptance was frequently the only possible choice during difficult times, but she was pleased she'd now thought of a more attractive course. "We mustn't let anything come between us, Evan, for surely there is no problem so great it can part us."

"No, I'll never let anyone part us, beloved." Evan drew her closer still, the fire in his blood making him again her slave. He needed the brightness of her smile, and the tenderness of her love far too greatly to ever let her go for any reason. He swung her up into his arms and carried her easily back to her bed, and then, finding her pose seductive, he tore off his clothes with frantic haste, thinking himself a great fool for spending so much of the evening alone when she'd been waiting so eagerly for him to return.

Bianca tried not to laugh as her husband threw his boots clear across the room as he removed first one and then the other with vicious yanks. "I'm not going to fall asleep, nor will I leave this bed. You needn't rush so."

Not heeding her advice, Evan pulled his shirt over his head rather than waste time on unbuttoning it. He removed his pants with a careless tug, and after kicking them aside, he joined his bewitching bride on the wide bed. She'd not bothered to button the tiny buttons at the neckline of her nightgown, and he slipped it off her shoulders easily, revealing the soft fullness of her breasts. Their light pink tips were already firm, but he stretched out beside her, caressing first one rosy peak and then the other, taking them into his mouth so his tongue could tease her flesh as the very sight of her lovely body teased him. He had not imagined he'd ever fall in love. That he now loved such an incredibly beautiful and loving woman was still almost beyond his comprehension. Looking up for a moment, he saw the warm glow of love in her half-closed eyes and whispered hungrily. "You taste delicious, every last bit of you does."

While he'd savored her flesh, Bianca had suddenly become curious. "Evan, is it possible for me to kiss you as intimately as you kiss me?" So he'd not misunderstand her question, she reached out to caress him lightly, her fingertips merely brushing his hardened flesh with a teasing promise of something far better.

Evan's breath caught in his throat for a moment. Bianca had never seemed in the least bit shy with him. Her hands often roamed over his body, inflaming his desire as she welcomed his every advance, but there were things he'd not taught her. He finally found his voice to reply. "Yes, but only if it is something you truly wish to do."

"Why not?" Bianca answered with a coquettish smile, and before he could offer any further suggestions, she'd slipped off her gown, had playfully pushed him down upon the pillows, and had moved between his outstretched legs. She then imitated his teasing sequence of caresses, with light kisses and a feathery touch moving slowly up the inside of his thighs before using her lips and tongue to capture his now-throbbing manhood in a deep kiss. He was so responsive, she swiftly sensed what pleased him most, although now his words were slurred with passion and almost incoherent. With the tip of her tongue she brought him to the brink of ecstasy. She could feel the rapture searing through him, fighting to be free, so she quickly moved astride him so his peak of pleasure would come deep inside her and she could feel it burst forth from his body into hers. She stretched out upon his chest then, and he wrapped her tightly in his embrace as their lips met. Their closeness complete, their loving play continued far into the night.

As soon as Evan had left for his shipyard the next morning, Bianca wrote a note to Nigel Blanchard to inquire if the Marshall property were still available. She invited him to call at her home so they might discuss the matter, which she wanted held in the strictest confidence. She sent the note to his home since it was so close, and the next afternoon he appeared on her doorstep. Viola showed him into the parlor, where Bianca offered him refreshments, and when he'd declined them, she turned the conversation immediately to the purpose of his call.

"Thank you so much for coming to see me so promptly. I have been thinking about the house you described to me, and if it is still for sale, I'd like to see it."

"I have approached no one else since I last talked with you, Mrs. Sinclair. As I said, it is a wonderful buy, but one few residents of Newport News can afford. I have time this very afternoon if you can spare it. I know you ride, and it is not a great distance from here."

Despite this man's handsome appearance and ready charm, Bianca was certain his interest was a purely monetary one, and she had no objection to riding with him without a chaperon. "Give me a moment to change into my riding habit while Nathan saddles my mare. I'll be only a moment."

"I have all afternoon, Mrs. Sinclair." Nigel smiled widely as she left the room, then he walked over to a window to enjoy the splendid view which extended down to the James River. His plan was working almost too smoothly. He doubted Evan would ever give up this magnificent house to move into Sarah Marshall's, but he could sense how keenly Bianca was interested in making a change. All he had to do was play her desires off against her husband's to set the stage for some bitter confrontations between them. When he'd inquired about Marion Grey, the attractive blonde had merely stated that her mother-in-law was resting, but it was obvious to him there was far more to that story than she'd been willing to relate.

"Mr. Blanchard," Bianca called softly from the doorway, "shall we go?"

She was dressed in the attractive green outfit in which he'd first seen her, and Nigel immediately came forward, eager for their ride to begin. "As I told you, the property is extensive, but as it also fronts the James River, it is not far. In fact, you and Evan may have ridden by it on one of your outings."

"He did not mention it if we did." Bianca tried to recall how far they'd ridden up the river, but she didn't remember seeing any homes which appeared unoccupied. Nigel helped her to mount Moonbeam and they left, leaving Nathan staring after them and wondering why Mr. Sinclair's wife would want to waste her time with a dandy like Nigel Blanchard.

The day was pleasant, the sky cloudless, and the ride so enjoyable Bianca saw no reason to make conversation with her escort but he kept up a steady stream of remarks ranging from comments on the fall weather to outright gossip. Since she knew none of the people involved, she didn't listen closely, but she made a mental note never to tell Nigel anything she wanted kept secret. When at last they reached the Marshall estate, they followed a wide path lined with stately oaks which led all the way from the river to the house. Set upon a gentle rise, the handsome three-story brick structure had a mansard roof with dormer windows. Its portico was supported by Grecian columns, which provided a balcony for the second story as well as an imposing entrance to the home. Nigel tied their mounts' reins to an iron ring driven into the tree closest to the house, and after escorting Bianca up the steps, he paused a moment so she could appreciate the beauty of the home's location.

"The river view is spectacular, don't you agree?" Truly, he did think the house and its grounds exceptionally appealing.

Bianca swept a stray curl from her eyes, attempting to hide her delight but failing. She'd known the instant she'd glimpsed the house through the trees that it would suit her tastes perfectly. "Yes. I am used to the sea, but the waters of the James River have a beauty of their own."

The entry hall was dominated by a wide staircase, and Nigel moved swiftly to point out its fine craftsmanship. "The staircase is made of native walnut and pine, a work of art really, but you'll find everything here just as handsomely made. When Sarah passed away the house was closed. I think we'll be the first visitors in several months. Let's see this floor first, then work our way up."

As Bianca walked slowly around the parlor the aftenoon sun lit the room with a soft golden glow, and she tried to imagine how festive it would look decorated for a party. The furnishings were covered with muslin sheets, but Nigel tossed aside the one covering the sofa.

"Most of the furniture is Chippendale, and as fine as this piece. You'll find ready buyers for whatever you don't wish to keep."

As they continued through the house, Bianca merely nodded in response to most of his comments, for she could appreciate the delicate plasterwork adorning the high ceilings, the fine cut-glass chandeliers, and the spaciousness of the well-proportioned rooms without his running commentary. The rooms on the second floor were as well designed as those on the first, and when they reached the master bedroom, she imagined herself sharing the massive fourposter with Evan and could barely suppress her smile. It was a very beautiful home, elegantly furnished, and although it was obvious that it had not been maintained properly for some time, she knew with a fresh coat of paint and with the furniture reupholstered, it would be a far more lovely home than the one she currently occupied. She did not want to appear too eager to buy it, however, as she was certain that would only drive up the price. "This is a very charming house, Mr. Blanchard, but it is going to need quite a bit of work."

"That's certainly true, but the effort would be well worth your while. Now, let's go up to the third floor where we can overlook the rest of the plantation." Nigel led her into a corner room which had once been used for sewing, and after walking over to the windows he pointed out the various buildings nearby. "During Aaron Marshall's time this was a very profitable tobacco plantation, but Sarah had great difficulty employing an honest overseer and finally gave up the enterprise entirely during the last few years of her life. Financially that was a serious mistake. It depleted her resources considerably. While you can not see them all from here, there is a separate structure for the kitchen, a forge, a smokehouse, a dairy, storehouses, a washhouse, and a coach house and stables. They all need substantial repair, that I'll readily admit, but the profit from your first tobacco crop would easily cover it, and provide additional income as well. The slave quarters will have to be rebuilt, but—"

"I'm sorry, Mr. Blanchard, but my husband will never use slave labor. That is out of the question." At the mention of slaves, Bianca's heart had fallen. The Marshall house was not simply a lovely home, but the home of the owner of the surrounding plantation. That was something she was certain her husband would never be.

"Must I ask you again to please call me Nigel?" The dark-eyed young man teased warmly. "I'm well aware of Evan's opposition to slavery on moral grounds, but it would be impossible for him to maintain this home for any length of time without the revenue tobacco will produce. I'm sure once he looks at it as strictly an economic proposition, he'll see what must be done."

"You expect him to compromise his convictions in order to make a profit?" Bianca asked sharply, certain her husband was too fine a man to do such a dishonorable thing.

Nigel recognized his mistake instantly. He'd not meant to anger Bianca, merely to encourage her interest in owning the house. She was so lovely a young woman he found the afternoon had passed all too quickly, and he dared not allow it to end on a disagreeable note. He reached out to grasp Bianca's arm, hoping both his words and caress would prove soothing. "What I expect Evan to do is to buy this house to please you. If he adores you as I think he does, that's exactly what he'll do. How he wishes to support the venture is his own business, my dear."

Deeply offended by his ingratiating tone as well as by his fawning touch, Bianca turned toward the door. She had only one choice, it seemed, and that was to forget any hope of owning that particular house for she would not put her husband in an awkward position. "I'd like to go now. There's no point in our staying even a minute longer as I've no interest in this house. It is attractive, but apparently far too costly to maintain so I'll not mention it to my husband." She went out the door and crossed to the top of the stairs, where Nigel overtook her and, hoping to make her reconsider, flashed his most charming grin as he again reached for her arm. "Bianca, you mustn't act like a silly child. You can make Evan do whatever you wish, and it's plain to me you want this house."

"I most certainly do not! Now let me go this instant, I wish to leave!" Bianca tried to brush his hand aside as she started down the stairs, but when he hesitated a moment before letting go, she lost her balance and although she grabbed for the railing her foot missed the step. With a terror-filled shriek, she fell headlong down the steep flight of stairs, her frantic efforts to catch herself proving fruitless once her feet became entangled in the thick folds of her skirt. Knocked unconscious by the violence of her mishap, she landed in a crumpled heap at the bottom of the stairs and lay still.

Thinking that he'd inadvertently killed this lovely young woman, Nigel nearly fell himself as he rushed down the stairs. His eyes filled with tears as he knelt by Bianca's side, and his hands trembled as he felt for the pulse in her throat. When he found a faint but steady beat, he relaxed for no more than an instant for he could tell by her deathly pallor that she'd been severely injured. He had no way to transport her to her home, where he knew Evan was sure to blame him for this ghastly accident. And it was his fault. While he'd not actually shoved her down the stairs, he might just as well have. He knew Sheila would be elated to hear how badly Bianca had been injured, but he was thoroughly sickened. His touch still far from steady, he felt carefully along the pale blonde's slender limbs seeking an indication of broken bones, but he found none. There was a deep purple bruise above her left eye and a gash in her lip, so he feared she might have suffered internal injuries which he could neither discover nor treat.

"Bianca! Bianca!" He called her name repeatedly without success. "God in heaven, how am I to get you home?" he asked in a strangled cry. Then he suddenly recalled that Sarah Marshall had owned a carriage he didn't remember selling. If it was still in the coach house, he had two horses to pull it. He waited a moment longer, uncertain whether he should risk leaving Bianca's side even for the short span of time such an errand would require, but deciding he had no other choice, he dashed out the front door and tore around the side of the house, praying as he ran that the carriage had not been stolen.

Chapter XVIII

"You bloody bastard!" Evan screamed as he grabbed the lapels of Nigel Blanchard's blue velvet coat and lifted him clear off his feet. Then, disgusted with the miserable banker's whimpered pleas for mercy, he released him with a rude shove which sent the young man crashing back against the wall.

Stunned by the harshness of Evan's treatment, Nigel nonetheless considered himself lucky the enraged man had not simply broken his neck with his bare hands. He'd brought Bianca home in Sarah Marshall's carriage, but since Moonbeam was apparently unaccustomed to being harnessed to any sort of vehicle he'd had to walk beside her, leading her all the way to the Sinclair house. He'd tugged continually on the dapple-gray mare's bridle since she'd chosen to behave with the stubbornness of an old mule while his own mount was forced to do the major portion of the work of pulling the heavy carriage. He'd not taken the time to do more than hurriedly dust off the leather seats before he'd placed Bianca inside, and that he'd delivered her to her home badly hurt and in a filthy carriage was more than Evan could abide. Nigel tried to stand up straight, determined to take whatever beating he'd have to suffer as bravely as he could. Although he knew Bianca's injuries were his fault, he dared not admit that fact to Evan and again he protested his innocence. "It was an accident, Evan, I swear it was!" he insisted, his voice unnaturally high and quaking with terror.

"My wife is the most graceful creature ever born. She would never fall down a flight of stairs, never! I'll have to wait to hear her version of this so-called accident to learn the truth." Evan again shoved the hapless banker back against the wall as he lowered his voice to a threatening snarl. "If she has suffered any permanent injury, no matter how slight, I'll make you pay and pay dearly. I don't want you coming anywhere near my wife ever again!"

Nigel forced back the painful lump fear had formed in his throat as he reached into his coat pocket for the note Bianca had sent him. He thanked God he'd thought to bring it with him for he needed every shred of evidence he could muster to prove the innocence of his actions and to avoid being blamed for this terrible calamity. "You don't understand, Evan. Bianca sent for me. We only went to the Marshall house because she asked me to take her there. Here. See for yourself." He thrust the note into Evan's hands and then stepped back out of range of the taller man's fists.

Evan scanned the brief note quickly, and was astonished to find Nigel's description of its contents accurate. "How did she even hear about the Marshall estate?" he asked sharply.

"Well, that is, I believe I mentioned it to her the night you two were at our home. Yes, I'm sure that's when it must have been, at our party," Nigel stuttered nervously, fearing Evan would know exactly why he'd done it.

"What possessed you to take it upon yourself to try to interest my wife in purchasing another house? There is no finer home than this in all of Virginia!"

Nigel nodded in agreement as he searched his mind

frantically for some plausible excuse Bianca would not dispute the moment she regained consciousness. "I believe her interest was in having a home of her own rather than having to share this one with her mother-in-law. Naturally I encouraged her to approach the subject with you. In fact, that was exactly what we were discussing when she fell. I'd scarcely encourage her to purchase the house herself without your knowledge."

Evan's perceptive gaze swept slowly over Nigel's trembling figure. Sweat was pouring off the banker, dripping off his face and soaking his clothes although the temperature that late in the afternoon was cool. "You're lying," he stated simply. "I can only speculate as to why you'd wish to lure my wife to that house since you won't tell me the truth. She is a very beautiful woman. Are you merely taken with her, or were you simply trying to create a problem between my wife and me?" Without giving Nigel the opportunity to respond, Evan continued in the same hostile tone. "That would certainly please your insipid sister, but I won't know what really happened today until Bianca can tell me herself. Now get out of my house before I decide to make short work of you right now!"

Nigel didn't utter another word. He dashed out the front door, and to his immense relief he found his horse saddled and waiting for the ride home. The Marshall carriage was nowhere in sight, but he knew Evan would probably simply set it on fire and he didn't tarry to see the blaze. He dug his heels into his mount's flanks and rode home at a furious pace. He knew Sheila would instantly begin praying for Bianca's death, while he feared such a tragedy would swiftly bring about his own demise.

Still clutching Bianca's note, Evan sat down on the stairs and held his head in his hands. Nigel Blanchard was an obnoxious pest, but he doubted the man would be so stupid as to try to rape Bianca. Had he even the slightest suspicion his wife had been injured resisting an unwanted advance he would never have let the rascal leave. No. Nigel was scarcely the type to force himself upon a woman, not when he worked so damned hard to be charming. He'd most likely merely been trying to stir up trouble. "As if I didn't have more than my share already!" he exclaimed loudly. Viola and Mattie were with Bianca now, attempting to make her comfortable until Dr. Stafford arrived. He'd left them to tend her while he'd tried to shake the truth out of Nigel. It was a good thing he'd come home early. He'd wanted to spend some extra time with Bianca, perhaps take her out for a late ride, but he'd arrived only seconds before Nigel, and far too late to protect his lovely wife from harm. Wearily he rose and climbed the stairs, not wanting to leave her alone with even two loyal servants when she would surely call for him the moment she awakened.

While Marion seldom left her bed, she was nevertheless acutely aware of everything that went on in her home. She'd overheard only bits and pieces of her son's confrontation with Nigel Blanchard, but she could barely hide her delight. If Bianca had been severely hurt while alone in Mr. Blanchard's company she would suffer not only the pain of that injury but the sharp stings of gossip as well. If that disgrace wasn't enough to send her back to Venice, perhaps something else would. Despite Evan's order, Marion hadn't replaced Charles's journal in Lewis's hiding place. She kept it with her and read from it frequently for her son's words were filled with his youthful exuberance and she felt close to him again when she reviewed his thoughts. Evan was wrong, she was sure of that. Bianca had killed Charles, and Marion did not intend to allow her to escape punishment for so heinous a crime.

While John Stafford's examination was much more thorough than Nigel's, he found no broken bones either.

Bianca had suffered numerous bruises, the worst being the one to her forehead, but he thought she'd require no more than a few days' rest to recover from her ordeal. She was awake, and her replies to his questions were lucid. As he straightened up, he had only one last concern. Evan was pacing distractedly up and down by the foot of the bed, so worried about his bride that John was tempted to give him a generous dose of laudanum to calm him down if not to put him right to sleep. "You have been married several months, Mrs. Sinclair. Do you have any suspicion that you might be pregnant? A fall as bad as the one you suffered could easily bring on a miscarriage within a few hours."

Evan stopped in midstride, as startled by that question as Bianca whose pale cheeks had instantly flooded with a bright blush. His lovely wife's body had a predictable rhythm which was as regular as the phases of the moon, and he knew as well as she did that she was not pregnant. It was the way the doctor had phrased his question that annoyed him, however. They had been married sufficiently long enough for her to conceive, that was certainly true, but he didn't want her to feel any less of a woman because she hadn't. Actually, he'd considered it fortunate that they weren't expecting a child since he'd been so deeply ensnarled in problems he'd scarcely had the time to contemplate the joys of fatherhood. It suddenly became clear to him why Bianca would want a home of her own. Surely one day they'd become parents, and he couldn't imagine trying to raise children where their grandmother's hysterical rages would terrify them before they were old enough to understand the cause of her behavior.

Bianca's eyes filled with tears as she shook her head. "No, I'm not pregnant, I'm certain of it."

Evan moved to her side and took her hand in both of his. "Since a miscarriage is not a concern, is there anything else which might cause a problem? I want to be certain Bianca receives the best care possible." If the doctor had any other questions, he hoped he would ask them more tactfully, but he dared not voice that request.

John pursed his lips thoughtfully. "Bruises simply require time to heal, but I'd like for you to remain in bed for several days, my dear. You've obviously suffered a slight concussion and I'd not want you to be injured again should you faint while walking about. There's no real need for me to remain with you tonight. I'll leave some laudanum in case you are too uncomfortable to sleep, and I'll stop by tomorrow to check on you again. Don't hesitate to send for me, however, should you have any severe pain. My wife always knows where I am, and should I be away on another emergency she will send for me."

Bianca felt very foolish as she looked up at the two men. "I'm sorry to have caused such a fright. I'll be fine in a day or two. I don't want you to worry about me a moment longer." While she had many aches, the pain in her head was by far the worst, and she hoped if she just lay still it would soon go away. She didn't want to be treated as though she were at death's door.

John Stafford reached into his bag, handed Evan a small bottle of laudanum and then bid them both good night. "I wish all my patients were so confident of a swift recovery, Mrs. Sinclair. Now, if you'll excuse me, I think I'll look in on Marion before I leave."

"Thank you again for coming over so quickly, John." Evan walked the doctor to the door, wishing his mother shared Bianca's optimistic view of life, but he soon hurried back to his wife's side.

Delighted by the doctor's unexpected visit, Marion sat up, eager to greet him. "I have been so worried about my daughter-in-law, John. Will she be all right?" she asked breathlessly, though she hoped Bianca wouldn't survive the night.

"Yes. She's had a bad fall, but she's young and quite healthy and will be up and around in a week or so. However, I must tell you again that you need to get up out of that bed and resume your rightful place as the mistress here. With Bianca unable to leave her bed, you'll work poor Viola and Mattie to death if you don't. Think about the rest of your household for a moment, Marion. It's high time you put your grief aside and began to live your own life once again."

Marion's smile faded instantly at that piece of unwanted advice. "I scarcely have the energy to sit up and read; there's no way I can run the house as I used to, John."

The doctor was nearly as tall as Evan, although far more lean. It was close to supper time, he'd had a long and tiring day, and he was ravenously hungry. He had slight interest in listening to Marion's excuses for not taking the suggestions he gave her so often. "Then get up for just an hour each morning. Help Viola plan the meals, see that the silver is polished, whatever, but take it upon yourself to be of some help to everyone for a change. Invite your friends in for tea as you used to. It will not overtax your strength to see them again, and I'll wager you'll feel all the better for it. I've simply no desire to continue to visit this house and find all the women in bed!" Knowing she'd probably ignore his comments as usual, he stormed out of the room and rushed home, hoping his wife had prepared a plump roast chicken or one of his other favorites for the evening meal.

Marion pouted angrily for more than an hour before realizing Dr. Stafford's advice was not entirely bad. By staying in her room she'd given Bianca free run of the house and who could say what mischief the young woman had caused? She still considered herself the rightful mistress of the house, and felt that it was hers regardless of what Evan claimed. Marion straightened her shoulders proudly, trying to think how best to turn Bianca's accident to her own advantage. Evan already knew she hated his wife, but it would not do to appear jubilant because Bianca had been hurt, she was smart enough to realize that. No, she would have to pretend to be as saddened by this latest misfortune as the rest of them. Stealthily she rose from her bed and replaced Charles's journal in her husband's room. It wouldn't do for Lewis to discover she'd read it. At least, not yet it wouldn't. If everything went according to her plans, she would tell him the truth later, but not now. Convinced that fate was at last on her side, she returned to her bed, picked up the novel she'd been reading earlier in the day, and became surprisingly absorbed in it, her conscience clear despite the darkness of her thoughts.

Bianca had slept badly. She'd dozed off soon after the doctor had left, but since there wasn't an ounce of her supple body that didn't ache it had been difficult for her to find a position comfortable enough to provide a good night's rest. Now it was morning and she was still so tired she felt as though she'd not slept at all. Evan was snuggled close beside her, his warmth very comforting, and she was touched by the thought that he'd still wanted to share her bed. She tried to shift her position slightly, but that made her head throb so painfully she had to give up the effort. She could remember the first few seconds of her fall; the rest was a merciful blur. Dr. Stafford had said she had no broken bones, but she could not imagine feeling any worse than she already did. She wondered what Evan had done to Nigel, for surely he'd blamed him for it. Blanchard was a slender young man. Certainly he'd be unable to defend himself if Evan chose to give him a beating. She suddenly wondered why she should be concerned about Nigel Blanchard, but as sleep overtook her again thoughts of him slipped from her mind.

Evan heard the persistent tapping at the door and rose quickly to open it before Bianca was awakened. He grabbed his robe, hastily tying it around his waist, and when he found his mother, fully dressed for the first time in months, he could only gape at her, too surprised to speak.

Marion peeked in to see if Bianca was sleeping before she whispered to her son. "I think one invalid in this house is enough, don't you?"

"Well yes, but—" Evan could not believe the transformation in his mother. There was color in her cheeks, a bright sparkle in her eyes, and best of all, her smile was the one he remembered so fondly and had not seen since his return home. "Are you certain you're well enough to be out of bed?"

"Positive. John has been telling me for months to get up and get busy. It's high time that I took his advice. With Bianca unable to leave her bed, you'll need some help and I should be the one to give it."

Evan glanced toward Bianca and saw that she was awake and watching them. "I do not want to appear ungrateful, Mother, but—"

"Oh, I know how badly I've behaved. You needn't remind me. I'll go and tell Viola you two need some breakfast. Just give me a minute." Marion hurried away, hiding her smile of triumph. It was all going to be so easy. First she'd help Bianca regain her strength, and then she'd make certain the little blonde hussy wanted to go straight back to Venice.

"Was that your mother?" Bianca asked in disbelief as Evan returned to her side.

"Yes, it seems she feels her help is needed. I don't

understand it, but I won't argue with her since this is the first time I've seen her looking well since we returned home."

Bianca closed her eyes, uncertain whether or not she would remind him of what had happened the only time she'd tried to speak with his mother. "Don't leave me alone with her," she said softly.

Evan sat down on the edge of the bed and took her hand in his. "I won't leave you, not even for a minute. Are you feeling well enough this morning to answer a few questions? I've not been in the Marshall place in years, but I don't recall the stairs being especially steep."

"It was not the fault of the stairs that I fell," Bianca hastened to admit. "What did you do to Nigel?" she asked apprehensively.

"Nothing as yet, but if it was his fault that you fell, I'll make him suffer for it," Evan promised with a determined frown.

Bianca hesitated a moment; then fearing Nigel would have her husband arrested should he give the man what he deserved, she made the incident sound as innocent as possible. "We were arguing, neither of us paying close enough attention as we started down the stairs," she explained sheepishly, her expression very contrite. "Isn't that what he told you?"

"More or less," Evan agreed although he was still puzzled. "I just wish I had known that you were interested in the Marshall house. Had I gone with you, I'm certain the accident would not have happened."

As tears welled up in Bianca's eyes she made no effort to suppress them. She knew the whole idea had been impossibly foolish. He had no need for a plantation, and she was sorry she'd not understood that it would be impossible to buy the house for innumerable reasons. "I just wanted a place where we could be happy, Evan, that's all."

Evan leaned down to kiss away Bianca's tears, sorry he'd failed so completely to give her a pleasant life. "We are going to be deliriously happy, my love, I promise you that. For now, all you need do is get well. Then we can decide where we'd truly like to live. Please don't cry so; you'll soon be well and everything will be better than it was before. I'm sure it will."

"I'm just so terribly tired," Bianca whispered.

"Go to sleep, love, I'll stay with you." Evan stepped into his own room to get dressed, and then remained by her side all day.

When Mattie brought them something to eat, Bianca refused it, but, ashamed to be so hungry, he asked her to bring him more. He'd not felt like eating supper the night before and was ravenous as a result. His mother came into the room several times, and on each visit she'd been lucid. She had displayed only concern for Bianca, not a trace of the hostility he'd come to expect.

When John Stafford returned in the late aftenoon, he thought it only natural that Bianca had spent most of the day napping, but he insisted she make more of an effort to eat. He coaxed her into swallowing a small sip of soup and then handed the bowl to her husband. "It's the concussion that's causing your queasiness, but you need nourishment to regain your strength. I'm going to insist you don't get out of that bed for at least a week."

Bianca listened calmly as the doctor continued to give her advice, but she was so upset by the stupidity of her accident, she just wanted to be left alone. She'd eat when she got hungry, not a moment before, regardless of what the man said.

Evan saw the sparkle of tears in his wife's eyes and couldn't understand why talking about food would make her cry. Perhaps she felt far worse than she'd admit, but he hoped rest was truly all she'd need. When John paused for a moment he spoke up quickly. "I'll see that Bianca has plenty of good food." He set the bowl of soup on the nightstand and hurried the man toward the door, for he doubted that his wife truly needed advice on a healthful diet. "Would you mind looking in on my mother again before you leave?" As soon as he'd closed the door behind John he returned to the bed. "I'll not force you to finish that bowl of soup unless you really want it. Is that what's upsetting you? Do you think I'd force you to eat? Or is it something else?"

Her husband looked so concerned that Bianca dared not give in to her tears. She did not want to make him feel worse. "John is a physician so he's undoubtedly right. If I don't eat I probably won't get well, but I'm just not hungry now."

Evan could only marvel at his wife's spunk, and he broke into a wide grin. "If you do not want soup, perhaps Viola has something else."

"I don't want anything," Bianca insisted stubbornly.

"Do you want some laudanum? I don't want you to be in pain."

"No, thank you. I don't mind the pain. It's not so bad."

She looked so small and frail, so battered and bruised, that again Evan suspected something more than her injuries was troubling her. He sat down on the edge of the bed and asked casually, "So what did you think of the Marshall house? It used to be quite a showplace as I recall."

Bianca was mortified at that question, but she could do little more than cringe inwardly before she replied, "I shouldn't have gone there, Evan. Can't we just forget that I did?"

Evan considered her request for a moment and then shook his head. "No, I'd really like your opinion of the place. Is it in ruins, or could it be remodeled rather easily?"

Bianca looked away, uncertain how to respond. "I suppose that would depend on your taste in houses."

"Oh really." Evan nodded thoughtfully, wondering what in the world she meant by that remark. "Perhaps I'll ask Nigel to give me a tour of it tomorrow so I can see for myself."

"You wouldn't!" The bedridden blonde gasped in surprise.

"Why not? If he is so intent upon selling the place that he'd show it to you, why wouldn't he be interested in showing it to me?"

Bianca quickly looked up at her husband, for she feared he was planning something far more desperate than merely looking at the house. "Nigel's an ass, that I'll readily admit, but I don't want you to punish him for this, Evan. It was as much my fault as his."

Evan chuckled as he rose to his feet. "What do you think I mean to do, take him to the Marshall house and push him down the stairs? It would serve him right, of course, but I'm not nearly so crude in my methods, my love. Now I'm going downstairs to get myself some supper, but I'll bring it back up here to eat with you. Are you sure I can't bring you something as well?"

"No," Bianca insisted again, but when he returned with a dish of freshly baked custard topped with several spoonfuls of brandy she found it so delicious she ate every last bite.

Sheila saw Evan riding toward their house and rushed into her brother's room to awaken him. "Wake up, Nigel!" She grabbed his shoulder and shook him hoping he'd not been too drunk when he'd fallen asleep to be brought around. "Damn it, Nigel, wake up!" she called even more loudly, and finally he opened one eye to look up at her. "Evan's here and I know he's not coming calling to see me. I'll stall him for as long as I can, but you'll have to come downstairs and speak with him yourself."

"Oh dear God," Nigel moaned. He pulled an extra pillow over his head, trying unsuccessfully to escape his sister's insistent nagging, but she grabbed it away from him and started beating him with it.

"Get up, you lush. Get up!" Sheila heard the bell. It would be answered, but she knew Evan Sinclair would just as soon come upstairs looking for Nigel as sit in the parlor and wait for him to appear. "He's already at the door. You'd better get yourself downstairs and fast!"

As Nigel tried to sit up slowly so the pain of his hangover wouldn't overwhelm him, Sheila gave him one last bash in the face with the feather pillow before leaving his room. He fell back across the bed. "Was he carrying a gun?" he called after her, wondering if this would be the last day of his life. Then, suddenly, he no longer cared.

Sheila swept down the stairs as though she were making a grand entrance at the governor's ball. "Why Evan, I'm so pleased to see you. Nigel told me about your wife's accident. How is she feeling this morning?" She'd left her dressing gown slightly open to display the fullness of her breasts, which were barely contained by the lace on her chemise. She'd had no time to dress before greeting him, but she thought perhaps her casual disregard for propriety would work to her advantage since she knew she was a very attractive woman, especially when partially clothed.

Evan paid not the slightest attention to Sheila's seductive garb. "Tell your insect of a brother that I want to see him immediately." He clasped his hands behind his back and stared down at her with a menacing glare. "I'll give him no more than five minutes to dress, and if he's not ready then, I'll take him with me in his nightshirt."

"He doesn't usually bother to wear one," Sheila

replied coquettishly. "Do you?"

"That's none of your business, Sheila. Now go and fetch Nigel. I'm in a hurry."

"I've already told him you're here. I saw you from my window. Now I insist you tell me what's happened to your wife. Is she dead?"

"What?" Evan was astounded that Sheila would be so rude as to ask that question with a gleeful smile. "She is feeling as well as can be expected two days after taking a bad fall. That she might die due to Nigel's carelessness wasn't even a remote possibility. Did he give you that idea?"

Sheila shrugged. "Well, you've come barging into my home at a very early hour, demanded to see my brother, and refused to answer my politely worded question as to Bianca's health so what else could I think but the worst?"

"Well, you're wrong. Now where's Nigel?" Evan started toward the stairs, but Sheila grabbed at his arm.

"He's had but a moment to dress, he'll need a few minutes more. Would you like some breakfast while you wait?"

"I've already eaten." Evan had left Lewis sitting with Bianca since he'd promised not to leave her alone. His mother had continued to be the sweet person she'd been before Charles's death, but he didn't trust her to remain calm if she found Bianca defenseless in her bed. He left his hand upon the banister, ready to go upstairs to look for Nigel himself if the man didn't soon appear.

Nigel had shaved the evening before so he merely splashed cold water on his face and then grabbed the first suit of clothes in the closet. If Bianca had accused him of causing her fall he'd probably not live to see noon anyway, and he knew Sheila would make certain he was buried in something fashionable. He pulled on his stockings, jammed his feet into his shoes, and raced down the stairs, greeting Evan breathlessly as he reached the bottom step. "I would have come to see Bianca, to ask about her, but since you forbade me to visit her, I respected your wishes and stayed away. How is she?"

"Recovering nicely, thank you." Evan had forgotten Nigel was several years younger than he, but this morning Blanchard looked no more than sixteen and he couldn't help but feel sorry for him. Nigel's eyes were badly bloodshot, and his hands were shaking. He'd undoubtedly drink himself into an early grave. "I'd like to see the Marshall Estate. If it is as wonderful a buy as you insisted to Bianca, then I think I'd be a fool not to consider purchasing it."

Nigel looked first at his sister's startled expression and then back at Evan's confident smile. Never had he dreamed the man would actually consider buying the place. "Why yes, it is indeed a superb buy. Do you wish to go now?"

"If you have the time before you go to the bank." Evan raised an eyebrow quizzically as his glance traveled over Nigel's hastily assembled outfit. He'd never seen the man so poorly dressed, and he realized Blanchard must have been badly frightened to come downstairs in such a sorry state.

"It will be a pleasure," Nigel replied with a relieved grin.

"Good. I took the liberty of ordering your horse saddled when your groom came out to tend my mount. I think we should be able to leave immediately."

Sheila frowned angrily as the two men left the house. Another of Nigel's schemes had obviously gone awry! "Oh, why couldn't that little bitch have broken her neck?" she opined, and furious that she'd not got so much as a smile from Evan, she raced back up the stairs and slammed her door soundly so none of the servants could hear her angry sobs.

Nigel stayed close beside Evan as they toured the Marshall house. He pointed out the splendid arrangement of the spacious rooms, the wealth of exquisite detail in the finely carved hardwoods, and the elegant plasterwork of the ceilings; but as they came to the staircase leading up to the third floor, his mouth grew so dry he could no longer speak.

Evan climbed the stairs slowly, then turned back to look down at the landing. "Is this where Bianca fell?"

"Yes," Nigel whispered nervously.

Evan turned away to inspect the rooms, enjoying the view from each before finally returning to the staircase. "Tell me exactly how she happened to fall, Nigel. I want to know precisely how it happened."

Nigel pulled out his handkerchief and mopped his perspiring brow. He had no idea what Bianca might have said. She might have accused him of anything, and he knew Evan would never take his word over hers. Deciding he'd stick as close to the truth as he had before, he tried to speak calmly. "We had been in the sewing room. I pointed out the function of the numerous buildings we could see from there. The storehouses, the dairy—you saw them all."

"Yes, go on," Evan urged matter-of-factly.

"Well, Bianca complained that the house needed considerable work, which I admitted, but I told her a tobacco plantation is a very profitable enterprise."

"That's certainly true," Evan agreed. "Bianca said you were arguing, however. What caused the disagreement?"

"Well it was not actually a disagreement," Nigel hurriedly explained, his heart pounding more rapidly with each beat as his fear increased tenfold. "Your wife apparently hadn't realized the estate was more than the house. The prospect of owning a plantation upset her, and she asked to leave. We walked to the stairs, here, where I suggested she speak with you."

"Just exactly where was she standing when she fell?"

"On, on the first step I believe," Nigel stuttered nervously.

"And where were you?" Evan inquired softly.

"Well I was right here, still at the top."

Evan took Nigel by the arm. "Stand on that first step for a moment so I can visualize this better." When Nigel stepped down, he grabbed immediately for the banister as if he feared for his very life. "If you two were discussing whether or not she should speak with me, did she turn back to look up at you?"

Nigel nodded, his eyes wide with fear. He knew Evan was going to shove him down the stairs, he just knew it. He was absolutely terrified of the taller man and he could think of no way to dissuade him from committing murder.

Evan looked down at the trembling man, then stepped back a moment to get a better view of the staircase. "She turned back to reply to something you'd said and fell. Is that how it happened?"

"Yes, exactly. It was an accident, Evan, an accident," Nigel insisted in a voice choked with tears. He stared into Evan's eyes, fascinated by their golden gleam and no more able to move than a bird paralyzed with fright is able to escape a snake's lunge. The seconds ticked by with maddening slowness as Evan simply stared down at him before he spoke.

"Then I must remind her to be more careful in the future. The figure you quoted is much too high, but I'm certain we can negotiate a more reasonable price with little difficulty, aren't you?"

"You mean you wish to buy the old plantation?" Nigel was so shocked he almost relaxed his hold on the banister, but suspecting a trick, he immediately tightened his grip.

"Why yes. This is a beautiful house with ample property." Evan was amused by Nigel's quivering lips, and amazed that the man hadn't fainted dead away when he'd asked him to reenact his wife's fall. "Are you feeling unwell, Nigel? I swear your skin looks positively green this morning," he said. Then he started down the stairs, not looking back until he reached the second-floor landing. "Well, let's go. Perhaps we can agree upon a price as we ride home."

Nigel nodded, unable to recall what figure he'd named. "Whatever you feel is fair, Evan. The church will be grateful for whatever sum you can afford."

As the banker reached his side, Evan extended his hand. "Good, I'll consider the estate mine then."

"Yes, it's yours," Nigel agreed with a giddy laugh. He was so pleased to have survived the morning in one piece he decided to donate his commission on the sale of the Marshall estate to the church, an action so generous he knew Sheila would never approve, but that morning he didn't give a damn what she thought. "I must find a husband for my meddlesome sister," he said. "Can you think of any good prospects?"

Evan's laugh was even louder than Nigel's as he shook his head. "No, but I'll definitely give it some thought." As they started down the stairs to the first floor Nigel slipped, but Evan caught him by the scruff of the neck before he fell. "Really, Nigel, you must be more careful," he cautioned him, and with a jaunty whistle he led the way down the stairs and out the front door into the sunshine.

Chapter XIX

When Evan heard the sound of male voices coming from Bianca's room, he quickened his stride, fearing the doctor had been summoned, but upon reaching the open door, he found Will Summer talking with his stepfather and his wife. "Will, how nice of you to call. Has the whole town heard about Bianca's accident?"

Will leapt from his chair and reached out to shake his friend's hand. "That I wouldn't know. I heard about it when I stopped by the shipyard this morning so I came right on out here to see if your wife felt up to having visitors."

"And I said yes, of course," Bianca replied, smiling warmly at her guest. "Please bring another chair, Evan. This is almost like a party."

"No. I'll give him mine," Lewis offered graciously. "I think I'll go on into Newport News since I'm no longer needed here." He stepped close to the bed to take Bianca's hand lightly in his. "I don't think Dr. Stafford would approve of a party, my dear, but I'm grateful that you're feeling well enough to suggest one."

"Thank you for staying with me," Bianca replied sweetly. "It is tiresome to lie here in bed, and I appreciated your company."

Evan waited until his stepfather had left the room before he sat down and made himself comfortable. "Has Will been keeping you well entertained, or did you miss me?" he asked with a teasing grin. He'd already decided he'd wait until his pretty bride had completely recovered from her fall before he told her he'd purchased the Marshall estate. She'd be busy the entire winter redecorating the house, but they should be able to move in by spring. Pleased with that prospect, he hoped he'd be able to keep his purchase a secret for a few days at least.

"I'll not insult your best friend by saying I missed you," Bianca replied with a teasing laugh. "We were having such a nice time I barely noticed you'd left the room."

Will had to chuckle at that remark since he knew quite well he was a poor substitute for Evan. Actually, he had been enjoying himself immensely, but he wasn't at all certain that Bianca had been having as good a time. She'd seemed very nervous, but now that her husband had returned she'd become far more relaxed. Despite being preoccupied, she had conversed as easily with him as she had aboard the *Phoenix*, as always he'd been impressed by her intelligence as well as her beauty. He still felt more than a twinge of envy because she was Evan's wife, not his, and some shame at how often he compared Lily to her, for other than their fair coloring there was truly no likeness between the two young women. Each was unique, and he vowed to keep them separate in his mind from that moment on, though he was not altogether certain he could make the same distinction in his heart.

"You are feeling better then?" Evan hoped aloud.

Bianca raised her hand quickly to cover a yawn. "Yes, I'm much better," she lied sweetly. Her head still hurt and her back ached, and though she'd enjoyed seeing Will, she was tired and hoped he'd not stay much longer.

"I think it's time my wife took a nap, Will. Why don't

we step into my room for a moment? There's something I need to speak to you about." Evan rose and gave Bianca a kiss upon the cheek before leading his friend into the adjoining room, but he left the connecting door slightly ajar so he could hear Bianca should she call. "It's too early for a drink. Can I get you something else?" he offered politely.

"No, thank you," Will replied as he glanced toward the door. "Will we disturb her?"

"I don't think so. She's been sleeping quite a bit, but I'd like to be able to keep an eye on her all the same. I took Nigel over to the Marshall house this morning so he could explain exactly how she happened to fall. I'm not entirely satisfied with his story, he's far too nervous about it for one thing, but since Bianca insists her fall was an accident there's little I can do to punish him."

Will took the chair nearest the window as he agreed. "Nigel wouldn't deliberately hurt anyone, especially not a pretty young woman. Had she been alone in that house with Sheila, I'd never believe her fall was an accident."

"Neither would I. Now was there something important you needed to see me about today?"

"With Bianca so badly hurt this is going to sound very silly, but I'd rather not leave Lily until I absolutely must. I need the work of course, so if you have a voyage planned for the *Phoenix*, I'll gladly take it. However, I was hoping there might be a job for me at the shipyard so I could stay in Newport News until spring."

Evan nodded thoughtfully, and seeing no reason not to tell his friend of his plans, he lowered his voice to a discreet level and began to describe them. "I'm buying the Marshall place, Will. My mother has been up and about the last few days, but even if she completely recovers her former zest for life, I want to give Bianca her own home. She's made the best of a difficult situation here, but I think it would be good for all of us if she and I moved into that place. It will require a great deal of work, and I'll need a knowledgeable foreman to supervise it. There's little difference between handling a crew of carpenters and painters and one of sailors. Would you like the job?"

Will didn't even stop to think about it before he replied, "Of course! I just never thought I'd see the day you'd retire from the sea to become a gentleman farmer. Are you really going to devote yourself to raising tobacco now?"

Evan shook his head emphatically. "No. I've no interest in farming any crop. I plan to keep enough land to provide the home with a sufficient surrounding for gracious living, but I'll sell the rest of the acreage off as small farms that single families can manage. I'll not own a tobacco plantation, merely a fine home with many good neighbors I hope."

"Evan," Will was so excited by that statement he hardly knew where to begin, "there's nothing Lily would like more than a little house of her own but I didn't think I'd ever have the money to buy her one. Would you consider selling me a few acres? I'm no farmer either, but I'd like a house with a little bit of land so I'd know Lily would have a secure home even when I'm away at sea."

"Give me a few days to get everything settled with Nigel and the deed recorded; then if Bianca is well enough to stay by herself, we'll go out and survey the entire estate. I'll give you first pick of the property I decide to sell. I'm certain the work you'll do for me will cover the price of the land and the construction of a house."

Will glanced out the window for a moment to give himself a chance to catch his breath. "I can't agree to that, Evan. You're always so generous, and I'll never be able to pay back all the favors you've done for me."

Knowing he'd unintentionally embarrassed his good

friend, Evan leaned forward, his expression a serious one. "Look, Will, you've a lifetime to repay favors, and I'm certain there will be plenty of times when I'll need one from you. This is simply a good business venture. I will not only own a magnificent home, I'll make a considerable profit on the sale of the land as well. Frankly, Nigel was so afraid that I was going to wring his neck this morning he sold me the estate at a rock-bottom price. I'll have the home I want and a dozen or so families will be able to afford farms they'd not otherwise have been able to buy. You'd be doing me a favor by taking one of the plots as I don't relish the thought of being totally surrounded by farmers. I'd like to have someone nearby who could converse about sailing when I feel the need. You'd be doing me the favor, not the other way around."

Will grinned sheepishly. "You don't really expect me to believe that story do you?"

"Why not? It's the truth. Since you seem so taken with your Lily, ask her what she thinks of the idea. I'm sure she'll agree it's a fine one. I've been too distracted to secure cargo for the *Phoenix* for a last voyage before winter anyway, and I'm sure Lily will be pleased you'll not be leaving town anytime soon."

Will rose to his feet and shook Evan's hand once again. "I'm fairly certain she will, although she's not nearly so open as Bianca. She doesn't say much so it's difficult to tell exactly what she's thinking. I do know it's her dream to have a little house of her own though."

"She sounds very sweet. I'll look forward to meeting her," Evan replied sincerely.

"I'd like you to meet her, I really would, but what will Bianca think of her?" Will asked with an anxious frown.

Evan shrugged. "If you love Lily, I'm sure we will too. Why wouldn't we?"

Will began to blush at that question. "You know what she was, not everyone will forgive her for it. I'd rather you didn't tell Bianca about Lily's past if she doesn't already know."

Why the man was so damned concerned about his wife's opinion, Evan dared not guess, but he didn't like it one bit. "Do you plan to marry Lily?"

Will hesitated a moment too long before answering. "She's so damn helpless at times I don't know how she managed to survive this long without me, but I'm not certain marrying her would be the right thing for either of us. She might just be grateful to me, and that's not what I want in a wife."

"Just what is it you do want, Will?" Evan inquired softly, certain in his own mind that his friend wanted an exact duplicate of his own wife though he was positive there wasn't another woman like Bianca anywhere on the face of the earth.

"I guess I'll know when I find her," Will responded with a sly grin. "In the meantime, I'd like to build a house for Lily, but I'm going to argue with you some more about how I'm going to pay for it."

"Fine, you can argue all you want, but it won't change my mind." Evan walked Will out to his horse, promising he'd let him know when they could go to the Marshall estate to begin their surveying. Upon turning back to the house, he looked up and saw his mother standing at Bianca's window and he realized instantly that he shouldn't have left his wife upstairs alone. He raced back up to her room, where, to his surprise, his mother began to scold him.

"How are you going to hear your wife calling for you if you're outside talking with friends? Really, Evan, you should have let me know you'd not be in here. I'd have been happy to sit with Bianca for a while." Marion smiled sweetly at him and then excused herself, leaving the still-sleeping blonde unaware she'd had another visitor who had used the few minutes she'd been alone in the room to pocket the unopened bottle of laudanum she'd found on the nightstand. Marion planned to put it to good use. Taking John Stafford's advice to heart she'd made frequent trips out to the kitchen, and she knew it would be a simple matter to add tiny amounts of laudanum to Bianca's food. Not enough to do her any harm, just enough to make her feel so tired her recuperation would be more lengthy. Time was what Marion needed most at the moment, time to gain her son's trust as well as Bianca's so her tale would be all the more devastating when she finally had the opportunity to tell it.

The doctor, who continued to stop by the Sinclair home each afternoon, could not decide which of his two cases was the most perplexing. Marion Grey's recovery was nothing short of miraculous, while Bianca's progress was so slight he feared she'd suffered more serious injuries than he'd first diagnosed. She seemed to be resting comfortably, but she had so little stamina she could not take more than a few steps away from her bed without becoming so fatigued she quickly had to return to it. She still had no interest in food except for the delicious custard Marion had Viola make for her each morning, and although that was a wholesome dish, it certainly couldn't comprise her sole diet. Because she had not been active, she didn't appear to have lost weight, but he feared she would grow frail if she didn't soon regain her appetite.

Bianca now knew each of John Stafford's speeches by heart and she tried to eat, but she was never sufficiently hungry to take more than a bite or two of her meals. "I'm sorry to be such a nuisance," she apologized. "I want to get well so badly but—"

Evan was far more worried than he'd let his wife see, but he didn't want her to brood over her health so he spoke in a cheerful tone as he interrupted her. "It's been just a week since you fell, my love. I'm sure in another few days you'll feel as well as before and we'll be able to go out riding together again since the weather is still good. You mustn't be so impatient with yourself, I'm not." He prayed that for once John would keep still and to his great relief the doctor did. Once they were out in the hall, Evan said what was truly on his mind.

"Have you any idea why Bianca is doing so poorly? I'll force her to eat if you think it's only a matter of her needing better nutrition, but could it be something more serious?"

The lanky physician shrugged helplessly. "Perhaps you'd like someone else to examine her if she still shows no improvement by the end of the week."

Evan frowned impatiently. "There's no better doctor than you, John. Don't be ridiculous. I trust your judgment, but Bianca was so lively, always so full of fun, and it just isn't like her to stay in bed unless she is really ill."

"Oh, do not mistake me, I think there's a good reason she's so tired, but I simply don't know what it is."

Evan remained at the top of the stairs as the doctor saw himself out. He was feeling so discouraged he didn't want to return to his wife's room until he'd regained some of the optimism he always made a point to affect in her presence. He was anxious to get started with the Marshall house, their house, he reminded himself, but until Bianca began to improve he didn't see how he could be away from her long enough to begin the project.

Marion paused at the top of the stairs, surprised to see her son standing in the shadows. "Evan?" she called softly. "Is anything wrong?"

As his mother approached, smiling prettily, he realized she'd begun looking younger each day. She was positively glowing with health, and while he was pleased with that, he made no attempt to hide his concern. "Bianca's not any better at all today, Mother. At first she seemed to be making good progress, but the last few days she's been as weak as a kitten."

"Perhaps she overdid it then, Evan. Your friend Will was here that morning you were out. They were laughing together, I don't think she was ready for that. Isn't that when her recovery began to slow? In fact, you probably tire her out yourself by spending so much time with her each day. I'm sure she doesn't want you to worry about her and that must be a strain. I'll bet if you left the house for a few hours tomorrow, she'd be able to get some real rest and you'd see an improvement in her condition as soon as you came home."

"I don't want to leave her, Mother," Evan explained simply, still convinced that her accident had been a needless tragedy which she'd never have suffered if he'd given her more attention. "Not yet."

"Well why don't you ask her what she thinks?" Marion suggested sweetly. "I'm sure she knows what would be best."

"I already know what she'd say were I to ask such a question. She'd say she'd be fine alone."

"Well why don't you believe her?" Marion asked slyly. "Perhaps more rest and less company is all she needs."

While he hated to admit it, he thought his mother might actually have discovered the problem he'd been too close to see. Whenever Bianca was awake they talked. He told her about some of his more adventuresome voyages, related a few incidents of the war, even discussed his ideas to improve the lines of the Baltimore clipper without sacrificing either speed or cargo space. He simply enjoyed being with her so greatly that he'd not even considered he might be overtiring her himself.

"I'll speak with her about it in the morning. There are several things I need to do, and I could finally see to them if she'd really like some time alone to rest."

"Yes. Let her decide what's best." Marion reached up to kiss her son's cheek before slipping into her room where she could barely restrain herself from whooping for joy. Had she discovered Charles's journal sooner she would have had the little slut out of her house long ago, she thought. If Evan actually did leave her unattended the next morning she'd have a long talk with the girl. She'd also stop lacing her dishes of custard with laudanum so Bianca would swiftly regain her strength. With any luck, the Venetian would be gone in less than a week. Delighted with her own cleverness, Marion danced a spritely jig around her room, no longer feeling a bit tired herself.

"Tell me the truth, do you mind if I leave for a few hours this morning, or would you really appreciate the peace and quiet?" Evan inquired with a ready grin, wanting his bride to make her own choice.

Bianca no longer suffered from painful headaches and most of her bruises had faded away, but she knew she'd have to remain in bed until she felt more like herself. Evan's question made her fear she'd become a burden to him since he'd completely neglected his business interests to be with her since her accident. Rather than ask him to keep her company when he clearly wished to be elsewhere, she sent him on his way. "I love being with you, Evan, you know that, but were you to leave I would just take a nap so I'd not miss you."

Evan bent down to kiss her lips lightly. He'd shared her bed each night, but knowing she lacked the strength to leave it, he'd not pressed her to make love. He'd merely held her tenderly in his arms enjoying that loving closeness for the time being. Still, he was so anxious for her to get well he was willing to give his mother's suggestion a try. "I'll have Viola check on you frequently, or if you'd rather, I'll ask Mattie to stay here with you."

Marion stopped by Bianca's room so often she no longer had any fear of being alone with her. In fact, she did not even think of the woman. "No, I'll be fine." Yawning again, she snuggled down into her pillows. "You'll promise to wake me when you come home though, won't you?"

"Yes." Evan remained at her bedside for a moment, not wanting to leave but thinking now that he'd said good-bye he must. "I won't be gone long."

"You needn't rush. I'll be fine," Bianca insisted again.

After one last kiss, Evan forced himself to leave, but he instructed Viola to visit his wife's room often so she'd not want for anything. When he did so, his mother was in the kitchen too, sampling the latest batch of custard which had just been set out to cool, and he stopped to kiss her good-bye. "It's lucky we found one thing at least that Bianca will eat."

Marion set aside her spoon and wiped off her hands before returning his kiss. "Everyone always loves my custard, that's why I knew Bianca would. Don't worry. We'll take care of everything here. You stay in town as long as you like."

While he had no intention of riding into town, Evan didn't say so. He'd told no one but Will that he'd bought the Marshall estate, but he wanted to visit it again before he invited his friend to go with him. "Let's hope your suggestion works, Mother." He left the house then, eager to run his errand and get back to his charming bride.

Marion let Viola check on Bianca once before she made her way upstairs. The young woman was asleep, but Marion planned to have her wide awake during their talk. First she got Charles's journal and the neatly folded handkerchief she'd found tucked inside it; then she went into the Venetian beauty's bedroom. She placed a chair at the side of the bed, sat down, and reached out to give Bianca's arm a gentle shake. "My dear, you must wake up. We have but a few minutes to talk privately, and I've something very important to say."

Startled by the sound of her mother-in-law's voice, Bianca awakened instantly, and seeing the woman seated at her side with a book in her hands, she thought she'd come to read to her. "Good morning." She offered Marion a shy smile.

Marion patted her daughter-in-law's hand lightly before sitting back. "We've not much time so you must pay close attention. I was too ill to greet you properly when Evan brought you home, but now it is my hope you will become the daughter I never had. For us to be close, however, you must learn the truth of why you are here."

The woman's compelling gaze and mystifying words had captured Bianca's attention instantly, but they had also thoroughly confused her. "I'm here because I am Evan's wife and he loves me. What other truth could there be?"

"That is what I mean to explain," Marion revealed dramatically. "Evan told me you didn't know Charles, but how can that be true when he was so deeply in love with you? Here, let me read a page or two from his journal. These are the last entries he made before his death." Marion looked up frequently to be certain Bianca was listening closely. She'd read the book so often she could recite the neatly penned passages from memory but she did not want to appear that familiar with her son's last thoughts. "He has described you perfectly, don't you agree? Your hair is like spun gold and your eyes have the fiery sparkle of fine emeralds. You would seem a goddess to any young man with so poetic a soul as my Charles. Indeed, you two would have been a most charming pair, but alas, apparently you had so many suitors you do not even recall his name."

Bianca had been deeply touched by Charles's words for indeed he must have adored the woman he'd described in such exquisite detail. While not written in verse, his journal had the melodic tone of poetry, and that he'd loved this beautiful lady so intensely but had died without leaving any indication that his love had been returned was heartbreaking. However, she knew the young woman could not possibly have been she. "Mrs. Grey, your son was obviously a fine young man and a very talented writer, but I am positive we never met."

Marion dismissed Bianca's denial as unimportant. "Whether you knew Charles or not is irrelevant now, my dear. What matters is that he paid with his life for loving you. When Evan went to Venice last spring to find you, it never occurred to me he'd bring you home. I am afraid I've behaved very badly toward you thus far, although now I am certain you can understand why I was reluctant to accept you into our family. Since my son has forgiven you for causing his brother's death, I have now decided I can do no less and I hope we'll be able to become close friends."

Stunned to be forgiven so generously for a crime in which she was positive she'd played no part, Bianca struggled to sit up so she could face the woman squarely. "Are you saying that Evan thought I had something to do with Charles's murder?"

Appearing the very soul of discretion, Marion lowered her voice to a conspiratorial whisper. "It was no mere suspicion, he knew from reading Charles's journal it was indeed your fault. He went to Venice solely to avenge his brother's death. What better revenge could he take than to wed the woman who'd caused it? Even though Charles had failed to win your heart, Evan soon did, didn't he?"

Bianca could barely catch her breath, she was so shocked by Marion's calmly worded accusation. "No, what you're saying can't possibly be true, it just can't. No man could be as cold blooded as that."

"Oh, my son isn't in the least bit cold blooded. He's

quite hot tempered in fact." Withdrawing the lace-trimmed handkerchief from her pocket, she unfolded it so Bianca could see the elaborately embroidered initial. "You were surprisingly easy to find, my dear. I believe Antonelli is your maiden name, is it not?"

Bianca stared at the elegantly swirling lines of the neatly stitched letter until it was branded in her mind although her vision blurred by tears. "No, no, there's been some horrible mistake," she whispered, her voice hoarse with emotion.

"The only mistake was that Evan did not tell you of his true motives for seeking you out in the beginning. I begged him to tell you this story himself, but he refused. I don't think it's proper for a man to keep such a dark secret from his wife, do you? Naturally he's reluctant to let you see how ruthless he is, but you would have discovered it soon enough on your own, I'm certain."

As tears spilled down her cheeks Bianca lay back against her pillows, fighting with all her inner strength not to accept so ghastly a tale as the truth, yet her own memories swiftly confirmed it. Her first meetings with Evan had been filled with drama, with an excitement so intense she'd been unable to resist his insistent invitations. Her desire for him had grown stronger with each new day until her need to be his had overwhelmed her resolve to obey her parents' command that she marry Paolo. Evan's love had seemed so real to her, as deep as her own, but had his courtship been motivated by a lust for revenge instead of by love? Had the fire of the passion which had sprung up between them so quickly been fueled by his hatred? She could not bear the pain of that thought. "Please go. I'd like to be alone."

"My dear, you must not make yourself more ill than you already are. Evan has forgiven you for your part in Charles's death; we all have. I would not have told you the truth today had I thought you'd take it so badly."

Marion rose slowly, glad the slender young woman couldn't see her mocking smile. She leaned down to place the handkerchief in her trembling hands. "Here, you may need this and my memories of my dear Charles are complete without it."

While Bianca clutched the linen handkerchief tightly, she did not use it to dry her tears. Her head now ached with a far sharper pain than the one which had resulted from her fall and her mind was bombarded by images of the most excruciating sort. She could recall with crystal clarity the moment she'd first met Evan. His tone had been mocking, his hatred clear as they'd been introduced, yet she'd been so stupid she'd mistaken his hostility for a reaction to her British heritage. How could she have been so naïve? She tortured herself with that question, asking it again and again. Perhaps inadvertently he'd allowed her a glimpse of his true feelings, but she'd later thought him so handsome she'd believed his lies. Was she so incredibly vain she had accepted his compliments on her beauty without once doubting his motives? How could she have been such a fool? The frequent darkness of his moods on their voyage home had a ready explanation now. He had simply used her body because he'd needed a woman, but inside he must have felt as though he were embracing some hideous serpent. She understood it all now, how his passion had gradually grown more tender, how he'd come to love her despite the fact that he held her responsible for his only brother's murder. Such an inner conflict would have killed a lesser man, but in time Evan had simply forgiven her, absolved her of the crime so she'd be worthy of his love. Now his mother had forgiven her too, only she had a far higher regard for the value of honesty than her son.

Bianca struggled to focus her eyes on the delicately embroidered *A* which adorned the lace-trimmed handkerchief. She traced it again and again with her fingertips. The linen still held a faint trace of some woman's seductive perfume, a beautiful woman with golden hair and eyes so vivid a green they'd set Charles's soul aflame with desire at first glance. Evan had thought the lace-trimmed handkerchief all the proof he needed of her guilt, yet Bianca had never seen it before. It was not one of hers. What would Evan do now, she wondered, when he realized he'd avenged his brother's murder by marrying the wrong woman?

Chapter XX

Exhausted by tears, Bianca was sleeping so soundly when Evan returned home that he dared not wake her. Instead he chose to work at the desk in his own room where he knew he would hear her when she first began to stir. It seemed obvious to him now that his mother's theory had been correct: he'd simply provided such splendid company he'd not allowed Bianca to get the rest she needed to get well. An unfortunate error he'd not repeat, still, he wanted to remain nearby, even if he did not stay in her room.

A cursory examination of the land surrounding the Marshall mansion had allowed him to become familiar with the natural variations in the terrain which could be used to form logical boundaries. He'd use them to create farms of sufficient size to support single families and allow for a reasonable profit as well. He admired Will for wanting to provide a secure home for Lily as he'd heard his share of complaints from men who made their livelihood in the merchant marine and knew it was difficult for them to be separated from those they loved for long periods of time. He'd never regretted his former solitary way of life, but now that he and Bianca were so happy together, he doubted he'd ever want to make another lengthy voyage. The thrill of launching a ship he'd designed and built gave him the greatest surge of pride. He didn't need to endlessly traverse the globe in order to be content. Yet, he'd never thought the prospect of creating a home would excite him so, and he prayed Bianca would soon be well enough to share his enthusiasm. He went into her room to check on her again, but she was still sound asleep so he let her rest.

Bianca did not awaken until midafternoon, and though Evan was eager to talk with her, she found it nearly impossible to respond coherently to his attempts at conversation. Marion's news had destroyed the snug world she'd thought they shared. Evan had taken such care to create that world, she reminded herself once again. If the tenderness she'd mistaken for love in the beginning had, in fact, been tightly controlled hatred, she dared not even imagine what Evan thought of her now, or how swiftly his feelings for her might change if he suspected she knew the truth. When Viola served her a steaming portion of vegetable soup, it required Bianca's full attention simply to guide the spoon to her lips, she was so badly frightened. She was surprisingly hungry, however, and that provided sufficient motivation for her to make the effort to eat. Any distraction was welcome when she found her husband's presence so unsettling. She had hidden the embroidered handkerchief beneath her pillow before she'd fallen asleep, unwilling as well as unable to question him about it until she'd regained her strength. Marion had described her son as ruthless, and Bianca knew if she simply accused Evan of lying to her, he would be furious, perhaps even violent. No, she'd have to be far more clever than that. She wanted desperately to learn the truth, but she feared the price of that knowledge might well be her marriage.

Despite his best efforts to chat politely with his wife, Evan found his thoughts taking an increasingly erotic turn. They had been so close, the love they shared so natural in its expression, and he had missed her affection more than he'd thought possible. "You slept so long today, I hope you won't have difficulty falling asleep tonight." While his smile was sweet, his thoughts were wild, for he'd grown weary of having to restrain his passions. Secretly he hoped she'd be as wide awake as he knew he was going to be. He knew how to make love tenderly so as not to cause her the slightest pain, and he hoped she'd missed him so greatly she'd allow him that opportunity.

Bianca looked up only briefly and finding his loving gaze impossible to return, she sipped another spoonful of soup before replying, "Eating soup always makes me sleepy. I'll be lucky to finish this before I doze off again."

Evan straightened up, disappointed to think that night would be no different than the last. "Your headaches are gone, aren't they?" he asked bluntly.

"Yes," Bianca admitted softly.

"That bruise over your eye is now faint and most of the others have faded away completely," he pointed out, not understanding why she didn't feel as well as she looked.

"I know it's taking too long for me to get well, Evan. You needn't catalog my injuries." She tossed her pale blonde hair impatiently. "I'm sorry, but I thought I'd be well long before this and I'm as unhappy about the situation as you are."

Astonished by that unexpected rebuke, Evan decided she'd be better off by herself until her mood improved. He forced himself to display a calm he didn't feel and rose slowly to replace his chair near the wall. "Would you like more of that soup? It smells delicious."

"It is good, but no. This is all I can eat. Would you take the tray back to the kitchen, please?"

"Of course. Shall I bring you a book to read, poetry perhaps?"

"No, thank you." Bianca tried to smile, but she knew her expression was far from cordial. She needed more time to think about this man who was her husband, more time to consider his actions in the new light in which she now saw them. "I'd just like to rest."

"I think maybe I'll eat supper downstairs tonight if you don't need me to stay with you." Evan was ashamed of himself for wanting more than she seemed ready to give, but she was so lovely he could not look at her without the heat of his desire causing him considerable pain. "Will you be all right?"

"I'm sure I will." Bianca watched him go, uncertain if that was what she should have said or not, but she was relieved to be alone again. Later Viola helped her to prepare for the night and when Evan came into her room she pretended to be asleep rather than risk speaking with him again when her thoughts of him were in such turmoil. When he finally joined her in the bed, he stayed on his own side of it as though he suspected his embrace would not be welcome, and that confused her all the more. He had always been so dear, but now that she knew his true motives for marrying her, the beauty of the love she'd always thought he had for her was obscured by a thick cloud of doubt. She had to speak with someone she could trust, someone who would understand her dilemma and help her solve it. She already knew Marion's point of view, and although Lewis had a warm and friendly nature, she didn't want to bring back the pain of his only son's death by confiding in him. Then she recalled William's offer of friendship. Of course! He was the perfect choice; he'd know exactly what Evan's motives had been and she knew instinctively he'd tell her the truth. She decided that the minute she could leave her bed she'd go into town to see him, and she fell asleep praying that the answers he gave her would be reassuring ones.

Much to her delight, Bianca's recovery began to progress far more rapidly. She kept her secret to herself, however, and continued to remain in her room, though not abed, and each day she felt stronger. When Evan announced one morning that he'd be working at the shipyard all day, she immediately made plans to go into town. Lewis had gone into Newport News, and when Marion went to her room to rest after lunch, Bianca rushed down the stairs and summoned Nathan, instructing him to drive the carriage into town. The man was startled by her request, but he dared not disobey and he took her straight to River's End.

"I won't be long, Nathan. Please wait for me right here," Bianca instructed him breathlessly before sweeping through the front door of the modest inn. Despite the improvement in her health, the excitement of her errand had made her slightly dizzy, and when she reached the desk she had to grip the edge tightly to steady herself. "I've come to see William Summer. Which room is his, please?"

It took an astonished Rachel Kelly several seconds to find her voice. She was not used to seeing so beautiful and finely dressed a young woman in her establishment. That this lady had asked for Will Summer was also a shock. Since she was obviously no whore looking to ply her trade, Rachel could think of no reason not to reply truthfully. "He's in number twelve, but whether he's in or not I can't say."

Bianca bit her lower lip anxiously. "Well, I'll go up and see if he is. If he isn't, he told me I might leave him a note here at the desk."

"Yes, I take his messages," Rachel offered with a smile, hoping she'd be able to read the one this beauty left.

Bianca lifted her skirts and started up the stairs, but when she reached the landing, she had to stop and rest a moment to catch her breath. She prayed that Will would be in his room, but when she rapped lightly at his door, there was no reply. Thinking he might possibly be asleep, she knocked again more insistently, and in a moment the door was opened by a slender blonde.

"Oh, I'm sorry. I thought the clerk said room twelve belonged to Mr. Summer." Bianca apologized quickly, thinking she'd made a mistake.

"Yes, this is his room," Lily replied with a puzzled frown. The stunning visitor was about her height, but her blonde hair was a more golden shade, and she wore it in a glorious cascade of gleaming curls. The thick fringe of her long lashes veiled eyes of a vivid green rather than pale blue ones. Lily had the strangest sensation, a tingling chill that shivered down her spine. She felt as though she were looking into a mirror, but reflected there she saw a woman far more beautiful and poised than she could ever hope to be. She'd had little experience speaking with women so obviously wealthy and cultured as this one, but she stepped aside to allow her to enter. "Would you like to come in and wait for him? He should be back soon."

Badly shocked to have discovered Will shared his quarters with this young woman, Bianca hesitated a moment before deciding what to do. "No, I really haven't the time to wait. If you have paper and ink I'd like to leave a message for him, though."

"Yes. They're in the desk." Lily gestured toward it and then excused herself. "I'm in the next room," she stated pleasantly. "Since I knew Mr. Summer wasn't in, I thought I'd answer his door for him." With that hasty excuse, she returned to her own room and closed the door.

Bianca thought the girl must be stupid indeed to imagine she'd believe that ridiculous tale. She was obviously Will's mistress, but so what? The man was attractive and single, and if he wished to keep a dozen women, she'd not fault him for it. She'd just been surprised to find that he was living with someone. She sat down at the desk and, after a moment's hesitation, wrote a brief note asking Will to come to see her at his earliest convenience. She reminded him of his generous offer of friendship, and requested his silence on the matter. After signing only her first name, she left the note open on the desk, knowing the girl would probably read it even if she sealed it in an envelope, but she was too worried that her husband would discover why she'd come into town to care whether or not the note remained private. She let herself out, hurried down the stairs, and with only a slight nod to Rachel left the inn to return home, where she made Nathan swear he'd never tell a soul where he'd taken her.

Lily heard Will's door close, and unable to contain her curiosity, she stepped back into his room. She read the note on the desk several times, trying to discern if there was a deeper meaning than the words first seemed to impart. Will had spoken of only one woman named Bianca, so she knew this must have been Mrs. Sinclair. "I should have introduced myself. She must have thought I had no manners at all," she mused absently. It seemed plain that the lovely Bianca Sinclair had gotten herself into some grave trouble and she expected Will to get her out of it without telling her husband. Lily sighed softly, perplexed by the young woman's demand. Will worked for Evan; how could he possibly help his wife without telling the man? Leaving the note where it lay, she strolled over to the window to look out at the street, recalling the day she'd watched Evan leave the hotel. He'd not only been handsome, he'd carried himself with such obvious pride that she knew without a doubt he'd not want any man, especially not his best friend, interfering in his marriage. Why hadn't Bianca known that? Or was she so spoiled she just didn't care? Lily turned then as she heard Will insert his key in the lock. "You had a visitor," she called out softly by way of greeting. "She left you a note."

"She?" Will asked with a bewildered frown, but the instant he saw Bianca's signature he grabbed the message and read it eagerly. "When was she here?"

"Ten, maybe fifteen minutes ago."

"Damn! If only I'd been here!"

Lily leaned back against the window, her pose relaxed even though she was terrified that what she was thinking was true. "You'll go to see her then, without telling her husband?"

"Of course. If she needs to speak with me, I'll go tomorrow. I only hope this isn't what I think it is."

"And what is that?" Lily asked curiously.

Unwilling to relate the tale, Will simply shook his head. "I'd rather not say. I told you she'd been badly injured in a fall. How did she look to you? Is she completely recovered?"

"She appeared to be. She's very beautiful, isn't she? She was wearing a gown of pale rose satin, and her hair was beautifully dressed. I'll bet that emerald ring she wears cost a fortune."

Will recognized the tinge of jealousy in Lily's voice, but at that moment he was more concerned about Bianca's request than her feelings and he didn't take the time to reassure her that they were groundless. "I've told you more than once that Evan is an extremely generous man. That he wishes to dress his wife in fine clothing and expensive jewels should come as no surprise."

"Just how far does his generosity extend, Will?"

"What's that supposed to mean?" Will responded angrily.

Lily turned back toward the window. "Will it cost you your job if he discovers you're seeing his wife?"

"I am not 'seeing' Bianca!" Will protested immediately. "She's just asked to talk with me, that's all. Don't make something more out of this."

"Do I remind you of her?" Lily asked wistfully.

For an instant Will was certain his heart had ceased to beat, and he had to struggle to force back the wave of fear which had swept through him in response to her question. "You're both pretty blondes, is that what you mean?"

"No," Lily responded simply.

Since there was nothing he could do about Bianca's request until the next day, Will set her note aside and went over to Lily. He bent down to kiss her throat softly as he whispered. "Bianca is Evan's woman and you are mine. There's no other comparison."

Lily closed her eyes as she leaned back against his broad chest, praying that what he said was true, but her doubts returned when he left the next morning without revealing his destination. She'd not bothered to ask where he was going since she was certain it was to see Bianca Sinclair. She sank down upon the bed and pouted angrily. "Maybe I ought to tell Evan myself just what his pretty little wife is up to." She was sorely tempted to do it too, but fearing Will would be the one to suffer rather than Bianca, she gave up the idea.

"I've had so little opportunity to leave the house since the accident, would you mind if we walked down to the river, Mr. Summer?" Knowing he'd not object, Bianca took his arm and led him toward the front door.

"I'd be delighted." Will escorted her some distance from the house before he felt safe in speaking, and even then he whispered. "I'm sorry I missed you yesterday. I came as quickly as I could."

"Yes, I knew you would. Thank you." When they reached a bench that offered an excellent view of the river, Bianca sat down, fidgeting nervously as she waited for Will to take his place at her side. "Evan's mother told me something. I need to know whether or not it's true."

Will shrugged helplessly. "I know she's feeling better, but I doubt I can back up anything she might have said." The young man could not help but notice the subtle changes in his pretty friend. While she was no less attractive, she was so nervous he ached to put his arms around her to reassure her everything would be all right, yet he dared not touch her when someone might be watching them from the house.

Bianca turned toward him, her expression intense as her perceptive gaze focused upon him. "Did Evan marry me because he thought I had something to do with his brother's murder? A simple yes or no will do."

Will gasped sharply, the breath forced out of him as though he'd been kicked. "That's not so easy a question to answer as it seems, Bianca."

Bianca looked away, her eyes filling with tears as she understood why he'd not reply. She'd prayed that her mother-in-law had been mistaken about Evan's motives. Now she was positive Marion had spoken the truth. She felt as though her whole world had come to end, for nothing would ever be mroe precious to her than Evan's love which she now knew had been a sham. "He has the wrong woman, Will. Marion showed me Charles's diary, but the woman he described in such lavish detail wasn't me. The initialed handkerchief wasn't mine either."

"What?" Will didn't know which was worse, that Bianca knew why Evan had married her, or her discovery of her husband's dreadful mistake. He knew he'd have to do some fast talking to save his friend, yet he feared he wasn't nearly eloquent enough for the task. "Let's take this one step at a time. Just what did Marion tell you?"

Bianca gave him a disgusted glance. "Exactly what I said. Evan went to Venice for the sole purpose of avenging his brother's death. For some reason he thought he'd done that by marrying me. He was wrong."

Wrong on two counts, Will thought to himself. Apparently Evan had married the wrong woman for the wrong reason. "Have you told Evan what his mother said?"

"No, of course not," Bianca scoffed. "That would be suicidal."

"Surely you can't think he'd harm you!"

Bianca lifted her chin proudly. "I know he'd never harm me, Will, but he'd not be happy to know I've discovered why he married me. Everything he told me was a lie, every single thing. Only the joke's on him, isn't it? He told me he loved me when all he wanted was revenge. What's he going to do when he learns he made a terrible mistake and married the wrong woman?"

Will leaned forward, resting his arms across his knees as he tried to reason with the distraught young woman. "What difference does it make why he married you, Bianca, when you love each other so dearly?"

"Oh, do we?" she snapped angrily. "The man married me for revenge, Will, not love! He couldn't have felt the slightest bit of love for me and done that. Why didn't you warn me before I'd married him? You've always seemed like an honest man, even if my husband isn't."

Will had done his best to dissuade Evan from marrying her, but since he'd not succeeded he offered no excuse now. "Do you want me to talk to Evan? Is that what you want?"

"No!" Bianca responded forcefully. "He must not even suspect that I've learned the truth. I want to go home, and if he knows I want to leave him he'll never allow it. Can you book passage for me on a ship bound for the Mediterranean? I've jewelry I'm sure will cover my fare and something more for you."

"Oh, Bianca, you can't want to leave Evan, you just can't." Will began to argue with her, but he could tell from the flames of anger glowing in her eyes that she was determined to do just that.

"I need your help, Will. You promised me that someday I'd need it, and now I know why. You knew I'd learn what had really happened in Venice sooner or later, didn't you?"

"Yes," Will admitted reluctantly, "but I didn't think you'd leave Evan over it. Not when he loves you so deeply. I know he adores you, Bianca. How can you doubt his feelings for you are sincere?" Will knew his friend hadn't told his wife about the Marshall estate yet so he dared not mention it. "He has so many wonderful plans for your future. You have your whole lives to share. How can you even consider leaving him?"

Bianca leapt to her feet and turned to face him. "If Evan lied to me from the moment we met simply to lure me into a marriage motivated by a desire for revenge, I do not want him for my husband! You say he loves me now, but he couldn't have loved me then, and who can predict how he'll feel about me tomorrow when he has so little regard for the truth? How can you consider asking me to stay with a man who spoke of love, who made love, when all he felt for me was contempt? Why should I have to suffer with that knowledge for the rest of my life? I'd never be certain whether the love he was showing me was real or merely part of some sinister plot."

Will rose quickly and took her arm to guide her back up the path. She was trembling all over, and he patted her hand lightly in a vain attempt to restore her to calm. "I know what he did was wrong, I told him so at the very beginning, but isn't your marriage worth saving? Isn't Evan's love worth more to you now than your pride?"

Shocked by his question, Bianca came to an abrupt halt. "This is not a question of love and pride, but one of revenge and a hatred so deep I can scarcely comprehend it. What he did was unspeakably cruel, and if you won't help me return home, then I will have to go to Nigel Blanchard and ask for his help. It is only because you offered your assistance should I ever have need of it that I went to you first."

Will drew the trembling young woman into his arms and hugged her tightly, no longer caring if anyone saw them and thought his gesture too bold. The scent of her perfume was so inviting he dared hold her only briefly, but he enjoyed having her in his arms so greatly it was a while before he finally stepped back. "This will take some time to arrange, you realize. Ships bound for the Mediterranean do not sail from Newport News every day."

"They do transport tobacco from here to England, though," Bianca reminded him. "If I could get that far, I'm certain I could travel aboard a European ship for the remainder of the journey."

Will nodded. "That's undoubtedly true, but this late in the fall, I still may have difficulty arranging passage for you."

"You will try, won't you? Oh, please, say you will," Bianca begged with tear-filled eyes.

Will would have done anything to please her, but he felt as badly now as he had when Evan had asked him to perform their marriage ceremony. "Don't you realize what you want to do to Evan is every bit as wrong as what he did to you? If only you two would sit down together and talk this over I'm sure—"

"No," Bianca responded firmly. "He'd never tell me the truth. My only choice is to end this now, before he causes me any more pain with his lies."

Will could not argue when the mist of her tears had given the green of her eyes the brilliance of emeralds. He was fascinated by her, and it wasn't simply her beauty which exerted such a strong hold upon his emotions. The fire of her spirit enflamed him with desire. He had never wanted to kiss any woman as he longed to kiss Bianca, but he knew if he showed her how deeply he cared for her he'd only add to her mental torment and he'd no wish to create another problem for her. He could only pray that by the time he found a captain willing to take a passenger to England, Bianca would have changed her mind about returning to Venice. He escorted her back to the house, bid her a polite good day, and, with a heavy heart and a troubled conscience, rode slowly back into town.

Marion smiled to herself as she stepped back from the window. She knew if Will Summer had come calling on Bianca he'd undoubtedly first made certain Evan wouldn't be home. The two men were close friends. It would have been a simple matter for him to stop by the shipyard to chat with Evan before he rode out to their house. Furthermore, although Bianca had not mentioned her trip into town, Marion also knew she'd left the house the previous afternoon, and now she realized exactly where she'd gone. She wondered just how close Bianca and Will truly were. The girl had obviously turned to him for support of some kind, whether it was emotional or financial didn't matter. Eventually Evan would discover what she was up to and he'd be furious over her duplicity. Things were going almost too well, and Marion was delighted. First, she'd made Bianca suspicious of Evan and now she had evidence of a friendship which would make Evan equally suspicious of his wife. At dinner that night she made her comment in an offhand manner and then sat back to watch the sparks fly.

"I'm sorry I had no chance to speak with William Summer while he was here this morning. I always liked that young man," Marion remarked with a smile.

"Will was here?" Evan looked toward his wife for an

explanation. "I saw him myself this morning and he didn't mention that he planned to come out here."

Bianca lay her fork aside. She was so nervous she knew she'd have dropped it in another second. "He was here only a few minutes, just to say hello."

Evan hoped his friend hadn't let anything slip about the Marshall house. That was a surprise he wanted to reveal to Bianca himself. "Will is a very considerate fellow, but I hope his visit didn't tire you."

"He was only here a few minutes, as I said," Bianca explained again.

Evan took a sip of his wine and tried to pretend he hadn't seen something which looked remarkably like fear in his wife's gaze. He couldn't imagine why she was so terribly tense. She seemed completely well, but she was as nervous as a cat and he was still very worried about her since her mental well-being was every bit as important to him as her physical health. Apparently her accident had upset her more deeply than they'd first thought. She was high strung, delicate in both her appearance and manner. Somehow he'd thought her to be far more resilient than she was proving to be. They'd still not resumed that portion of their marriage he cherished most, and he knew he simply could not wait much longer for her desire to again equal his.

When Lewis Grey changed the subject to a matter concerning new merchandise for his shops, Bianca sighed with relief. Nonetheless, she had difficulty finishing her dinner for she was certain Evan would ask her about Will's visit later, when they were alone. Each time she glanced his way she found him looking at her with a puzzled stare, and knowing she was a very poor actress, she prayed Will would find her a ship leaving the very next day. She had to get away from Evan, she simply had to. Each time she looked at him she was reminded of what he'd done and that pain was nearly unbearable. She'd loved him with all her heart, but she'd never really known him until the afternoon his mother had come into her room to make friends. As tears welled up in her eyes, she forced them away, knowing she'd never be able to leave her husband unless she fooled him completely.

Bianca knew how badly Evan wanted her, and although she prayed that this would be the last time they made love, when he joined her in bed she moved into his arms.

"I have missed you," she forced herself to say, glad that he'd doused the lamp before coming to bed for she knew her troubled expression would have given away her true feelings.

While he was delighted to find his wife in so receptive a mood, Evan tempered his own enthusiasm for her affection with tenderness. He covered her face with light kisses and then drew back slightly. "If there's something still troubling you about your accident, I wish you'd tell me. You needn't shield Nigel any longer if he was truly to blame. I won't tear him limb from limb, I promise."

Bianca was surprised that he thought she was upset because of Nigel, but she didn't use the man as an excuse for her nervousness. "Nigel is as innocent as I told you he was. If I do not seem myself, it is not his fault, but mine. I am just so unaccustomed to being ill I was a difficult patient, but I will try to make it up to you."

"Bianca, there's nothing to make up. Now come here." Evan silenced any further apologies she might have wished to make with a lingering kiss. His whole body ached with the need of her, yet he slowly aroused her passions, his gentle caresses leaving her trembling with desire. He loved to touch her lightly perfumed skin, to enjoy the softness of her breasts, to savor the warm moist sweetness her body created solely to welcome his. He had never taken such pleasure from a woman as from his slender bride. She had been born to be his, he was certain of that, and as she enfolded him in her arms, he lost himself again in her loving, thinking himself the luckiest man alive.

Chapter XXI

Will barely tasted his supper. Lily kept glancing up at him, her blue eyes bright with curiosity, and although she made no comment on his obvious distress, he couldn't bring himself to confide in her. Although performing a wedding ceremony for Evan when he'd mistrusted his motives had pained his conscience badly, that torment had been slight compared to what he was suffering now. Evan was the best friend he could ever hope to have, but Bianca, well, Bianca was simply the most delightful woman he'd ever known. Her innocence as well as her radiant beauty had captivated him the moment they'd met and he wanted to do what was truly best for her, but it seemed there was no way that could also be what was best for Evan. When they had finished eating he excused himself, rather rudely he was afraid, and went out for a walk hoping the chill of the night air would help to clear his mind.

Were he to help Bianca leave, Evan would swiftly learn she was gone and just who had arranged her departure. He could imagine how angry the man would be, and he knew there would be no way to escape his wrath. To help Bianca meant betraying Evan, yet how could he refuse to help the young woman he admired so highly? That she would even consider turning to him for help was so flattering he wanted desperately to please her, no matter what the price. It all came down to the price he'd have to pay, he finally realized. Was Bianca Sinclair's admiration worth the price Evan would extract? She'd be gone and he'd probably never see her again, but there would be no way for him to escape the power of her husband's influence. In helping Bianca he knew he'd not only be sacrificing his friendship with Evan, but his career as a sea captain as well. The house he'd hoped to build for Lily would remain no more than a dream. It seemed his whole life hung in the balance, and he longed to make the right decision. He walked so far the moon was high in the sky before he returned to the hotel. He'd searched his heart for an answer to his dilemma, but each possibility caused him only new avenues of pain. He doubted he was clever enough to solve so difficult a problem as Bianca presented, yet he vowed to do his best to try. There is a correct answer to every puzzle no matter how complex, and he was certain there was a fair solution to this problem too. He'd not give up trying until he found it. He might lack Evan's keen intelligence, but he did possess tenacity and he swore to make that trait count for all it was worth.

When she heard Will enter his room, Lily pretended to be asleep. He was always so talkative, but clearly he had no desire to share his present problem with her. Even without an explanation she knew exactly what was troubling him. Bianca Sinclair had decided she had some use for him. She'd simply crooked her prettily manicured finger, beckoned to him with a toss of her golden curls, and he'd gone running to her like a devoted pet. That he was in love with his best friend's wife was so pathetically obvious, Lily knew her only real choice if she wanted to save her own pride was to leave him. She knew she'd been a fool to stay with him so long, yet when he joined her in the bed his kisses were so eager she feared come dawn she'd find some excuse, no matter how pitiful, to remain.

It took Will the better part of an agonizing week to put together a scheme which satisfied both Bianca's desire to return home and his own need to placate his conscience for meddling in his best friend's marriage. In the end, the choice he made seemed the only logical one, and he prayed all concerned would eventually agree. Since repeated calls at the Sinclair home would raise too many questions, he waited until the last possible moment to visit Bianca. He carefully timed his arrival so that Evan and Lewis were away in Newport News and Marion was upstairs taking her afternoon nap. He told himself for the thousandth time that he'd made the only decision he possibly could, but his heart ached with uncertainty.

Bianca hastened down the stairs to meet her friend, breathless with excitement, her eyes bright with more than a trace of fear. "I have been so terribly worried you'd not be able to help me, Will, but I pray your news is good."

Will took her arm and pulled her close as he whispered softly in her ear. "Go upstairs and gather only as much as you can bring without alarming the servants. Tell Viola I'm taking you into town to shop and that you'll come home with Evan. Now hurry, there is no time to lose. The captain of the *Aurora* is prepared to set sail the moment you step aboard."

"You mean I can leave today? This very afternoon?" Bianca clung to him, needing his strength for she was terrified now that the opportunity to return home had actually presented itself.

"Have you changed your mind about leaving your husband?" Will would see her inner turmoil clearly mirrored in her frightened glance, but he hardly dared hope she'd suddenly choose to stay with Evan.

Instantly Bianca's expression changed to one of fierce

determination, the clear green of her eyes darkening with rage as she replied, "My choice was made for me when I first discovered what a rogue my husband is. I'll not be but a moment." She tried to leave the parlor with a gracefully sedate walk, but her thoughts were churning at a frantic rate. She could still feel the tenderness of Evan's last caress upon her breast, the pressure of his lips upon hers as he'd kissed her good-bye that morning. Before he'd left he'd returned to her bed and made love to her with a devotion that would once have moved her to tears, but now the memory of his lovemaking failed to lift the veil of sorrow which enveloped her proud spirit like a shroud. While the pleasure he had given her had been deep, it would never make up for the treachery she knew filled his heart. She forced herself to think only of his deceit as she sorted through her wardrobe to select the garments she couldn't bear to leave behind. The bundle grew far too large to carry down the stairs, however, so after only a moment's hesitation, she opened the window and let it drop to the grass below. Holding her jewels, which were wrapped tightly in a scarf, her cloak thrown over her arm, she then descended the stairs, her forced calm born of stark terror. When she went out to the kitchen to give Viola Will's message, she was relieved to find the housekeeper and her daughter so busy preparing for the evening meal they paid her scant attention. She returned to the main house then and found her friend restlessly pacing the parlor. Bringing her fingertip to her lips, she whispered, "I dropped my things on the lawn. We can get them on the way to the carriage. Let's hurry before Marion wakes up and sees me leave."

"Did you write Evan a note?" Will asked in a hushed tone as he came forward to help her don her cloak.

"What could I possibly say to him?" Bianca replied with bitter sarcasm. "That I won't live with him now that I know the truth about why I'm his wife? The fact that

I've left him will be message enough."

Will was stunned by the depth of her anger, but he knew it was pointless to argue. He escorted her out the front door, paused to grab the neatly wrapped bundle she'd made of her belongings, and then quickly helped her to enter the carriage he'd rented. Once she was comfortably seated and her possessions were concealed in the luggage compartment in back, he climbed up into the driver's seat and grabbed the reins, eager to be on their way.

As the carriage lurched into motion Bianca turned to look back at the house. Bathed in the warm glow of the afternoon sun, the beautiful home looked like such a happy place, and it was all she could do not to burst into tears as she recalled the months she'd spent there. She'd worked so hard to be a good wife to Evan, not only to love him but to be his best friend as well. How could he have married her for so despicable a reason as revenge? She'd asked herself that question over and over, wanting to understand the answer, but it was all too plain. He'd simply used her, turned his hatred into the passion she'd so innocently satisfied. She'd taken bath after bath, but she'd not truly felt clean since the afternoon her mother-in-law had told her the truth. That she'd fallen in love with Evan had been a tragic mistake, and she would never again allow any man access to her heart when openness caused such agony. When they at last reached the docks, she was still frightened about the impending voyage, but she trusted William Summer and knew he'd place her life in the hands of a most capable captain. As he opened the carriage door, she fired a barrage of questions at him

"Have you ever sailed on the *Aurora*, Will? Do you know the captain and crew well? Will there be other passengers?"

Readily appreciating the cause of her anxiety, the sandy-haired young man hastened to explain. "I've not sailed on her myself no, but she is a sturdy ship, a Baltimore clipper like the *Phoenix*. She's reliable, if not nearly so well designed and sleek. She's bound for England with a hold full of tobacco. You'll be the only passenger, I'm afraid, but the captain is an agreeable sort who'll see you don't become bored."

"This is no pleasure cruise," Bianca reminded him smartly. "I want only to be left alone. I'd consider that the most agreeable thing the man could do."

"I've already told him your preference is for privacy and he'll respect your wishes." Will then added somewhat awkwardly, "I said you'd pay for your passage with jewelry."

"Of course. He'll want it now, won't he?" Without a second's hesitation the lively young blonde yanked her emerald wedding ring from her finger and placed it in Will's outstretched palm. "That should more than cover my expenses."

"Yes, indeed," Will agreed as he shoved the sparkling ring into his coat pocket. "Now put up your hood to hide your hair, I don't want anyone to recognize you while you're walking across the deck."

Will saw her to her cabin, then returned in a few minutes with her bundle of clothing. When he placed it upon the bunk the reality of what she was doing suddenly overwhelmed Bianca. Will had been such a good friend, yet she knew they'd never meet again. "I have other jewels, will you let me give you something for your trouble?" she asked hesitantly, afraid he'd be too proud to accept.

"Absolutely not," Will insisted. They were alone now, and he could no longer fight the flames of desire the mere sight of her frightened expression kindled in his blood. He wanted so badly to be the one to soothe away her fears. Since that was an impossible dream, he asked for all he could hope to have. "Would you let me kiss you good-bye?" he asked hoarsely, the pain of his longing clear in his deep voice.

Bianca was surprised by that question, but as Will's expression softened she realized it would mean a great deal to him if she granted his request. Moving close, she placed her hands upon his shoulders and lifted her lips to his. She'd expected only a light kiss, a very gentle one, but she was swiftly enveloped in a warm embrace as his tongue parted her lips for a deep, searching kiss which left her badly shaken when he finally drew away. No one but Evan had ever kissed her so passionately, and she was deeply shocked to find that Will had wanted to take so much from her.

Will's smile was a rakish grin, for while he'd enjoyed kissing Bianca, it had not been the shatteringly blissful experience he'd expected. He'd surprised her, he realized, given her no time to return his lavish display of affection in kind; nonetheless, there had been such a slight degree of warmth in her response, he thought himself very foolish for having placed such a high value on the experience. He knew she'd loved Evan, and her kiss made it plain she loved him still. He relaxed, confident that the manner in which he'd chosen to solve her problems had been the correct one. "Stay put today at least. I know this cabin is small, but you dare not be seen on deck until you're well out to sea."

Bianca nodded nervously, uncertain what to expect from the young man after such a shockingly intimate kiss. "I understand, and I'll stay right here. I'll not cause the captain a single bit of trouble the whole voyage. Thank you so much for convincing him to take me, I know it couldn't have been an easy task."

Will shrugged, too modest to take any credit for arranging her passage. "It was nothing. Now I've got to go or I'll find myself forced to work off my passage." He reached for the door, suddenly eager to be on his way.

"I'll never forget you, Bianca. I hope you have a happy life."

"I wish the same for you," the lovely young woman replied, but she dissolved in tears the moment he was gone. She felt so lost and alone, utterly abandoned. It would be a long and tiring voyage, and she was uncertain what to expect when she arrived home. The best she could hope for was a stern lecture from her father while her mother wept with joy at her safe return. She would have no choice but to accept whatever punishment her father wished to mete out, but she knew her life would never again be the carefree one she'd given up by marrying Evan. Overcome with tears of regret, she moved her belongings aside, curled up on the narrow bunk, and cried herself to sleep like a heartbroken child.

Will stood on the dock until the *Aurora* rounded the southern tip of Newport News, her sails filled with the afternoon breeze as she made her way through the calm waters of Hampton Roads prior to entering the Chesapeake Bay. His heart was light now that he was certain he'd done the right thing, and he couldn't wait to get home to see Lily and explain the reason for his sullen moods this past week, to apologize to her. He'd shut her out of this intrigue for a good reason. Now that it no longer existed, he wanted to explain everything to her so she'd understand why he'd been so glum. He hurriedly returned the rented carriage to the livery stable then walked home with a long, brisk stride. He whistled merrily, his spirits soaring as he entered the River's End, but before he reached the stairs Rachel Kelly called to him.

"I've a note for you."

Will grabbed the folded sheet of paper on his way up the stairs, not caring what it might be in his eagerness to see Lily. He called her name as he unlocked his door, but though she usually came quickly from her room to greet him, today he was met by stony silence. "Lily?" he called again. Still hearing no reply, he opened the connecting door to her room but found it empty. Cursing softly under his breath, he went over to the window to use the last of the sunlight to read the note he'd been given, and he was shocked to find it was from Lily. She'd spelled more than one word incorrectly, and while Bianca's handwriting was a fluid script filled with elegant swirls, this message was penned in a childish scrawl. It took him no more than a few seconds to read it for it was painfully brief. She was leaving him without providing any explanation, saying good-bye in no more than a few short sentences. Where she was going he could only guess. He swore then, an outrageous stream of vile oaths, for he knew he'd hurt her without meaning to. He'd planned to make it all up to her that very afternoon, but she'd not given him the chance. That was what infuriated him most: she'd picked the worst possible time to go. He wanted desperately to see her. He wanted to hold her in his arms, to taste the sweetness of her kiss now that he'd found Bianca's so wanting. He could never hope to have Bianca's love, that had been no more than a foolish dream, but Lily's emotions were real. He'd realized only that afternoon that he loved her. Why hadn't she waited to hear him say it?

When Will approached her, Rachel Kelly shrugged helplessly, unable to provide any information on Lily's whereabouts. "She just handed me that note as she went out the door, Will. She didn't waste any time in telling me good-bye." That oversight obviously displeased the friendly woman.

"Well, when did she leave? Did you at least notice the time?" Will asked impatiently, certain Rachel must know far more than she would admit.

"She left right after you did. It's been several hours now," Rachel reported nonchalantly.

Will glanced toward the door of the inn, having no clue as to where Lily might have gone. "Was someone waiting for her with a carriage?"

Rachel smiled slyly as she replied, "A man, you mean?"

"Whomever!" Will responded angrily. He was in no mood for verbal sparring. "Did someone meet her or not?"

"I didn't take any notice," Rachel insisted. "Where'd you meet her? Maybe she went back there."

Will's frown deepened into a hostile scowl, for the thought that Lily might have returned to Fanny Burke's was more than he could bear. That possibility disgusted him completely, yet the more he thought about it, the more logical that choice seemed. She had no friends in town other than the women at Fanny's. Where else could she have gone if not there? It was a place to start at least. "Thanks for giving me her note, Rachel," he mumbled absently before turning toward the door. It was already growing dark, and if Lily had been so foolish as to return to Fanny's, he certainly didn't want her to be there long enough to entertain her former customers.

As he hurried along the walk he couldn't think of anything to say to Lily except that he expected her to return home with him. A hotel room wasn't a proper home certainly, but he was working on providing her with one soon. There was much he'd never told her, he realized, things he needed to say, things he knew she needed to hear; but if she wasn't at Fanny's, he wouldn't have the chance. He quickened his stride, nearly running as he climbed the steps of Fanny Burke's. It was still early, and the parlor was unoccupied so he went straight to the madam's office. Finding the door ajar, he stepped in without bothering to knock. "Good evening," he remembered to say. "I'm looking for Lily. Is she here?"

Fanny looked up from her ledger, her glance more curious than hostile as she turned toward him. "Now what would Lily be doing here, Mr. Summer?"

Not put off by that evasive reply, Will persisted. "You damn well know what she'd be doing here. The same thing the rest of your girls will be doing tonight. I just want to know if she's here or not. You might as well tell me the truth now because I intend to find Lily even if I have to search your place from top to bottom to do it."

Fanny raised her right hand to sweep a stray curl back into her elaborately styled coiffure, making her dozens of bracelets jingle merrily. "I don't like trouble here, Will. You know that, so if you're planning on causing me any, I suggest you think again."

Will knew the madam always had at least two young brutes on her payroll. Where they'd been the morning he'd helped Jacob take Nigel home he didn't know, but he'd no interest in taking on any of her boys in a fist fight. All he wanted to do was speak with Lily. "I didn't come here to cause you any trouble, I just came to ask if you knew where I might find Lily."

Fanny leaned back in her chair, crossing her legs to show them off to the best advantage. "Lord knows I warned you, Will. I told you that girl would cause you no end of trouble. Just be glad you got out of it so quickly and be on your way."

Her protective attitude meant only one thing to Will: Fanny knew exactly where Lily was. He was positive she was upstairs dressing for the night. As he moved toward the door he called back over his shoulder, "Is she still in the same room?"

Fanny was out of her chair in an instant, following him into the hall. "Don't you dare go upstairs bothering my girls, Will Summer!"

"I've no intention of bothering them, Fanny. I just

need to talk with Lily, that's all." He kept right on walking, but before he could reach the stairs Fanny had shouted a man's name and he heard the sound of running feet. They weren't light footsteps, but a thunderous pounding, and he turned quickly, prepared to block a blow. To his dismay there was not one man running toward him but three. They were tough-looking young brutes barely out of their teens, and while he could have defended himself quite well against one of them, he knew he had little chance to hold his own against all three. Nonetheless, he was determined to try. He fended off the first few punches, but the trio soon overpowered him. Two of the bullies swiftly grabbed his arms and pinned them behind his back so the third could land his brutal punches without interference. He tasted blood in the back of his throat and was certain his nose was broken. He kicked his assailant then, the toe of his boot landing squarely in the man's crotch. While that took care of him for the moment, Will still couldn't pull his arms free, and the two men behind him simply slammed his head into the wall, splattering blood from his broken nose all over the silk brocade wallpaper.

"Be careful!" Fanny shrieked. "Just toss him out in the street. Don't tear up the place!"

Stunned by his savage encounter with the wall, Will felt his legs weaken, and he doubted they'd support him when the men let him go. He'd be damned if they'd leave him sprawled in the street, however, and when he felt the pressure of one man's grip slacken as they hustled him toward the door he broke free. He managed to hit one fellow hard enough to send him reeling, but the other's fist caught his cheek with a force which nearly snapped his neck. As he staggered back against the wall Lily ran toward him. She was crying, but he couldn't imagine why.

"Leave him alone!" Lily screamed as she leapt between

Will and the three husky men who were now regrouping in order to shove him out the door. "Just leave him be!"

The stairs swiftly filled with girls in various stages of undress, all eager to see what had caused the commotion. They began to laugh and call teasing insults to the three young men whom Fanny employed just to avoid such troublesome scenes. Will concentrated solely upon keeping his balance for he was barely conscious and hurting badly. It might appear he'd gotten the better of the three young men, but he surely didn't feel like it.

Lily's eyes were filled with tears, but she brushed them away as soon as they spilled over her lashes, embarrassed to be so transparent in her feelings for Will. "You shouldn't have come here," she scolded him crossly, but she didn't let go of his arm for fear he'd suffer another awful beating the moment she stepped aside.

Fanny put her hands on her hips, thoroughly disgusted with the scene she'd just witnessed. She spoke sharply to one of the men. "Frank, I want you to get a pail of water and clean the blood off the wallpaper before it sets. Can't expect our customers to just ignore that sight; it's bad for business. As for you Will, go on home. Lily came back of her own free will. When you paid me that thousand dollars for her, I didn't make any provisions for a refund so you just learned yourself an expensive lesson. Now get out of here and don't ever come back."

Lily gasped sharply, unable to believe what she'd just heard. "You paid Fanny a thousand dollars for me? You just bought me as though I were a slave?"

Will could barely find the breath to argue. "No, it wasn't like that at all, it was—" He blinked his eyes as his vision began to blur. Suddenly the floor seemed to be slanted at a peculiar angle, and he reached out to grab hold of Lily, afraid he might fall. "Help me," he whispered hoarsely.

Lily screamed to one of the other girls to help her get

Will up to her room. As hurt as she was by what she'd just learned, she'd not allow him to be tossed out into the street when he was barely conscious. "I'll get him out of here in a little while, Fanny. Just let me clean him up first."

Fanny threw up her hands in disgust. "You've got one hour, Lily, and not a minute more!" She then turned to the girls standing on the stairs. "Well what are you all gawking at? Hurry up and get dressed. I'll not have men kept waiting while you preen in front of your mirrors!"

Most of the girls turned away, but one more came to help Lily. Will tried to get up the stairs on his own power, but he soon found he had to allow the three young women to assist him or he would never have made it. He was dizzy and felt sick to his stomach, so he sacrificed his pride rather than fall where he stood. "Just let me lie down for a moment," he heard himself say, but his voice sounded so distant he wasn't certain he'd actually spoken.

"Let's just get him to the bed," Lily directed her friends, sounding far more confident than she felt. Will's face was a mess, but while it hurt to look at him, the fact that he'd paid Fanny for her caused her nearly unbearable pain. The minute they got him comfortably stretched out upon the bed she sent the other two girls away with a breathless thanks, but she hardly knew where to begin with Will. The front of his shirt was marred with bright red blotches, but she didn't bother to ask him to remove it so she could rinse it before the bloodstains became permanent. She'd never done his laundry and she saw no reason to begin now. She'd let him rest a moment, help him get cleaned up, and then send him on his way. That was more consideration than he deserved. She dampened a towel with water from the pitcher on the washstand, then sat down beside him. "I'm afraid I'll hurt you, but you can't go home looking like that."

Will took several deep breaths and began to feel slightly better, but he was in no mood to return to the River's End alone. Rather than argue, however, he rested quietly as Lily did her best to rinse the blood from his face. He knew exactly how he'd look in the morning. His eyes would be black and his features so swollen he'd not be able to go out on the street for several days, but that would present no hardship for him. When Lily had finished washing his face, she moved away and he could hear the hem of her skirt sweeping the floor as she paced the small room restlessly. Finally, when he felt up to talking, he spoke. "I didn't buy you, Lily. I paid Fanny to let you go. I was taking away a good source of income from her and she wanted compensation. I never felt as though I owned you. I'm sorry you found out about that. It was just mean of Fanny to mention that when she must have known how badly it would hurt you."

Lily stopped moving momentarily and turned to face Will. He sounded so sincere that in spite of her initial embarrassment she believed his motives had been good. Still a thousand dollars was a great deal of money for him to have given Fanny and she wished he'd told her about it sooner. "Even if she won't give you your money back, I will. It will take me a while to earn it, but I'll see that you get every cent."

"No!" Will shouted angrily, but that outburst renewed the stabbing pains in his head and he could say no more.

Lily stood watching him for a moment, not understanding why he'd refuse her offer. "I will pay you back, Will. I mean to do it."

Will was furious with himself, not her. There'd been a time when he could take on three men in a fight and win, but that was obviously long over. "I'm getting too old for this," he mumbled sadly.

"What? You're not old, Will. Don't be silly." Lily came back to the bed and after a brief hesitation sat down by his side. "I'm sorry you came here. You didn't deserve this. Did you think Fanny would give you your money back?"

Will opened his eyes, and was grateful he could see Lily's face clearly again. "Frankly I'd forgotten all about the money, but did you honestly think I'd just let you walk out of my life like that?"

Lily bit her lower lip nervously, forcing herself to say what was truly on her mind. "You don't have to lie, Will. I know you're in love with Bianca Sinclair. I'm just in your way."

Will started to swear; then he caught himself. "Look, I know I've not told you anything about Bianca, but—"

"Please don't try and explain. It was wrong of me to go with you in the beginning. This couldn't have ended any other way so it's better that it's over. I'll see you get back your money."

As she started to rise, Will reached out to catch her hand and then pulled her back down beside him. "The money doesn't matter to me, but you do. I didn't tell you the reason for Bianca's visit because I couldn't. I didn't even know what I was going to do about it until a few days ago. She wanted to go home to Venice, and she begged me to help her do it. She didn't want me for a lover, Lily; she just needed someone to arrange for her passage home. I put her on board the *Aurora* this afternoon and by now the ship's well out at sea."

Lily's gaze grew wide with wonder. "But surely Evan will kill you for this!"

Will's smile was faint. "When you walked out on me this afternoon you couldn't have cared what happened to me. Are you telling me now that you do?"

Lily turned away to hide her tears. "Of course I care about you," she whispered softly.

"You'll have to speak up, I can't hear you." Will was almost certain she'd said what he wanted to hear.

"If you feel better, I'll get Jacob to drive you home in the carriage. I've caused you nothing but trouble, Will, cost you a lot of money and, oh, just look at you! You could have been killed coming here, and for what? I'm simply no good and you're lucky to be rid of me."

When she again tried to rise, Will pulled her down beside him with a forceful yank. "Just stay put, Lily, because I'm not leaving here without you. Your father was an idiot and David was no better, but if it takes me a lifetime, I'm going to teach you that you deserve to be loved. I'm positive no one has ever loved you as much as I do, honey. Won't you at least give me the chance to prove it to you?"

"You love me?" Lily asked in a startled whisper. "Truly?"

Will tried to remember when the concern he'd always felt for her had begun to deepen into love, but he simply didn't know. He'd thought her a sweet kid, one he couldn't bear to see hurt, but how long had he loved her? It now seemed as though he always had. "I should have said so long before now. I'm going to build that house you want, you know. Come spring I should have it finished and I hope you'll want me to share it."

Lily didn't know what to say, she was so thrilled by his words of love. Still, he hadn't offered marriage, and how long could he possibly be content with her? One year, two? Then what would happen? She'd have her own home at least if not him, but that was hardly a comforting thought. It terrified her in fact, and she pushed it from her mind, preferring to concentrate on the happiness she'd have now rather than let her fears for the future spoil the present. "Yes. I'll always want to share my home with you."

"I hoped that's what you'd say," Will replied with a

wide grin which swiftly turned into grimace when his battered face brought him a fresh wave of pain. "Now gather up your things and we'll go. I hope you don't mind waiting a few days to get married. While I know I'm not handsome, I can at least look better for you than this."

"You want to marry me?" Lily asked in an excited squeal. "You really want to marry me?"

Will could not recall ever seeing Lily so happy, and he was sorry he'd waited so long to propose. He could scarcely remember what his life had been like before he'd met her. It had taken him quite a while to win her confidence. She was still sometimes perverse, but more often than not loving and dear now that she'd allowed him to really come to know her. "I love you," he said again. "I've been a fool not to tell you that again and again. If I had, you'd not have been so jealous of Bianca and—"

Lily leapt to her feet. "Oh, my God, I'd forgotten about Evan! What are we going to do, Will? When he finds out Bianca is gone he'll tear you limb from limb. Whatever are we going to do?"

Will sat up slowly and was relieved to find he wasn't too dizzy to walk back to the inn. "First let's get out of here. I'll answer all your questions once we get back home."

Unconvinced, Lily continued to worry aloud. "Maybe we'd be better off staying here. He probably won't think to look for you in this place." She wrung her hands as she tried to think of some way to protect him.

"Lily, I forgot to ask. Do you love me?"

"What? Why of course I love you, and you're wrong, you are very handsome, even now," she insisted. "But we can't let Evan find you. He'll be furious because he's lost his wife! Now where are we going to hide?"

Will struggled to his feet and reached for her hand. "Just pack up your things, and I'll tell you the whole story as we walk back to the inn." When the slender blonde simply stared at him, too frightened to move, he reached out to encircle her waist, then pulled her close. "If I am going to be your husband, Lily, you must trust me."

"I do trust you, but I can't bear to see you take another beating," Lily explained tearfully.

"Evan and I are about an equal match so it's by no means certain that he could give me a beating. There's no danger of it, however, so just do as I say and please get packing!"

"You're certain?"

"Positive. I'll tell you all about it on the way home. I promise. I'm only sorry I couldn't tell you everything before now. It's a very interesting story although it will be awhile yet before I can tell you how it ends."

Eager to hear the tale, Lily gathered up her belongings for the second time that day. She pulled on her cloak; then, deciding she'd done all she could to make Will look presentable, she moved toward the door. "Let's use the back stairs. Most of the girls should be downstairs by now and Fanny won't want any more trouble."

"Neither do I," Will remarked with a sly chuckle. For some reason he felt too happy to care that his body ached in more places than he could name. Luck was with them and they left the brightly lit house without being seen. He then put one arm around Lily and carried her bundle of clothes in the other. "Now the beginning of this story is very sad, and while I can tell you only that and the middle, I do hope someday for a happy ending. At least when I'm finished you'll understand why I've no need to fear Evan."

Lily looked back over her shoulder, grateful it wasn't far to the inn. They were not being followed. The night was chilly and she pulled her cloak up closer to her chin to keep warm. "No matter how the story begins and ends,

I want to hear it," she said encouragingly.

"All right. The story begins last year, when Evan's younger brother, Charles, left on a voyage to Venice." Although he tried to be brief, Lily asked so many questions it was quite late before he finished his tale. By the time he'd bathed and had supper, his mood was so mellow he was able to celebrate their engagement with all the enthusiasm he truly felt. He held Lily close as he savored her deep kisses, memories of the lovely Bianca Sinclair not once crossing his mind. The woman in his arms was the only one he wanted. He knew that now and he planned to devote the rest of his life to making her believe how dearly she was loved.

Lily raised her hand to sift the thick curls at his nape. "I was so afraid to love you. Each time we made love I feared it would be the last."

"Oh, Lily, you've nothing to fear from me. I could not bear the pain of losing you so I'd never go. Tomorrow I'll take you to see the land I've asked Evan to set aside for our home. It's a beautiful spot, and if you can tell me exactly what sort of house you want me to build, I'll see that you have it. Maybe when I carry you over the threshold into your own home you'll finally believe my love will last forever."

Lily pulled his mouth down to hers as if to seal that promise with a kiss. "It was never the house I wanted, Will, simply you."

"You already have me," Will pointed out again, "but we'll need a home."

"Yes, a home. That sounds very nice," Lily mused thoughtfully.

"How does the word husband strike you?" Will asked playfully, delighted as always by the innocence of her manner.

"That is a very nice word too, even better I think."

"Let me show you something nice that needs no words," Will whispered huskily as he shifted his position slightly to bring her closer still.

"Please do." Lily wrapped him in a warm embrace, the last trace of her fears melted away by the warm glow of his love.

Chapter XXII

Bianca didn't awaken until long after dawn. Sometime during the night she'd grown cold and, tossing her wrinkled gown aside, had slipped under the covers, but she'd been too exhausted by her tears to want supper. Now that the *Aurora* was well underway, she thought of numerous questions she'd neglected to ask Will. She supposed the captain expected her to share his table. Although it would be rude of her to refuse such an invitation, she had no desire to answer the questions the man would surely ask. She pushed back the covers, resigning herself to the task of storing her belongings and then passing the day as best she could. She was sorry she'd not thought to bring along something to read, but she hoped the captain would have a library of some sort aboard. In no hurry to rise, she sat for a long while on the edge of the bunk, deeply depressed by the wretched turn her life had so suddenly taken. She missed the beautiful view of the James River which had greeted her from the windows of her bedroom, but she struggled to force that image from her mind since she'd never again awaken to that charming sight. With diligent effort she was certain she could forget the life she'd led in Virginia. She had no choice but to put it all behind her, every last bit of it: the people she'd met, the interesting places she'd visited with Evan. She closed her eyes then, unable to suppress the memory of her husband. No, she'd never be able to forget Evan, no matter how hard she tried, for his handsome features were permanently engraved upon her heart. His smile had usually been a rakish grin, while his golden glance could tease or smolder with undisguised passion. "If only Evan had loved me as dearly as I love him," she whispered softly to herself, her sorrow now beyond tears. "If only—" But there had been dozens of ifs, she realized sadly, and Evan had failed to use any of the numerous opportunities he'd had to confide in her. Her thoughts grew so black then that she knew she'd have to get up, get busy, and stay busy or she'd swiftly lose the tenuous hold she had upon her composure. It was pointless to dwell on Evan's treachery now that she had left him. Maybe she'd call herself a widow; that would serve him right for treating her so badly, for stealing not only her innocence but her heart as well. She could kill him in her mind, if not her heart, and that would just have to do. A sharp rap at the door startled her, and she leapt to her feet as she called out, "Yes, what is it?"

"Your breakfast, ma'am," a deep voice replied.

"Please leave it by the door, I'm not dressed," Bianca replied nervously, hoping the man wouldn't insist upon serving it.

"Yes, ma'am. I'll put it right here. The sea's getting rough, and the captain wants you to stay in your cabin where you'll be safe. If he can join you for dinner, he'll send for you," the sailor explained in a lazy drawl.

"Thank you, I understand." Bianca waited until the sound of the man's footsteps had died away before she opened the door slightly. When she peeked out and found him gone, she picked up a tray bearing a pot of tea, rolls, and jam, and quickly brought them inside, relieved she'd not had to face anyone yet. She doubted she'd feel up to being charming company that night either, but after spending the whole day in the small cozy cabin she was quite bored. When the weather became too rough for the captain to entertain, she was surprised to find herself disappointed. The man who'd left her breakfast and lunch trays outside her door returned with her supper, and she opened the door this time to thank him. When she recognized him as a man who'd been on board the *Phoenix* she gasped in surprise. "I'm so sorry, I've forgotten your name, but weren't you on the last voyage of the *Phoenix?*"

"That I was, ma'am." The friendly sailor carried the tray through the door and set it upon the small shelf which served as both desk and table for the cabin. "My name's John Clark, but just call me John."

Bianca blushed deeply from embarrassment for he obviously knew she was Evan's wife. Then, straightening her shoulders proudly, she decided she'd simply not justify her actions to anyone. "Are there any more of the crew from the *Phoenix* on board?"

John paused a moment, frowning as he concentrated upon providing an accurate reply. "Yes, ma'am, there are quite a few of us, but that's not unusual. The *Aurora* had a cargo, the *Phoenix* didn't, and we all needed the work."

"Of course. I didn't mean to pry." Yet Bianca felt increasingly uneasy at the thought that she was surrounded by men she knew to be loyal to her husband. Nothing could be done about that unfortunate circumstance, however. "I don't mean to be a burden, but if the captain has some books, do you think you might bring me one or two? It would help to pass the time."

"You want a couple of books?" John asked as he moved through the door. "I'll see what he can spare."

"Thank you, I should have thought to bring my own." Bianca felt very foolish. She'd vowed not to cause any problems and she hoped John wouldn't trouble the captain unnecessarily on her behalf. When he returned in a few minutes with not one book but three worn volumes, she took them eagerly. They were books by British authors, and at first glance appeared frightfully dull. Nonetheless, she thanked John profusely for his trouble, and chose a novel which appeared to be somewhat interesting, she began to read as she ate her supper. The story was set in Cornwall, and as the wind buffeting the sails increased in volume she could almost feel the damp mist through which the heroine walked down to the sea to await the return of her lover's ship. It was a melancholy tale, filled with loneliness and longing, not at all what she needed to raise her spirits. She couldn't imagine why the captain would have had such a dreary novel on board, but grateful for any diversion, she curled up on the bunk and read long into the night. ,

The weather did not improve for several days, and by the time the captain finally sent word that he would be charmed to have her join him in his cabin for supper Bianca was delighted to accept. She was so grateful for the opportunity to escape the close confines of her cabin she didn't care how many questions he might ask. She'd asked John for paper and ink, and had tried to write down every query he could possibly make, along with a properly evasive reply. The man must know Evan, at least casually if not well, and she didn't want to discredit her husband in the eyes of his friends because of what he'd done to her so she dared not reveal the truth no matter how sympathetic a soul the captain might prove to be. She dressed in one of her prettiest dresses, a pale blue satin, and smiled easily at John's conversation as he walked her the short distance to the captain's cabin. He was a pleasant man who served as the cook's helper. Since the *Aurora* had no cabin boy, he'd somehow been assigned the extra duty of looking after her, but he didn't seem to mind. He knocked upon the captain's door and, hearing a welcoming call, opened it for her, then stepped aside to allow her to enter.

"Oh, John, what's the man's name?" Bianca whispered softly, suddenly realizing she'd never heard it.

John raised a brow quizzically. "You can't have forgotten it, Mrs. Sinclair." With the grace of a fine gentleman he escorted her across the threshold, then left her to face the captain of the *Aurora* alone.

As her eyes met his, the color drained completely from Bianca's face, leaving her light golden skin deathly pale, and for a moment she thought she'd surely faint. The captain, readily sensing her distress, rushed forward to take her hand and led her to her seat at his table. He filled her goblet with wine, then waited until she'd taken a sip to steady herself before he spoke.

"Since you are obviously too overcome with emotion to speak, allow me to welcome you aboard the *Aurora*. She is unfortunately not nearly so comfortable a ship as the *Phoenix*, but since she was already loaded with a profitable cargo and ready to sail, I decided she would have to do. Had you only given me more notice of your impending departure, I could have secured a cargo for the *Phoenix* as well." Evan took the chair opposite Bianca's, filled his own goblet with wine, and raised it in a toast. "To a safe voyage," he said, and drank the rich red wine in one long swallow.

Bianca felt utterly defeated and she was numb with shock. Will had betrayed her confidence so completely he'd helped her escape her husband's home only to have returned her to his care within an hour's time. "Was it only the storm which kept you from inviting me here before now?" she finally had the presence of mind to ask, but she forced back the vile string of insults she was sorely tempted to hurl.

A slow smile lifted the corner of Evan's well-shaped

mouth. "Your door has never been locked, Bianca, nor has mine. You could have paid me a call at any time you wished. Night or day," he added slyly.

While the intent of that remark swiftly brought the color back to Bianca's cheeks, it didn't serve to ease the fright she'd suffered. The table was set for two with silver as fine as he had in his home, but she doubted she'd be able to eat a bite. "Just what did Will tell you?" she asked, her curiosity suddenly keen about what had transpired between them. She already knew she'd been betrayed, but she felt a perverse need to know how far that betrayal had extended.

Evan shrugged. "You mustn't blame Will for the embarrassment you're suffering now, my love. He had your very best interests at heart when he came to me. I think the man is more than a little in love with you, but he understands you belong to me, even if you find that impossible to remember."

Bianca sat back in her chair, finding it difficult to catch her breath, let alone to argue with the wit her husband was so cleverly displaying. "It isn't a question of my belonging to you, Evan, because you deserve absolutely no loyalty after what you've done. You lied to me from the moment we met, made a mockery of our wedding vows, continued to deceive me even after we reached your home. You can't expect me to be your wife after the despicable way you've behaved."

"Despicable?" Evan seemed to find that term highly amusing. "That's a very beautiful gown you're wearing tonight, one of my favorites actually. You'll find all the things I had made for you, everything you had no time to pack, stored in the trunk at the foot of my bunk. Should you need something you'd left behind, just come and get it." He removed her wedding ring from his vest pocket and laid it upon the table. "I'll return this to you now.

You are my guest, and there is no charge for your passage."

Bianca was not only confused by his offhand manner, she was outraged as well. "This isn't some game, Evan. I don't want a husband who tells me nothing but lies. I won't be your wife any longer so keep the ring and give it to the next woman you deceive so cleverly she never doubts the honesty of your love."

Before Evan could respond to that insult, John returned with their meal. He'd been careful to knock upon the door, and Evan had quickly admitted him. When they'd been served, John again left them alone, and while Evan ate with a hearty appetite, Bianca simply sat staring at him, unable to find the savory meal attractive in her present mood.

Evan was as upset as his wife, far more so in fact, but he'd be damned if he'd respond to her insults in kind. He forced himself to chew each bite of the succulent stew at least twenty times so he'd be in no danger of choking, but it took more restraint than he'd known he possessed to control the fury of his temper. When Will had first come to him with Bianca's preposterous request to return to Venice, he'd wanted to go straight home and talk as long as it took him to force his wife to see reason, but his friend had prevailed upon him to consider his options more thoughtfully. Finally he'd come to accept the fact he and Bianca would never have any happiness as long as Charles's murderer remained unpunished. He decided to return to Venice to accomplish that goal, and since that was where she was so determined to go, he'd take her there himself. In his view, Bianca was still the only key he had to the dark mystery surrounding Charles's death, a mystery he was now determined to solve. When John had again left them after clearing away the dishes, Evan leaned back in his chair to make himself comfortable, preparing himself for a lengthy chat. "I will not question my mother's reason for telling you what she did since it's obvious her grief is still coloring her decisions. The real problem is that you no longer trust me, but I'd like you to consider for a moment what it was I was hoping to do when I went to Venice. Please do so before you judge my motives for our marriage so harshly."

"I understand what you wanted to do," Bianca replied with an impatient sweep of her hand. "You wanted to trap your brother's murderer and you used me for bait!"

Immediately Evan disagreed. "No, my dear. I used myself as the bait for that trap. I thought if I courted you as Charles had, whoever had killed him would come after me. I'd have an advantage Charles hadn't had, however, for I'd be waiting for him."

The moment he'd begun to speak of his brother's death, Evan's expression had grown so hard and cold Bianca felt chilled despite the cabin's warmth. He appeared so utterly ruthless she became frightened for she knew she'd never be able to escape him once he'd drawn her into his plot. He'd caught her in a net woven of flattering lies, and she'd never once questioned his love when in truth she'd been no more than a pawn in a senseless game of revenge. "Evan, can't you understand why I am so hurt by what you did? You simply used me, used my love for you, and all the while you had the wrong woman. It's like some ridiculous joke, only I don't find it the least bit amusing."

"Nor do I," Evan responded calmly. "Regardless of why I originally wished to meet you, Bianca, I swiftly fell in love with you and I still want you for my wife. Marrying you was the smartest thing I've ever done, regardless of how misguided my reason. There's no need to throw away our marriage because your pride certainly isn't at stake. I love you very much. Isn't that all you really wanted from me?"

"No!" Bianca cried out unhappily, her eyes growing bright with the sting of unshed tears. "It's not enough, it just isn't. Why couldn't you have told me the truth in the beginning? I would have been happy to help you. We could have found Charles's murderer together, I know we could have. But we had no chance at all when you told me only lies!"

As Evan studied his wife's furious reaction to what he'd considered a poignant declaration of his love for her, he reminded himself that despite her beauty and usual poise, she was very young still and often a captive of her own tumultuous emotions. Indeed, it had been her fiery spirit which had intrigued him so greatly when first they'd met, and he realized he'd have to be far more patient with her. "What choice did I have, Bianca? You seemed constantly to be warning me to stay away from you so I was certain you knew who'd killed my brother. What I didn't know, however, was whether or not you'd warned that man as well. I couldn't possibly have confided my plans to you when that might have meant signing my own death warrant. Your father is an extremely powerful man and—"

"You can't mean you suspected him of murdering Charles?" Bianca asked in shocked disbelief.

"Yes, either him or Paolo," Evan admitted calmly.

"But that's absurd!" Bianca insisted angrily, deeply insulted as well as hurt.

"Is it? Someone killed Charles. It could easily have been one of them." Evan got up to get a bottle of brandy. He poured Bianca no more than a taste but was quite generous with his own portion. He hadn't been lying. He loved her and he wanted her as his wife. It had been a struggle all week to stay away from her, but he'd hoped she'd used the time she'd had to herself more wisely than she had. He'd missed her terribly, but clearly she'd not missed him at all. Returning to his seat, he turned their conversation in the only direction he could. "All right, let's try it your way this time. When we reach Venice, let's simply turn back the clock and pretend it's last spring. I need your help even more than I did then, and this time I'll be completely honest with you. If I can find the woman who entranced Charles so completely, I'm certain she'll lead me to his murderer. Do you still have her handkerchief?"

That he would be so matter-of-fact about his plans was a further shock to his fragile blonde wife, and it took her a moment to reply. "Yes. I don't know why I brought it with me, but I did."

That admission brought a smile to Evan's face. "Perhaps you wanted to help me without realizing it. I really do need your help, Bianca. You must have some idea who the woman Charles loved is since you seem to be positive it wasn't you. I was just so certain that it had to be you when I first saw you I didn't even consider any others. Your beauty was the perfection he described, and your name was Antonelli, accounting for the *A* on the handkerchief."

Bianca shook her head. "Oh, Evan, how could you have made such a foolish mistake? Men use the first letter of their last name for a monogram, but women frequently prefer to use the first letter of their first name since their last name will change when they marry. In my haste to leave home with you I didn't even bring any of my handkerchiefs, but they were all embroidered with a *B* not an *A*. You're looking for a young woman whose first name beings with *A*."

Evan did not enjoy feeling like a fool, and he most assuredly felt like one. However, if he'd not made such a silly error, he'd not have married Bianca and that possibility concerned him far more. "Whether it was a mistake or a trick wrought by fate, I'll not complain since it brought me you," he remarked with a slight smile. "I still want you to be my wife. I want you to share this cabin and my bed for the rest of the voyage, but I'll not force myself upon you. I've never raped any woman, and I'll not begin with the one I love."

Bianca wanted to believe him. With all her heart she longed to believe his declarations of love were true, but what if they weren't? What if all he wanted was exactly what he'd wanted before: her help in catching his brother's murderer? Once he'd caught the villain, would he have any further use for her devotion? He might finally tell her the truth, kiss her good-bye, and return to Virginia alone. That possibility was far too painful to contemplate for she'd simply not survive a betrayal of such monstrous proportions. It would be like dying twice, and she lacked the courage to take such a risk. If he was sincere in his love for her, he would do as she asked. "I would rather stay in my cabin," she replied hesitantly. "I'll do what I can to help you, but until we find Charles's killer, I'll not be your wife."

Evan took a deep breath and then let it out slowly, not understanding why she'd not forgive him for lies he'd told so many months ago, before he'd come to love her for her inner beauty as well as the perfection of her face and figure. There was nothing he could do but let her have her way for the time being, but he was wretchedly disappointed in her decision. "Speaking of lies," he began in a caustic tone, "I wish you'd had the decency to come to me with my mother's tales rather than go running to Will Summer. I thought you loved me as much as I love you, but it's clear you don't understand the meaning of the word, nor are you aware of the respect which should exist between husband and wife." He rose then, ending the evening abruptly for he was in danger of losing his temper completely. "I'll escort you back to your cabin, where I hope your dreams will be pleasant despite having spent what you must regard as a disagreeable evening since you were sharing it with me. I will be happy to entertain you each evening, but just how lavishly will be up to you. If you can give me any help in bringing Charles's murderer to justice, no matter how slight the clue might appear to you, I will be very grateful."

"I will be glad to help you in any way I can, just as I would have last spring," Bianca reminded him, her tone as sarcastic as his. She bid him a hasty good night before slipping through her door, not trusting either herself or him to accept the separation she'd just demanded. She leaned back against the door, knowing it wasn't her pride but her very soul which was at stake. If she trusted him again and he failed her, that would break what was left of her heart and leave her an empty shell.

Evan spent another restless day. He knew that in many respects Bianca's anger was justified, but he was certain he didn't deserve to be shut out of her life completely. She'd had a difficult time the last few weeks, first being bedridden after her fall and then having to cope with the hurt his mother's revelations had obviously inflicted. At least now he understood why she'd been so distracted, and why though he'd done his best to put her mind at ease by being as affectionate as he could, he'd gotten nowhere. He'd never forget the last morning they'd spent together. He'd prayed the tenderness of his loving would sway her, convince her she belonged with him, but she'd left him anyway as though there were nothing between them worth saving. When he sent John to her cabin to escort her to dinner that night, he doubted she'd join him, but to his immense delight she did.

Bianca had again taken the time and trouble to dress in a pretty gown and to style her hair attractively, but she'd done that for her own pride, not in an attempt to seduce

Evan. As soon as John had served their meal, she lay the embroidered handkerchief upon the table. "Since this and Charles's description are the only clues we have, I have been trying to think of every possible name which begins with the letter *A:* Angelina, Anna-Maria, Antonia, Aida, Allegra, Alexandra, Anabelle, Andrea, Aurelia, even Aurora. If the young woman were a foreigner, then we should consider other names as possibilities too."

Evan was somewhat startled that Bianca was so businesslike, but since she'd offered her help so generously, he did not refuse it. "It might be more helpful if you thought not simply of names, but of blonde women. She has to look remarkably like you. Have you ever been mistaken for someone else?"

Evan was dressed very handsomely that evening too. Just looking at him made any sort of serious contemplation difficult so Bianca concentrated upon her supper rather than her companion's charm. She wondered what had become of her emerald ring since she'd left it lying on the table. "My mother and I look very similar. She's quite young too, but her name is Catherine and she and my father are very happily married. She is not the woman we seek."

"I doubt Charles would have fallen so desperately in love with a married woman. Oh, I know it's a possibility, but let's not consider any such women now. We have plenty of time to think before we arrive. Why don't you just jot down any thoughts you might have on the young woman's possible identity, and when we reach Venice, we'll talk about each one and see what we can learn."

Bianca hesitated a moment before agreeing to part of his suggestion. "I will be happy to give the matter thought, Evan, but once we reach Venice I plan to live with my parents. I'll give you whatever help I can, but I don't think it would be wise for us to be seen together."

"Not wise?" Evan responded sharply. "You are my

wife, Bianca. Why shouldn't we be seen together?"

"My parents will never recognize our marriage since it was not a Catholic ceremony performed by a priest." Bianca spoke slowly, emphasizing each word with care. "In their eyes I have never been married, Evan, and that's a fact I'm prepared to accept."

Evan had taken all he could on that subject for the evening, and he could no longer hide his anger. "If the legality of our marriage was a problem for you, why didn't you tell me so? I would have married you again in a religious ceremony, a dozen times if that was what you wanted."

Bianca laid her fork carefully upon the side of her plate, needing time to think of a reply which wouldn't enrage him all the more. "I never gave the circumstances of our wedding any thought, Evan, since I thought I'd be your wife forever. Now that everything has changed between us, the fact that I've set you free to wed another should please you."

"What?" Evan couldn't believe his ears. "Why do you think I'd marry another woman when you're the one I love? Do you think me so stupid as that?"

"Of course not. I don't regard you as stupid at all. It is just that since things have turned out so badly, perhaps we are both lucky that our marriage vows can be so easily forgotten."

Evan considered his choices with great care. He could either leap to his feet, strangle Bianca and be done with her, or get a hold of his temper and pray she would soon see how ridiculous the idea of dissolving their marriage truly was. He chose the latter option. "As I said before, this will be a long voyage and we needn't spend all our time at each other's throats. I agree with you actually; I think we might be better able to find the man we want by working separately. I can grow a beard, and if I call myself something other than Evan Sinclair, I'll probably not be recognized."

Bianca simply stared at her husband, surprised that he'd allow her to see how easily his mind could turn to deceit. "What is it you'll want from me?"

"Names, just as you've given me tonight. But I want the names to be those of attractive blondes. I doubt there are any women in Venice so beautiful as you, but there must be a few good possibilities; and we can narrow them down to young ladies with names beginning with *A*. That will help circumscribe our search."

Bianca nodded, what little appetite she'd had now completely gone. "The last morning I spent in your house, you knew I planned to leave you, didn't you?"

Surprised by so unexpected a question, Evan nevertheless told her the truth. "Yes, but I hoped you'd change your mind so I did all I could to influence your decision in my favor. Obviously I failed."

"The next time you wish to impress a woman, Evan, I hope you'll consider telling her the truth rather than relying upon your talents as a lover."

Evan rose as Bianca left his cabin, but he knew she'd not come to harm on the way to her own so he let her go. He'd brought along a generous supply of brandy, and he now knew he was going to need every drop. She saw each of his actions in the poorest possible light but at least she was still speaking to him even if most of her comments were insults. It would be a lengthy voyage, and time would work more to his advantage than hers. He was confident he could regain her trust. He just hoped it wouldn't be long before he did as he'd no desire to spend even one more night alone.

The following morning Evan carried his wife's breakfast tray to her cabin himself. "Bianca? I've an idea. May I please speak with you for a moment?"

Bianca had been awake only a few minutes. She was still clad in her nightgown, and her long curls were as yet unbrushed. "No. I'm not dressed!" she called out in a frantic whisper.

"That's all the better," Evan replied with a deep chuckle.

Bianca recognized that laugh all too well. Whatever Evan was up to might be pleasing to him but she was certain it wouldn't be to her. Forgetting her appearance because she was so angry, she yanked open the door. "I thought we had more than ample time. What is so terribly urgent that it can not wait until I'm dressed?"

Evan carried her tray into the cabin and set it down upon the unmade bunk. He'd forgotten she had such small accommodations, but he did not again offer to share his own. "I want you to make a chart showing everyone you know in Venice. Prepare a map of the canals if it will help you to remember, but I want the name and location of every family you can recall plus a list of their daughters' names."

"Not just the blondes?" Bianca clenched her fists at her sides, far more upset than she'd let him see. It was easy to be furious about his duplicity, but as always the warmth of his smile had a powerful influence on her. If only the man weren't so damn handsome, she thought to herself. But because she had a weakness for him, she didn't have to give in to it.

"No. I'd like to know all the women's names since we can't be certain from which source the information we need will come. Your cabin is much too small for that sort of work so I want you to use mine. I'm seldom in it during the day and you'll need the table to lay out the map. I've an old chart and you can use the back. Just roll it up when you've finished working each day."

"I'll admit the idea seems like a good one." Bianca still felt as though she was being manipulated, but she knew the only way to end the wretched mess in which she found herself was to help Evan catch his brother's killer.

That done she could discover whether or not he truly loved her. "I'll begin right after breakfast then. Just leave the chart you wish me to use out on your table and I won't trouble you for anything more than pen and ink."

"You shall have all you need." Evan turned to go, more to hide his triumphant smile than out of any urgency to leave. He planned to involve his lovely wife in every step of his plans until her life was so entwined with his she'd no longer wish to leave him. He had little patience, but it was a trait he'd cultivate for he wanted her to love him as she once had. However, he knew if he never had anything more than her hatred, he'd never let her go.

Chapter XXIII

Bianca didn't know if she was pleased or disappointed when Evan kept his word and left her alone each day while she worked in his cabin. She'd found the task he'd given her surprisingly diverting. The serpentine curves of the grand canal resembled a reversed letter *S*, and were lined on both banks with splendid palaces. While she'd loved to draw as a child, she'd had no formal training. Nonetheless, she found it a simple matter to sketch in the details of the façades of each of her friend's homes. In only a few days' time her map took on the appealing appearance of a work of art, and she was inspired to expand the drawing to include several of the smaller canals leading into the one on which she'd lived. She added the Piazza San Marco and other points of interest, making the map not only accurate but informative as well. The time passed quickly while she was working, but she enjoyed herself so thoroughly she was always surprised when Evan returned to his cabin in the late afternoon. Since she knew he'd wish to bathe and dress before supper, she quickly put her materials away and went to her own cabin although on more than one occasion he invited her to remain. They had once been so close, but now she was careful to maintain a discreet distance between them, in both her actions and her words. She did not respond in kind to his teasing, and although she was far from immune to his charm, she did not once let him see that the depth of her feeling for him had not changed. She knew all she need do was forgive him for deceiving her and they would again share the indescribable pleasure he'd taught her to crave, but she refused to indulge that weakness. She still suspected that he'd simply use her in a ridiculous plot which had backfired upon them both, and she feared he might try to use her again. She sat at his table each night and made polite conversation, but she'd never admit to him that, once she'd returned to her cabin, more often than not she cried herself to sleep.

Evan had not expected Bianca to throw herself into making a map of Venice with such unbridled enthusiasm, but he was pleased to see that the project had not only offered a way to fill the hours, it had lifted her spirits as well. While she never seemed to truly relax in his presence anymore, she would at least discuss what she'd done each day and he was grateful for that. "I'm going to have this map of yours framed and hang it in my study when I get home," he remarked proudly, "It really is very good."

"You want to keep it?" Bianca asked shyly, for she'd planned to save the map for herself.

"Yes, of course. I'm unlikely to ever return to the cursed place and this would make the perfect souvenir." Evan noted the buildings she'd added that day, and then he remembered the morning he'd followed her after their meeting in the Piazza San Marco. "Do you recall where you went the morning after I spoke with you in the cathedral? It was a modest home, probably a bright yellow once, but now the color is quite faded." He pointed in the general location of where he thought it had been. "I believe it was about here, near the Arsenale."

"You followed me?" Bianca asked in a sudden fit of temper. "You had the audacity to follow me?"

Evan raised his hands to plead for mercy. "Please, you needn't be so angry with me. I was just curious as to what you did with your day. I thought I'd be following you back to your home. When you went in the opposite direction, I was puzzled. I hoped for the chance to speak with you again, but when you remained inside a long while I gave up and went on back to the *Phoenix*. I'd not have embarrassed you, or done you and Raffaella any harm."

Bianca thought such admirable restraint on his part highly unlikely. "How many times did you follow me? Dozens?"

"No, just that once," Evan replied truthfully, but he knew had he had other such opportunities he'd certainly have used them to study her behavior. "Who lives in the little yellow house?"

Finished for the day, Bianca rolled up her map and crossed the cabin to put it with Evan's charts, where it was kept. "To keep you from annoying him, if for no other reason, I'll be happy to tell you who lives there."

"You two were visiting a man?" Evan asked, his understandable shock showing clearly upon his even features.

"Yes, a man, an artist," Bianca explained matter-of-factly. "His name is Stefano Tommasi. He was just completing my portrait and was about to begin Raffaella's when we left Venice."

"Is he good?" Evan wanted to know. His face was serious now, the matter obviously of some importance to him.

"Why yes, he is excellent. He's done portraits for many of the wealthier families. He is quite expensive, but his work is well worth the price."

Evan did no more than nod slightly, but he planned to remember the artist's name so he could consult with him should he need additional help Bianca couldn't supply. An artist working for wealthy patrons would surely know every beautiful woman living in Venice, and perhaps he just might know one Bianca didn't. "Well I'm certain his portrait of you must be among the best. I hope I'll have an opportunity to see it."

"You can not possibly expect my parents to entertain you, Evan, so I doubt you'll ever see the portrait," Bianca told him as she moved toward the door, but he called out to stop her.

"I never met your parents, so they'll not recognize me. I did say I'd grow a beard, and I suppose I might as well begin now. I rather like the idea of disguises though, so who knows? You may find me at your parents' table on more than one occasion." Evan smiled as he teased her, but the prospect of meeting her father was enormously appealing. His glance wandered slowly down her figure, but there were no changes that he could discern. He'd been hoping he'd finally succeeded in making her pregnant that last morning they'd been together. It was a slim hope, he realized, and it was probably still too soon to know if she'd give him an heir, but he'd use any excuse to keep her. Should she be carrying his child it would aid his cause tremendously.

Bianca stared at him, amazed that he'd be so reckless. "Do not make the mistake of confronting my father, Evan. He'll be no more likely to forgive you for what you've done than I am."

Evan didn't argue, but let her go without comment, hoping she'd eventually tire of baiting him when he steadfastly refused to respond. He'd never met a woman so headstrong as his wife, but he was certain that, as with most people, there was a limit to her stubbornness. He had only to find it, he reminded himself, amazed at his own determination where she was concerned.

When Bianca finally finished the last details of the map she numbered each of the palaces and began to list their residents on separate sheets of paper. It was a laborious task for most families were far larger than her own and she didn't want anyone forgotten. Whenever she remembered a blonde woman or one whose name began with an *A* she circled that person, but even after she'd listed nearly half the people she knew there wasn't a single name with the required two circles. She sat staring at the project which had consumed so many of her hours, knowing something was definitely wrong. She could feel it as her fingertips moved between the map and her lists. It was no more than a vague uneasiness, but it persisted all through that day and into the next. Finally, when she could hide her anxiety no longer, she spoke to Evan about it.

"I've tried to remember everyone I know, Evan, but my circle of friends was limited to my father's choice and I can't help but feel the woman you want just isn't listed here."

Bianca seemed so genuinely concerned that she'd failed him Evan was touched. He'd thought involving her in his search a clever ploy; now he wasn't so certain since it had obviously caused her additional worry he knew she didn't need. "She's in Venice somewhere and we'll find her. If nothing else, you've told me where she isn't. That is invaluable information in itself." He stood beside her, so close their shoulders were almost touching, almost but not quite. He was as careful as she to keep his distance, but he really wanted to pull her into his arms and make love to her until she remembered the joy he couldn't forget. "I asked only for your help, my love. I didn't expect you to lead me directly to the woman."

Since he clearly didn't share her disappointment in the lack of substantial clues, Bianca rolled up the map and the lists of names. She put them away, uneasy still, but unable to describe her feelings of foreboding. Perhaps it was only his preoccupation with revenge which caused her such distress, but she knew criticizing him for that would be pointless.

"Today was quite warm. There's still time if you'd like to go up on deck. You've been working too hard on that map, and I'm certain you'd feel better if you got some exercise." Without waiting for her to agree, Evan reached for Bianca's hand and pulled her through the door. He paused at her cabin only long enough for her to fetch her cloak; then he led her up on deck. The wind was brisk, but not bone chilling, and he placed her hand upon his arm so she'd be in no danger of falling as they strolled around the deck. When at last he felt her begin to shiver, he drew her over to the rail and stood behind her to block the wind as he whispered in her ear. "You used to love spending your time on deck. Why is this voyage so different from our last?"

Bianca felt the answer to that question was too obvious to merit a reply so she kept still. As always, the vastness of the Atlantic Ocean was a compelling sight, and she was content to stand between Evan's outstretched arms for a long while before she turned to look up at him. The beard he'd begun to grow was neatly trimmed. If anything, it made him all the more handsome. She reminded herself that his goal was deception, not to enhance his appearance, and that brought her thoughts swiftly back to practical ones. "How much longer before we reach England?"

Evan smiled slyly. "We were never bound for England, Bianca. I can sell tobacco in Venice as easily as in Southampton, and we've no time to lose. We're traversing a southern route, making straight for the Mediterranean, and although the *Aurora* is as heavily armed as the *Phoenix* I hope we'll escape the Barbary pirates' notice."

Bianca had not even considered another confrontation with those villains and she was frightened, although Evan had made that remark with his usual supremely confident manner. Murderers, pirates, nothing seemed to bother the man in the least. She suddenly recalled Will's description of the hero Evan had been during the Revolutionary War. It was not his bravery she questioned, but his sense of honor. Since he'd never actually told her where they were bound, she could scarcely accuse him of lying to her again, but she still felt that he had deceived her and she turned back to enjoy the view of the sea a while longer. When he asked if she'd like to return to his cabin for tea, she was too cold to refuse his invitation.

As soon as John had brought a fresh pot of the brew, Bianca took a grateful sip of the steaming tea, keeping a hold on her cup to warm her hands. "Why didn't Will come with us? I thought you disliked assuming the duties of the captain yourself."

"I do." Evan hesitated a long moment, then decided explaining why he'd not brought Will along would help to pass the remainder of the afternoon in a pleasant fashion. "Will didn't want you to know about Lily, but I think you met her, didn't you?"

"His mistress you mean?" Bianca asked bluntly, still not pleased about the way Will had betrayed her trust.

"I think she'll soon be his bride, but yes, when you met her she was his mistress. I've not met her myself. Do you think she's pretty? He certainly does."

Bianca frowned slightly, remembering the slender blonde quite well. "Yes. She is attractive, but there was something rather strained about her manner. Perhaps she was as embarrassed as I was. I don't know how to describe our conversation, other than to say we each seemed to want it over quickly."

Evan smiled knowingly, his golden glance teasing. "She must have been very jealous."

"But she'd no reason to be!" Bianca protested sharply.

"Of course not. You merely wished to enlist Will's aid so you could leave me. Why should such a thing upset Lily?" Evan's smile vanished as he asked that question, but he'd not meant to begin a fight and quickly changed the subject before Bianca could repond with an insult of her own. "No matter, whatever fears Lily had were groundless. Will is devoted to her. I was waiting for you to recover your health to tell you this, but I bought the Marshall house for our home. I left Will in charge of the needed repairs and renovations although I wanted you to select the color scheme for each room and whatever new furnishings were needed."

Bianca was so startled she had to take great care to place her teacup on the table before she spilled the last of her tea. "You bought the Marshall estate for us?" She'd not even dared hope he would be interested in the house since it included a large plantation as well.

"Yes, despite the low opinion you have of me, I knew you weren't happy in my mother's house and your happiness means a great deal to me. I would do anything I possibly could to insure it."

In the soft light, Bianca could see that Evan's smile was a very melancholy one, and her eyes filled with tears which swiftly spilled over her thick lashes despite her best efforts to brush them away. That he would have bought the lovely home simply to please her overwhelmed her with sorrow for it was a sweet gesture that was totally wasted now. "I'm so sorry, Evan, so terribly sorry," she apologized. "It must have cost you a great deal of money, and now—"

Evan knew better than to tell her he planned to cover the cost of the house by selling off parcels of the land for farms since a shrewd business deal had not been his primary motivation for purchasing the estate. He didn't want to impress her with his cleverness, but with his devotion. He rose to go to her side, and pulling her gently to her feet, he enfolded her in his arms, pressing her cheek close to his chest while he attempted to soothe away her sorrow. "It will be a beautiful home, Bianca, but not without you. I want only to share it with you," he whispered softly, "only with you." She seemed near hysteria although he didn't truly understand why his purchasing the Marshall home would have upset her so badly when he'd explained that he'd done it just to please her. Nonetheless, she clung to him, weeping pathetically, and all he wanted was to dry her tears with tender kisses which he hoped would swiftly turn her mood to a romantic one. He put his fingertips beneath her chin to raise her trembling lips to his, kissing her gently at first and when she didn't instantly draw away in revulsion deepening his kiss to a far more passionate one. He slid his fingers through her wind-tossed curls, remembering the beauty of the first voyage they'd taken together when their love had still been new. Her affection was even more delicious now, he realized, and like a man dying of thirst, he savored her honey-sweet kisses until he felt the heat of his own desire being returned in full measure. He swept her up into his arms to carry her the short distance to his bunk, where he was delighted to find the light woolen gown she wore had required no corset. He'd thought he'd remembered her exquisite beauty perfectly, but he realized now as he peeled away her soft green gown and then her filmy lingerie that his memories had been woefully incomplete. Her fair skin was seductively soft and smooth, inviting his caress. Her tawny curls fell about her shoulders, spilling over the fullness of her breasts and making the lush curves of her figure all the more alluring. He was captivated by the freshness of her youthful beauty, yet it was the sorrow so clearly reflected in her tear-brightened eyes which drew him near. She lay back against his pillows, silently regarding him as he hurried to undress himself, but had she offered any protest to what he wished to do, he knew he'd not have been able to heed it. He needed her too badly now to play the part of a gentleman any longer and as he joined her in his bunk he gave free rein to the passions which had burned too long within him without release.

Bianca closed her mind to the strident voice of her conscience as she slid her arms around her husband's neck and drew him close. She welcomed his kisses eagerly, so hungry for his loving she refused to consider the consequences of such recklessness. She knew only that she wanted to feel the hardness of him deep within her, to enjoy the strength of his superbly conditioned body as he moved over her with a grace which would fill not only her body but her soul with the rapture of his loving. She relaxed in his embrace, inviting him to take whatever pleasure he desired since she knew how greatly they would share that bliss.

Evan fought the wild impulse to take her swiftly, and instead he began with deliberate care to explore her body's most charming secrets. As his lips moved to caress the tender tips of her breasts, his fingertips slid down between her thighs, parting them gently as he sought to arouse her fully to enable her body to prepare a lush welcome for his every advance. The rhythm of his motions was slow, knowing, for he wanted solely to please her, but all too quickly her beauty worked an exotic magic upon him and he found his own desires impossible to control. His lips teased the smooth flesh of her belly, then strayed lower to the inviting triangle of blonde curls as he sought to conquer her spirit with ecstasy's most stunning gift. He spread his fingers to cup her hips, lifting her slightly to allow his tongue to plunge deeper still, his fevered kisses setting his own blood aflame as well as hers. He could feel the tremors of pleasure within her lovely body become increasingly more intense until at last the final shudder of splendor rocked her to the very marrow. His own satisfaction still to come, his lips returned to hers then, as he took her with a rapid series of deep driving thrusts which swiftly carried him aloft to share with her the rapture of their union. They were finely matched lovers, a perfect pair whose passions flared again and again before they finally surrendered to the deep warmth of contentment and fell asleep in each other's arms.

Evan awoke as John, ready to serve supper, knocked lightly upon his door. He sat up slowly, perplexed to find himself alone in the narrow bunk. His temper threatened to explode in a fiery burst of blistering insults he knew the man truly didn't deserve, but he got his anger under control by telling himself Bianca might have wished to be alone for a dozen reasons, none of which were necessarily an insult to him. He got up quickly, pulling on his pants and grabbing his shirt as he went to open the door. He made no excuses for his appearance, but continued to dress as the cook's helper set the table. John was clever enough to hide his smile, and when he left, Evan lost no time in going to Bianca's cabin, where he had to rap several times before he heard a faint reply. Not understanding her response, he tried the handle and, finding the door unlocked, opened it and looked in.

Bianca was sitting upon her bed. Despite his hopes, she'd not bathed and dressed for supper but was wearing the same light green dress she'd worn earlier in the day. She'd not bothered to comb her hair since leaving his bunk, and its wild disarray framed her sorrowful expression. "I said, 'Go away.' Just leave me alone," she repeated once again.

"Leave you alone?" Evan cried out in disbelief. "You can't ask that of me after the afternoon we spent together. I thought you'd come back to me. Or at least that's what I felt in your—"

"Stop it!" Bianca cried, her gaze dark with anguish. "Blame that interlude on me if you must. I'm sorry it happened. It was a grave mistake on my part and one I'll not repeat. I'll not go near your cabin again, much less your bed," she explained apologetically.

"Have you lost your mind?" Evan was past anger now. He strode through the door, took a firm grip upon Bianca's wrists and, unmindful of her frantic protests, pulled her off the bunk. "You will dine with me tonight, as indeed you will every night until we reach Venice. I am the captain of the *Aurora* and my word will be obeyed, my invitations accepted without argument!" He slipped his arm around her waist and escorted her to her place at his table with a haste that allowed no time for refusal. "The food smells delicious and I expect you to eat every bite." He served their plates himself then, and made her portions as generous as his own as if daring her to defy him.

Bianca stared at her husband, fearing that her company at dinner would not be all he required that night. "I apologized. It was my fault we made love again when I'd told you I didn't wish to do so. I said I'm sorry. You needn't behave like such a bully."

Evan stared at her coldly as he spoke with fierce determination. "I am still your husband, Bianca, and I have certain rights. Whether or not I'll choose to exercise them is up to me, not you! All I've asked you to do is eat your supper, and I suggest you do it before I change my mind and ask for something else I want far more!"

Bianca gripped her napkin tightly, then thrust it into her lap, desperately sorry she'd allowed herself to become carried away by her emotions that afternoon. It was no wonder Evan was so angry, for it must seem to him she'd simply used him and nothing could be further from the truth. Rather than argue anymore she took a bite of her supper and chewed it slowly, wondering how she'd be able to get herself out of this terrible trouble she'd brought on herself. She'd taken the blame since it was rightfully hers, but clearly that meant nothing to him.

Evan had to force himself to sit quietly, to behave as the gentleman he'd always tried to be with her. He was so thoroughly disgusted with his willful wife's unreasonable moods, however, he simply didn't know what to do with her anymore. He'd tried patience and tenderness, which only that afternoon had enabled them to recapture the love they'd once shared, but that bliss had been all too brief and now she'd again retreated behind a shell of silence he couldn't break. What secrets did she keep hidden in that pretty head of hers? Would she never again trust him or confide in him? When he finally gathered his thoughts enough to speak, it was to make a hostile accusation. "You wish me to forgive you for being unable to control your passions where I'm concerned, is that it? When you'll not forgive me for my desire to see justice done or for involving you in my efforts to trap my brother's murderer? I may have used you last spring, Bianca, but that was before we fell in love and were married. It was you who used me this afternoon, and I'll never forgive you for that insult. The map's finished.

Spend your days in your cabin, or up on deck, but each night I expect you to be at my table and if ever you refuse that invitation, or any other I might wish to extend, I can guarantee you will swiftly regret it!"

Bianca did not reply. She simply rose from her chair, leaving her supper barely touched, and returned to her cabin where she quickly bolted the door. Then she leaned back against it, afraid Evan would follow her. When he didn't, she began to relax. In no way could she have explained to Evan that she'd not left his bed to insult him, but to protect her own badly bruised emotions. It was clear that what was important to him was finding his brother's murderer. That was what he wanted, while she sought only proof of his love. God help her she'd married a stranger and come to love him so dearly, but she still didn't feel she knew him, not when he'd threaten her as cruelly as he just had. The answers they sought were all in Venice, they had to be, but she knew it would take every ounce of strength she had simply to survive the voyage home without giving in to Evan's demands. She wondered if she had the will to continue to deny the love she felt for him. When his slightest touch filled her with such desperate longing, how could she hope to survive without him?

Evan was no less confused than his wife and he found brandy an extremely poor substitute for her presence in his life. She appeared at his door each evening, her beauty radiating from a deep inner glow, but he made no effort to understand the complexity of her moods which continued to keep them apart. He wished a thousand times he'd chosen to take the *Phoenix* unladen as the *Aurora*'s time was anything but swift, but when they finally reached the Mediterranean, he knew the voyage would soon be over and that caused him even greater agony. He'd made no demands upon Bianca, other than that she share his table; yet he could not bear to spend the last night they'd be together alone, and when she excused herself after they'd eaten, he simply refused to let her go.

"I beg your pardon?" Bianca asked breathlessly, certain she had heard him correctly the first time but wanting to make him say it again.

"I said there's no need for you to return to your own cabin tonight." Evan made his comment in an offhand manner, sounding nonchalant, but he was determined to have her that night and not by force either. "You are my wife, Bianca, and you're going to spend tonight with me. I'll tie you to my bunk if I must, but why don't you save us both that embarrassment and come to me willingly?"

Not a day had passed without Bianca expecting this demand. That he'd finally chosen to make it was actually a relief. He'd given her some brandy, and she took a sip and then another before she rose unsteadily to her feet. She'd learned how to lace up her own corset out of necessity and without asking for his help with her garments she slowly began to disrobe, not realizing her natural grace made her actions superbly erotic.

Evan waited until she was completely nude to remove his own clothing. "I want it all tonight, Bianca. Everything we've ever done together, we'll do again. Then if you still wish to leave me in the morning, I will let you go." Yet even as he spoke Evan prayed she'd not recognize his promise for the boldfaced lie it was. He reached out to draw her near and she came into his arms without hesitation, yet he felt that her surrender was only partially complete. She was holding back the one thing he wanted from the very beginning: her trust. He'd have no choice but to let her go, if only briefly. He realized that now as her long curls brushed against his bare chest. The price of that night would be her freedom, but he vowed it would be only temporary, and never complete.

Bianca lost herself completely in the warmth of her husband's embrace. He'd asked only for affection, and that she could easily give for it filled her heart to overflowing. She made love to him for hours with a slow teasing sweetness, but before the first glimmer of dawn lit his cabin, she again left him to return to the privacy of her own.

Chapter XXIV

As the gondola pulled away from the side of the *Aurora,* Bianca could not resist the impulse to turn back for one last glimpse of Evan. Still standing at the rail, he waved to her as though he'd been expecting her to give him some last sign of farewell. With his impressive height, auburn hair, and unusual golden brown eyes, she doubted anyone he'd met on his previous visit to Venice would be fooled by his newly grown beard. He was still the handsomest man she'd ever seen, and leaving him now was the hardest thing she'd ever done. She remembered then that her first impression of her husband had been most unfavorable. She'd thought him an arrogant ass. Now, after several months of marriage, she still didn't quite know what to make of him. Although Evan had given her no choice about where she'd spend her last night aboard the *Aurora,* he had been more than merely kind to her the next day. He'd kept his word, and had summoned a gondola to take her home as soon as they'd docked. He'd told her good-bye with such obvious regret she'd been sincerely touched, but he'd promised he'd keep her informed of the progress of his investigations so she knew she'd see him again before he returned to America. "Alone," a tiny voice whispered in her heart, but she shoved that painful thought aside as she attempted to devise an excuse which would present the truth without infuriating her parents unnecessarily. While he'd not asked her to use the name he'd invented, Captain Jonathan Wright, she planned to use it anyway rather than admit she'd spent the last few weeks on board her husband's ship. She'd spent many an hour attempting to come up with a clever and convincing tale, but now as she saw the Ca' Antonelli in the distance she could recall none of those imaginative stories and she was badly frightened that she'd be turned away by her parents.

The gondolier helped Bianca from his boat to the marble steps of her home, then unloaded her luggage. Evan had already paid him, tipping the man generously, but he waited to be certain that she'd be welcomed into the elegant Gothic palace before he went on his way. When the servant who came to the door squealed in delighted surprise and hurriedly summoned the rest of the household staff, he considered his work done and returned his craft to the Grand Canal.

Disturbed by the noisy confusion downstairs, Catherine left her bed and peeked over the balcony railing to see what was causing such a stir. When she saw her daughter standing in the entranceway she could scarcely believe her eyes. "Bianca!" she called excitedly, unwilling to come down the stairs when she wasn't fully dressed but not wanting to be left out of the boisterous celebration everyone else was enjoying.

Bianca lifted her skirts and ran up the stairs, but as she reached the first landing she was so shocked by the changes in her mother's appearance she could do little more than gape. Her mother's fair beauty was undiminished, but the soft folds of her lace-trimmed nightgown failed to conceal her advanced pregnancy.

Catherine saw the focus of her daughter's glance and began to laugh as she placed her hands upon her swollen abdomen. "It is about time I gave your father another child. You must hurry. Come into my room so you can tell me everything before he returns."

Bianca rushed the rest of the way up the stairs and hugged her mother tightly. She was so grateful she'd not been immediately banished from the house, she couldn't find her voice to say thank you. They walked arm and arm to her mother's room where Catherine returned to bed, insisting it was a precaution of her physician's she thought totally unnecessary. Bianca climbed up on the foot of the high bed, a perch she'd loved but had not occupied since her childhood. She still did not know where to begin.

"You have been gone for months! Now tell me all about this man you married. Why isn't he with you?" Catherine asked, curiosity making her pretty green eyes sparkle brightly.

Bianca swallowed nervously. "I don't want Papa to hurt him, I couldn't bear that, so I'd rather not say where he is," she finally explained, knowing she was making no sense at all. "I've left him, but perhaps not forever. At least I hope not forever."

Fascinated by her incomprehensible statements, Catherine stared at her lovely daughter for a long while without speaking. She was a clever woman in her own right, and needed to ask only one question to know all the answers she required. "Do you love him?"

Bianca bit her lip savagely to force back the flood of tears which now seemed to be perpetually threatening to overwhelm her. She could no more lie to her mother than she could lie to herself, and she readily admitted the truth. "Yes, desperately, but—"

"My dearest, if you love the man, 'desperately,' then why have you left him? Is it only a matter of pride? If so, then you must go to him immediately and beg his forgiveness, for I know you are no fool and it would be very foolish indeed for you to leave the man you love."

Bianca nodded, knowing all her mother said was true. "It is not a question of pride, but of a desire for revenge, a desire so all-encompassing it led him to deceive me. He is the one who must make peace within himself before we can again be husband and wife. It is all up to him."

Catherine found that belief difficult to share. "I did not realize Americans pursued vendettas as men do here. Are you certain that this isn't precisely the time he needs you most?"

"He is a proud man, Mama, but the only help I could provide was of scant use to him."

Since her daughter's distress was obviously becoming more acute, Catherine let the matter drop. She was certain Evan Sinclair must be in Venice too, and she hoped this time she'd have the opportunity to meet him before he left since everything she'd heard about the man was enormously intriguing. "Was he good to you, angel?"

"Yes, he was very good about most things, if not all." Bianca was afraid she'd reveal more than she wished to if she didn't keep still so she lifted her chin proudly, her resolve to be silent quite clear in her posture.

"I think I understand," Catherine mused softly, making no attempt to speak her thoughts aloud. "While I have the chance, I must warn you that your father was furious that you defied him so willfully."

"And you weren't?" Bianca asked with a hesitant smile.

"Francesco was not my father's first choice although he was mine. I tried to remind him that our own love story was a tumultuous one, but unfortunately I failed to impress him with that memory. I was certain someday you would return to us, if only for a visit. I knew you'd come home and I didn't want him to turn you away. If that does happen, however, I want you to go straight to

Raffaella as she will surely take you in."

"Isn't Raffaella here?" Bianca asked in surprise.

"Of course, you would have no way of knowing. She married Marco Ciani. Your father provided a generous dowry for her, not quite what he'd planned to give you, but a goodly sum all the same. They are a charming couple who visit us frequently. Do you remember which home is his?"

"Why yes. I've been there many times."

"Good. Then if the worst happens, you must go there. Raffaella will get word to me that you are safe."

Bianca doubted she'd ever feel safe with Evan prowling the city in search of the mysterious blonde whose identity she'd been unable to supply. "Mama, do you know of a young woman who resembles me, no matter how slightly?" Although she attempted to make her description complete she realized Charles had left them pitifully few clues to relate.

Perplexed by so unusual a question, Catherine took some moments to consider the possibilities, but she could provide no new ideas. "I know but a few blondes, none are nearly so pretty as you, and none have names beginning with the letter *A*. Is this some sort of a puzzle?"

"It certainly is a puzzle, one I hope to solve, however, and soon." Since Bianca wanted Evan to find the murderer quickly, she hoped she'd be able to find someone who could give him the assistance he needed. "Just keep thinking about it, maybe someone will occur to you later."

As Bianca talked with her mother, she tried to prepare herself for the worst, but even her lively imagination did not provide an adequate preview of the scene which transpired when her father returned home. He was not simply angry to find her there, he was livid. The fury of his temper was undimmed by the passage of time, and she was instantly reminded of the night Paolo had pulled her from Evan's arms and had returned her to her home with the demand that she marry him within a few days' time. That was the night she'd fled her home with Evan, and now despite her father's rage she thought only of her husband and did not respond in kind.

Francesco Antonelli had learned of his daughter's arrival the moment he'd set foot in his door. Knowing she'd be with her mother, he'd dashed up the stairs, eager to tell her exactly what he thought of her for disgracing them by disregarding their choice of a husband. Not wanting to upset his wife, however, since he regarded her health as fragile, he insisted Bianca discuss her homecoming in the privacy of his room so Catherine would not be a party to it. He closed his door behind them, then spoke in a menacing whisper. "There is only one excuse I'll accept from you, Bianca. If that scoundrel, Sinclair, raped and kidnapped you, then I will welcome you home with unrestrained joy, but if you left this house by your own choice, I'll not waste another minute on you. Just go!"

When he'd come into her mother's room, Bianca had rushed forward to kiss him, but he'd pushed her away with a savage shove and had hastily escorted her into the adjoining suite. Coming home had been an impossible dream, she realized sadly, but she'd not demean Evan's good name simply to restore her own. "If those are your conditions, I'll have to go because Evan did not force me to leave. I went with him out of love," she explained softly. She waited a moment, hoping he'd relent, but he turned his back on her and remained silent. Knowing her mother would swiftly learn what had happened as well as where she'd gone, Bianca didn't risk upsetting her by returning to her room to tell her good-bye before she went downstairs. For the second time that day she watched her luggage being loaded aboard a gondola, and her heart was no less heavy when she left her former home than when she'd left her husband. Would the love and acceptance she craved never be hers again? Her choices seemed very few, and if Raffaella's welcome was no more sympathetic than her father's, she feared she'd have a very difficult time indeed. She'd defied her family by eloping with Evan, also tradition which repaid daughters harshly for disgracing their parents as she had. At least her father had not called her a whore, but that was scant consolation to the tearful young woman.

Having no time to waste, Evan swiftly found a buyer for his cargo of tobacco and then began the tiresome process of unloading it. A veteran of countless voyages, he found the riffraff inhabiting the docks of Venice no different from that in any other port in the world. There were men who were eager to provide services of any nature, for a price. They were puzzled when Evan insisted he wanted only information on a certain green-eyed blonde, but he had the cash to provide them with an incentive. He'd used the map and the lists Bianca had made to good advantage. Since it stood to reason she would know every wellborn young lady, that left another segment of Venetian society unexplored. The lace-trimmed handkerchief had fooled him. Surely a courtesan, as well as a respectable woman, would have expensive things. It was a fantastic idea perhaps, but he was willing to pursue it until it came to a dead end. Charles's green-eyed goddess was here somewhere, and this time he'd sworn to remain in Venice until he found her and brought his brother's murderer to justice.

He missed Bianca terribly but as he ate supper alone in his cabin, Evan realized he could visit her whenever he wished. He then found it difficult to pass the next few hours, but when he was certain the rest of her household would be asleep he made his way by boat to the Ca' Antonelli, again scaled the intricate stone façade and entered her room. He waited in the darkness, his heart pounding with excitement as he listened for the sounds of her breathing, but when he heard only a deep silence he found the lamp at the bedside and lit it. There had been no lights showing in any of the windows, so he'd assumed his wife would be asleep in her room. To his amazement, he soon discovered that the elegantly furnished bedchamber was unoccupied, and that it held none of Bianca's belongings. Alarmed, he paced the room with an anxious stride as he tried to imagine where his lovely bride might be. He'd not even considered having one of his men follow her since he'd known exactly where she was going, or at least he'd thought he'd known where she was bound. Greatly frustrated that she'd somehow eluded him, he sat down upon the bed, recalling his first visit to her boudoir, and that bittersweet memory reminded him that his reason for coming here had been anything but honorable. He'd wanted only information regardless of the cost to her, but he'd swiftly lost his heart. Had Bianca been in the house now, he was certain she'd be using her former room since it had obviously not been given to another. Since it was pointless to remain, he left the Antonelli mansion quickly and returned to the *Aurora*, knowing he'd made a grave mistake in offering money for the whereabouts of only one golden-haired beauty when clearly he must seek two.

Bianca found Raffaella's questions as difficult to answer as her mother's, for nothing she was willing to admit made the slightest bit of sense, even to her own ears. Marco was astonished to find her a guest in his home, and he apologized profusely for introducing Evan to her in the first place.

"Believe me, Bianca, I had no idea the man had so little in the way of character. I called at your home repeatedly in the hopes your parents would forgive me for unintentionally allowing you to fall into his hands." Marco had to pause and smile at Raffaella then. "At first your father refused to see me, but I found your cousin such charming company I soon returned only to see her."

Bianca knew exactly why Marco had needed her father's forgiveness. He was an ambitious young man who dared not make an enemy of a man so close to the Doge. She'd known her parents were hoping to find a suitable mate for their niece, but she prayed taking Raffaella as a bride had not been the price Marco had had to pay to regain her father's favor. From the adoring looks the young couple constantly exchanged it seemed unlikely that Marco had married Raffaella for any reason save love, however. Still, she feared her presence in their home might cause them trouble her mother had not foreseen. Venetian society was always alive with intrigues and scandals, and she did not want to see them hurt by the talk her return would surely cause. It was too soon to know which action would seem the greater disgrace, that she'd eloped with an American sea captain or that she'd left him.

"I'll not become a burden to you," Bianca insisted. "I've many nice pieces of jewelry, perhaps you can arrange for the sale of them for me, Marco. Then I will have sufficient funds to rent a small house for myself, although I'm not quite certain how I'll manage to maintain it."

"You are my cousin!" Raffaella protested immediately. She knew from bitter experience the perpetual problems a home with little money faced. "I'll not have you living in some tiny house with no servants and not knowing how you'll survive from day to day. You'd soon become hopelessly in debt to merchants for every single item you require, and then you'd be at their mercy. You'll stay here with us. Tell her she must stay, Marco, please do."

With Marco's love, her cousin had blossomed into the lovely young woman she was meant to be. Her glossy brown hair was now attractively styled, her pretty yellow gown was new, and her manner was that of a young woman who is confident her opinions are valued. The portrait Stefano Tommasi had done of her hung in the parlor, and Bianca noticed immediately that the artist had captured the new beauty love had given her.

"Of course," Marco agreed. "You will always be welcome here with us, Bianca, always."

"Thank you." As the couple again exchanged glances, Bianca looked away. Evan had offered her a generous sum of money, but she'd refused to take it, thinking she might as well learn how to get by on her own since she might have to in the future. She slept poorly, although the room she'd been given had a comfortable bed. It was enormous compared to the bunk she'd slept in during the voyage, and she felt all the more alone. During the next few days she enjoyed accompanying Raffaella when her cousin went shopping, but she asked to be excused from paying social calls or speaking with her cousin's guests since she knew any remarks she made would be used to fuel the fires of the gossip Venetians so loved to spread. Through servants, she managed to reply to the letters her mother sent to her. Catherine still hoped her father would soon forgive her, but Bianca doubted he ever would. She felt he was much too proud a man to forgive her for the disgrace he'd suffered, but when her troubles began in earnest, it was not he who caused them, but Paolo Sammarese.

While Marco was still cordial, his manner became increasingly preoccupied and Bianca thought she'd done something to offend him although it had been quite unintentional. She thought perhaps she was spending too much time in his wife's company when he'd undoubtedly prefer to have Raffaella to himself. She made it a point then to return to her room the minute they'd finished eating supper, and she did not leave it in the morning until she was certain he'd left the house for the day. She did her best not to infringe upon the privacy he and Raffaella had so obviously enjoyed before her arrival, but she still feared her presence in their home was an intrusion. When she could no longer ignore the strain she was so clearly causing in her cousin's household, she knew she'd have to discover its source for fear that she might create the same discord no matter who took her in unless she knew the cause. When Marco had left for the day and the two young women were alone in the parlor, Bianca quickly seized the opportunity to learn the truth. "You have been so kind to me, Raffaella, which is very generous of you considering the way I used to tease you, but I can tell that something's wrong. Won't you please tell me what it is? If you'd like for me to go elsewhere, I wish you would just say so."

Raffaella was mortified by her cousin's request, and her eyes quickly filled with tears as she forced herself to explain her fears. "Bianca," she began hesitantly, ashamed to admit what she could no longer hide, "it's Paolo. He knows you're here and he's threatened us. He means to ruin Marco; he has the influence to do it too. If we continue to allow you to live in our home we'll soon face the worst of financial difficulties. Everyone is afraid to defy Paolo, and if he wishes to discourage the trade Marco normally has—"

Instantly understanding her cousin's dilemma was her fault even though Paolo had caused it, Bianca raised her hand to halt her confession. "I knew you and Marco were upset, but I had no idea it was something as serious as this. Why didn't you and he tell me about Paolo's threats immediately?"

Proud of her husband's actions despite their inherent risk, Raffaella hastened to defend him. "Marco would never send you away, never, no matter what it costs him. He still feels partially responsible for what happened to you. You see, Evan asked to meet the most beautiful young woman in Venice, one he'd heard had golden blonde hair and green eyes. Marco knew he would be here only a few days and unfortunately he saw no harm in indulging that request but he never dreamed Evan might take you away with him."

Bianca knew Raffaella loved Marco dearly, and she did not question her motivation for revealing a secret he'd obviously wanted to keep hidden. As her glance fell upon her cousin's portrait, she had a sudden inspiration. "I'd like to go upstairs and begin packing right now. I've an idea of where I might go, but I'd rather not reveal it. Tell Marco this was entirely my idea. Don't let him suspect you told me about Paolo's threats since that would only upset him. It is enough that he showed the courage to stand up to that dandy Sammarese, I'll not allow him to suffer by making him continue to do so. This will all be resolved soon, and I promise neither of you will suffer for helping me."

"Oh Bianca, this is such a dreadful mess. If only Evan Sinclair had never come here!"

For the first time since she'd returned home Bianca smiled, really smiled, and her expression was positively radiant as she thought of her husband. "Knowing him, loving him, was worth every bit of this pain, Raffaella. Now let's not waste any more time on regrets. Come and help me pack." She took her cousin's hand as they mounted the stairs. "Did Marco ever mention any other women to you? Was I the only one he planned to introduce to Evan or were there other blondes he might have named as possibilities?"

"Others? Whom do you mean?" Raffaella asked innocently.

Bianca laughed. "If I knew their names I would not have to ask you!"

Realizing how silly her question had sounded, Raffaella blushed deeply. "I'm sorry, but no, although he has often said he wondered how Evan managed to describe you so perfectly when you'd never met. Do you know how he did it?"

"Yes, but that's a secret I dare not reveal yet." Despite her cousin's insistent complaints that her silence was unfair, Bianca did not mention Charles or his diary as she gathered her belongings. The more she thought about the dearth of clues, the more she realized how helpful the artist, Stefano Tommasi, might be. His eye was trained to observe every nuance of beauty, and she was sorry she'd not thought of visiting him sooner for surely a man with his appreciation of women would know the one who'd bewitched Charles. "I'll not tell you where I'm going just yet. I'll stop and change gondolas several times. That way if Paolo has men watching me I'll lead them on a merry chase before I reach my destination. Please don't worry about me. There's something I must do for Evan before I make plans for my own life."

"For Evan?" Raffaella's eyes widened in alarm. "You mean he's here again, he's in Venice?"

"I didn't say that," Bianca replied evasively for she'd

not meant to give her cousin that suspicion. Then, although Raffaella continued to plead with her to remain with them regardless of the consequences, Bianca refused to change the plan she'd just made. She borrowed money for gondolas, kissed her cousin good-bye, and left.

Stefano was thoroughtly bored. He'd just completed a portrait of a kindly woman in her sixties, and although he'd done his best to make the goodness of her spirit shine forth from the light in her eyes, there had been no way he could make such a homely individual attractive. Her children had loved the portrait, however, and had paid his fee without argument, but this was not the type of commission he enjoyed accepting and he hoped to find some far more amusing subjects soon. When Bianca knocked upon his door, he could not believe his good fortune. "Bianca! I had heard a rumor that you had returned to us, but I considered it untrue. So you are here after all, come in, come in."

Bianca ignored Stefano's bright glance, which had already begun to stray down her figure. She'd not forgotten the hunger in his eyes when he'd looked at her, but she hoped his appetite for pretty women would work to her advantage this time. "I've nowhere to go, Stefano. If you will allow me to stay here for a while and help me locate a woman I wish to find, I'll pose for that portrait you wanted to do of me."

Upon hearing such an intriguing proposal, Stefano's smile changed to a lecherous grin. "I think you better come inside so we can discuss the details of your offer in more comfortable surroundings. I can think of little I'd refuse to do for an opportunity to paint you again."

As he brought her things inside, Bianca hoped she'd not just made the biggest mistake of her life. She sat perched on the edge of her chair, attempting to make her offer clearly a business proposition. "First, I need a place to stay, and I know you have extra rooms. Second, I wish to locate a young woman who resembles me to a great degree. She is a green-eyed blonde, and her name begins with the letter *A*. Since you have painted so many portraits of lovely women, I know you're my best hope of finding her. If you'll allow me to stay here, and help me to locate her, I'll pose for you, but only for one portrait."

"That is all you want, a room and the name of some pretty blonde?" Stefano leapt from his chair to refill his glass, although Bianca had had no time to take the first sip of her wine. "Surely you are joking. How could I possibly know someone that you do not?" he asked flippantly.

Bianca thought his reluctance to accept her proposal odd, for the advantage was clearly his. "I'm sorry. Have I offended you in some way? I meant only to strike a bargain which would be beneficial to us both."

Instantly Stefano became contrite. "I am not offended, but neither am I made of stone, Bianca. Were you to live under my roof, to pose for me in the nude, I could not promise my reactions will always be those of a gentleman. Do you wish to take that risk?"

"No," Bianca replied firmly. "If you make the slightest advance to me, I will leave immediately, and I will see that both my father and Paolo Sammarese are informed of the reason why."

Stefano scoffed at that show of bravado. "From what I've heard, neither of those fine gentleman would care."

"Perhaps not, but do you want to take the risk that one of them might break your hand, or even your neck, should they learn you have insulted me?"

Stefano returned to his chair and, stretching his legs out before him, crossed his ankles to get comfortable, but his excitement was barely contained. "Why must I worry about your father and Paolo? It is my understanding you are a married woman now."

Bianca licked her lips slowly, certain there was a better way to go about what she was doing and wishing that she'd found it. "I have left my husband, and I'd prefer you did not mention him to me ever again."

Stefano shrugged, knowing the scandal currently surrounding Bianca's return to Venice would make any painting he did of her all the more valuable. Her figure was so splendid clothed, he doubted it would be anything less than exquisite in the nude. "Perhaps we will be able to come to terms after all."

"There should be slight difficulty in that for there is little to discuss. I need a room and information, you want me to model. It is a fair exchange."

The wily artist drew his fingers through his dark curls. He considered her offer too good to refuse, yet he was reluctant to accept it for the risks he'd run were considerable. "A room will be yours for as long as you wish to stay. I will try to help you locate the woman you are seeking, but since that may require some time, I would like to begin making sketches of you immediately. I am between commissions, and it would be foolish for us to waste any of the time you are here."

Bianca stared at the dark-eyed man a moment, knowing his suggestion was a reasonable one no matter how greatly she'd hate posing for him. What do I want most, she asked herself, to retain my modesty, or to find the blonde Evan is seeking? When she posed the question in those terms, the answer was easy. She raised her still untouched glass in a salute. "Agreed."

"Good," Stefano replied with unabashed glee. "Since the light is perfect now, remove your gown and we'll begin. There will be plenty of time later for you to put away your things."

Bianca knew it would be futile to stall for more time since posing in the nude would be no less disagreeable if postponed. She quickly finished her wine, grateful for its numbing warmth, and reached for the hooks at her bodice, wishing she were undressing for the man she loved rather than an artist whose appreciative glance was an outright leer.

Chapter XXV

Thanks to the creativity of his hired informants, Evan met nearly three dozen comely young women. Most were very pretty, some were actually blonde, and a few even had green eyes. All claimed to be named Angelina or Anna-Maria, although he doubted any had had that name for more than a few minutes. None of these willing-to-oblige women bore the slightest resemblance to his wife, but he paid the agreed-upon amount for each introduction and promptly sent them on their way. The men of his crew undoubtedly thought him daft for bringing such a parade of females on board and promptly sending them away, but he didn't care what their opinions of him were. Obviously the description he'd given the enterprising Venetians had been incomplete for all of them had set their sights too low. He decided to send only the best of them out again with firm directions to secure the names and addresses of the mistresses of the city's wealthiest men. He made it clear he'd not pay out any more money unless one of their leads actually provided him with the correct name. That assignment proved more challenging by far, but each informant assured him he would be the first to secure the name of the woman sought.

That worrisome task taken care of for the moment,

Evan took up the far more important quest of locating his wife. He couldn't call upon Marco Ciani for help again after the mockery he'd made of their friendship. He knew everyone he'd met in the spring must regard him as a bastard indeed, yet he had no one to blame but himself for having no friends in Venice who'd be willing to help him. That fact didn't bother him, however, for he had no interest in involving anyone else in his plans. The more people who learned of his true purpose in returning to Venice, the more dangerous his mission would become. Finally it occurred to him that the Antonellis were a possible source of information. They'd not recognize him, so he could go to their home, ask for Bianca, and appear to be surprised when he was told she was no longer living there. If luck was with him, they'd reveal where she'd gone. It was undoubtedly unwise to go to her parents' home, he knew, but since he had no other promising alternative he decided to give it a try.

When Lucia said that a Captain Jonathan Wright wished to speak with her, Catherine was sufficiently intrigued by the maid's description of the man to invite him up to her room. She saw immediately that the servant's praise of the man's appearance had been much too modest, for the captain was far more than merely handsome. He was tall and well built, with the unusual golden brown eyes and auburn hair that fit Raffaella's description of Evan Sinclair perfectly. Indeed, Catherine was certain that was exactly who he was, and she wondered why he'd chosen to lie rather than rely on the truth. Then, remembering her daughter's comments, she realized he was apparently prone to do just that. "You must forgive me for receiving you here, Captain Wright, but my physician has forbidden me to leave my bed prior to the birth of my child. Bring a chair close so I can talk with you for a few minutes at least."

Bianca had described her mother as young and beautiful, but Evan had not expected her to be so near his own age. She was as lovely as her daughter, and despite her physician's precautions, she appeared to be glowing with health, her pregnancy obviously a source of great pride to her. It took him a moment to recall the story he'd planned to tell, he was so charmed by the warmth of her smile. "I am very pleased to meet you, Signora Antonelli. I am the captain of the *Aurora*, and your daughter was my passenger on the voyage here. I had planned to pay a brief call on her, but I understand that isn't possible for some reason. I hope she's not ill."

He had placed his chair near the side of her bed, at a respectful distance, and Catherine found his appearance no less pleasing now that he was closer to her. She could easily understand how such a dashing individual could have won her daughter's love in mere days. While his manner was relaxed and pleasant, she saw no reason to continue to pretend to be taken in by him. She was, after all, not nearly so naïve a woman as Bianca. "I dislike being deceived as greatly as my daughter does, Captain Sinclair. If you're not prepared to speak the truth with me, I'd rather you simply said good day and left my home now."

Not embarrassed because he'd been caught in his ruse, Evan threw back his head and howled with laughter. It seemed Catherine and Bianca were very much alike, not only in appearance but in their thinking as well. "I hope you'll forgive me for laughing. I did not mean to lie to you, only to avoid an angry confrontation. I need to speak with Bianca and I expected her to be here," he explained with a ready smile, lying again he realized, for he'd known damned well his wife wouldn't be at the Antonellis' before he'd arrived.

Catherine hesitated a moment, but knowing her

daughter loved this man despite his casual regard for the truth, she decided to be honest with him. "Bianca's father is not an unreasonable man, but he can not forgive his daughter for defying his wishes and eloping with an American she'd known but a few days instead of marrying the man to whom she'd been engaged for some time."

Insulted by that remark, Evan replied heartily, "That engagement was a sham, signora, and you know it. Bianca had no love for Paolo Sammarese, none whatsoever, and from what I saw he had even less for her. She'd have been miserable as his wife. It disgusts me to think you, her own parents, would plan such an empty life for her, and believe me, that I could prevent such a travesty from occurring is to my credit." Thinking it was pointless to prolong their conversation if it was simply going to deteriorate into a disputation, he began to rise, but when Catherine reached out her hand to stop him, he sat down once again.

"I meant only to offer an excuse for the way my husband has chosen to treat our daughter, not to question your behavior, although I, too, think it was most improper. When Bianca left here, she went to Marco Ciani's home since he and her cousin Raffaella are now married. I'd hoped she'd be able to stay there until you and she worked out your differences, but apparently she's gone elsewhere."

Evan frowned slightly, not understanding how Catherine could have thought he might have influenced her daughter's actions. "I didn't think Bianca would tell anyone I was here."

"Oh, she didn't tell me. She and I have always been very close; it was merely something I sensed by her reluctance to reveal what was troubling her so greatly. She asked if I knew any women who resembled her, but with a wife like Bianca I can not imagine why you would be seeking other women. Is that what you did to break my daughter's heart, were you unfaithful to her?"

He could tell by the blush which lit her fair complexion with a soft pink glow that she was angry with him, and he knew she had every right to be furious when she was thinking what she did. But he'd never hurt Bianca intentionally, and he said so. "I have never been unfaithful to my wife, and I never will be. The woman I am seeking has nothing to do with an illicit love affair. She was involved in a personal matter I am not at liberty to discuss."

Catherine relaxed against her pillows, trying to remain calm instead of insulting him again by pointing out the error in his thinking. "Bianca is unique. No one here remotely resembles her except me."

Evan nodded. He was beginning to wonder if Charles had filled his journal with fiction instead of fact, but he was still unwilling to admit defeat. "It's possible she's a woman you and Bianca do not know. Someone's mistress perhaps or—" As Catherine's expression changed to one of horrified disbelief Evan halted in midsentence, thinking something must be terribly wrong. "Signora Antonelli, are you in pain?" He knew his visit had upset her, but he prayed it hadn't brought on her labor prematurely.

Catherine reached for the crystal decanter at her bedside, poured herself a goblet of water, and, gripping it tightly with trembling hands, managed to take several deep swallows before she set it aside. "I'm sorry to have frightened you, but I suddenly realized I know the woman of whom you're speaking, and it was something of a shock. When Bianca asked about her, I thought she was referring to someone her own age, someone I would have met socially. It did not even occur to me she might be describing Allegra Netti. If you have any sense at all, Captain Sinclair, you will find my daughter and return to America immediately. Believe me, Allegra is the last person in Venice you should wish to meet."

The fragile woman seemed so badly frightened that Evan moved closer and took her hand tenderly in his. "I am quite capable of taking care of myself, signora. Won't you please tell me what you know of this woman? If you do, I may be able to leave Venice as promptly as you say I should."

Catherine was reluctant to say anything further, but Evan was so sincere in his interest, she knew he'd pursue Allegra himself if she weren't cooperative so she dared hold nothing back. "Allegra is no more than the beautiful daughter of a baker, but she is a clever young woman who used the remarkable assets with which nature had blessed her to every advantage. In her early teens she attracted the notice of the artist, Stefano Tommasi, and she frequently modeled for him. His art work is magnificent, and many say he did some of his finest paintings with her as his subject. Allegra shunned the boys of her own modest neighborhood, preferring to accept the favors of the older, far more successful and influential men she met through Tommasi. She used each of her romantic conquests to further her own status, always moving on to more powerful benefactors. She must be in her late twenties now, and Bianca would have no knowledge of her, or others of her kind, since we never discussed such women in her presence. Had you described her to my husband or any of his friends, however, they could have instantly supplied her name. As I said, she is both beautiful and clever. She now owns her own palace on the Grand Canal, and for the last few years she has been the mistress of the Doge."

Evan slumped back in his chair, certain the man who

ruled Venice would be difficult to kill. But no death is impossible to arrange, he thought; then he felt strangely elated for he'd finally learned the name of his target. He could see what had happened so clearly in his mind. Somehow Charles had met Allegra. She was undoubtedly an enchanting creature with many charms, but she had been merely toying with his affections, leading him on as an amusing diversion which had most certainly failed to amuse the Doge. Charles had never had a chance to leave Venice alive. "May I assume she is a green-eyed blonde?" he finally asked in a hoarse whisper.

"Yes, but her beauty is merely a veneer, a thin surface which covers the soul of a heartless tramp. No matter what your reason for wanting to meet her, I beg you to put it aside. My daughter is worth ten thousand of her, and you mustn't risk losing her over someone as worthless as Allegra Netti."

"Actually, I don't even need to speak with her now that you have told me so much about her." Nonetheless Evan planned to make a point of doing so. He owed Charles that much. "I did not mean to upset you; please forgive me for that. I wanted only to see Bianca when I came here. Do you have any idea where I might find her if she's no longer at Marco's?"

Catherine shook her head, "No. I expect her to let me know where she's staying, but she hasn't done so yet and I'm very worried about her. My husband and I do not agree about her, you see. He knew I wanted her here with us, especially now; yet he sent her away. If you find her, will you please come and tell me where she is?"

"Of course." Evan had never expected to have such an attractive and sympathetic mother-in-law, and when he leaned down to kiss her forehead lightly his affection for her was quite real. "I love your daughter very much. I realize you and your husband will probably never forgive me for taking her away from you, but I could never have allowed her to marry Paolo Sammarese when I loved her so." Even if that had not been the truth in the beginning, it was now, and Evan thought that was all that mattered.

"Will you come to see me again?" Catherine asked shyly, hoping he'd soon find Bianca and make things right between them.

"I will try." Evan gave her hand a warm squeeze, thinking it doubtful he'd be able to return, but perhaps Bianca could. When he returned to his ship, he found one of his informants waiting on the dock and took him along to his cabin. He knew it was unlikely he'd be the only man in Venice willing to pay for information, and he wondered how long it would be before one of the rascals he'd hired gathered the courage to go to the Doge and sell information about him. Taking pen and ink from his desk, he made the man a new proposition. "I'm going to write a name here. If it is the same one you write, I'll have another assignment for you. Agreed?"

The slightly built man shrugged, his knowledge of English being somewhat limited, but he understood they were going to compare names. He took the pen when Evan had finished and printed in a neat hand: Allegra Netti. To his delight, he found that was exactly what Evan had written.

Evan was certain he'd repeat the scene he'd just played several times with other men who hoped to be paid for what they'd learned. Since he'd dared not press Catherine Antonelli for the directions to Allegra's home, he took out Bianca's map and encouraged the man to point to it's location. Just as he'd thought, the fellow indicated a spot along the Grand Canal, one Bianca had left blank. That information was worth quite a bit to him so he paid the man handsomely for his trouble, then said that in a few days time he'd have another job for him, thinking the lure of more easy money would insure his silence.

Bianca had never enjoyed posing for Stefano, and she'd expected modeling in the nude to be even worse. She wasn't surprised when it was. He'd asked her to recline upon a chaise draped with red velvet so at least she'd been comfortable, but despite the grace of her pose, she had never been more ill at ease. The preliminary sketches he'd done were so good he'd been inspired to begin a large canvas immediately, thinking he'd include a swan and call it a portrait of Leda, the Greek goddess whom Zeus had visited in the form of that graceful bird. Knowing she had no reputation left to protect, Bianca made no objection to his choice of subject, for Leda seemed more acceptable than many other women his keen interest in mythology might have inspired him to select.

The second time she posed for him was no less awkward than the first, but Stefano worked quickly, using charcoal to block in her figure on his canvas. He'd taken great care to position her upon the chaise, achieving the most sensuously provocative pose possible, but he'd been wise enough to do so by spoken directions. He had not touched her. "If you'll bend your left knee just slightly please. Ah yes, that is perfect. The proportions of your limbs are so elegant I want an especially flattering pose. Do you recall that I told you you had the beauty of Venus but unfortunately you lacked her patience? I imagined you like this even then, but I never dreamed I'd have the good fortune to actually paint you as I saw you in my mind. I know holding any pose is difficult for you, so the moment you become tired we will stop for a rest."

Bianca tried not to listen as Tommasi continued to praise the beauty of her unclothed form; his effusive compliments simply made her feel unclean. She'd asked him several times about the woman Evan hoped to find, but appearing excited by using Bianca as a model, he'd changed the subject each time, not once supplying any useful information. He was clearly getting what he wanted from their bargain, but she wasn't. Bianca thought that extremely unfair. True to his word, Stefano stopped after an hour, and after tossing her a light blue silk robe to wear for a few minutes, he brought her a cup of tea. As she waited for it to cool, she again tried to focus his attention upon her quest. "Which do you prefer to paint, Stefano, blondes or brunettes?" she asked in a casual tone.

"Blondes of course," Stefano replied with a hearty chuckle. "I adore beauties with your exquisite golden hair and fair complexion, for the public sees such a woman in the role of a goddess. You do most of my work for me you see, and I am very grateful for that."

"Then a man with your passion for fair beauties would surely know the woman I'm seeking. She must be a few years older than I, possibly married. Won't you please try to remember which woman you've painted looks most like me?"

Stefano pursed his lips thoughtfully, appearing to give the matter deep thought. "Why are you so certain this woman is still in Venice? If she was here at one time she may be gone now, or she may be dead, although, if she is truly as lovely as you say, I hope that is not the case."

"Do you keep a log of your commissions? I could simply use it for a reference and not trouble you unless I came across a name which might be hers," Bianca said sweetly, thinking he must keep records of some kind.

"My accounts are a hopeless muddle!" Stefano

exclaimed with a frustrated sigh. "I have never kept an accurate record of my work. Perhaps that is something you might help me begin. Now if you have finished your tea, let us continue. I must go out at noon, so do not fear that I will make you model for me all day."

Bianca took the last sip of her tea, then reluctantly removed the silk robe. She had difficulty assuming the same pose, and this time Stefano came over to give her precise directions. Again he was careful not to touch her, but she could see in the warmth of his glance that he certainly wanted to. He was proving to be no help at all, and she was furious with herself for agreeing to pose before Tommasi had provided her with the names of several women who fit the description in Charles's journal. Every decision she made seemed to be the wrong one, but she realized she'd had few decisions to make until she'd wed Evan. Her life had been so carefully structured that she'd had little control over her own destiny. Now she was all alone, with no one upon whom to rely for guidance, and the frustration of being unable to help Evan was causing her endless sorrow. Bianca was so lost in the complexity of her problems it seemed to her she'd posed for just a few minutes when Stefano suddenly thanked her and began to put away his things. Wrapping the robe around herself, she quickly went to her room, grateful to have a place to be alone so she could give in to her tears.

The room he had given her was at the back of the house, and surprisingly neat, for his studio was cluttered and most of his home was filled to overflowing with the paints, brushes, and canvases he used to ply his trade. In the small room adjacent to hers Stefano stored a large collection of props. He had no housekeeper at present, and he seemed to spend most of his spare time with other artists. Just now he'd gone out to buy fresh groceries for himself. Tommasi had told her to prepare her own meals, and he saw to his own. Since she had little to occupy her other than worrying, which had proven totally unproductive, as soon as Bianca had finished dressing, she sat down to write her mother a note. She hoped Catherine was feeling well. Since her baby was due soon, Bianca didn't want to be the cause of concern. Nonetheless unable to bring herself to admit where she was living, she merely stated that she was well and would contact her again soon. Since she had no money to hire a gondolier to deliver the note, and Stefano had no servants, she had no choice but to deliver it to her home herself although she knew it would be a tiresome walk. However, as she was donning her cloak, she heard a loud knocking at the front door. Not wanting Tommasi to miss an important client, she went to see if she could take a message for the prolific artist.

Thinking the house unoccupied at the moment, Evan had just turned away when his wife opened the door. He was so surprised to find her there he spoke without thinking. "What in God's name are you doing here?"

"Good afternoon," Bianca replied sweetly, too happy to see him to respond to his question in the angry tone he'd used. "Stefano is away, but if you'd like to come in for a moment, I'm sure he'd not mind." She wondered if he'd come there looking for her, but remembering his shocked expression upon seeing her that seemed unlikely.

Evan followed her inside, and was surprised to find the front portion of the house given over to the artist's studio. "Is Signora Tommasi at home?" he asked with a puzzled frown.

"There is no Signora Tommasi as far as I know. Now, if you'd like to sit down while we talk, the two chairs over near the windows aren't covered with paint. Apparently

Stefano does not entertain here often, for he has devoted little space to anything not connected to his art."

Evan doubted he could restrain his temper sufficiently to be seated for long, but he hoped that was possible. "Your mother is very worried about you. Why haven't you let her know where you are?" As he spoke he surveyed the studio with a critical glance, still not understanding what she could possibly be doing there.

"You've met my mother?" Bianca asked calmly.

"Yes. She's beautiful and charming, and she's worried about you, as I am. Tell me what you're doing here. Surely you don't want your portrait painted again."

Bianca blushed at that remark, since he'd unintentionally discovered exactly what she was doing. "My father forbid my mother to hang the last one Stefano did of me so I'll not need another."

"Well, if he doesn't want it, I do," Evan assured her quickly, although he doubted her father would make him a present of it. "That's really beside the point now. I hope you haven't told your friend Stefano why I'm here."

"Why no. I said nothing to him about you," Bianca replied nervously. She feared there might be some reason why she shouldn't have mentioned the blonde they were seeking. "Did you want to see Stefano about something, or were you looking for me?" she asked suspiciously.

"I was hoping Tommasi might know where you were. I was just surprised to find you here that's all." Evan smiled happily, too pleased to find her to worry about what help the artist might be. "I think I've found our goddess, Bianca. Her name is Allegra Netti. Since I doubt she speaks English, will you come with me to pay a call on her?"

"Do you think that's wise?"

"Perhaps not, but I think it's imperative that I meet her. This time I want to be absolutely certain I have the right blonde before I use her to find Charles's killer." Evan had taunted her with that, not even knowing why, but upon seeing the shock with which she received that remark, he apologized. "Forgive me. I did not mean to hurt you again. I've been so worried about you, and to find you living here with Tommasi—"

"I am merely his guest for a few days, Evan. I don't plan to make my home with the man," Bianca pointed out calmly, knowing if he'd truly found the woman he sought, she had no reason to remain in Stefano's care. She'd simply tell the painter good-bye and let him complete his new Leda from memory. "We're wasting time. If you wish me to translate for you, let's go now."

Evan watched in wonder as his pretty wife left the room. She returned in a moment, wearing her cloak, and he went quickly to her side. "I have a gondola waiting," he said. "Our destination isn't far from your home. We can stop there to leave some word for your mother if you'd like."

"I would, thank you. I have a letter for her. Had you arrived a few moments later, I would have already gone to deliver it." Before she stepped into the waiting gondola, Bianca took the precaution of putting up her hood to protect her curls from the breeze. The day was chilly, and when Evan put his arm around her shoulders to hold her close, she didn't draw away. "I hope this is the woman you want Evan, but I'll be terrified if she is. You might be killed."

Bianca was so very dear to him, Evan could not help but be moved by that expression of concern. "I am a very cautious man, my love, and not given to heroics of any kind. If it appears the price of the revenge I seek is my own life, I'll not make the attempt for we would all lose far more then than the murderer. I have no intention of leaving you a widow so please put that thought from your mind. I merely want to talk with Allegra, to see what sort of person she is. You'll help me do that, won't you?"

"Yes, I agreed to do so." Having said this, Bianca reflected that each time she agreed to do something she found herself deeper in trouble. She wanted to believe her husband, but from Will's stories she knew what other men would describe as heroics he considered routine. They were not merely going to pay a social call upon Allegra to satisfy his curiosity as he wanted her to believe, but to learn the murderer's identity, and she had no doubt he'd make the most of that information. Following her directions, the gondolier approached the Antonelli home by traversing a series of narrow side canals. He stopped only long enough for Bianca to drop off her note, then took them to the palace that reportedly belonged to Allegra Netti. When Evan requested that she give her maiden name to the butler who came to the door, Bianca realized why she'd make such an excellent interpreter. Few people in Venice had the nerve to turn away the daughter of Francesco Antonelli, and apparently Allegra was not one of them.

Dressed in a low-cut gown of soft pink silk which complimented her fair beauty superbly, the stunning blonde seemed to float as she moved gracefully down the stairs to greet her guests. Bianca glanced up at Evan, but found his expression impossible to read. He appeared to be studying the woman's features a bit too intently, yet this did not faze Allegra Netti. Clearly she was used to captivating men's hearts wherever she went, and she smiled seductively at him, scarcely noticing that he was not alone. When they were seated in her parlor, a delicious assortment of pastries was served. Allegra ate the small sugar cakes in tiny bites, all the while eying Evan as though she regarded him as an even more tasty morsel, as Bianca relayed their polite greetings in English and Italian.

Allegra's gestures were filled with a sensuous grace, and her voice was honey smooth as she questioned Evan about his impressions of Venice. Catherine's description of the woman had been perfect, he realized. Her hair was soft and golden blonde like his wife's, her complexion was petal smooth, the green of her eyes vibrant, and her features were delicate yet well defined. She had the same individual assets which made his wife such a great beauty, but in Allegra they seemed as artificial as her sickeningly sweet personality and Evan had taken an instant dislike to her. Her insipid charm reminded him too much of Sheila Blanchard's suffocating affection. Swiftly becoming bored with her calculated teasing, he waited until she'd licked the sugar from her fingertips before he turned to Bianca. "Ask her as nonchalantly as you can if she remembers meeting Charles Grey last fall. I simply want to see her reaction." Evan was amazed then, for the moment his wife spoke his brother's name, Allegra's mask dropped, revealing such deep sorrow he no longer doubted that beneath the attractive shell she'd so artfully created there beat a woman's heart. Suddenly she looked like a small child who'd been caught playing dress-up in her mother's finest clothes. She was obviously a consummate actress, but such an unveiled display of emotion was not something he'd expected from the Doge's whore and he was quite taken aback by it. "Since it's obvious she does recall him quite vividly, see if she'll tell you what their relationship was."

Bianca had not expected Evan to be so cruel, for it was clear that the mere mention of Charles's name had pained Allegra. To probe what was clearly an unhealed wound was not a task Bianca wanted to perform, yet she wanted to know the truth as badly as he did. She reached out to touch the young woman's knee lightly in a soothing gesture of sympathy. "We look enough alike to be sisters, don't we? Please think of me as your friend. I've read Charles's journal, and his love for you is expressed in every line. We merely wish to know if you loved him in return."

Allegra began to cry then, with hoarse racking sobs, her tears streaming down her cheeks as she nodded. "I adored him, but we had so little time. I was to leave with him, we had everything planned, and then—" Too distraught to continue, she put her face in her hands and continued to weep as though her heart had not merely been broken by his death but crushed.

Encouraged because this unhappy woman had confided in her, Bianca quickly translated Allegra's remarks for Evan. Then she asked, "Who could have hated Charles enough to kill him?" As she did so, she realized that she knew nothing about this woman. "Your husband perhaps, another lover? Who could it have been?"

Allegra shook her head emphatically. "It was a thief. It had nothing to do with me." When she rose unsteadily to her feet, Evan and Bianca rose as well.

"I'll help you upstairs to your room," Bianca offered quickly, and with a conspiratorial glance toward Evan, she slipped her arm around the tearful young woman's waist. She was the taller of the two and easily guided Allegra up the stairs. As they entered the attractive courtesan's bedroom Bianca immediately noticed the portrait hanging near the bed. Without having to read the signature, she knew it was one of Stefano's. Surely he could not have forgotten a woman who was as close to his ideal for a goddess! "Allegra, Charles described you as a goddess. Did he have some special reason to call you that?"

Allegra sank down upon the bed. Although she tried to wipe away her tears, there seemed to be no end to them.

"My maid would translate for us although we never seemed to need words. He asked about that painting, and she told him the artist always referred to me as his Venus, his goddess of love. Then Charles said that I was his goddess now. I had never been in love before I met him, and we thought we'd have forever. It was no more than a week."

While Allegra seemed sincerely convinced that a common thief had taken her lover's life, Bianca certainly wasn't, and she persisted in questioning the distraught blonde. "Who knew you'd fallen in love with Charles, Allegra? Anyone besides your maid? Could she have told someone?"

"Teresa would never betray such a confidence. No one else knew I'd fallen in love with Charles. It was far too precious a secret to share."

Bianca sat beside Allegra, comforting her until she fell asleep. She then covered her with a light blanket before returning to the parlor, where she found Evan standing at the windows and staring out at the traffic upon the Grand Canal. She was so utterly confused by Stefano's refusal to admit knowing a woman with whom he'd clearly been very close, but she wanted him to provide her with some explicit answers before she told her husband what she'd learned about Allegra's relationship with the artist. "She was too upset to say anything more than that a thief had killed Charles. She appears to think his death had nothing to do with her. I'm sorry we were able to learn so little."

Evan smiled slightly as he turned toward her. "Actually, we learned a great deal. Charles's love was returned in full measure; somehow I didn't expect that."

"Does that change things for you?"

Evan shook his head slowly. "No, it only makes me all the more determined to see the bastard who killed my brother in his grave, no matter who he might be."

"I see." Bianca pulled up her hood as they returned to the waiting gondola, but it was not the chill of the breeze off the canal which made her shiver, nor was it the icy calm of her husband's ruthless stare. It was the heady realization that she might know exactly who that bastard was.

Chapter XXVI

Evan was silent as they returned to Stefano Tommasi's faded yellow house. The canals the gondolier chose were narrow and, by the afternoon, veiled in deep shadows that gave the brief voyage a sinister atmosphere, further depressing Evan. He looked up at the bright earth colors of the homes they passed, wondering what types of people chose to spend all their lives confined upon these tiny crowded islands. Venice was a magnificent city in many respects, and entirely unique for its industrious founders had chosen to build a town upon small sandy islands they'd connected by a series of ingenious canals and bridges, but he was overwhelmed with longing for the lush forests and rolling meadows of Virginia. Homesickness was not something which usually bothered him, but his memories filled him with melancholy now. Most of all, he wanted the wretched obligation to avenge Charles's murder to be fulfilled so he could devote himself to the happy life he planned to share with Bianca.

When they arrived at the artist's door, Evan asked the gondolier to wait as he followed Bianca inside. He was disappointed to find that Stefano had not yet returned home for he wanted to meet the man. "I appreciate your coming with me today, Bianca, but I certainly don't want to leave you here. Come back to the *Aurora* with me now. Venice is your home, but I am lost here without you. You are not only a wonderful guide, but you know what it is I'm trying to do and I need your help to accomplish it." Evan paused then, knowing he was giving her all the wrong reasons. "I really need you with me because I love you; it's as simple as that."

Bianca turned away in order to hide the confusion that would surely be revealed in her glance. "Just who is Allegra Netti, Evan? Her home was lovely. I'd noticed the house before, but I'd never been there. I've never met a family by the name of Netti, and when I asked about a husband she didn't respond. She didn't say she was planning to leave anyone to go with Charles, only that she wished to be with him. Does she have a husband?" Bianca was afraid she'd sounded completely incoherent, but if a man other than Stefano might have had reason to want Charles dead, she had to know who he was.

"I believe she is unmarried," Evan replied softly, disappointed that Bianca had changed the subject without giving him an answer. "I shouldn't have involved you so deeply in this, but since I have it is too late to pretend otherwise. If I am to do anything about what happened to Charles, I'll have no time to tarry here in Venice while you make up your mind about whether or not you wish to continue our marriage. I want you aboard the *Aurora* because if I have no choice but to flee I'd be risking my life to come here after you. This is, indeed, no game as you told me once. My business here is serious, possibly deadly, and I can't risk failing in what I must do because of you."

Bianca turned around slowly. "But I'd not do anything to jeopardize your life, you can't believe that I would!"

"The tides in the lagoon dictate when a ship may enter and leave Venice. If the slightest thing should go wrong, I'd be trapped here. Don't do that to me, Bianca. Come with me now."

Bianca swallowed hard to force back the scream of angry frustration which filled her throat. "I need more time, Evan, another day at the very least. Please don't be angry with me."

Evan could not honor a request so impossibly silly as that. "I've asked you to come with me because I love you. It's possible my very life may depend on your being on board the *Aurora*, but you say you can't make it for a day or two? You can't possibly mean that!"

Bianca clenched her fists tightly at her sides, her expression as hostile as his. "Just who is it you plan to kill? Allegra gave us no clues at all. She thinks Charles was murdered by a thief! If she doesn't suspect anyone she knows, then who do you think the murderer is?"

That his wife would be so preoccupied with Allegra Netti infuriated Evan all the more. "The woman has been mistress to many men, Bianca. Even if it isn't obvious to her that her current lover killed my brother, it is damned obvious to me! Now are you coming with me or not?"

"Who is this lover? If he can provide so fine a home as that he must be fabulously wealthy indeed! You'll not find such a man strolling about Venice alone and unarmed," Bianca shouted back at him. "What is it you really want from me, to use the name Antonelli to get to him?"

A fiery red haze obscured Evan's vision for a fraction of a second, and had she been a man, his fist would have found a mark. However, he did not dignify so insulting a question with a response. As he turned to go, the covered canvas upon the easel, the one on which Stefano had been working that morning caught his eye. As he strode by it, he yanked away the sheet of cotton cloth draped over the painting, then halted abruptly, his stare one of pure horror. While the artist had finished only his preliminary sketch, the model was clearly his wife. His glance dark with hatred, Evan turned back toward her. "How could you possibly choose to stay here and pose for Stefano rather than come with me? Do you prefer him to me?"

"Evan, you don't understand anything!" Bianca cried out in an anguished protest.

"The model for this is you, isn't it?" he queried angrily, and when she did not deny it, he left without bothering to say good-bye.

Bianca rushed after him, then stopped at the doorway. She watched him climb into the waiting gondola without making any effort to call him back. He was a hot-tempered man, but she'd had no choice about provoking him since she'd dared not leave without the information only Stefano could provide. Somehow she had to wring it out of him that night. She closed the door and hurriedly replaced the cloth over his easel. If he and Allegra were as close as the young woman had said, Bianca was certain he'd have something of her about, sketches or paintings, so she began a methodical search. Since his bedroom seemed the most likely place for him to display a painting of Allegra she went right to it, but a quick glance around the room revealed no artwork of any kind. A painting would be too large to hide easily. As she turned to go, however, she noticed a place on the wall where the paint appeared newer than the rest of the room. If a painting had hung there, Stefano must have removed it recently. Had he sold it, or had he hidden it so she'd not see it? Inspired by that possibility, she went to the most logical place for him to conceal something from her: the cluttered room where he stored his props. There were marble columns upon which to place decorative vases, oriental carpets tightly rolled up, yards of velvet—the same material he'd used to cover the chaise when she'd posed—and, hanging upon a wrought iron rack, more than a dozen elaborate costumes he'd designed for

Carnival. She ignored the pieces of furniture he'd stored, and she didn't bother to unwrap several cartons of small items. Instead she went over to the stack of new frames leaning against the wall, awaiting paintings he'd yet to complete. They were partially wrapped in coarse paper but she sorted through them, thinking this would be the ideal way to hide the missing painting. When she found a hauntingly beautiful portrait of Allegra Netti, she wasn't at all surprised. It appeared to have been done several years earlier for she was hardly more than a pretty child, but Stefano had succeeded in capturing the vibrant coloring which would eventually make her beauty so striking. If he was in love with her, did he not mind the fact she was another man's mistress? Perhaps he had resigned himself to sharing her love with others, but had murdered Charles to keep her from leaving Venice? It was such a logical assumption that Bianca did not recognize the danger she was in until Stefano spoke.

The artist was leaning against the open door. "I see you are a very curious creature, Bianca. What is it you wished to know about Allegra? If you'll tell me the truth, perhaps I'll give you an answer."

Bianca instantly regretted her decision not to confide in Evan for Stefano's manner was coolly threatening, and though he'd have been no match for her husband, she knew he would find it easy to beat her senseless, or worse. "Is this Allegra?" she asked innocently, her manner deliberately charming as she stalled for time while she tried to think of some plausible reason for her interest in the woman.

"Don't you recognize her?" Stefano asked in dismay. "You've done nothing but pester me with questions about her; I thought you'd recognize her portrait the moment you saw it."

"She is very lovely," Bianca offered sweetly.

"She is more than that, Bianca. She is an exquisite

beauty," he declared as he approached her slowly. "I might just as well return that to my room since you've found it."

"Why would you have put it away?" Bianca attempted to smile warmly, as though she had no reluctance to discuss the woman.

Stefano reached out to caress the velvet smoothness of her cheek lightly before he reached for the painting, but his gesture held no affection. "My relationship with her is a private one. Now, tell me why you are so interested in her." He was effectively blocking the exit as he waited impatiently for her to reply, his gaze and his stance menacing.

Bianca smiled brightly, hoping the tale she'd suddenly been inspired to spin was too audacious to fail. "I had never heard her name, only that there was a young woman in Venice who resembled me and that she had done extremely well for herself. I know nothing about her actually. I've merely overheard comments from time to time and I've been curious since I'd never seen any such woman myself. I made a terrible mistake in marrying Evan Sinclair so I returned home at the first opportunity, hoping my parents would forgive me and welcome me. When they did not, I remembered the whispered comments about someone who looked like me, a woman who had succeeded on her beauty alone. I wanted only to learn her name so I might consult her and learn how I might provide for myself as she has."

Startled by so candid an admission, Stefano shook his head in disbelief; then he turned and carried Allegra's portrait back to his room and rehung it. Bianca followed him but remained in the hall until he was finished. "We must talk," he said simply, and led her out to his studio where he swiftly brought her a goblet of wine. They made themselves comfortable on the two chairs on which she and Evan had sat earlier. "I knew you must have been desperate when you came to me, Bianca, but you have spent a night and nearly two days in my home without suffering too greatly, haven't you?"

Pretending to respond to his playful mood, Bianca smiled again. "Why yes you've been very nice to me. Thank you."

"I would like to be nicer still," Stefano offered as his glance strayed hungrily over the fullness of her bosom. "But first let me tell you a little something about Allegra Netti."

Bianca didn't need to pretend an interest in that subject. She took a sip of her wine and sat forward slightly. "Yes, please do tell me about her."

"What you saw was the first portrait I did of her, done almost ten years ago. I recognized her then for what she was: a great beauty. But her nature was so innocent she had no idea how to use her remarkable gifts to her own best advantage."

"And what would that advantage be?" Bianca asked eagerly.

"She is the mistress of the Doge," Stefano explained with a shrug. "No small accomplishment for the daughter of a baker. I taught her how to please a man with her body, how to dress stylishly, and what to say so she'd appear intelligent although she's far from that. I took her when she was no more than a piece of clay, molded her into a goddess; and she has repaid me a thousandfold."

Bianca was so stunned by Stefano's calmly worded revelations that she scarcely knew how to reply. She was now certain Evan knew Allegra was the Doge's mistress, and she realized who he was plotting to kill. She finished her wine in an attempt to steady herself before she had the presence of mind to ask, "How has she repaid you, Stefano?"

Stefano chuckled. "We have always been very discreet so this confession is meant only for your ears, Bianca. Allegra has been the mistress of many men, but all the while she has been my wife. Others may have enjoyed my creation briefly, but she will always belong to me."

"Your wife!" Bianca set her now-empty goblet aside and gestured helplessly. "But how could you have allowed her to be another man's mistress? How could you bear to—"

The dark-haired artist raised his hand in a request for silence. "My art is my life, Bianca. I earn a good living, but I have extravagant tastes and swiftly squander whatever I'm paid for my paintings. That my prices are high makes no difference; it simply allows me to spend more foolishly. I could no more provide the elegant home that Allegra deserves than I could fly. This is the perfect arrangement for us, especially for her as it allows her to live a pampered life, and since no man can afford to devote more than a few hours each week to his mistress, she always has more than enough time for me."

Bianca sat back, every bit as shocked as she seemed. "How do you know when it is safe to visit her?" she asked in a hushed whisper.

"Her maid, Teresa. She can travel about unnoticed. When Allegra wishes to see me, she sends a message with her. Over the years, Teresa has proved invaluable to us both."

"She keeps you informed you mean?"

"Exactly," Stefano admitted with a sly grin. "As I say, Allegra is a beauty, but she lacks your ready wit and has never realized Teresa is as much my servant as hers."

"How convenient," Bianca remarked sweetly, now knowing exactly how he'd learned of Allegra's love for Charles. "What would you do if your wife ever did something of which you don't approve?"

Instantly Stefano's relaxed manner vanished. His openness turned to hostile reserve as his dark eyes regarded her with a forbidding stare. "I would promptly see that such behavior didn't continue. She knows the difference between being the Doge's mistress and being my wife."

Bianca did not have to ask what he would do should his "goddess" fall in love with another man. He encouraged Allegra to sleep with wealthy men but she had made the mistake of falling in love. The young woman might not be overly bright, but she'd been smart enough not to tell Stefano she was leaving him. To distract him from what she was afraid he was thinking, Bianca said the first thing which entered her mind. "I knew many of my father's friends kept mistresses but—"

"What makes you think that he does not?" As Stefano got up to get more wine, he tossed this question over his shoulder.

"He would never do that to my mother!" Bianca scoffed. "Never!"

Stefano came back to refill her goblet and then his own before he sat down again. "I was only teasing you. I have never heard any rumor about your parents so if he has a mistress, or she a lover, then it is a well-kept secret."

"There are no secrets there, Stefano. They love each other too dearly to look to others for affection." As she spoke, her mind dwelt on her present dilemma. She had to get to Evan, tell him what she'd learned, before he launched some wild scheme to kill the Doge! If only he'd told her earlier that Allegra was the Doge's mistress . . . She was certain he'd known it. "While Allegra's story is interesting, we have little in common other than what appears in your painting to be a slight similiarity in appearance. I believe I already know everything you taught her. I'm merely uncertain of how to go about becoming a man's mistress."

Stefano frowned slightly, surprised such a lovely young woman would have such a practical nature. "I can assist you there as I did Allegra. I have a passion for beautiful women, also for gambling and I am frequently in the company of wealthy men at the gaming tables. Were I to mention you have no one to look after you, it would not surprise me if someone stepped forward to assume that responsibility quite eagerly. Your beauty is well known, you've forsaken your husband, been disowned by your parents. Yes, I think such a pitiful story told by a clever friend might bring you several offers. You'd have a choice."

"I would be ever so grateful for your help, Stefano. Would you be willing to mention my plight to those who are in a position to offer me the most benefits?" Bianca asked that question in the businesslike tone she'd used when bargaining for Allegra's name, although she wanted only to get him to leave the house so she'd be able to go to Evan. "Tonight would not be too soon since my situation is truly desperate."

"It just so happens I did plan on going out this evening. I think I would be better able to describe your charms, however, if I've sampled them first." Stefano rose, and placing hs fingertips beneath Bianca's chin, he lifted her lips to his for a possessive kiss she struggled to end. "I thought you were prepared to sell yourself to the highest bidder? Your reluctance to reward me doesn't inspire me to exert myself to help your cause," he remarked in a taunting whisper, his lips still brushing hers.

Bianca blushed deeply. She had forced herself to disrobe in front of this vulture, but she'd never climb into his bed. Since she knew that wasn't what he wished to hear, however, she lied. "You've made me too nervous to want to make love, Stefano. Surely I don't need to prove anything to you, not after the way I've posed for you the last two days. I'd prefer to have you see what interest there is for me before I show my gratitude."

Thinking her request surprisingly astute, Stefano stepped back. "You are a clever wench, Bianca, always driving bargains of one sort or another. Well, tonight you are in luck for I have already made plans to be at the gaming tables and I've come home only to change my clothes. You needn't wait up for me. I'm as likely to go on to Allegra's as to come here."

Relieved by that prospect since it would buy her more time, Bianca asked the most obvious question. "Aren't you afraid you might find the Doge there?

"No. We established a signal many years ago. Allegra places a flower pot on her balcony when he is there. If I do not see that sign, I know it is safe to go in."

"How clever of you." Bianca paid him the compliment easily, although her hatred of Stefano was becoming more intense with each passing second.

"Yes, I am a very clever man, in addition to being the finest artist in Venice. I have talents which you do not even suspect as yet, but perhaps I will show them to you later," he boasted, a proud smirk on his face.

Bianca did not flinch this time as his mouth covered hers, but only a few minutes after he'd left her she donned her cloak and with a quick step started off for the docks. The streets of Venice, meant only for foot traffic, are narrow, and since the canals are used for going from one island to another, she had to pursue a winding course and double back when she missed taking the proper turn to reach a bridge. Had she had the means to hire a gondola, she'd not have found one in that area at night, so although it took her almost an hour to reach the *Aurora*, she had no other choice. The man on watch seemed startled to see her, but he bid her a polite good evening and stepped out of her way so she might go directly to Evan's cabin.

Now that she'd arrived, Bianca realized Evan might not be all that glad to see her, but certain he'd want the information she had, she rapped lightly upon his door praying he'd not send her away before she could reveal it.

In as foul a mood as when she'd last seen him, Evan yanked open his door, expecting to be confronted by one of his men. When he saw Bianca, her cheeks filled with a bright blush, still quite breathless from the haste of her journey, he quickly drew her inside and smothered her face with hungry kisses. "I prayed you would not make me leave you behind," he whispered hoarsely, so thrilled to have her in his arms again he could not recall why he'd walked out on her.

Bianca enjoyed his lavish display of affection, but at the first opportunity she slipped from Evan's embrace. "Please, I have something important I must tell you."

"You're here," Evan responded with a satisfied chuckle. "What could possibly be more important than that?" He reached out to catch her around the waist and, pulling her close, kissed her once again, but when he felt her stiffen slightly in his arms he stepped back. "All right. Since you're obviously unable to concentrate upon our reunion as fully as I'd like you to, tell me what news you have."

Bianca looked up at him, loving him so she wanted only to make him happy but fearing what he might do. "The Doge didn't kill your brother. If only you'd told me what you were thinking this afternoon, we'd never have had that horrible argument."

"What?" Evan scarcely knew how to respond. "What makes you think I suspect the Doge?" he asked with genuine surprise. He'd spent the hours since he'd left her wondering how he could get close enough to kill the man, but he couldn't understand how she'd discovered what he meant to do.

Bianca took off her cloak and tossed it aside. "May I have some brandy please?"

"Of course." Evan found the bottle quickly and poured them each a generous amount. As he touched the edge of his silver goblet to hers in a mock toast, he suddenly decided that while he was in Venice he should purchase some crystal snifters to use aboard ship no matter how unpractical their fragility made them. That thought was so irrevelant to their present topic he wondered why it had occurred to him. He was so excited to see his wife he knew he wasn't thinking clearly, so he sat down and pulled her across his lap, intending to hold her while they talked. "Now tell me why you think I'm after the Doge," he said, being careful not to deny it.

First Bianca took a swallow of brandy to enhance her courage. It went down smoothly, relaxing and warming her. "Allegra Netti is the Doge's mistress. Something I'm certain you knew when we went to see her. Why didn't you tell me that?" She was tempted to accuse him of lying to her again, but for once she succeeded in holding her tongue.

Evan gave her a warm hug. He feared she'd not believe his excuse for not revealing everything he'd known about the woman they'd visited. "I thought it would be better if you didn't know. Then if something happened to me, if I was caught, you could not be accused of being my accomplice."

Bianca closed her eyes as she took a deep breath. "That was so incredibly stupid of you, but I was stupid too so I forgive you."

"Thank you," Evan replied teasingly. He was hardly able to contain his joy at having her with him again.

Bianca turned toward him, the intensity of her gaze instantly making him serious. "When I went upstairs with Allegra I saw a portrait of her. It was Stefano's work. He calls her a goddess. That's what inspired your brother to use that term to describe her. I went to him because I was certain if anyone in Venice knew such a woman it would be he. Yet when I described her, he pretended complete ignorance of her."

"Why would he lie?" Evan asked perceptively.

"When I went back to his house this afternoon, I searched until I found another portrait he'd done of her and he finally admitted he knew her. She modeled for him years ago, but he doesn't want anyone to know they are still close. She is his wife, Evan, and I'm certain he killed Charles to keep her from leaving Venice with him."

"Oh, dear God!" Evan was appalled by the knowledge that Bianca had knowingly put herself in such a dangerous situation. "You're right, of course. Neither of us has been truthful with the other, and this time it might have cost you your life!"

"Or yours if you'd gone after the Doge!" Bianca pointed out swiftly. She threw her arms around his neck, as frightened as he by their narrow brush with death.

While he returned her warm embrace, Evan's thinking became crystal clear. "Have you any proof that he is the murderer, or is it merely your suspicion?"

Bianca leaned back so she might watch his reaction to her words. "Stefano said Allegra's maid keeps him well informed. Apparently she has done so for years, although Allegra doesn't suspect she's being spied upon."

"Where is the man now?" Evan asked pointedly.

"Gambling somewhere. Why?"

"I think I may go to his house and wait for him to come home. He'll expect you to be there, won't he?"

"Yes, but I doubt he'll return until a late hour. He said

he might go to Allegra's tonight."

"I see. Then perhaps that would be the best place for me to wait for him."

Bianca knew exactly what he was thinking. "Please Evan, let's go to my father with what we've learned about Stefano. He'll see that the man is arrested and tried for Charles's murder, and I can assure you justice will be done without you risking your life."

Evan plucked his distraught wife from his lap and stood her upon her feet so he could rise. "We have not a shred of proof, Bianca. We merely suspect Stefano is the murderer because he had such a good motive. Besides, do you really think the Doge will want to see Allegra involved in a scandal of this sort? I doubt it. If justice is to be done, it will still be up to me to arrange it."

Tears filled Bianca's eyes as she looked up at her husband's determined scowl, but she knew he'd made up his mind to seek revenge when he'd first learned of his brother's death and nothing she could ever say or do would sway him. "I love you, Evan. More than anything I want to be your wife and to make the Marshall house our home but—"

"Hush," Evan whispered softly as he drew her into his arms. "You must trust me, Bianca. Trust me to do what is right, not only tonight, but always."

Bianca's slender figure melted into his then as the intensity of his affectionate embrace stilled all thought of resistance. He was indeed the rogue she'd first thought him to be, but she loved him desperately and as she lifted her lips to his no other thought entered her mind.

Evan made his decision quickly. If Stefano was not due at Allegra's for several hours, he had no reason to go there now. His wife in his arms, and he'd not waste such a splendid opportunity to make the most of what could well be the last night of his life. With slow sure movements, he peeled away her gown and then the many soft layers of her lingerie. His fingertips strayed over her breasts as he reached for the ribbon which held her chemise in place, and he felt her shiver with the same delight which filled his heart. "You must never leave me again; we belong together like this."

Bianca slipped her hands beneath his shirt, finding the warmth of his skin so comforting a sensation she could not wait for him to cast off his clothing. She unbuckled his belt to encourage him to show some haste, but he continued to move with such slow graceful motions she thought he might simply be teasing her. Two could play that game, however, so she ran her hands across his broad shoulders, down his back and over his hips before her fingers slid under his belt to caress him with a possessive touch she knew he'd be unable to resist.

She had never been coy, and Evan was especially glad she'd no desire to become so that night. Seizing her wrists he gave her a graceful turn to propel her toward his bunk. As soon as he'd removed his clothing, he stretched out beside her and waited for her to come to him, the softness of her breasts cool against the hardened muscles of his chest. They were opposites who complemented each other so well he knew exactly when her kiss would become demanding and, without waiting for that unmistakable signal of desire, slid his hand over her hip and down between her thighs. She was warm, her flesh smooth, the sweetness of her scent inviting, and he found this type of play immensely enjoyable but her hands were giving him no respite. Her slow, steady caresses were drawing him dangerously near the limit of his self-control. He wanted to possess her too badly to delay a moment longer, and she arched her back to meet his first deep thrust. He silenced her welcoming sigh with his lips, holding her locked in his embrace as the exquisite tension of their passion filled his senses. Then, lost in the ecstasy of their loving, he shuddered as their passion overwhelmed them. He wanted nothing to spoil the night's enchantment. Each kiss and every caress was filled with the devotion he'd never been able to express in words, a devotion he now knew was understood and was returned in full measure.

Chapter XXVII

Bianca lay nestled in Evan's embrace, her fingertips toying with the dark curls that covered his chest as she tried to find the words to express what was truly in her heart without insulting or hurting him. "We've come full circle, haven't we? We're back in Venice and so deeply involved in plotting revenge we nearly lost each other. I'm so frightened, Evan, because I don't want to lose you again."

"You've never lost me, my love." She had kept him off balance for a damned long time, however, but he'd not admit that. "Perhaps if I had confided in you when we first met, we could have begun our lives together far more happily, but I'll not waste time on regrets. I'll take care of Stefano tonight, and we can begin the return voyage to Virginia tomorrow. Venice will then be a closed chapter of our lives, one we need never reopen."

Bianca raised up on an elbow, wanting to watch his reaction closely as she spoke. "You'll not even consider doing as I ask and requesting my father's help to prosecute him?"

Evan sighed deeply as he closed his eyes; he knew she could read too much in his glance. "There's not enough evidence for a trial, Bianca, and even if there were, the

Doge would suppress it because the scandal would make him a laughingstock. Don't forget, Allegra was planning to leave him as well as Stefano."

"You don't even know the Doge, so how can you presume to predict what he will do?" Bianca inquired with her usual stubborn persistence, but she did not demand that he do as she thought best for in the time they'd been apart she'd decided never again to allow anything to separate her from the man she loved.

"I can't trust him to do what is my duty to accomplish, Bianca. Now don't ask me to walk away from it when it is finally within my grasp." Evan sat up, but his lovely wife reached out to pull him back into her arms and covered his face with such tender kisses. He hugged her warmly as he tried to reassure her. "Please don't worry so. I'll be back soon. I'll get your things and the painting Stefano began so there will be nothing to connect you to him after we're gone."

He seemed to have all his plans made, but Bianca instantly devised one of her own. "I'm coming with you!" she declared in an excited rush. "This isn't something you can do alone!"

That prospect was so ridiculous it immediately brought a smile to Evan's lips. "I have killed more than my share of men, Bianca, without your assistance. I'll not need your help tonight."

Unmindful of his words, Bianca scrambled off the end of his bunk and hastily began to pull on her clothes. "You don't even know what Stefano looks like. I'll not have you out murdering whomever you meet!"

"Bianca!" Evan threw back the covers and rose to his feet, certain no man had ever had to put up with so willful a wife as he'd had the misfortune to marry. What annoyed him most was the fact that she was right. He had no idea what Stefano looked like, and he didn't want to take the life of some innocent man out for a midnight stroll. "Describe him to me," he ordered as he pulled on his breeches. "That will give me a clear idea of the man I want."

"There are hundreds of dark-haired, dark-eyed men here of like build. It would be impossible for you to recognize him from my words alone." Without thinking, Bianca turned toward Evan so he might tie the laces of her corset for her, and he did it without comment. "You'll have to take me with you. It's the only sensible thing for you to do."

For several seconds Evan thought he'd actually have to put her in chains as he'd once threatened to do; then he realized she was right. He needed her too badly to leave her behind. "Can you promise me you'll identify him and then stay out of my way? You'll be scant help to me if you end up between us."

Since he had apparently just agreed to take her along, Bianca didn't argue. "Yes. I'll simply wait with you, and point him out. The rest will be up to you." She continued to dress hurriedly so she'd not keep him waiting. To so calmly plot Stefano's death bothered her until she recalled that he'd spoken of Allegra as a prized possession while clearly he had no real regard for her as a person. He'd murdered Charles in cold blood, simply to protect a valuable piece of property. That thought disgusted her so greatly her hatred nearly equalled her husband's.

Evan took care to dress in well-worn, dark clothing as he didn't want to be hindered by the constraints of more fashionable garb, not on such a deadly errand. Once dressed, he resembled a handsome highwayman more than the wealthy sea captain he was. "We'll go first to his home. If he is there, so much the better. I'll finish him off. If not, we'll gather your things and go on to Allegra's. If he has gone to visit her, surely he'll leave well before dawn and we'll be waiting for him."

"That sounds like a good plan." Bianca tied her cloak

securely beneath her chin, then took his arm as they moved toward the door.

"My God, did I just hear you agree with me?" Evan asked with a hearty chuckle.

"Hush! This is no time for you to tease me!" Bianca glared as she looked up at him, but he swiftly pulled her into his arms for a last lingering kiss which made any criticism of his behavior seem irrelevant.

"I love you, Bianca, and I have from the very first moment I saw you. There has never been another woman for me except for you."

Surprised by the tenderness in his voice, Bianca realized he was telling her good-bye. Should their plan end disastrously, he wanted her to know how deeply he had loved her. "Evan, please, I will never love any man but you, however, let's just do what we must and be done with it."

"That, my dear, was exactly what I had planned." Evan swept her out the door, keeping her tiny hand in his as they made their way to the small boat he'd planned to use for his midnight excursion. He'd not trust a gondola, but a rowboat suited his purpose quite as well. He had brought a lantern for the night was too dark for them to be able to find their way without one. After helping her seat herself in the bow, he handed her the lantern to hold, then took his own place and began to row with a strong steady rhythm which swiftly propelled them through the pitch-black waters of the harbor to the city's deserted canals.

Bianca shivered not simply from the chill of the night air, but from the danger inherent in their plan. She could hear the rhythm of Evan's breathing increase as he quickened his pace, and she knew he was as anxious as she to see the night end. She guided him through the silent waterways, her heart beating so loudly she feared it might awaken the residents of the homes they passed, but it did not. When they reached Stefano's, the little house was veiled in darkness and she didn't know whether that was a good sign or not. After Evan tied up the boat and helped her up the steps to his door, she said, "If he is home, he left no lamp lit for me." She held their lantern low so they would not be recognized if anyone had observed their arrival.

"Perhaps he did not notice that you were not in your room," Evan replied in a hushed voice. "Let's go in. Just walk by his room and see if he is there. If he is, tell him good night in a voice I can hear."

Bianca swallowed nervously, uncertain that she could do as he'd bade her when she was trembling so badly, and Evan put his arm around her shoulders as they entered the house. "There's a lamp here by the door," she whispered softly before lighting it. It gave off only a small amount of illumination, but threw menacing shadows upon the walls of Stefano's studio. In Bianca's present tension-filled mood, the shadows seemed to be weaving back and forth in some strange ritualistic dance of the dead. "See to the canvas first; then we can leave quickly," she suggested, hoping she'd be able to gather enough courage to do her part.

Evan nodded, but as he moved toward the easel the toe of his boot struck one of the three legs holding it upright and easel and canvas fell to the floor with a loud clatter. Evan swore loudly; then, catching himself, he whispered to his wife, "If that didn't wake him, nothing will. Go and see if he's here. Well, go. Hurry before he walks in on us!"

Since she had had to convince him he'd be wise to bring her along, Bianca knew she must be of some use to him. Carrying their lantern, she turned down the hall, tiptoeing stealthily. She paused outside Stefano's door, straining for the sounds of deep breathing which would tell her he was asleep in his bed. When she heard nothing, she reached for the doorknob and turned it slowly. As the door opened, the hinges gave a low moan and she froze once again, certain Stefano would at any second leap out at her, ready to plunge his knife into her heart. Again there was only silence, and as she lifted the lantern, its warm glow fell across Stefano's bed. It was neatly made as it had been that afternoon when he'd rehung Allegra's painting. Closing the door, Bianca hurried back to the studio to tell Evan what she'd found.

"He's still gone!" she whispered anxiously.

Evan had cut the new canvas from its frame and had rolled it up neatly. "Then we needn't whisper. Gather your things. I'll stay here in case he should come home in the next few minutes."

"What will you do if he does?" Bianca asked softly, still worried that someone would overhear them.

"I'll introduce myself politely, explain why I'm here, and then I'll slit his throat. Now hurry. We've no time to waste discussing my choice of tactics!" Evan said crossly. The tension of the night was affecting him too.

Bianca turned away without responding, her mood as ill-tempered as his. When she reached her room, she placed the lantern on the floor and quickly gathered up her things, caring little that she was wrinkling the fine garments. She tossed her gowns and lingerie in the center of the bed, then folded the blanket over them to make one cumbersome bundle which she then carted down the hall.

Evan rushed forward to meet her. "Here, give me that. You take the lantern." He followed her out the door, then set her belongings on the steps while he helped her get back into the boat. After placing the bundle and the canvas at her feet, he climbed down onto his seat and gripped the oars. "I have only the barest idea of how to reach Allegra's from here. Do we dare take the Grand Canal?"

"No!" Bianca insisted firmly. "No, we must go up this one until we reach the first canal to cross it. Turn to the west. That will carry us into the Grand Canal just below Allegra's house."

"Is this the way we came yesterday?" Evan inquired as he began to row, setting the boat onto a course which would take them down the center of the narrow canal.

"That gondolier knew shortcuts, but I do not. It is better to go a bit out of our way than to become lost." She held the lantern out so she could see what lay ahead in the canal since he was facing her and could not. "I'll tell you when it is time to turn. Don't worry, I'll not lead you in the wrong direction."

"Let's hope not." Evan concentrated solely upon rowing the small boat. The darkness of the night made the brief trip appear treacherous for he could see little of where they had been or where they were going. Three-story houses towered above them, like the sturdy legs of giants, on both sides of the canal, and he did not recall, even in wartime, ever making so torturous a journey for the walls of the canal seemed to hold them in a watery grip. He could not tolerate confinement of any sort, least of all during an ordeal such as this and in the dead of night. He lost all sense of time as he rowed through the darkness, but he prayed that his path would intersect with Stefano's, for this was not the type of pursuit he wanted to repeat.

"Here's the other canal," Bianca pointed out quickly. "Now there are no more turns until we reach the Grand Canal." She looked up at the heavens, but the night was so overcast no stars were visible. It was cold too, the dampness of the canal seeping beneath her cloak and making her shiver. She'd had no time to bathe so the fragrance which still clung to her skin was Evan's rather than her own, but she found that pungent aroma comforting. She wanted to savor every bit of him she could, and it pleased her that his heady masculine scent covered her body like a warm caress. While she knew rowing the small boat was hard work, he seemed not to mind but pulled the oars with a methodical rhythm which carried them swiftly toward their goal. When they at last reached the wide waters of the Grand Canal he stayed near the bank, easing the boat silently past Allegra's home to the next place where he could tie it up without being observed. "How does Stefano come here, by foot or on the canals?"

"He has a boat, but he'd no more dare tie it up at Allegra's dock than we would. I think he must leave it nearby and approach the house on foot. He told me he watched her balcony for a signal that it was safe to visit her, but as we passed, it was too dark for me to see anything clearly."

Evan had had several opportunities to traverse the narrow streets of Venice so he knew the impressive palaces along the Grand Canal had main entrances, which faced the water, and smaller entrances on the side streets. He helped Bianca from the boat, then took her hand and led her along the walk. They finally positioned themselves on the corner opposite the house so they could see someone leave by the side exit, and could step out quickly to block his path. "We shouldn't have long to wait now." Evan doused the lantern and set it at their feet. "If someone leaves by the side door, he'll have to come right by us. If it is Stefano, call his name. He'll not be expecting you and will naturally stop to ask why you are here."

"Oh, Evan, I did not even think about Allegra. If she tells him we came to see her today, he'll know everything I told him was a lie!"

Evan gripped Bianca firmly by the shoulders, ready to shake her if necessary to insure her cooperation. "She'll not mention it because Stefano is the last person she'd want to know about Charles."

Bianca took several deep breaths, trying to force her thoughts away from the act they were about to commit. "Of course. I'm sorry." She slipped her arms around her husband's waist and hugged him tightly, wanting only to feel his comforting warmth once again.

Evan used a fingertip to tilt her chin up, and he silenced her fears with a slow, deep kiss before he spoke. "We'll wait only until sunrise, if he doesn't appear by then I'll take you back to the *Aurora*. No matter what Stefano discovers about you, I'll see that you come to no harm."

Bianca stepped back into the shadows, not wanting to be shut out of this adventure no matter how frightening it proved to be. She shifted her weight nervously from foot to foot in an attempt to keep warm as they waited for the artist to leave his wife's elegantly furnished mansion to return to the humble dwelling which housed his studio. When her back began to ache, she leaned against Evan slightly and he hugged her again, but the sky was already growing light before they heard the door at the side of Allegra's home open and close. The sounds of a man's footsteps echoed in the deserted street, and as he came near, Bianca had no difficulty recognizing him as Stefano Tommasi. When she called his name he halted abruptly.

"Bianca? Is that you?" he called out softly, his desire for secrecy as great as hers.

Evan stepped forward to greet him, and instantly realizing by the man's befuddled expression that he spoke no English, he called to his wife. "Would you introduce us please? I'd like him to know exactly who I am before I draw my knife. I want him to know why I have a score to settle with him."

Bianca didn't know how she got the courage to speak, and she did not abide by her husband's request. She chose not to reveal his identity for should his attempt to see justice done fail, Stefano would survive to name him as his attacker. "Last fall you killed a young man named Charles Grey," she told the artist calmly, "a man Allegra loved dearly. That's a crime which cries out for punishment, Stefano, but you feel not the slightest degree of remorse, do you?"

"I don't know what you're talking about," Stefano replied in a hoarse snarl. He drew a knife from his belt, clearly ready to defend himself as he began to back away toward the impressive home he'd just left.

Evan started toward him, his own knife now in his hand. He had no need to tell the artist anything more before he killed him. Dressed all in black, wisps of the early morning mist curling about him, he was a fearsome sight indeed, and Stefano's eyes widened in terror as he drew close.

"I killed him because he had no right to seduce my wife! Tell this man Allegra is my wife, Bianca!" Stefano screamed in his own defense. She translated that pitiful excuse, but it did not stop the tall bearded stranger's relentless pursuit. Panic-stricken, Stefano ran to the side door through which he'd just left Allegra's house, and finding it locked, he beat upon it helplessly as he pleaded for someone to let him in. Fearing the awesome stranger would use his knife to impale him against the old wood as easily as he'd pin a butterfly in a glass case, he dared not tarry there, however. Since Evan blocked the narrow street, he had no choice but to move toward the low wall which kept the waters of the canal from flooding the island upon which they stood. He crept slowly to his left, toward the sanctuary offered by Allegra's house. The balconies on the second and third stories extended all the way across the front of the imposing structure. Stefano's gaze filled with terror as he realized there was no way to climb up to the safety they'd provide. He had no choice but to stand and fight.

Evan watched Stefano's expression closely, pleased to see the bastard tremble with fear. "You cowardly swine, you'll never have the chance to stab me in the back as you did my brother," he called out in a threatening whisper, caring little whether the man could comprehend his words for he knew Tommasi would understand the harshness of his tone. "I should hack your carcass into tiny bits and toss them into the canal to feed the fish who thrive on garbage."

Stefano called out to Bianca, his only hope for salvation now. "I did nothing more than protect my wife!" he shouted hoarsely. "He had no right to take my wife from me!"

Since the man had readily admitted his guilt when confronted with the crime, his sniveling protests that he'd been justified in killing Charles sickened Bianca. He'd not challenged the young man to a duel, but had struck him down from behind like the coward he so obviously was. The sky was growing lighter in the east, making the mist which enveloped them sparkle with the reflected brightness of the rising sun. She caught sight of someone standing at the corner of the topmost balcony, a shadowy figure that must be Allegra. Bianca wondered if she'd heard Stefano's confession, but she had no time to worry about that young woman's feelings for Evan made his first lunge at the artist. While he was much shorter in stature, Stefano was wiry and quick, and he managed to duck out of Evan's reach. The tip of the American's blade only sliced through the fabric of his jacket, leaving him unscathed.

Evan was in no hurry to finish the fight he was sure to win. He'd given Tommasi an opportunity to defend himself, and that was far more consideration than the man had given Charles. Now he toyed with him, parrying his thrusts easily because of his greater reach, taunting him with playful nicks which drew bright red drops of blood. Stefano had considerable skill with a knife, Evan would give him that, but the artist was simply no match for a man as determined as he. Evan was merely wearing him down, waiting for the moment when Tommasi would face his own death, and know why, but as Stefano stumbled and crashed into the wall at his back Evan did not advance. He suddenly saw him for the pathetic creature he was, a heartless soul who'd sell his own wife to the highest bidder. Thoroughly sickened, he knew there would be no honor in taking the life of such vermin. He changed his tactics then, and sought only to disarm the artist. He'd decided to take his wife's advice and turn the miserable wretch over to the authorities to be tried. They had heard his confession, and that should be evidence enough. Surely the Doge would be as disgusted as he and would swiftly bring the villain to trial. Evan lunged at Stefano's wrist, and when the artist cried out in pain, he knocked the blade from his hand with a savage kick. While the man's eyes widened in horror for he was thinking his next breath would surely be his last, Evan stepped back and called out to his wife. "Tell him I'll not kill him. I'll do as you ask and take him to your father to hand over to the proper authorities."

Surprised that Evan had suddenly seen the wisdom in her request, Bianca was nonetheless enormously relieved by his change of heart. She spoke sternly as she approached the men, again telling Stefano that they knew he'd killed Charles and that they would see he was brought to trial and severely punished for his crime.

For a moment the arrogant artist seemed not to understand that he was not to be immediately executed by the tall stranger with the menacing golden gaze. Then he threw back his head and taunted them with an evil laugh. "You have no proof!" he cackled with insulting glee. "No proof at all. I will go free."

Bianca's eye caught a flash of movement on the balcony overhead, but before a sound escaped her lips Allegra had sent the flower pot she'd used to signal her husband crashing down upon him. Hurled from the third-floor balcony the heavy ceramic container was a deadly missile. As Stefano was bent forward with laughter, it tore away the side of his head. By the time his crumpled body toppled into the street, he was quite dead.

Evan was too stunned to move for an instant. If Bianca had not rushed forward, grabbed his arm, and pulled him away, he would still have been standing in the widening pool of blood which flowed from the gaping wound in Tommasi's head. Bianca understood why Allegra had done it.

"She must have heard what he said about Charles," she whispered breathlessly.

"Obviously," Evan agreed, but when he looked up, he found the balcony deserted.

As soon as he had spoken, Allegra, still dressed in her lace-trimmed nightgown, joined them on the walk. Following her were her maid and butler, also dressed in their nightclothes. "Is he dead?" she asked with a cool detachment, giving no sign of the tears the mere mention of Charles's name had evoked.

Bianca did not bother to feel for a pulse in Stefano's throat, but shuddering with revulsion, she replied, "I'm sure he is."

"He did not deserve to live when Charles is dead," Allegra declared. "You two must go now. We'll take care of this ourselves." She paused a moment, then presented them with a plausible explanation of what had happened. "It was an accident you see. A scuffle below my window awakened me. I went out onto the balcony to see what was happening and in the darkness upset the flower pot. Unfortunately that resulted in Stefano's tragic death."

When Evan tightened his grip upon her arm, Bianca

quickly explained what Allegra meant to do. "Stefano trained her to cope with the demands of the luxurious life her beauty won for her, but I doubt he realized his creation would one day turn on him."

"Will she be all right?" Evan asked with a worried frown.

"Oh yes. I'm certain her servants will corroborate her story, and she has the protection of the Doge as well. Stefano's death will be investigated and classed as an accident, I have no doubt of it."

"You'd better warn her about the maid," he suggested softly.

Thinking that idea imperative, Bianca drew Allegra aside as though to comfort her and whispered that Teresa was not to be trusted. Allegra smiled only slightly, but nodded, the message understood. She looked up at Evan then, wanting to know why he had cared so deeply about the man she had loved. When Bianca explained that he and Charles were brothers, Allegra reached up to kiss him lightly upon the cheek before she told them both good-bye.

Evan was still reluctant to leave, but when he saw Allegra turn back to her servants and issue a series of lively commands he realized she was in complete control of the situation. "I meant to see him tried for murder, Bianca, I really did."

"I know, and I'm grateful for that. Come, let us go before any of the neighbors awaken and become curious about our presence. It has been too long a night. I want only to go back to the *Aurora*, to sleep, and to forget this whole ghastly nightmare ever took place."

Evan did not argue. The nightmare was now at an end for him as well. He was exhausted, but the thought of sharing his bunk with Bianca gave him sufficient strength to row their small boat back to the ship. He carried her things into his cabin, then dropped them and kicked them aside.

"I absolutely forbid you to put those away now," he said.

Bianca tossed her cloak over a chair and sat down to remove her slippers. "Believe me, that is the last thing I want to do. Is it too early to heat water for a bath?"

"No, I'll see to it," Evan offered generously, realizing he could use one as well. But before he could reach the door someone began to pound upon it with a frantic staccato rhythm. He turned back toward his wife, certain something had gone wrong with Allegra's plans and they were about to be arrested for murder. Not about to be dragged off his ship for a crime he didn't commit, he drew his knife as he reached for the knob. When he saw a silver-haired stranger before him, he was startled. Something about the well-dressed man was familiar, but he couldn't quite place what it was.

Looking past Evan, Francesco Antonelli spoke to his daughter in the language only she would understand. "It's the baby," he revealed with an anguished sob. "The birth is not going well and your mother wants you to be with her."

"Of course, I'll come right now!" Bianca jammed her feet back into her slippers and grabbed her cloak as she told Evan she was leaving with her father.

"I'll come with you," he declared, although he could tell by his father-in-law's hostile glance that he was unwelcome.

Chapter XXVIII

Evan sat opposite his wife and father-in-law as the Antonellis' sleek gondola carried them up the Grand Canal to the elegant palace which bore their family name. As they glided through the haze of dawn, he was glad that they'd not pass Allegra Netti's house, but he would have preferred to be well out to sea before the sun rose rather than still in Venice. That he'd been up all night and was dressed in the dark garb of a bandit didn't please him either. Since Francesco did not speak English, he thought it unlikely they'd be able to strike up a friendship at this late date though they'd undoubtedly be spending the next few hours together, but he gave the man a reassuring smile. In return, Francesco simply looked away as if the mere sight of his son-in-law turned his stomach. Evan thought that reaction predictable, but he was annoyed that Antonelli would give him so little opportunity to prove himself when clearly he was his daughter's choice. "Do you have any knowledge of childbirth whatsoever?" he asked Bianca softly, thinking it highly unlikely that she'd received any such training.

Bianca shook her head. "No, but I know my presence will be a help to my mother and I'll gladly give that."

"Of course," Evan agreed.

But when they reached her home and she left him to go to her mother's room, he found himself at a loss for he was unable to break through her father's hostile reserve.

"Come with me," Francesco ordered curtly, his English softly accented with the sounds of his native tongue. Surprised that he spoke English, Evan followed him into his study, where he indicated a chair and then unlocked a cabinet cleverly concealed in the ornately carved paneling that decorated the walls of the room from floor to ceiling. The older man withdrew a bottle of brandy and two crystal snifters. "While my mind will not be focused solely upon our discussion, I think it is imperative that we have one."

Evan sank down into the chair the man offered, hoping he'd not insult him by falling asleep during what was sure to be a difficult conversation at best. At least they had a common language in which to converse, which was more than he'd dared hope. Trying to be as considerate of the man's feelings as possible Evan spoke first. "Did your wife tell you we'd met? She's a very lovely woman and I'm sorry she's having a difficult time. Was Bianca's birth also very trying for her?"

Francesco handed Evan a brandy and then took the chair opposite his. His manner was still stiffly formal as he replied, "My wife is no longer in her teens, Mr. Sinclair, and her enthusiasm for motherhood is unfortunately far greater than her strength. The babe should have been born hours ago, and if he's not born soon I fear I will lose them both. You have taken my daughter. Now it appears God may take this infant from me and my wife as well."

Francesco had also been up all night, Evan realized, but he'd be damned if he'd sit in a comfortable study while Bianca gave birth alone. "Then why aren't you with her? If it is strength Catherine needs, why not give her yours?"

Francesco eyed Evan even more suspiciously then. "I am no midwife!" he snorted derisively.

"Neither is Bianca," Evan pointed out sarcastically, but instantly regretting that show of temper he apologized. "I'm sorry. That remark was totally uncalled for." He took a sip of the brandy and found it exceedingly fine, smooth as it was it nevertheless warmed him clear through. He relaxed enough then to realize they'd have to remain in Venice for several days, and he hoped it would be to celebrate the birth of a child rather than to bury a tiny babe and his mother-in-law. He recalled that Venice had one island, San Michele, which was entirely devoted to a cemetery, and he prayed they'd have no reason to go there. From what he'd seen of Catherine, she had a will to survive as strong as her daughter's. Perhaps she'd soon give birth to a healthy child. Since he could do nothing to help her, however, he chose to deal with a problem he could do something about. "While it is far too late for me to ask your forgiveness for the way I spirited Bianca out of Venice last spring, I hope after your child is christened, we might arrange another wedding ceremony to be held here so you and your wife might attend." He'd not forgotten Bianca's comments about the ease with which their wedding vows could be forgotten, and not wanting to hear that argument again, he'd decided to marry her as promptly as a religious ceremony could be arranged, thinking she'd regard the vows they spoke then as a permanent bond.

Before Francesco could reply, Marco Ciani opened the door and peeked in, when he saw Evan he was so startled his hand slipped off the doorknob and sent the heavy door flying open with a thunderous crash. "Forgive me," he mumbled, "I thought you'd be alone."

Francesco beckoned for the young man to join them. More than a little drunk, he lifted his glass toward Evan. "This rogue has the audacity to ask my permission to marry Bianca now. What do you think of such manners as those?"

Evan rose to offer Marco his chair since he felt the young man would obviously be more agreeable company for Francesco. "I did not ask your permission as she is already my wife," he said. "I merely want to marry her a second time in a religious ceremony. I'd like you and your friends to share in our happiness. If you wish us to marry alone, however, we'll do so."

Marco was surprised by the American's plan, but he noted that while he was obviously determined, he'd spoken in a soft sincere tone which inspired confidence rather than hostility. Evan had impressed him favorably at their first meeting the previous spring, but then he'd been appalled by the part he'd unwittingly played in Bianca's elopement. Since she had so recently been a guest in his home, however, Marco could not understand how any discussion of a second wedding could possibly be appropriate. "Will Bianca agree to another ceremony?" he asked curiously, not realizing the answer to that question was none of his business.

Evan shrugged. "I certainly hope so." He'd do his best to convince her, he knew. "I am a gentleman, despite what you might have thought of me when I eloped with your daughter. I can give her a lovely home and a pleasant life. Whatever Paolo Sammarese could have offered her, I can match, and I am the man she loves."

At the mention of Sammarese, Marco swore a bitter oath, but he preferred his native tongue when using language of such a base nature so Evan couldn't understand his exact words, though he got the meaning. "No matter what you just called him, I think I agree wholeheartedly."

His interest now piqued, Francesco wanted to know why Marco disliked Paolo so intensely. "What has Paolo done now?" he inquired as he rose to offer his new guest some brandy.

Marco shook his head, reluctant to answer such a question. "He disagrees with the way I run my life, but that is no business of his and I'll not change my ways no matter what it costs me in trade."

"Marco," the older man sighed wearily, "I feel as though I've been awake for days. If Paolo and you are engaged in some sort of a dispute, you'll have to explain it more clearly than that. If he's threatened you in some fashion, I'll be happy to give him a taste of his own medicine, but I'll have to know why."

When Marco was obviously reluctant to share his burden with Francesco, Evan provided what he was certain was the correct answer. "It's Bianca, isn't it? I'll bet he disapproved of your taking her in when she wasn't welcome here." Although Francesco's obstinate refusal to welcome his daughter still angered Evan, he thought his father-in-law had enough problems that morning without adding to them by telling him what he thought of him for turning his back on Bianca.

Francesco appeared surprised for only a moment and then he nodded. "Of course. He tried to hurt Bianca through you, didn't he, Marco?"

"I would never have asked her to leave our home. She left of her own accord while I was away," Ciani explained hurriedly. "If I'd had to choose, I would have preferred Bianca's friendship rather than Paolo's for his is based on the prospect of profit alone. He has no regard for me as a person."

Francesco poured himself more brandy and then raised his glass in a toast. "To Catherine," he stated before sinking back down into his chair, nearly in tears over his inability to help his dear wife. "I can handle Paolo's pettiness easily, he'll soon regret having threatened a member of my family, but only God can give Catherine the courage to endure what she must."

As Marco drew up another chair and nodded toward him, Evan realized that the two Venetians had accepted him into their midst, and he sat down again to wait with them, his expression as worried as theirs.

Bianca found Raffaella with her mother, but she could see that her cousin was so badly frightened she'd be little help. As she'd hoped, her own presence gave her weary mother's spirits the lift they'd sorely needed. Taking her cousin's place beside the bed, Bianca wiped the perspiration from her mother's brow, lay the damp towel aside, and then gripped Catherine's trembling fingers tightly.

The midwife was a competent woman of unfailing good cheer, and Catherine did her best to follow the woman's directions and push with each contraction. But they were now so intense, she could no longer stay ahead of the agonizing pains, and she feared she could not stand many more. Tears streamed down her cheeks as she gasped for breath. When she looked at her daughter she regretted asking Bianca to share in her labor. "I'm sorry," she whispered hoarsely. "So sorry."

"You've no reason to apologize, signora, when you're being so brave. The babe's nearly born, now give it your best this time and he'll be here," the midwife encouraged warmly.

Bianca was certain her mother had already been giving her best, but she'd not allow her to quit doing so. "You can do it, I know you can!" With the next contraction her mother gripped her hand so tightly she thought she'd scream out herself with pain. Instead she watched in rapt fascination as a tiny head emerged from between her mother's thighs, the babe's face drawn up in an angry pout as though it had been suffering quite badly too. The midwife began to speak excitedly to Catherine as she cradled the infant's head and turned its tiny shoulders to carefully lift the baby free of his mother's body. He began to cry then, his lungs gulping in air which swiftly turned the blue cast of his skin a healthy pink.

"It is a son, Signora a handsome son!" She exclaimed with delight. "Let me tie off the cord, clean him up a bit and I'll hand him to you to hold."

Bianca was so excited her tears were swiftly mixed with her mother's. She reached out to Raffaella who'd been shyly standing aside, and the three women clung to each other and wept for joy.

"Papa will be so thrilled!" Bianca declared. Then she wondered if he'd be happy enough now that he had a son to forgive her for failing him. She and Evan were together again, she had a brother, and she wanted them all to be happy, to be a family. When at last her mother and the baby were ready to receive visitors she went downstairs to call her father. She found him in his study. He and Marco were sitting on the edges of their chairs, spellbound, as Evan finished the tale which finally gave them both a clear understanding of the matter of honor which had brought him to Venice. The three men turned to look at her and saw by the beauty of her smile that the news was good. "You have a son, Papa. He's perfect and while mother is very tired, she is fine."

Evan and Marco pulled Francesco to his feet and began pushing him toward the door, their loud whoops of excitement drowning out whatever protests he might have wished to make over their clowning. As he reached his daughter's side, Francesco broke free from them and gave her a warm hug. "Thank you for coming to help your mother. After the way I had treated you—"

Bianca kissed his cheek swiftly as she lifted her fingertips to his lips to still his apology. "Go on up and see your son. We can all talk later."

Francesco turned back to look at Evan, his glance now

warm. "You may marry Bianca again as you'd wished, but this time I want it done properly. You will live on board your ship until I send for you. She will stay here until you are truly man and wife. I'll give you my word it will be within a week."

"Yes, sir," Evan replied with a rakish grin, too happy to have won the man's confidence to argue over his terms. He waited until his father-in-law and Marco had left the room before he pulled Bianca into his arms. Her hair was tangled, the first two buttons of her bodice were undone, and she looked as tired as he felt; but he thought she'd never been prettier. "I love you, Mrs. Sinclair, and I'm so glad you have a brother."

Bianca thought that comment unbearably sad coming from him, but there was not the slightest bit of sorrow in her husband's sparkling golden glance. "He is very cute. Don't you want to come see him?"

"Of course I do. Then I am going back to the *Aurora* and sleep until your father lets me know the priest is here."

"You'll accept his conditions?" Bianca asked in surprise, for she did not want to be parted from him for an instant, no matter what the reason.

"I think I owe him that much, don't you? He's being very gracious about giving you to me," Evan teased with another loving hug.

"But I will miss you too greatly, Evan," Bianca protested. However her handsome husband silenced her complaints with lingering kisses which left her too content to be dissatisfied about the arrangements for their wedding.

After Evan had gone, Bianca ate, took a warm bath, and went straight to bed. She slept right through the dinner hour, but the household was too excited by the birth of her brother to notice she'd not left her room. Snuggled in her comfortable bed, she might have slept until dawn, but before the first rays of the sun lit the sky with pink she felt her husband's warm breath upon her cheek as he leaned down to kiss her. She stretched languidly as she came fully awake, her smile one of delighted surprise. "How did you—" she began; then, looking toward the doors of the balcony, she knew. "You never meant to stay alone aboard the *Aurora* did you?" she asked with a mischievous giggle.

"No, but that's our secret. We needn't share it with your father now that I've finally managed to impress him favorably."

Bianca moved over to make room for her husband in the massive bed. He'd changed somehow since she'd last seen him. His clothing was far more elegant, he'd bathed, and his hair sparkled with a deep red glow in the dim light cast by her lamp. His grin was so enticing she couldn't wait for him to peel off his clothes and join her, but she suddenly realized what the difference was. "Evan, you've shaved off your beard!" she whispered excitedly, feeling very foolish because she'd not noticed that immediately. "I liked it. It was quite handsome."

Evan laughed as he cast his breeches aside, and lifting the sheet to slip in beside her, he teased her in return. "You never told me you liked it, not even once. How was I to know that you did."

"I never told you?" Bianca asked in dismay, certain she must have.

Evan wrapped his arms around her to hold her tightly. "No, but if you liked my beard, I'll simply grow another. I only want to please you, my love. I made many mistakes when I came here last spring, but thank God I met you. You've taught me what is really important, and nothing will ever mean more to me than your love."

Bianca combed his hair back from his temples with a

feathery touch while she attempted to give her question the proper inflection. "Just what did you tell my father and Marco? I'd like to know because when they question me I want to give the right answers."

Evan leaned back slightly, but his glance teasing, not hostile. "I told them the truth, what did you think I'd do?"

"The truth?" Bianca was skeptical. "All right, how much of the truth?"

"Well, if you put it that way, it's another story." He pulled her close then, to nuzzle her throat with playful nibbles. "Can't I explain that later?"

"Hm." Bianca purred contentedly. "We're getting married the day after tomorrow. Will you come to me again tomorrow night?"

"What makes you think I plan to leave?"

"But, Evan, you must! I'll not have my father angry with you again."

"I imagine he is so ecstatically happy over the birth of his son, he would forgive me anything."

"Let's not give him anything to forgive." Bianca wrapped her arms around his neck to pull his lips down to hers for a delectable kiss.

As Evan drew away, he grew thoughtful. "I hope you weren't frightened this morning. I know having a child is sometimes difficult, but I don't want you to dread it."

Bianca readily admitted her feelings. "I was frightened, and badly, although I did my best to give my mother confidence. But once the babe was born, we were all so relieved to see that he was healthy and she was fine my memories of the birth will be happy ones. You needn't think I'll be afraid to have your child, Evan, because I won't."

Noting the sly satisfaction in his wife's expression, Evan quickly said, "Bianca, if you are pregnant I want you to tell me immediately! I want the truth from you, right now!"

"Hush, Evan. Someone will hear you!" Bianca cautioned him in a frantic whisper.

"Blast it all, woman, you are my wife! Now tell me the truth!"

"While I am almost certain, I'll not have you telling everyone you'll soon become a father when it might not prove true."

"I am the soul of discretion," Evan boasted proudly. "But don't you want to tell you parents before we leave?"

"I thought I'd wait until after our wedding if you don't mind," Bianca remarked demurely. "That seems a more appropriate time."

"When did it happen? That afternoon you became so upset that I'd bought the Marshall house?"

"Yes, it must have been then," Bianca agreed softly. "I couldn't bear to think you'd bought us a home that we'd never live in together."

"Neither could I. I told you that several times as I recall."

"Yes, but there was still the matter of avenging Charles's murder." She shivered then, as she remembered Stefano's death.

"Well, that deed is done, even if I can not take the full credit. When we go home there'll be no more sadness, and I know I can make you happy this time. I'll not let anything distract me now."

Bianca moved her whole body against his in a seductive caress, as always wanting more of his inviting warmth. "I was happy before, Evan. There was a magic between us despite all the pretense, and we've never lost it."

"Nor will we." Evan promised as his lips brushed hers softly. He made love to her then with exquisite tenderness, enfolding her in a fond embrace, his kisses deep, his mouth never leaving hers as his hands moved slowly over her luscious curves to enflame her passions which then consumed him in a fiery burst of rapture that fused their souls as well as their splendid bodies. This was where their marriage had first begun, and it pleased him to think it would now begin again, only this time with the beauty of truth instead of his cunning lies.

Bianca was sleeping soundly as he left her bed, dressed quietly, and strolled out upon her balcony. He lingered there for a moment before climbing down to his boat. The city of Venice lay stretched out before him, its splendor still veiled in shadows. "We'll name our first son for you, Charles," he promised softly. It was a vow he knew Bianca would want him to keep. He turned then, to steal one last glimpse of the radiant beauty who'd won his heart when he'd mistakenly believed his passion could only be fired by vengeance. She'd simply bewitched him with her magic, turned a quest fueled by hatred into one fed by love. He knew then she was truly a goddess for she had made each moment they shared a paradise indeed. With her golden hair and emerald gaze, she'd enrich his days forever.

"Until tonight, my love," he whispered in farewell, and as the bright glow of dawn burst over Venice, he was gone; but the warmth of his love still lit Bianca's dreams.

HISTORICAL ROMANCES BY EMMA MERRITT

RESTLESS FLAMES (2203, $3.95)

Having lost her husband six months before, determined Brenna Allen couldn't afford to lose her freight company, too. Outfitted as wagon captain with revolver, knife and whip, the single-minded beauty relentlessly drove her caravan, desperate to reach Santa Fe. Then she crossed paths with insolent Logan MacDougald. The taciturn Texas Ranger was as primitive as the surrounding Comanche Territory, and he didn't hesitate to let the tantalizing trail boss know what he wanted from her. Yet despite her outrage with his brazen ways, jet-haired Brenna couldn't suppress the scorching passions surging through her . . . and suddenly she never wanted this trip to end!

COMANCHE BRIDE (2549, $3.95)

When stunning Dr. Zoe Randolph headed to Mexico to halt a cholera epidemic, she didn't think twice about traversing Comanche territory . . . until a band of bloodthirsty savages attacked her caravan. The gorgeous physician was furious that her mission had been interrupted, but nothing compared to the rage she felt on meeting the barbaric warrior who made her his slave. Determined to return to civilization, the ivory-skinned blonde decided to make a woman's ultimate sacrifice to gain her freedom—and never admit that deep down inside she burned to be loved by the handsome brute!

SWEET, WILD LOVE (2834, $4.50)

It was hard enough for Eleanor Hunt to get men to take her seriously in sophisticated Chicago—it was going to be impossible in Blissful, Kansas! These cowboys couldn't believe she was a real attorney, here to try a cattle rustling case. They just looked her up and down and grinned. Especially that Bradley Smith. The man worked for her father and he still had the audacity to stare at her with those lust-filled green eyes. Every time she turned around, he was trying to trap her in his strong embrace.

Available wherever paperbacks are sold, or order direct from the Publisher. Send cover price plus 50¢ per copy for mailing and handling to Zebra Books, Dept. 3193, 475 Park Avenue South, New York, N.Y. 10016. Residents of New York, New Jersey and Pennsylvania must include sales tax. DO NOT SEND CASH.